REDEEMED

REDEEMED

A House of Night Novel

P. C. CAST and KRISTIN CAST

ST. MARTIN'S GRIFFIN
NEW YORK

REDEEMED. Copyright © 2014 by P. C. Cast and Kristin Cast. All rights reserved. Printed in the United States of America. For information, address St. Martin's Press, 175 Fifth Avenue, New York, N.Y. 10010.

www.stmartins.com

The Library of Congress Cataloging-in-Publication
Data is available upon request.

ISBN 978-0-312-59444-2 (hardcover)
ISBN 978-1-4668-5849-7 (e-book)

St. Martin's Griffin books may be purchased for educational, business, or promotional use. For information on bulk purchases, please contact Macmillan Corporate and Premium Sales Department at 1-800-221-7945, extension 5442, or write specialmarkets@macmillan.com.

First Edition: October 2014

10 9 8 7 6 5 4 3 2 1

This book is dedicated to Matthew Shear—publisher, friend, father figure, and champion. Kristin and I often say that St. Martin's is our family. Well, Matthew was the heart of that family. We miss him.

ACKNOWLEDGMENTS

It is with great love, respect, and affection that we acknowledge our agent, Meredith Bernstein. Without Meredith there would be no House of Night. Thank you for giving me the idea of a series set at a "vampyre finishing school." Thank you for your integrity and business savvy. And thank you for your friendship. We love you!

St. Martin's Press is a dream publisher. Our family there is spectacular! From the very first book we have had the support and enthusiasm of our team. Thank you to everyone who has worked so hard to make House of Night such a success, especially: Jennifer Weis, Anne Marie Talberg, Jennifer Enderlin, Sally Richardson, Steven Cohen, Jeanne-Marie Hudson, Sylvan Creekmore, Stephanie Davis, Bridget Hartzler, and a very harried production staff. Also, we appreciate so much the beauty and design of our books, covers, posters, etc. Thank you, Team SMP! We heart you!

Thank you to the House of Night fans! We have the most creative, loyal, and enthusiastic fans in the world. We love and appreciate you!

From P.C.: Thank you to my brainstorming partner, Christine, who has pulled my butt out of plotting fire more times than I can count during this series.

Thank you to my father, Dick Cast (Mighty Mouse!), who was invaluable as I was creating the biological foundation of the HoN vampyres.

Thank you to Kristin, my wonderful and talented daughter, who is the best teen-voice editor in the universe!

And thank you to my very patient life partner, Dusty. He knows why.

REDEEMED

CHAPTER ONE

Zoey

I've never felt this dark.

Not even when I'd been shattered and trapped in the Otherworld and my soul had begun to fragment. Then I'd been broken and battered and well on my way to losing myself forever. I'd felt dark inside, but the people who loved me most had been bright, beautiful beacons of hope, and I'd been able to find strength in their light. I'd fought my way out of darkness.

This time I didn't have any hope. I couldn't find a light. I deserved to stay lost, to remain shattered. This time I didn't deserve to be saved.

Detective Marx had taken me to the Tulsa County sheriff's office instead of sticking me in jail with the rest of the criminals who were newly arrested. On the seemingly endless trip from the House of Night to the big brown stone sheriff's department building on First Street he'd talked to me, explaining that he'd made a call—pulled some strings—and I was going to be put in a special holding cell until my attorney could make arrangements for my arraignment, so I could get released on bail. He'd looked back and forth from the road to my reflection in the rearview mirror. I'd met his eyes. It didn't take more than a glance to read his expression.

He knew I had no chance for bail.

"I don't need a lawyer," I'd said. "And I don't want bail."

"Zoey, you're not thinking straight. Give it a little time. Believe me, you're going to need a lawyer. And if you could get out on bail, that would be the best thing for you."

"But it wouldn't be the best thing for Tulsa. No one is going to let a monster loose." My voice had sounded flat and emotionless, but inside I was screaming over and over and over.

"You're not a monster," Marx had said.

"Did you see those two men I killed?"

He'd glanced at me in the mirror again and nodded. I could see that his lips had pressed into a line, like he was trying to keep himself from saying something. For some reason his eyes were still kind. I couldn't meet them.

Looking out the window, I'd said, "Then you know what I am. Whether you call it monster, or killer, or rogue fledgling vampyre— it's all the same. I deserve to be locked up. I deserve what's going to happen to me."

He'd quit talking to me then, and I'd been glad.

A black iron fence surrounded the sheriff's department's parking lot, and Marx drove to a rear entrance where he had to wait to be identified before a massive gate opened. Then he stopped and led me, handcuffed, through a back door and a big, busy room that was sectioned off with cubical dividers. When we walked in, cops were talking and phones were ringing. As soon as they saw it was Marx and me, it was like an off switch had been thrown. The talking stopped and the gawking started.

I stared straight ahead at a spot on the wall and concentrated on not letting the screaming that was going on inside me come out.

We had to walk all the way through the room. Then we went through a door that led to one of those rooms that look like the ones you see on *Law & Order: SVU* where awesome Mariska Hargitay interrogates the bad guys.

It had given me a jolt to realize that what I had done had made *me* one of the bad guys.

There was a door at the far end of the room that led to a little hallway. Marx turned left. He'd paused to swipe his ID card, and a massively thick steel door opened. On the other side of the door, the hall dead-ended in just a few feet. There was another metal door on our right, which was open. The bottom was solid, but about shoulder high bars started. Thick, black bars. That was where Detective Marx stopped. I glanced inside. The room was a tomb. I suddenly had trouble breathing, and my eyes skittered away from the horrible place to find Marx's familiar face.

"With the power you have, I imagine you could break out of here." He'd spoken quietly, as if he thought someone might be listening to us.

"I left the Seer Stone at the House of Night. That's what gave me the power to kill those two men."

"So you didn't kill them by yourself?"

"I got mad and threw my anger at them. The Seer Stone just gave me a boost. Detective Marx, it was my fault. Period, the end." I'd tried to sound tough and sure of myself, but my voice had gone all soft and shaky.

"Can you break out of here, Zoey?"

"I honestly don't know, but I promise I'm not going to try." I'd drawn a deep breath and let it out in a rush, telling him the absolute truth. "Because of what I did, I belong here, and no matter what happens to me, I deserve it."

"Well, I promise you that no one can bother you here. You'll be safe," he'd said kindly. "I made sure of that. So whatever is going to happen to you, it won't be because a lynch mob got to you."

"Thank you." My voice had broken, but I'd gotten the words out.

He took off my handcuffs.

I hadn't been able to move.

"You have to go in the cell now."

I'd made my feet move. When I was inside, I turned, and just before he closed the door I'd said, "I don't want to see anyone, especially not anyone from the House of Night."

"Are you sure?"

"Yes."

"You understand what you're saying, don't you?" he said.

I'd nodded. "I know what happens to a fledgling who isn't around vampyres."

"So basically, you're sentencing yourself."

He hadn't phrased it as a question, but I'd answered him anyway. "What I'm doing is taking responsibility for my actions."

He'd hesitated, and it seemed like he had something else he wanted to say, but Marx had ended up shrugging, sighing, and saying, "Okay, then. Good luck, Zoey. I'm sorry that it has come to this."

The door closed as if sealing a coffin.

There was no window, no outside light except for what peeked in from the hallway between the bars on the door. At the end of the cell there was a bed—a thin mattress on a slab of something hard attached to the wall. There was an aluminum toilet sticking out of the middle of a parallel wall, not far from the bed. It didn't have any lid. The floor was black concrete. The walls were gray. The blanket on the bed was gray. Feeling like I was in a waking nightmare, I walked to the bed.

Six steps. That's how long the cell was. Six steps.

I went to the side wall and walked across the cell. Five steps. It was five steps across.

I'd been right. If you didn't count the distance to the ceiling, I was locked in a tomb the size of a coffin.

I sat on the bed, drew my knees up to my chest, and hugged them. My body shook and shook and shook.

I was going to die.

I couldn't remember if Oklahoma was a death penalty state. Like I'd actually paid attention in history class while Coach Fitz played movie after movie? But that didn't matter anyway. I had left the House of Night. Alone. With no vampyres. Even Detective Marx understood what that meant. It was only a matter of time before my body began rejecting the Change.

Like I'd hit a rewind button in my head, images of dying fledglings played against the screen of my closed eyes: Elliott, Stevie Rae, Stark, Erin . . .

I squeezed my eyes shut even tighter.

It happens fast. Really, really fast, I promised myself.

Then another death scene flashed through my memory. Two men—homeless, obnoxious, but alive until I'd lost control of my temper. I remembered how I'd thrown my anger at them . . . how they'd crashed against the stone wall beside the little grotto at Woodward Park . . . how they'd lay there, crumpled, broken . . .

But they'd been moving! I didn't think I'd killed them! I hadn't meant to kill them! It really had just been a terrible accident! My mind shouted.

"No!" I spoke sharply to the selfish part of me that wanted to make excuses, wanted to run away from consequences. "People convulse when they're dying. They are dead because I killed them. It won't make up for what I did, but I deserve to die."

I curled up under the scratchy gray blanket and faced the wall. I ignored the dinner tray they slid through a slat in the door. I wasn't hungry anyway, but *whatever* that was on that tray definitely didn't tempt me.

And for some reason, the bad food smell reminded me of the last most awesome food smell I'd experienced—psaghetti at the House of Night, surrounded by my friends.

But I'd been too stressed out by my Aurox/Heath/Stark problem. I hadn't appreciated the psaghetti, not really. Just like I hadn't appreciated my friends. Or Stark. Not really.

I hadn't stopped to consider the fact that I was *lucky* to have two such amazing guys love me. Instead I'd been pissed and frustrated.

I thought about Aphrodite. I remembered how I'd heard her talking to Shaylin about watching me. I remembered how I'd stormed in and shoved Shaylin with the power of my anger focused through the Seer Stone.

The memory made me cringe in shame.

Aphrodite had been absolutely right. I had needed watching. It wasn't like she'd been able to reason with me. Hell, when she'd tried, I hadn't been anything close to reasonable.

I cringed again as I remembered how close I'd come to throwing my anger at Aphrodite.

"Ohmygoddess! If I had, I could have killed my friend." I spoke into my palms as I covered my face with my hands in shame.

It didn't matter that the Seer Stone somehow, without me really asking it to, amplified my powers. I'd had plenty of warning. All those times I was annoyed and the stone got hotter and hotter. Why hadn't I stopped and thought through what was going on? Why hadn't I asked someone for help? I'd asked Lenobia for boyfriend advice. *Boyfriend advice! I should have been asking for an anger intervention!*

But I hadn't asked for any help with anything except what my tunnel vision had been focused on: *me.*

I'd been a self-absorbed bitch.

I deserved to be where I was. I deserved my consequences.

The lights in the hallway went out. I had no idea what time it was. It seemed like years instead of months since I'd been a human—a normal teenager who had to go to bed too darn early on school nights.

I wished, with everything inside me, that I could call Superman and have him fly backward around the earth until time turned back to yesterday. Then I'd be home, at the House of Night, with my friends. I'd run straight into Stark's arms and tell him how much I love and appreciate him. I'd tell him I was sorry about the Aurox/Heath mess, and that we'd figure it out—all two point five of us—but that I was going to appreciate the love that surrounded me no matter what. Then I'd yank that damn Seer Stone off, find Aphrodite, and give it to her to keep it safe like she was my Frodo.

But it was too late for wishes. Turning back time is only a fantasy. Superman isn't real.

I didn't sleep. It was night, and night had become my day. Right now I should be at school with my friends, living my life, having what was (for me) a normal "day." Instead I lay there, hugging myself. I should have been smarter. I should have been stronger. I should have been anything except a selfish brat.

Hours later I heard the slot in the door open again, and when I turned over I saw that someone had taken away my untouched tray. Good. Maybe the smell would go away, too.

I had to pee, but I didn't want to. Didn't want to use the bare toilet sticking out of the wall in the middle of the room. I stared at the corners of the walls where they met the ceiling. Cameras.

Was it legal for wardens to watch prisoners pee?

Did the regular rules even count with me? I mean, I'd never heard of a fledgling or a vampyre being put on trial in human court, or going to human prison.

I don't have to worry about that. I'll drown in my own blood way before I go to trial.

Weirdly enough, that thought was a comfort, and as the light in the hallway came on, I fell into a restless, dreamless sleep.

It seemed like ten seconds later when the slot in the door banged open and another aluminum tray sloshed into my cell. The noise jolted me awake, but I was still groggy, still trying to fall back to sleep—until the scent of eggs and bacon had my mouth watering. How long had it been since I'd eaten anything? Ugh, I felt terrible. Blearily, I got up and walked the six steps to the door, picking up the tray and carrying it carefully back to my rumpled bed.

The eggs were scrambled and super runny. The bacon was beef jerky hard. There was coffee, a carton of milk, and dry toast.

I would have given almost anything for one bowl of Count Chocula and a can of brown pop.

I took a bite of the eggs, and they were so salty they almost made me choke.

But instead of choking, I began to cough. Within that terrible cough I tasted something, something metallic and slick and warm and weirdly wonderful.

It was my own blood.

Fear rocketed through me, making me weak and dizzy and nauseous. *It's happening so soon? I'm not ready! I'm not ready!*

Trying to clear my throat, trying to breathe, I spit out the eggs, ignored the pink tinge in the runny yellow, put the tray on the floor, and curled up on the bed, wrapping my arms around myself and waiting for more coughing and more blood—a lot more blood. My hands were shaking as I wiped fresh wetness from my lips.

I was so scared!

Don't be, I told myself as I tried to stifle a really awful cough. *You'll see Nyx soon. And Jack. And maybe even Dragon and Anastasia.*

And Mom!

Mom . . . I suddenly wanted my mother with a terrible, heartsick longing.

"I wish I wasn't alone," I whispered in a gravelly voice into the hard, flat mattress.

I heard the door open, but I didn't roll over. I didn't want to see the horrified expression of a stranger. I closed my eyes tight and tried to pretend I was at Grandma's lavender farm, sleeping in my bedroom there. Tried to pretend the egg and bacon smell was her cooking, and my coughing was just a cold keeping me home from school.

And I was doing it! Oh, thank you, Nyx! Suddenly I swear I could smell the scents that always lingered around Grandma, lavender and sweetgrass. That gave me the courage to speak quickly, before my voice was drowned in blood, to whoever was there. "It's okay. This is what happens to some fledglings. Just please go away and leave me alone."

"Oh, Zoeybird, my precious *u-we-tsi-a-ge-ya*, do you not know by now that I will never let you be alone?"

CHAPTER TWO

Zoey

I thought she was part of my dying hallucination, standing there at the door of my cell, dressed in a purple linen shirt and worn jeans, with one of her many picnic baskets in the crook of her arm, but as soon as I turned to face her, she rushed to me, sitting on the edge of my bed and enveloping me in her arms and in the scent of my childhood.

"Grandma! I'm so sorry! I'm so sorry!" I sobbed into her shoulder.

"Shhh, *u-we-tsi-a-ge-ya,* I am here." She rubbed a soft circle in the middle of my back.

My coughing had temporarily eased, so I said in a rush, "It's selfish of me, but I'm so glad you are. I don't want to die all by myself."

Grandma pulled back from me enough to take my shoulders in her hands and give me a stern shake. "Zoey Redbird, you are not dying."

Tears spilled down my cheeks. I ignored them and wiped at the corner of my mouth, holding my trembling fingers out to her so that she could see the blood.

She barely glanced at the proof I was trying to show her. Instead she opened her picnic basket and took out a red and white checked napkin and began dabbing at my tears and my nose, just like she had when I was a little girl.

"Grandma, I know you love me more than anyone in the world," I said, trying (unsuccessfully) not to cry. "But you can't stop my body from rejecting the Change."

"You are correct, *u-we-tsi-a-ge-ya,* I cannot. But they can." She nodded to the doorway behind me.

I turned and saw Thanatos and Lenobia, Stevie Rae, Darius, and

Stark—my Stark—all clustered in the doorway. Stevie Rae was bawling so hard I wondered how I hadn't heard her.

Stark was crying, too, but silently.

"But I said not to follow me! I said I deserved to face my consequences." I was crying as hard as Stevie Rae now.

"Then live and face them! And I'll be right here as close to you as I can get through the whole thing!" Stark hurled the words at me.

"I can't. I've already started rejecting the Change." I sobbed.

"Child, your grandmother spoke the truth. Unless your body's rejection of the Change was already fated, our presence will stop it," Thanatos said.

"You're *not* dying! I won't let you!" Stark shouted through his tears, and started to come into my cell.

"Hold on there, boy! I said only one of you at a time can go into her cell." A guy in a sheriff's uniform stepped up from behind my group of friends and placed himself between them and my cell. "Detective Marx told me I had to allow you vampyres in the building if you showed up, but I ain't bending the rules enough to let her have more than one visitor at a time. Her Grandma's family. The rest of you can wait in the interrogation room." He gave Grandma a stern look. "You have fifteen minutes." Then he slammed the door.

"Fifteen minutes." Grandma made a small sound of disgust. "That isn't a proper visit. That is a hard-boiled egg. Well, then, I'll not dillydally. Zoeybird, blow your nose and stand for me. You need a good smudging. Oh, the gentleman who searched this certainly made a mess of my basket."

She was already rummaging around in her bottomless picnic basket, so I had to take her hands in mine to stop her and get her attention focused on what I was saying.

"Grandma, I love you. You know that, right?"

"Of course, *u-we-tsi-a-ge-ya*. And I love you—with all my heart. That is why I must smudge you. I wish there was a bathtub in here, or even a sink, to help cleanse you even more. But the smudging will have to do. I worked all night and finally chose to smudge from this oyster shell you and I dug when we followed the Mississippi River to the Gulf the summer you turned ten. Do you remember?"

"Yes, of course, but Grandma—"

"Good. I've ground and mixed together sage, cedar, and lavender. Combined, they make a powerful smudge for emotional and physical cleansing." She was pouring dried herbs from a black velvet pouch into the oyster shell. "I've also brought an eagle feather and my favorite piece of raw turquoise. I know they might take it from you, but let us try to hide it within your mattress. It should serve to protect you while—"

"Grandma, please stop," I interrupted her. Meeting her eyes without flinching, I said, "I killed those two men. I don't deserve to be cleansed or protected. I deserve what was happening to me before you all showed up."

I hadn't meant to sound cold, but my words made her flinch, so I softened my voice, but not my resolve. "The vampyres may have made it so that I won't drown in my own blood, but that doesn't change the fact that I did a terrible thing—a thing that I have to be punished for."

She paused in the preparation of my smudging and her sharp eyes met mine. "Tell me, *u-we-tsi-a-ge-ya*, why did you kill those two men?"

I shook my head and brushed my tangled hair from my face. "I didn't know that I killed them until Detective Marx came to the House of Night. All I knew was that they'd made me mad—they were hanging around Woodward Park looking for people, mostly girls, to scare into giving them money." I paused and shook my head again. "But that doesn't make what I did okay. Once they realized what I was, they were going to leave me alone."

"And move on to find another victim."

"Probably, but not one to kill. They were panhandlers not serial killers."

"So tell me what happened. How did you kill them?"

"I threw my anger at them. Just like I'd shoved Shaylin earlier and knocked her on her butt. Only I was even madder in the park. Somehow the Seer Stone amplified my feelings and gave me the power to attack all of them."

"But you did not kill Shaylin," Grandma said logically. "I saw the child at the House of Night just before I came here. She looked very much alive to me."

"No, I didn't kill her. Not that time. Who knows what would have happened if I hadn't taken off and found my way to the park—and vented my anger on those two men? Grandma, I was out of control. I was a monster."

"Zoey, you did a monstrous thing. But that does not make you a monster. You turned yourself in. You gave up the Seer Stone. You allowed yourself to be imprisoned. Those are not the actions of a monster."

"But Grandma, I killed two men!" I felt tears well in my eyes again.

"And now you will have to face the consequences of your actions. But that does not mean you may give up and cause the people who love you even more pain."

I bit my lip. "My whole point was to take responsibility by myself so that I didn't hurt anyone else, especially not the people I love."

"Zoeybird, I do not know why this terrible thing has happened. I do not believe you are a killer." She held up her hand to quiet me when I tried to speak. "Yes, I am aware the two men are dead, and that you appear to be responsible for their deaths. And yet even you admit the Seer Stone played a major role in the accident, which means Old Magick is at work."

"Yes, I have been using it," I said sternly.

"Or it has been using you," she countered with.

"Either way, the results are the same."

"For the two men. Not necessarily for you, *u-we-tsi-a-ge-ya*. Now, stand before me. You need your mind cleared and your spirit cleansed so that you can analyze exactly what has brought you to this cell. You see, I am not here to help you hide from what you have done. I am here so that you may truly face it."

As always, Grandma was the voice of reason and of unconditional love. I stood and allowed myself the brief, small comfort of watching her cradle the oyster shell in one hand while with the other she placed a tiny round piece of charcoal on top of the herbal mixture and lit it. As it sparked, she said, "Three deep breaths, *u-we-tsi-a-ge-ya*. And with each, release the toxic energy that clouds your mind and darkens your spirit. Envision it, Zoeybird. What color is it?"

"A sick green," I said, thinking of the disgusting stuff that had come out of my nose last time I'd had a sinus infection.

"Excellent. Breathe out and envision ridding yourself of it along with your breath."

The charcoal had stopped sparkling and was beginning to gray around the edges. Grandma reached into the black velvet pouch and began sprinkling the herbs over the coal, saying, "I thank you, spirit of white sage, for your strength, your purity, your power." Sweet smoke began to lift from the oyster shell. "I thank you, spirit of cedar, for your divine nature, for your ability to create a bridge between earth and Otherworld."

More smoke lifted and I breathed deeply in and out, in and out.

"And, as always, I thank you, spirit of lavender, for your soothing nature, for your ability to allow us to release our anger and to embrace calm." Then Grandma began walking a clockwise circle around me, shuffling her feet in an ancient, heartbeat rhythm that seemed to electrify the fragrant smoke and pulse it into my body as she wafted it around me with her eagle feather. Not missing a beat in her dance, Grandma's voice paired with her movements, echoing through her blood to mine. "Out with what is toxic—green and bile-like. In with sweet smoke—silver and pure."

I concentrated as she moved around me, falling into the ritual as easily as I had throughout my childhood.

"Draw in healing. Draw in cleansing. Draw in calming. Green bile, gone it will be. Replaced by silver and clarity," Grandma sang to me.

I lifted my hands, guiding the smoke around my head, concentrating on the silver cleansing.

"*O-s-da*," Grandma said, then repeated in English, "Good. You are regaining your center."

I'd been lulled into a sleepy, trance-like state by the smoke and Grandma's song. I blinked, as if surfacing from a deep dive, and my eyes widened with surprise. Clearly visible through the smoke was a bright silver light that, bubble-like, surrounded Grandma and me.

"That is what you are projecting now, Zoeybird. It has taken the place of the Darkness that was within you."

I drew another deep breath, feeling an amazing lightness in my chest. Gone was the terrible tightness that had been there when I'd begun coughing. Gone was the awful sense of despair that had been with me for—

For how long? I wondered. Now that it was gone, I realized how smothering it had been.

Grandma had halted in front of me. She placed the still-smoking oyster shell between us at our feet, and then she took my hands in hers.

"I do not know everything. I do not have the answers you seek. I cannot do more than cleanse and heal your mind and spirit. I cannot take you from this place or change the past that has brought you here. I can only love you and remind you of this one, small rule that I have tried to live my life by: I cannot control others. I can only control myself and my reactions to others. And when all else fails, I choose kindness. I show compassion. Then, if I have made poor choices, I have at least not damaged my spirit."

"I failed in doing that, Grandma."

"Failed—that is past tense, and you should leave that failure in the past where it belongs. Learn from your mistakes and move on. Do not fail again, *u-we-tsi-a-ge-ya*. That means if you must stand trial and go to prison for this terrible thing that has happened, then you do so speaking with truth and acting with compassion—as would a High Priestess of your Goddess."

"I shouldn't push away the people who love me." I hadn't phrased it as a question, but Grandma answered me nevertheless.

"Pushing those away who love you and have your best interest at heart would be the action of a child, and not that of a High Priestess."

"Grandma, do you think Nyx still wants me to be her High Priestess?"

Grandma smiled. "I do, but what I think is not important. What do you believe of your Goddess, Zoey? Is she so fickle that she would love and then discard you so easily?"

"It isn't Nyx I question. It's myself," I admitted.

"Then you must look to yourself. Hold tightly to your center." She retrieved the raw turquoise stone she'd taken from the picnic basket earlier and folded it into my hand. "You have used the Seer Stone to focus your powers, whether willingly or not. Now I think you must find a focus within you, just as turquoise has its own protective power, you must find your own power—within yourself. This time do not look to anger, Zoeybird. Look to compassion and love."

"Always love," I finished for her, taking her stone in my hand and feeling its smoothness.

"Hold as tightly to your true self as you do this stone, and remember that I will always believe you are stronger, wiser, and kinder than you know you are."

I put my arms around her and hugged her tightly. "I love you, Grandma. I always will."

"As I will always love you."

"Time's up!" The guard's voice made me reluctantly let go of Grandma. "Hey, what's going on in here? What's that you're burning?"

Grandma turned to him, smiled, and in her sweetest voice said, "Nothing you need worry about, dear. Just a little cleansing and clearing. Do you like chocolate chip cookies? I have a secret ingredient that makes mine irresistible, and I just happen to have a dozen tucked into my basket." Patting him on the arm she herded him from the doorway, lifting a paper plate full of cookies from her magical basket and winking at me over her shoulder. "Now, dear, why don't we get you some coffee to go with these while you send that nice young vampyre named Stark in to visit with my granddaughter?"

Stark!

I sat on my bed, nervously straightening my clothes and trying to comb my fingers through my super-crazy hair. And then he was in the doorway, and I forgot about the way I looked. I forgot about everything except how glad I was to see him.

"Can I come in?" he asked hesitantly.

I nodded.

It didn't take any time at all for him to walk those six steps to me. I couldn't wait another second, though. As soon as he got within grabbing range, I threw my arms around him and buried my face in his shoulder.

"I'm so sorry! Don't hate me—please don't hate me!"

"How could I hate you?" He held me so tightly that it was hard for me to breathe, but I didn't care. "You're my Queen, my High Priestess, and my love—my only love." He let go of me enough to look into my eyes. "You can't commit suicide. I can't survive it, Zoey. I swear I can't."

He had dark circles under his eyes and his red vampyre tattoos looked especially brilliant against the unnatural paleness of his skin. He looked like he'd aged a decade in one day.

I hated how tired and sick he looked. I hated that I had caused it.

I met his gaze and spoke with all the kindness and compassion within me. "That was a mistake. I won't do it again. I'm sorry I put you through that—I'm sorry I'm going to put you through all of this." I gestured at the jail cell.

He touched my cheek gently, almost reverently. "Where you go, I go. We are Oath Bound for this lifetime and beyond, Zoey Redbird. And all of this is bearable if we have each other. Do we still have each other?"

"We do." I kissed him, long and hard. I thought I was comforting him but realized that his touch—his taste—his love was really comforting me.

It was that moment that I truly understood how much I love Stark.

"See," he said, covering my face in fast little kisses and brushing away the tears that were slipping down my cheeks. "Everything's better now. It's going to be all right."

I didn't want to tell him that I wasn't sure anything was ever going to be all right again. That wouldn't have been compassionate. Instead I led him to my hard, narrow bed. We sat, and I curled against him, resting in the crook of his arm.

"We're going to take turns staying here so that you don't start rejecting the Change again. From today on there will always be a vampyre just outside your door," Stark began explaining softly while he held me close to him. "They're putting a cot in the hallway."

"Really? You get to stay that close to me?"

"Yeah, Detective Marx made them let me. He's a really good guy. He told the chief of police that not letting a vampyre stay with you would be like giving a human prisoner a razor blade and then turning a blind eye to whatever he did afterward. He said it was inhumane, and that by turning yourself in you had the same rights as any of them."

"That was nice of him." I suddenly realized what time it had to be—midday at the latest. "Wait, you shouldn't be here. It's daylight outside." I sat up and began looking over his body, checking him for burns.

He smiled. "I'm fine. So's Stevie Rae. We drove here in the back of the school's van—you know, the one with no windows."

I nodded and smiled. "The Chester the Molester van."

"Yep, that's how I roll now." His smile turned cocky. "Marx let us pull into the covered parking attached to the sheriff's building. No sunlight got to any of us."

"Well, be careful, okay?"

He raised his brows at me. "Really? *You're* telling *me* to be careful?"

"Asking, actually," I said, remembering kindness.

He laughed and hugged me. "Zoey Redbird, you're a hot mess, but I love you."

"I love you, too."

Too soon he let go of me and his expression sobered. "Okay, I want you to tell me everything. I already know you got pissed at the two humans and threw some kind of power at them, but I need specifics."

"Stark, can't we just—" I began, not wanting to waste a second of being with him to talk about the terrible mistake I'd made.

He cut me off. "No, we can't just ignore it. Zoey, you're a lot of things, but you're not a killer."

"I slammed two guys against a wall, and they're dead. That makes me a killer, Stark."

"See, I have a problem with that. I think that makes your Seer Stone a killer. That's why you gave it to Aphrodite, isn't it? Because it was what channeled your anger at those two guys."

I'd opened my mouth to start trying to explain to him what I didn't understand myself, but the sound of feet running down the hallway interrupted me. The guard, red-faced and wide-eyed, appeared at the door.

"Let's go, let's go! Gotta get out. Now!" he told Stark, gesturing wildly at him. "One of you vampyres can stay, but it has to be out here in the hallway. The rest of you gotta get outta here—go back to where you came from."

"Wait, it hasn't even been five minutes, let alone fifteen," Stark said.

"Nothing I can do about that. Everything's going on lockdown. There's an emergency downtown."

I followed Stark to the door, feeling like an ice cube was making a trail down my spine.

"Where downtown? What's going on?" I asked.

"All hell's broken loose at the Mayo, and they need every cop the city can spare there."

The door to my cell slammed closed, leaving Stark and me to stare at each other through the bars.

"Neferet," Stark said.

"Ah, hell," I said in complete agreement.

CHAPTER THREE

Neferet

It had been midmorning on a sleepy Sunday when Neferet commanded her threads of Darkness to open their embrace and allow her to drift from their thick cloud of blood and death to the sidewalk in front of the Mayo. She straightened her white Armani suit and swept back her long auburn hair. Neferet was ready for her glorious return to the penthouse that awaited her amid marble and stone and velvet on the rooftop. She opened the vintage brass and glass door and then paused just inside the entrance, sighing happily at the vast ballroom that opened before her, resplendent in white marble, statuesque columns, grand 1920s fixtures, and a double staircase that curved up to the promenade with the grace of a goddess's satisfied smile.

Her dark brows lifted. Her emerald gaze sharpened. Neferet studied her surroundings with renewed interest.

"It is, indeed, a building exquisite enough to be the temple of a goddess." Neferet smiled. "*My* temple. *My* home."

"Miss Neferet! Is it really you? We have been so worried that something terrible happened to you when your penthouse was vandalized."

Neferet looked from the grand ballroom to the young woman who beamed at her from behind the reception desk.

"My temple. My home. *My supplicants.*" She knew what she must do. Why had it taken her so long to think of it? Possibly because she had never absorbed as many deaths at once as she had just moments before arriving at the Mayo. Like her faithful tendrils, Neferet was pulsing with power, and that power focused and clarified her thinking.

"Yes, that is exactly how it must be. Every human in this building must worship me."

"I'm sorry, ma'am. I don't understand what you mean."

"Oh, you will. Very shortly you will." The receptionist's beaming smile had begun to fade. With preternatural movement, Neferet glided toward her. She glanced at the girl's golden name tag. "Yes, Kylee, my dear. Very shortly you will understand me completely. But first you are going to tell me how many guests are currently staying in the hotel."

"I'm sorry, ma'am," Kylee said, looking thoroughly uncomfortable. "I can't give out that information. Maybe if you told me what you need I—"

Neferet leaned forward, stroking her hand along the rich marble top of the reception counter, cutting her off and capturing the girl's gaze. "You will not question me. You will never question me. You will do as I command."

"I-I'm sorry, ma'am. I didn't mean to offend you, but information about guests of the hotel is confidential. Our—our p-privacy policy is one of the things about which we are most d-diligent," she stuttered, her hands trembling nervously as she clutched at the gold chain that held a crucifix around her neck.

Even had Neferet not been psychic, she would have known the extent of the girl's fear—little Kylee reeked of it.

"Excellent! Now that you are going to be following my commands, I will expect you to be even more vigilant about privacy—*my privacy.*"

"I'm sorry, ma'am. Do you mean that you have purchased the Mayo Hotel?" Kylee's confusion intensified along with her fear.

"Oh, much better than that, and much more permanent. I have decided to make this lovely building my first Temple. But did I not just command you not to ever question me?" Neferet sighed and made a tsking sound. "Kylee, you are going to have to do much better in the future. But do not worry your little blond head. I am a benevolent Goddess. I intend to be certain you get the help you need to be my perfect supplicant."

As Kylee gasped like a fish bereft of water, Neferet turned her back to her and faced the sea of tendrils that, unseen by the doltish Kylee, lapped over the marble floor and washed caressingly against her legs. "Children, you have fed exceedingly well. Now it is time you repaid me for the bounty I provided." They writhed excitedly, a nest of mating adders, and Neferet smiled fondly at them. "Yes, I have given you my oath. That was only the beginning of our feasting. But you must work for your food. I refuse to have children who are miscreants." She laughed gaily. "Now, I shall need one of you to possess this human. No! You may not kill her," Neferet clarified when a dozen or so tendrils began to slither with excited and obvious purpose toward Kylee. "Follow my mind into hers. Use my pathway to her innermost thoughts, wishes, desires, then coil there, around her will, and squeeze. Not enough to kill her, or rob her of whatever she has that passes for reason. I won't have a Temple full of gibbering idiots. I will have a Temple full of obedient servants. Possess her, so that I may be certain of her obedience!"

Neferet whirled around to face the girl, whose face had paled so dramatically that her brown eyes looked like dark bruises within it.

"Miss Neferet, please don't hurt me!" she said, beginning to cry.

"Kylee, my dear, my first human supplicant, this really is for the best. Free will is a terrible burden. I had free will when I was a girl, not much younger than you, and yet I was trapped in a life not of my choosing and abused. Too often that happens to humans. Look at yourself—this menial job, that substandard clothing. Do you not want more from your life?"

"Y-yes," Kylee said.

"Well, then, it is settled. If I take away your free will, I also take away the unexpected terrors life can bring. From this moment on, Kylee, I will protect you from unexpected terrors." Neferet captured the girl's wide-eyed gaze and bored into her mind. She was too focused on Kylee to look down, but she knew a strong, faithful tendril had obeyed her and was slithering up the girl's body. Though she couldn't see what was crawling up her leg, Kylee could definitely feel it. She opened her mouth and began to scream. "End her terror and enter her!" Neferet commanded, and the tendril shot up and into her open mouth.

Kylee gagged convulsively, and only Neferet's grip on her mind kept her from fainting. "So very human. So very weak," the Goddess muttered as she probed the girl's mind, feeling the familiar presence of Darkness following. When she found the center of Kylee's will—her soul, her consciousness—Neferet commanded, "Encase it!" With that extra sense—the one gifted to her by another Goddess more than a century before—Neferet witnessed Darkness imprisoning Kylee's will.

The girl slumped, her body twitching spasmodically. "Remember well the pathway I just showed you, children. Kylee is only the first of many." Neferet clapped her hands together quickly. "Come now, Kylee. Pull yourself together, my dear. Your life has just become so much *more*, and I have other commands you must obey."

Kylee jerked upright as if she were a puppet on a string.

"There, that is so much better. Now, tell me how many guests are in the hotel, and remember, no more of that irritating screaming."

"Yes ma'am," Kylee responded instantly and mechanically.

Neferet's smile returned. She was filled to overflowing with power! Humans *must* worship her—with their feeble wills and their easily manipulated minds, they really had no choice. "And stop calling me ma'am. Call me Goddess."

"Yes, Goddess," Kylee repeated automatically, her voice utterly devoid of emotion. Then she began tapping at her keyboard while she stared, stone-faced, at her computer screen. "We currently have seventy-two guests, Goddess."

"Well done, Kylee. And how many residents are living here?"

"Fifty."

Neferet took one long finger and turned Kylee's chin so that she had to meet her gaze again. "Fifty, what?"

Kylee shivered, as a horse would to dislodge clinging insects, but her gaze remained open, blank, and she corrected herself immediately by saying, "Fifty, Goddess."

"*Very* well done, Kylee. I am going to retire to my penthouse. Remember, this building is now my Temple, and I insist on having my privacy, as well as my divine body, protected. Do you understand?"

"Yes, Goddess."

"You understand that means that if anyone comes looking for me, you tell them that you are absolutely certain I am *not* here, and then you send them on their way."

"I understand, Goddess."

"Kylee, you have been exceedingly helpful. I am going to allow you to live long enough to worship me properly."

"Thank you, Goddess."

"You are most welcome, my dear."

Neferet began to glide toward the gleaming elevator. She lifted her hand, beckoning. "Come, my children. I have a feeling we are going to need to redecorate."

Bloated and pulsating with the blood on which they had so recently fed, the tendrils of Darkness slithered eagerly after their mistress.

"Just as I thought. It has been left in ruins! This is utterly unacceptable." Neferet stalked around the overturned chairs and stained rugs of the living room that had once been a meticulously kept luxury penthouse apartment. "Stale blood! The room reeks of it. Clean it!" she commanded. The tendrils obeyed her, albeit more slowly than they did when the meal she provided was fresh. "Oh, don't be so picky. Some of that blood is from Kalona. Even stale, immortal blood carries power." That seemed to perk up the tendrils, and they slithered with more enthusiasm.

While they worked, Neferet went to her wine bar, only to find it empty. Not one bottle of the dark, expensive cabernet she preferred remained. "This is what happens when I am not here to oversee those lazy humans—they neglect their duties. I have no wine and my penthouse is left in a shambles!" Neferet's annoyed gaze found the scattered pile of turquoise dust that had sifted from the cage of Darkness in which her tendrils had encased the tediously stubborn Sylvia Redbird. "And that! Get rid of that horrible blue dust. It mars the beauty of the onyx marble floor even more than those stained Persian rugs." Several tendrils attempted to obey her command, but they shied away from the blue rubble, as if it still had the power to repel them. The boldest of the slithering threads scooped into the rock dust, only to shiver and cringe away, its slick, rubbery flesh smoking and oozing dark, fetid liquid. Neferet frowned, beckoning to the tendril. With one sharp fingernail, she pierced the flesh of her palm. "Come, feed from me and heal yourself," she murmured, welcoming the cold, painful touch of the tendril's mouth, stroking it fondly as it fed from her, quivering beneath her touch.

"This will never do. Cleaning up after a human's mess is a job too menial for my loyal children. Human supplicants to clean up after human messes—that is what I need surrounding me, doing my bidding, easing my workload. And, happily, we have more than one hundred of them beneath this very roof. All of them, except the ever so helpful Kylee, are as yet unaware of how busy they will be quite soon. Hmm . . . how best to go about initiating my new subjects?"

Neferet shook off the feeding tendril. "Not so greedy. You are healed." The tendril slunk away. Neferet stroked her long, slender neck, thinking. She must weigh the best way to move forward, and she must act quickly.

She had left no one alive at the Boston Avenue Church, but what she had left were several hundred mutilated, bloodless corpses.

"The authorities will go to the House of Night first, of course. Thanatos will insist none of her pristine flock would ever so such a thing. The crone will blame me. Whether they believe her or not, even the inept local police will eventually come here looking for me." Neferet drummed her long, pointed fingernails on the black marble countertop of her disappointingly empty bar. She didn't have the luxury of time, unless she chose to go into hiding.

"No. I will never hide again. I am a Goddess, an immortal, gifted with the ability to command Darkness. Nyx never understood me. Kalona never understood me. No one ever understood me. Now I will make them understand—I will make them all understand! *The residents of Tulsa should hide from me, and not me from them.*"

She must move quickly and decisively, before the police arrived to attempt, unsuccessfully, to arrest her—or before her feast at the church hit the news and began scaring away the Mayo guests: her future supplicants.

Neferet found the remote and clicked on the large flat-screen television that was wall mounted and had, luckily, come through the battle unscathed. Turning it to a local station, she muted the babble and began to pace, thinking aloud, as she kept her eyes on the screen.

"It is a shame that I cannot encage the humans as I did that old woman and release them when I require their worship or their services. It would be so much easier on them and, ultimately and more important, on me. I would wager a great deal on the fact that none of them would put up the fight Sylvia Redbird did. Normal humans could never enter or leave a cage of Darkness created by you, my darlings. And, from what I have seen thus far, my humans are *exceedingly* normal." Neferet stopped abruptly, considering. "*My supplicants are normal humans. Tulsa is filled with normal humans. And I have become so much more than a normal human or vampyre.*"

Absently, Neferet stroked a tendril that had wrapped itself around her arm. "I wouldn't be imprisoning the humans here. I would be *protecting* them, *allowing* them to exchange the tedium of their lives for the fulfillment of worshipping me, just as I have done for Kylee." She fondled the smooth tendril while it wriggled in pleasure. "I don't need to encage them. I need to cherish them!"

Throwing her arms wide, she beamed a smile at her Dark minions that was both exquisitely beautiful and terrifying. "I have an answer to our dilemma, children! The cage we created to hold Redbird was a weak, pathetic attempt at imprisonment. I have learned so much since that night. I have gained so much power—*we* have gained so much power. We will not cage people, as if I am a gaoler instead of a goddess. My children, we are going to blanket the very walls of my Temple with your magickal, unbreachable threads so that my new supplicants will be able to worship me unhindered. And that will only be the beginning. As I absorb more and more power, why not encase the entire city? I know it now—I know my destiny. I begin my reign as Goddess of Darkness by making Tulsa my Olympus! Only this is not a weak myth passed down as trite stories from schoolchildren to schoolchildren. This will be reality—a Dark Otherworld come to earth! And in my Dark Otherworld, there will be no innocents being abused by predators. All will be under my protection. I hold their fates in my hands—they have only to look to my welfare to be fulfilled. Ah, how they will worship mc!"

Around her, the tendrils writhed in response to her excitement. She smiled and stroked those nearest to her. "Yes, yes, I know. It will be glorious, but what I require first, my children, is room service. Let us summon my new minions. Some of them will clean and set my chambers to right. Some of them will replenish my wine. All of them will obey me without question. Ready yourselves. The time of Neferet, Goddess of Darkness, is here!"

It went smoother than even Neferet had imagined. Not only were humans ridiculously easy to control, they were also all as utterly defenseless as little Kylee against the infestation of a single tendril of Darkness. She had been absolutely correct. They needed her to order their lives as a babe needs its mother.

The only problem in her plan was that Neferet did not have access to an infinite number of tendrils. Only the most loyal, her true children, had remained at her side after she had shattered.

She briefly considered sending out a call for more threads of Darkness, but just as quickly rejected the notion. She would not reward betrayal—and the threads that had abandoned her in her time of need had betrayed her at her deepest level.

Neferet sipped her favorite cabernet from a crystal goblet as she paced around her penthouse, counting the humans who were laboriously cleaning and setting to right the mess Zoey and her friends had left. Six. There were four women from housekeeping and two men from room service. Neferet's lips tilted up. Actually, they were little more than boys—both blond and eager to answer her room service request. Stepping off her elevator, their expressions had given away their thoughts so clearly she hadn't bothered probing their minds. They wanted her. Very badly. They had obviously been hoping she wanted a little blood and sex with her wine. Fools! Now they moved mechanically, completing the commands she had issued with no complaints, no worries, and no irritating flirtatious glances. They were, as she preferred her human men, silent and biddable and young.

"Gentlemen, life is glorious. Don't you agree?"

The two blond heads lifted and turned in her direction. "Yes, Goddess," they spoke together, as if by rote.

Neferet smiled. "As I often say, free will is a terrible burden. You are welcome for relieving you of it." Then she commanded, "Get back to work."

"Thank you, Goddess. Yes, Goddess," they repeated, and obeyed.

So, she had used six threads already. No, seven, counting little Kylee at the front desk. Neferet glanced contemplatively at the nest of tendrils where they swarmed around the broken doors that led to the rooftop balcony, absorbing the last of Kalona's dried blood. How many were there? She tried to count, but it was impossible. They moved too quickly and too often, and they tended to merge together and then separate at will. There did appear to be many of them remaining, though. And they had all grown larger, thicker, markedly stronger, after feasting.

I must make sure they remain well-fed. They cannot waste away—thus will my absolute control over the humans waste away.

Decisively, Neferet lifted the phone and punched zero for the receptionist.

"Front desk. How may I help you, Neferet?" Kylee's perky voice answered on the first ring.

"Kylee, when I call you, the correct way to answer the telephone is to say, 'How may I serve you, my Goddess?'"

Kylee's voice flattened out, and with no emotion at all she said, "How may I serve you, my Goddess?"

"Well done, Kylee. You are such a quick learner. I need to know how many staff members are working here at my Temple today."

"Six housekeepers, two bellboys, four room service personnel, and myself. Rachel should be working the front desk with me, but she called in sick."

"Poor, unfortunate Rachel. But that leaves a lucky thirteen as my staff. Of course that doesn't count the restaurant, though. Is it open today?"

"Yes, we are open for brunch until two o'clock every Sunday."

"And how many staff are there today?"

Kylee paused and then counted off, "The chef, his sous chef, another cook who works the line, the bartender, who is also the manager, and three waitresses."

"For a total of twenty. Here is what you will do, Kylee. Close the restaurant immediately, but do *not* allow any of the workers to leave.

Tell them there has been a change in the management of the hotel and the new owner has called a meeting of all the staff."

"I will do as you say, Goddess, but the restaurant is not owned by the Snyders."

"Who are the Snyders?"

"The family who bought and renovated the Mayo in 2001. They own the building."

"Correction, Kylee, my dear, they *owned* the building that was known as the Mayo Hotel. I *control* the Temple it has become. No matter. It will all be made very clear, very soon. All I need you to do for me right now is to gather every one of the staff members, restaurant and hotel, and direct them to report to my penthouse in thirty minutes. Afterward, I will do away with the staff meeting title and call it what it truly will become: an opportunity to worship your Goddess. Doesn't that sound much more pleasant than a staff meeting?"

"Yes, Goddess," Kylee repeated.

"Excellent, Kylee. I shall see you and the rest of my new supplicants in thirty minutes."

"Goddess, I cannot leave the front desk unattended. What will happen if someone tries to check in or out?"

"The answer is simple, Kylee. Chain all of the doors through which one may enter or leave my Temple, lock them, and then join me with the keys."

"Yes, Goddess."

Neferet was going to have to find a different place in which to receive the supplications of her subjects. Her penthouse was far too intimate for so many humans. Nevertheless, she would have to make do temporarily. She'd positioned herself standing within the stained-glass doors that had been broken, now newly replaced by one of the two blond boys. She'd turned off all of the garish electric lights and commanded the housekeepers to bring candles to her chamber. Pillars and pots and votives covered the granite bar, the fireplace mantel, the marble art deco coffee table, and the large wooden dining room table. She'd also ordered the lanterns on either side of the doors to have the garish lightbulbs ripped from them and replaced with the warm, flickering light of two white tapers. She made a mental note to send one of her minions out for more candles—many, many more candles.

Neferet's gaze swept around her penthouse, and she was pleased. Everything looked so much better, and she was so enjoying her second bottle of cabernet, thinking how much more she would enjoy it later, privately, when one of her supplicants offered to mix his—or her—blood with it.

Neferet had dressed carefully, glad none of her clothes had been disturbed while she'd been gone. She chose a dressing gown made of golden silk that clung to her body as if it were caressing her. As usual, Neferet left her thick auburn hair falling free in glistening waves around her waist. She did not adorn herself with a symbol of any other goddess. No upraised, silver embroidered images would ever be allowed on her person again—she'd ripped the last of those threads out herself.

Neferet had a new symbol. She had been considering it carefully, and she could hardly wait until one of her supplicants ordered the custom piece from Moody's jewelry store and "surprised" her with a six-carat ruby shaped like a perfect teardrop. She would be effusive in her thanks and wear it always on a solid gold chain.

It was, indeed, going to be good to be Goddess of Darkness—Goddess of Tulsa—Goddess of Chaos.

The elevator chimed. "Children, come to me!" The threads of Darkness rushed to her, surrounding her, lapping against her naked feet with their comforting coldness. "Oh, and supplicants, you may return to my presence," she called over her shoulder to where she'd sent her servants to wait until she wished to command them again. They shuffled past her just as the elevator doors opened and Kylee led the rest of the staff into the penthouse.

"Welcome!" Neferet raised her glass and lifted her arms. "You are blessed to be in my presence."

Most of the group looked confused. Two women, dressed as waitresses, muttered questions to one another. Neferet's sharp eyes took note of them. One of the men, the one wearing the silly white chef's hat, spoke up. "Can you tell us what's going on here? We had to close the restaurant and make our patrons leave—even though they weren't finished with brunch. I can tell you, there are some pissed off *ex-customers* out there right now."

"What is your name?" Neferet asked him, keeping her voice pleasant.

"Tony Witherby, but most people call me Chef."

"Well, Tony, I am not most people. You see, *most people* call me Goddess."

He barked a patronizing laugh. "You're kidding, right? I mean, I can see your tattoos and I know you're a vampyre and all, but vampyres aren't goddesses."

Neferet was pleased to see that Kylee had stepped away from the chef as if she didn't want to be contaminated by his disobedience. Kylee really was becoming an excellent supplicant.

Neferet didn't waste even a glance at the chef. Instead she smiled down at her writhing children. "So eager," she half chided, half encouraged. "So smart." She bent to stroke a particularly precocious tendril that had wrapped itself around her leg and crawled almost to her thigh. "You will do nicely."

"Okay, you're gonna have to let us in on the joke or I'm gonna call the owner of the restaurant," the chef said. When she continued to ignore him, he began to bluster, "This really is ridicu—"

"Take him!" Neferet commanded. "And let yourself be seen."

The tendril became visible as it flew at the chef. It was so large that it easily coiled around his thick waist, moving quickly upward.

"What the fuck! Get it off me!" the chef shrieked, and lurched backward, beating impotently at the tendril with both of his thick hands.

Neferet thought he sounded like a young girl who had been frightened by a spider.

A tall, handsome black man dressed in a bellman's uniform moved to go to the chef's aid.

"Stay where you are or your fate will be the same as his!" Neferet snapped.

The man froze.

"Nooooo!" The chef's shrieks echoed with hysteria, and Neferet was relieved that it was at that moment the tendril slithered up his neck and surged into his mouth, causing it to open so impossibly wide that the corners of his lips split open and began to bleed before the thick length of it disappeared within the human's body. The chef slumped to the floor.

"I do think it is unfortunate when a grown man sounds like a frightened little girl, don't you?"

The humans who were not possessed by her children stared at her with mixed expressions of horror and disbelief. The whispering waitresses had begun to sob. Another woman, one of the housekeepers who hadn't answered Neferet's earlier summons, was praying in Spanish and clutching the crucifix that dangled around her neck from a rather cheap-looking silver necklace. The entire group, except for misguided Tony, were backing, herd-like, toward the elevator doors.

"No," Neferet said mildly. "You may not leave until I release you."

"Are you going to kill us, too?" one of the women asked, holding her friend's hands and trembling spasmodically.

"Kill you? Of course not. Tony isn't dead." Neferet addressed the chef, who was still slumped on the floor. "Tony, my dear, stand up and tell the others that you are perfectly fine."

Woodenly, Tony stood. He jerked around until he was facing Neferet. Then, with no expression on his florid, blood-spattered face he said, "I am perfectly fine."

"You forgot something," Neferet said.

Tony's body twitched spasmodically, as if he had been electrified from within, and he hastily repeated, "I am perfectly fine, Goddess."

"There, you see? It is just as I said. What is your name, my dear?" she asked the trembling woman.

"Elinor," she said.

"What a lovely old name. You don't hear names like that anymore, and it is such a shame. Where have all the Elinors and Elizabeths, Gertrudes, Gladyses, and Phyllises gone? No, no need to answer me. They have been overrun by the Haileys and Kaylees, Madisons and Jordans. I loathe modern names. You know, Elinor, I must thank you. Your tasteful name has helped me come to a decision about you, my new supplicants. I am going to rename any of you who have overly perky names." Neferet glanced at Kylee and smiled. "Except for you, Kylee. I like your gold name tag too much to change your name."

"Goddess?" Elinor whispered the name as a question.

"Yes, my dear."

"Are—are we working for you now?"

"Oh, much better than that. You are worshipping me now. The twenty of you are the first witnesses of my reign as Goddess of Darkness. You each will have a very special and important role to fulfill as you worship me and attend to my every need. You will offer gifts and sacrifices to me, and in return I will take from you the exhausting free will that has obviously repressed and depressed you all of your lives. Why else would you be working in such menial and meaningless jobs?"

"I don't understand what is happening." Elinor wept.

"Very shortly your confusion will be gone. Don't worry, sweet Elinor, it only hurts for a moment." Neferet raised her arm. "Children—" she began.

"Wait!" The bellman who had wanted to help Tony stepped forward and unflinchingly met Neferet's gaze. "You said if we tried to help Chef, our fate would be the same as his. I didn't help him. None of us helped him. So, according to your own word, you're not going to send those snake-things on us."

"And what is your name?"

"Judson." He paused and then added, "Goddess."

"Judson, that's a name from the Old South, did you know that?"

"No, I—I, no, I didn't," another pause, "Goddess."

"Well, it is. I won't change your name, either. And about what I said before? I lied. Take them!" Neferet commanded.

Thankfully, her children had anticipated her wishes and moved swiftly, so that the annoying shrieking ended very, very soon.

CHAPTER FOUR

Neferet

Neferet sent her new supplicants, each initiated into her worship by the possession of one of her children, and commanded that they rouse the hotel guests and residents, and have them gather in the grand ballroom.

Neferet had decided she would set up her offering room in the main ballroom. It was surrounded by marble columns with a lovely high ceiling, ornate art deco chandeliers, and a wide double staircase with a curved wrought-iron banister that had a landing between the ground floor—where her supplicants would stand—and the upper-level promenade, where only her closest worshippers, or those tending to her needs, would be allowed. The others would be confined either to their rooms or to the basement holding area, which Kylee had been so kind as to show her. Or if they were too much of a nuisance, and she didn't care to waste a tendril to possess them, they would become food for her children.

Neferet would, of course, only feed from those supplicants who captured her interest.

Kylee had been tasked with finding a chair that would have to suffice as a throne until she could have a proper one commissioned to be carved.

"You'll need to find a master craftsman to create exactly what I require. The wood must be stained the deep red of bull's blood," she spoke as she chose the setting carefully. "And with none of those wretchedly cold, hard seats that the crones on the High Council prefer. Pillows of golden velvet—that is what I will sit upon."

Neferet allowed two of the most attractive housekeepers to wrap her in a luxurious dressing gown of royal purple, and had just decided that she would not wear any shoes—she would be barefoot, as should befit a newly born Goddess, when she returned to her living room to refill her wine goblet—annoyed that there was no eager human waiting on her. She was already waiting, impatiently, for the guests and residents to be rounded up by her obedient staff so that she could make her entrance to the ballroom.

"Even for a Goddess, it is so difficult to find good help. But I shall let this mistake pass. There are only twenty of them. They must be quite busy herding the humans into my offering room. Though I shall only let it pass this one time." She was sipping the rich red liquid, enjoying the taste of the blood the handsome bellman had so graciously volunteered to slice open his flesh to flavor her wine with, when the television caught her peripheral vision. There was a breaking news feed going across the bottom of the screen, MURDERS IN TULSA, and the anchor, Chera Kimiko, was speaking with a somber expression.

Delighted, Neferet hit the mute button, expecting to relive the delicious details of her feast. But instead of the Boston Avenue Church, the screen filled with a picture of Woodward Park, in a terrible state of burned-out unattractiveness. Then the camera shifted and Neferet's brows lifted as they focused on the rock wall beside the grotto that had so recently been her sanctuary. She tapped impatiently at the volume in time to hear Kimiko, sounding oh-so-serious.

"This is the site of the gruesome murders of the two men, whose bodies were discovered by firefighters yesterday morning. As we reported earlier, the violent thunderstorm that created winds in excess of seventy miles per hour also carried with it deadly lightning. Lightning strikes in the Tulsa area have accounted for five deaths today, with ten more people still hospitalized in serious condition. But the death of these two men was, apparently, unrelated to the storm. Adam Paluka is live with Detective Kevin Marx, and we go to him for the details. Adam?"

The scene changed from the storm-ravaged park to a detective sitting behind a desk in a mundane-looking office. Neferet recognized him as the officer who had, annoyingly, seemed sympathetic to Zoey Redbird in the past. She scowled as she watched the brief interview.

"Detective Marx, could you please explain about the two additional deaths at Woodward Park, and have you truly ruled out storm-related causes?"

"The bodies of two men, both in their mid-forties, were discovered early yesterday. The cause of death was the same for both men—blunt force trauma and loss of blood."

Neferet smiled, deciding this was an excellent preshow rehearsal for the carnage they would soon discover.

"And is it true that you have taken into custody someone who confessed to the killings?"

Neferet's brows lifted. "Confessed to the killings? In custody? That is quite impossible."

"Yes, I am sad to report that a young fledgling, one I know personally, came forward of her own volition and confessed that she killed the two men."

"A fledgling!" Neferet exploded off the chaise, shouting at the television screen.

"May we have the name of this fledgling?"

"Zoey Redbird."

Neferet shrieked, picked up one of the electric lamps she had unplugged, and hurled it at the screen.

"That simpering, feeble child believes she killed those two men? I found them, barely stunned, mere feet from my sanctuary, and their blood served to feed me so that I could make my way to the grand feast at the Boston Avenue Church. Zoey Redbird kill two grown men? What utter nonsense! She doesn't have the will to kill anyone! And she actually confessed to their murder? That girl is a bigger idiot than even I could have imagined." Neferet threw back her head and mocking laughter filled the penthouse.

Neferet had taken her position in the middle of the graceful double staircase of the main ballroom of the Mayo Hotel. She loved the irony that she was standing in the very spot where so many deluded human couples had spoken their wedding vows.

"Boxed pasta lasts longer than most human marriages. Did you know that?" She smiled at the crowd assembled on the gleaming black and white marble floor. She had ordered that the chandeliers be dimmed and that large candelabrums be set and lit to the left and right of her on the landing. She knew her beauty was divine and complemented by the way her gown shimmered with the candlelight's caress.

She had commanded that half of her twenty supplicants surround her, though without actually entering her landing. The other ten possessed humans were stationed at the entrance to her Temple. She had given them one command: no one is allowed to enter or exit.

Her Dark children writhed around her, invisible to the gaping humans but comforting to her with their familiar eagerness.

"Ah, you are correct not to respond. That question really wasn't worthy of a Goddess's first address to her chosen people. Let me begin anew."

Neferet positioned herself in front of her throne, spread her arms wide, and said, "Behold! I am Neferet, Goddess of Darkness, Queen Tsi Sgili. I have made this hotel my Temple Dark, and you—you fortunate few—shall be my loyal supplicants, my Chosen Ones. I, in turn, shall reward your worship by removing the cares of the mundane world from you. You need no longer toil at your meaningless jobs. You need not return to tedious marriages and unappreciative children. From today until your deaths, your only purpose is to worship me. Rejoice, humans!"

Her speech was followed by a long moment of absolute silence, and then the crowd began to rustle nervously with whispers.

Neferet waited for what she knew would come, and that knowledge kept the beatific smile on her face. She did so enjoy teaching humans life lessons.

As expected, Neferet didn't have to wait long. A woman stepped forward. She was tall and brunette—probably late middle-aged, though she had the well-preserved, well-exercised look of a woman who worked diligently to maintain what was left of her youth. She was wearing a tasteful, meticulously cut dress that was a beautiful shade of emerald green.

"Wherever did you get that lovely dress?" Neferet asked the human before she could speak.

The woman blinked in obvious surprise at the question but answered, "It's a Halston. I bought it at Miss Jackson's."

"Kylee," Neferet called down to where the girl stood, looking serenely robotic, at the bottom of the stairs. "Make a note. I'm going to need you to go to Miss Jackson's and choose a variety of dresses for me. Be sure to include a Halston design."

"Yes, Goddess," Kylee intoned emotionlessly.

Neferet frowned, staring at Kylee. Did she really want the girl choosing her raiment for her? The child couldn't be more than twenty, and if her hacked-off haircut was an example of her fashion sense, it really could be a disaster to—

"Okay, you need to explain what is *really* going on. I don't have time for this." Recovering from her surprise, the emerald-dressed woman interrupted Neferet's internal contemplation. She rested one well-manicured hand on her slim hip and looked up at Neferet, tapping her foot impatiently. "I have early dinner plans at the Summit Club, and a plane back to New York to catch afterward."

"I have already explained the situation to you," Neferet said. "I am now your Goddess. You will not have dinner at the Summit Club, nor will you be returning to New York—unless I command you there on an errand for me. Your only job is to worship me. In return I take away your worldly woes and cares. What size is that dress? A four or a six?"

"Seriously, this is a bad joke. Frank Snyder is behind this, isn't he? Frank?" The woman ignored Neferet and called the man's name, looking around as if expecting him to appear. "She's dressed like a silver screen diva. Let me guess—she's going to sing "Smoke Gets in Your Eyes" for my birthday, right? How ever did you find a vampyre for hire? Or are those tattoos painted on?" The woman had completed a full circle and was facing Neferet again, peering up at her as if she was considering trying to wipe at her tattoos.

Neferet decided that her patience had come to an end.

"Chosen Ones, let this be a lesson for you. I am *not* a joke. I am your Goddess—powerful, possessive, immortal, and omniscient. I am almost completely devoid of patience, and I never, ever suffer fools." Neferet leaned forward, resting a hand on the iron banister. She met the woman's gaze and plunged into her unprotected mind. "So, your name is Nancy, and it is the day of your birth." Neferet's smile was catlike. "And you are fifty-three, though you tell your friends you are forty-five."

The woman's body spasmed and she gasped, shocked by the violation but powerless to resist. "How could you know that? And how dare you!"

Neferet made a tsking sound. "Such a life of self-deprivation in the name of beauty. Did no one explain to you that, no matter what you did, *you were human—you were meant to age?* Nancy, you should have eaten more pasta, drunk more wine, slept with your neighbor's young son more than twice, and left your loathsome husband when he had his first affair twenty-five years ago. And, Nancy, I know these things because I am a Goddess. I dare to say these things because I am *your* Goddess, though you are, obviously, undeserving of me."

The people standing around Nancy shifted, as if they wanted to move away from her, but still had dazed looks of confusion and disbelief on their bovine faces.

"It would be wise to stand away from Nancy. I know my Temple has laundry facilities, but there is no reason to unnecessarily stain your clothing." The people closest to Nancy took a few halting steps away from her. Neferet smiled encouragement at them as she bent and lifted one of the tendrils that lapped around her bare feet. It was satisfyingly thick and heavy, and its cold, rubbery skin pulsed against her flesh as it wound around her arm. "Kill Nancy. Make her suffer. She filled her life with suffering, so suffering in death should be a comfort to her." Neferet spoke fondly to her child. "And allow yourself to be seen."

She hurled the creature at Nancy. It became visible midair. There were gasps and exclamations from the crowd, which changed to screams when the tendril wrapped itself around Nancy's neck and began, slowly, to saw through her flesh and cut off her head.

The crowd unfroze all at once and, crying out in panic, they surged toward the exit.

"*I have not given you permission to leave my presence!*" Filled with immortal power, Neferet's voice echoed around the vast ballroom. "*Children, show yourselves to my people!*"

The nest of Darkness surrounding her rippled and became visible, but few of the people noticed them. They were too busy staring in horror at the black snake-like heads of the tendrils that had possessed her staff and who, at her command, had made themselves visible within the open, gaping mouths of each of the robotic humans guarding the exit.

Neferet made another mental note—she must be certain to reward those of her children who had volunteered for the tedious task of possessing her staff. They were being so obedient, so responsive. Another feast must soon be in order for them.

Neferet felt a small shaft of power slide into her body and she shifted her attention to Nancy, whose head had finally been sliced off. There was so much blood, though, that the one tendril couldn't feed fast enough. Neferet sighed. The shining marble floor was going to be soiled. Must she do everything herself?

"Feed from her—quickly!" Neferet commanded the children closest to her. "I cannot abide a mess in my Temple." Then she sighed again and turned her attention to the panicked crowd. "You are making a poor beginning!" she called to them. "In return for lives filled with new purpose, all I ask is your obedience and your worship. Nancy gave me neither, and you see what happened to her. Let that be a lesson to you—to all of you."

"What are those creatures?" a short, round man asked, obviously trying to control his fear as he stroked the arm of a woman who was likewise short and fat, and who had buried her face in his suit coat, sobbing.

"They are my children, formed of Darkness and loyal only to me."

"Why are they in those people's mouths?" he said.

"Because those people are my staff and they, too, must be loyal only to me. Possessing them is more efficient than cutting off their heads. Now, do you see how much simpler it is if you just do as I command?"

"But this is insane!" a man standing near the rear of the ballroom yelled. "You can't really expect us to stay here and worship you? We have lives, families. People will miss us."

"I am certain they will, but as they are *people* and not immortals, that does not concern me. Though, if you are very, very good, I may give permission for your families to join you."

"You won't be allowed to do this," said a woman between sobs. "The police will come for us."

Neferet laughed. "Oh, I do hope so. I look forward to the confrontation. Let me assure you, the Tulsa Police Department will not be victorious."

"What now? What are we going to do? Oh my god! Oh my god!" shrieked another woman.

"Shut her up!" Neferet commanded, and a tendril flew at the woman, wrapping around her face and closing her mouth. Writhing, she fell to the floor.

Neferet breathed a long sigh of relief when not just her shrieks stopped but all of the herd-like panic stilled as well. She straightened her already perfectly fitted gown and spoke calmly to her shocked and staring supplicants. "You should learn these lessons now." She ticked the lessons off with her long, slim fingers. "I cannot abide hysteria. I cannot abide disloyalty. I am also not overly fond of middle-aged white men. Now, I need sixty volunteers. Who would like to attend to some very important business in my penthouse?"

No one moved. No one met her gaze. Neferet sighed again and added, "I will not be feeding on any of those sixty volunteers." A young woman raised a trembling hand. "Yes, my dear. What is your question?"

"Are—are you going to tell the snakes to go into our mouths?"

Neferet smiled sweetly at her. "No, I am not."

"Th-then I'll volunteer," she said.

"Well done!" Neferet praised. "What is your name?"

"Staci."

"No, I shall call you Gladys. That is a much more dignified name, don't you think?"

The young girl's head nodded jerkily.

"So, Gladys, move over to the left side of my offering chamber. Now, I want fifty-nine more people to be as enthusiastic as Gladys, and to join her."

When no one else moved, Neferet filled her voice with anger and shouted, "*Now!*"

As if struck by a whip, a group of the humans bolted to join Gladys.

"Kylee, count them and let me know when I have sixty volunteers."

With increasing impatience, Neferet waited. Finally, Kylee called, "There are sixty volunteers, Goddess."

"Very good. Be a dear, Kylee, and take them to my penthouse. Have them wait on the balcony for my command. Oh, and open several cases of champagne. Pour generously. My volunteers must be rewarded!"

Looking confused but relieved, the sixty shuffled to the elevators. Neferet turned her attention to the remaining worshippers. They were staring up at her as if they were waiting for her to drop an enormous guillotine blade on them all.

"It would be easier to possess them all. Instructing modern humans on how to properly worship a Goddess is going to be unendingly tedious," Neferet muttered to herself as she drummed her fingers against the iron railing.

A woman who was standing close enough to hear her took several steps toward the staircase and then, catching Neferet's gaze, she sank into a deep, graceful curtsy. Neferet's brows went up. She studied the woman, who remained in a curtsy, head respectfully bowed. She was older than Nancy had been, but not by much. And though she was tastefully dressed in a well-cut, expensive suit, she looked her age.

"You may rise," Neferet finally said.

"Thank you, Goddess. May I have your permission to present myself to you?"

"You may, indeed," Neferet said, thoroughly intrigued.

"I am Lynette Witherspoon, owner of Everlasting Expressions. I would like to offer my services to you."

"Lynette. Yes, that name is inoffensive. You may keep it. And what exactly is Everlasting Expressions?"

"It is my company. I provide event planning, design, and coordination for a discriminating clientele," she said.

Neferet appreciated the pride and confidence in her voice. "And what is it you propose to do for me?"

"Everything," Lynette said firmly. She looked around the ballroom at the people huddled behind her before candidly meeting Neferet's gaze. "I believe the worship of a Goddess is an ongoing event of major importance that should be smoothly and tastefully run. If you allow me, I can assure you that your worship will be one spectacular event after another."

"Interesting . . ." Neferet mused. "Lynette, you will not mind if I take a brief and painless glimpse at your motives, will you?" Though she phrased it as a question, Neferet didn't wait for Lynette's response. She did move into the woman's mind more gently than she had Nancy's, though.

What she found made the Goddess smile. "Lynette, you are an opportunist."

"Y-yes," she said a little shakily after Neferet left her mind.

"And you loathe men." Neferet's smile widened.

"I am not divine, so I can only guess, but I think you understand that loathing," Lynette said.

"I like you, Lynette. I will allow you to manage the planning of my worship."

Lynette curtsied deeply again. "Thank you, Goddess."

"And what is your first order of business?" Neferet was almost unbearably curious about what this unusual human intended.

"Well," Lynette said, patting her chignon and studying the people who stood silently, stupidly behind her, "all events begin with two things—the correct clothing and the correct decorations."

"I have only one requirement—dazzle me," Neferet said.

"Yes, Goddess," Lynette said respectfully.

"And you, my supplicants"—she gestured at the rest of the herd—"do whatever Lynette commands." Neferet cut her eyes at Lynette and added, "As long as she doesn't command you to try to leave my Temple."

"I wouldn't think of it, Goddess," Lynette said quickly.

"Oh, my dear, you have thought of it. You just realized how unwise that thought was."

Lynette bowed her head. "Touché, Goddess."

"Now, I leave my subjects in your capable hands, Lynette. I am going to retire to my penthouse to prepare the—"

Neferet's departure was interrupted by the tall bellman, Judson, calling from where he stood in front of the chained and locked front doors of the Mayo. "Goddess! The police are here!"

CHAPTER FIVE

Lynette

"Help! Police! She's keeping us trapped in here!" A girl Lynette recognized as the maid of honor from last night's spectacularly expensive wedding screamed and, slipping around a snake-possessed staff member, began pounding on the thick glass of the front doors.

"Why must I always do everything myself? Staff, all of you except Judson take these humans to the basement!" Neferet's voice was filled with venom and the hotel staff reacted as if she had shot an electric current into them. As one, they began roughly prodding the group of terrified people toward a rear emergency exit. The vampyre floated down the staircase and drifted across the ballroom floor, passing so closely by Lynette that the train of her purple robe brushed over her feet. Lynette backed away, trying to blend inconspicuously with the shadows and avoid being culled with the rest of the herd, but Neferet snapped at her, "You, come with me. I wouldn't want you to miss the event *I* am planning."

"As you wish, Goddess." Lynette straightened her back, kept a tight hold on her fear, and followed Neferet. No matter what, she was not going to end like those poor staff schmucks who had the vampyre's disgusting snakes peeking out of their mouths. Nor was she going to do something stupid and get her head cut off. She'd survived an alcoholic mother and an abusive, white trash childhood to build an empire of her own. She had money and social status. She drove a Mercedes-Benz S-Class and owned a six-thousand-square-foot home in Eight Acres, the most exclusive, expensive gated community in midtown Tulsa. She vacationed in France and she only flew first class. She'd damn well survive a power-crazed vampyre who had delusions of immortality, *and* she'd figure out a way to profit from the situation.

Neferet had reached the shrieking girl. "You are not a proper supplicant!" With unnatural strength, she took a fist full of the girl's over-processed blond hair and pulled her head back until Lynette was sure her neck would snap. Then she pointed at the screaming girl's mouth. "Possess her!"

Lynette wanted to look away, but she couldn't. The black snake burrowed into the girl's mouth. Her eyes rolled in her head so that only the whites showed and her body went completely limp. Only Neferet's hold on her hair kept her upright. "I am going to name you Mabel. When I command, you will come willingly to me," Neferet snarled, lifting the unconscious girl's face so that it was only a finger's length from hers. The sightless eyes blinked. As if the vampyre had thrown a switch, the terror on the girl's face was gone, leaving only a wooden but attentive expression in her blank eyes.

"Yes, Goddess," she intoned emotionlessly.

Those horrid snakes are in complete control of whomever they possess, Lynette thought. *Not me,* she promised herself. *It will not be me. I'd rather die than end up like that!*

Neferet let loose her hold on the girl. She staggered, as if unbalanced, but remained standing. The vampyre smoothed her perfect hair and brushed an invisible speck of something from the shoulder of her robe. Then she glared at Lynette. "You know what will happen if you disappoint me and it turns out you aren't a proper supplicant."

Lynette did not look away from Neferet's emerald eyes. She did drop down in the deep curtsy the vampyre had appreciated earlier. "I will not disappoint you, Goddess."

She felt the sick slide of Neferet touching her mind and focused her thoughts on the truth—no damn way did she intend on doing anything that would cause the vampyre to turn against her.

"Soon, Lynette, you will believe that I am Goddess, and that your destiny is to serve me." Before Lynette could comment, Neferet had turned her back to her, commanding, "Judson, unchain the front doors. Lynette, you will join me. Children, do not allow yourselves to be seen, but attend me!"

With a swoosh that had long reminded Lynette of old money and opulence, the austere brass and glass double doors opened and Neferet strode out, with Lynette close on her heels, so close she could feel an awful chill that radiated from the invisible snakes.

There were two TPD cars and an unmarked town car idling in the small circular drive directly in front of the hotel. Four uniformed officers were talking to a tall man in plain clothes, who was obviously in charge, which meant he was a detective of some type. At Neferet's appearance, the group instantly shifted their attention to the beautiful vampyre. The detective nodded to the others. They fell in step behind him as, stern-faced, he began to approach Neferet.

"No, I want you to remain by your cars," Neferet said. She'd stayed close to the doors, standing under the wrought-iron awning that was the hallmark of the Mayo's entrance. She took a small step to the side and draped her arm around Lynette's shoulders—and shoved her.

Lynette didn't have to be psychic to know what the vampyre wanted her to do. Without hesitation, she stepped forward so that she was standing between Neferet and the police. Neferet's hand rested on her shoulder, and Lynette could feel the vampyre's hard, sharp fingernails pressing against the skin of her neck just over the artery that beat strong and fast there.

Lynette held perfectly still.

The tall man hesitated only a moment, though that moment seemed an eternity to Lynette. Then he and the officers took several steps back.

"There, that is so much better." Lynette could hear the smile in Neferet's voice. "Now we can chat more politely. Detective Marx, it is so nice of you to visit me. It has turned out to be a lovely afternoon, hasn't it? It is as if the tumult of yesterday's weather washed the city clean." Neferet spoke affably, one hand still resting on Lynette's shoulder.

"Neferet, I need to ask you some questions. Would you rather come down to the station than have me interview you here?"

Neferet's sigh was one of exaggerated disappointment. "So there are to be no social niceties between us?"

"Under normal circumstances, I have no problem with social niceties, as you well know. You and I have worked amicably together before. But what happened in Tulsa yesterday was far from normal, and I don't have time for much politeness." He paused and gestured at Lynette. "And I think it's pretty ironic that you're complaining about social niceties when you're holding a hostage in front of you."

The pressure from Neferet's fingernail was instantly gone, and the vampyre withdrew her hand from Lynette with an intimate caress of her cheek. "Detective, you are very mistaken. Lynette, are you my hostage?"

"No, Goddess," she said, shaking her head and doing her best to act as if it was an everyday occurrence to be a human shield for a psychotic vampyre. "I am your willing supplicant."

"There, you see. All is well. Lynette is simply here because she worships me. But why are you here, Detective Marx? Are the questions you are so curious about regarding Woodward Park or the Boston Avenue Church?"

Lynette saw the detective's eyes narrow. "What do you know about the Boston Avenue Church?"

Neferet laughed. "Everything! Ask me a question, any question at all. Would you like to know how long that mewing excuse for a pastor screamed before I killed him, or why the councilman's wife was missing her lovely white Armani suit, which was, coincidentally, just my size, when you found her drained, lifeless body outside the so-called sanctuary? You see, blood is very difficult to get out of fine linen."

As Neferet was speaking, Lynette watched the change in the police. First, their faces registered shock, and then, as they drew their guns, revulsion and anger.

The detective's gun pointed over Lynette's right shoulder. "Lynette," he called to her. "Walk directly to us. Keep your hands clear, where we can see them."

Lynette knew it didn't matter that Neferet wasn't touching her. She had absolutely no choice. "No, thank you," she said, managing somehow to keep her voice from shaking. "I'm happy staying here with the Goddess."

"What the hell are you talking about?" one of the cops blurted. "She's a fucking vampyre who murdered a church full of innocent people! She isn't a goddess."

"Lynette, I do not appreciate foul language. Do you?" Neferet asked.

Holding her breath, Lynette responded the only way she could. Shaking her head, she said, "No, I don't."

Neferet cocked her head to the side and studied the officer who had spoken. Lynette saw his body twitch. "Officer Jamison, does foul language fill your mind when you fantasize about your ten-year-old stepdaughter? How about when you watch her sleep and admit to yourself that you are mere days away from taking your desires for her from fantasies to reality?"

The color drained from the officer's face. "That's a fucking lie!" he sputtered.

"More profanity. Methinks the man doth protest too much," Neferet said, then she spoke conspiratorially to Lynette. "It is a misquote, yet it seems to fit the situation well, don't you think?"

"Yes, I do," Lynette said, watching the officer closely. The man was red-faced and looked as if he could explode at any moment—and Lynette realized Neferet hadn't been baiting him or making anything up. She'd slid into his mind and revealed his dirty little secret.

"You fucking bitch!" Officer Jamison yelled.

"That's enough of that!" Detective Marx commanded the uniformed man, then he refocused on Lynette and Neferet, speaking in a clear, calm voice that made Lynette wish she could run from the vampyre's insanity straight into his protection. "Lynette, if you choose to remain with Neferet, then you may also join her in a jail cell. Neferet, you are under arrest for the murder of the entire congregation of the Boston Avenue Church."

Neferet's laughter was humorless, cruel. "You cannot even get the charges against me correct, Detective."

"You just confessed to those murders!" Marx said. He'd lost the professional objectivity his voice had maintained until then. With a terrible tightening in her stomach, Lynette realized the unbelievable truth—Neferet had slaughtered an entire church full of innocent people.

She had to grasp her hands together in front of her to keep them from trembling.

"You are so disappointingly narrow-minded, Detective Marx. What I did in the church wasn't murder—it was sacrifice, and it was glorious!

I do so wish you could have been there to bear witness to it, but had you been *there,* you wouldn't be *here* to bear witness to the beginning of my reign. Oh, but I digress. Your charges are incorrect because they are incomplete. You forgot to add the little snack I made of your mayor a few nights earlier."

Detective Marx's face was a mask of loathing. "My gut said the House of Night vampyres were telling the truth when they said you were responsible for the mayor's death."

"For once, they were correct. But let me continue my *confession.* It is such a shame that there was no one yesterday at Woodward Park to witness my triumphant exit from my lovely, sheltering den and to watch me discover two deliciously stunned men who practically begged me to drain their blood from them." The detective's eyes widened and Neferet sneered. "I don't know what is more unbelievable, that that simpering Zoey Redbird somehow deluded herself into thinking she'd killed the men, and then rushed to give her pathetic self up to you, or that you actually believed the insipid child had the will to kill. Either way, the situation doesn't bode well for your skills of detection."

Lynette saw that the uniformed officers, even Jamison, had all paled at Neferet's flippant admissions of guilt, but Detective Marx's face hardened into stubborn lines. His spoke with calm authority. "Neferet, I will allow you to make one phone call to your High Council, but you must give yourself up to me and prepare to pay the consequences for your actions."

"The High Council has even less jurisdiction over me than do you," Neferet said. "I am no vampyre—I am Goddess of Darkness, Queen Tsi Sgili—and I will *never* again bow to any authority. You, Tulsa, and even the world will worship me as is my divine right. Watch and learn. Mabel, come to me!"

The girl obeyed immediately. She walked through the front doors that Judson opened for her and went to Neferet's side.

"More hostages won't help you get out of this, Neferet!" Detective Marx said.

"I said, watch and learn, humans! I have no hostages, only willing supplicants. Now gaze into your future!" Neferet opened her arms to the girl she called Mabel. Lynette had to step aside as Mabel hurried willingly into her embrace. "If I am your Goddess, sacrifice yourself to me."

Morbidly curious, Lynette watched, wondering what the girl was going to be compelled to do. She only had seconds to wonder.

"You are my Goddess," the girl said mechanically, and then Mabel began clawing at her own neck, gouging her flesh and causing blood to weep from the wounds.

"Now *that* is the behavior of a proper supplicant." Neferet bent to drink from her offering. The girl gasped and trembled, but instead of trying to escape, she cried, "Thank you, Goddess!" in a voice that was filled with ecstasy.

"How sweet of you," Neferet said, her lips inches from Mabel's bloody neck. Before she began feeding from her, she commanded, "Shield us!"

An instant later there was a deafening burst of gunfire. Lynette fell to the pavement, ducking into a ball and putting her arms up in a vain attempt to protect herself.

There was a cry of pain, and then the officers began shouting. Shaking violently, Lynette peeked up through her arms. Neferet was feeding on the girl, ignoring the chaos happening before them.

Apparently, the bullets meant for Neferet—and probably also Lynette—had bounced off whatever shield the vampyre had invoked and been deflected directly into the foul-mouthed pedophile officer's body.

"Oh my god," Lynette whispered in a rush.

"Do you not mean oh my *goddess*?" Neferet, lips scarlet from the girl's blood, smiled down at Lynette.

"Y-yes, I do," Lynette said, feeling light-headed.

Neferet let loose the girl, and Mabel fell heavily to the concrete. Then she held out her hand to Lynette, who took it and stood shakily. "Have no fear. I won't allow them to harm you. I won't allow them to harm anyone who is loyal to me," Neferet told her. She turned her attention back to the officers. They had dragged Jamison's bullet-ravaged body behind the cars, which is where the rest of the men were crouching. Lynette could hear their radios crackling as they called for an ambulance and backup.

"Do you understand now, Detective Marx? Have you learned your lesson?"

"We've learned that you're a killer!" he shouted. "We're not done here—this hasn't ended!"

"For once, you are correct. I am not done here—this has only just begun. Watch and learn, watch and learn," Neferet repeated. "Oh, and look up! Children, come with me!" she commanded. Linking Lynette's arm with hers, Neferet turned her back to the officers and reentered the Mayo.

"Judson, chain the doors again."

"Yes, Goddess. That will not hold them off for long, though."

"I know that! Just do as I have commanded. As always, I will take care of the rest of the details myself."

"Yes, Goddess."

"Lynette, I'd like you to join me on the balcony of my penthouse. A spectacular event is getting ready to take place there."

"Yes, Goddess," Lynette said, entering the elevator with her.

Neferet's smile was knowing. "You almost believe that I am divine."

Lynette didn't respond. What could she say that Neferet couldn't refute by probing her mind and finding the truth? So again, she said the only thing she could, "I'm here to serve you, Neferet."

"And so you shall."

The doors to the penthouse opened. "Kylee, Lynette's looking pale. Pour a glass of my best red wine and bring it to her on the balcony." Neferet swept past Kylee with Lynette following, opening the glass doors and joining the sixty people who stood in frightened groups on the balcony. Many of them were near the stone balustrade that framed the wide outdoor expanse, and it was obvious from their expressions that they had heard the shots from below and had been watching the drama unfold from above.

"Wait here, Lynette, and drink your wine. It will help the bloom return to your cheeks. I can't have my favorite supplicant looking sallow and ill," Neferet told her. Then she walked to the stone railing, causing the people closest to her to shuffle nervously aside. "Because modern education is abysmal, I feel it is my duty as your Goddess to tell you that this"—she paused and pointed at the carved stones—"is called a balustrade. The thick, evenly spaced supports, here and here and here"—she pointed again—"are called balusters. It is a happy coincidence that there are exactly sixty balusters spaced all around this rooftop balcony of my Temple. I want each of you to choose a baluster and stand directly in front of it."

"You—you aren't going to make us jump, are you?" asked a terrified old woman.

"No, Grandmother," Neferet said warmly. "That makes no sense at all. Did you not see how I protected Lynette from the deadly bullets the police fired at her?"

There was a long silence, and then someone called, "Yes, but you ate that girl."

"Mabel was disobedient. Would you like to share her fate?"

Her words worked like spurs on the people. They scattered, each taking a position in front of a baluster.

"Excellent! Kylee, refresh my supplicants' glasses of champagne while I have a private word with my Dark children."

Lynette appreciated expensive red wine, and she usually savored it, sipping slowly as it deserved. Not then. She chugged it, snagging the bottle from robotic Kylee as the girl passed her to return inside, fetching more champagne. Lynette was grateful for the surreal, detached feeling the alcohol was giving her as she watched the vampyre. She'd moved to a shadowy corner of the balcony, well away from the stone railing, and was bent, talking to what looked like nothing at all.

Lynette knew better. And, sure enough, only another second or two passed before the air around the vampyre's feet rippled, like heat currents lifting from a blacktop road in the summer, and Neferet's snakes became visible. Lynette was glad the vampyre was distracted by her "children," because she couldn't repress her shudder of disgust. Lynette was reminded of an old western she'd seen as a young girl. In it cowboys were on a cattle drive, and as they made a river crossing, a young man had fallen off his horse, landing in the middle of an enormous nest of mating water snakes to be killed by them, though not quickly enough. It looked like Neferet was standing in the center of that nest, only her snakes were bigger, blacker, and even more dangerous than the old west vipers.

What in the hell were they? Granted, Lynette didn't know much about vampyres. Though she would have welcomed their business— they were notoriously wealthy—she'd never been hired by one. She was far from a vampyre authority, but she felt sure she would have heard something about these deadly snake-creatures. Their familiars were supposed to be cats, for god's sake, not reptiles!

Lynette poured the remainder of the wine into her goblet and took another long gulp, feeling relieved that her face was warm. Good, the flush would bring back the "bloom" of her cheeks. Lynette had no doubt the vampyre was capable of killing her on a whim. Surreptitiously, she pinched her checks to be sure they were in full bloom.

How was she going to get out of this mess? She didn't even give a damn about profiting from the situation anymore. She just wanted to escape, without being chased down by one of the insane vampyre's children.

"Excellent!" Neferet straightened, turning her attention to the sixty people, each standing in front of a rooftop baluster. "Now that my children understand my wishes, I am ready to share them with you—my loyal supplicants." She took a position in the center of the balcony so that she could be seen and heard by everyone. "Kylee, that is enough champagne for now. Go stand by Lynette." Kylee, of course, did as she was commanded.

Lynette snuck sideways glances at the girl. Her mouth was closed, and she couldn't see any sign of snake infestation, but the girl was clearly on autopilot. Her eyes were open but blank. Her face was expressionless. This time Lynette did suppress her shudder of disgust. Who knew what the thing beside her would report to the vampyre?

"Now, I have a question for you, one that anyone may answer. What is your foremost concern right now?" Neferet was asking the people. Lynette thought how strange it was that she could sound so normal, even kind. It was all a façade, but it was a good one.

No one answered her question, and Neferet smiled warmly, encouragingly, saying, "Oh, come now! I am your Goddess. It is my duty and pleasure to hear your concerns—and as my supplicants, it is your duty to voice them to me. Please don't make me force you to do your duty."

A man spoke up. "My biggest concern is that I don't want to be killed—or worse," he said, giving the writhing nest of darkness that surrounded the vampyre a fleeting nervous glance.

"Good! Well said. Do any of the rest of you have the same concern?"

Neferet sounded like she authentically cared, and even Lynette felt her head nodding with the others.

"Perfect!" Neferet said. "I knew safety would be your key concern. Now, I'm not admonishing you, nor am I angry with you, but your key concern should be caring for and worshipping me." Several of the people started to protest, obviously out of fear for what the vampyre would do next, but Neferet lifted her hand and, with a regal gesture, quieted them. "No, no, I understand. Truly I do. And that is why I am going to make quite sure that no one can harm my supplicants so that they can then be free to truly worship me."

Lynette thought it was ironic that as Neferet made this pronouncement, the sound of multiple sirens screamed, ever closer, from below.

"In order to assure my supplicants of their safety, I need your help. Do exactly as I say, and I promise you my Temple will be impervious to harm."

Lynette sighed softly. Too bad someone didn't say what everyone was thinking: *It's not the outside world we're worried about—it's you!* But of course no one spoke because it was Neferet they were all petrified of.

"What you need do is very simple. First, each of you must turn so that you are facing outward." Slowly, reluctantly, the sixty people did as she commanded until they were all facing away from Neferet. "Now, raise your arms, close your eyes, and clear your minds by taking three deep breaths with me—in and then out . . . in and then out . . . in and then out." Lynette heard the people breathing with her. "I want you to concentrate on my voice and think of nothing else." Neferet paused, looking around the balcony as if to be sure everyone was in place. When her eyes found Lynette, her full lips turned up in a feral smile.

Lynette's stomach twisted in foreboding and she worried that she would throw up the wine she'd guzzled.

Neferet's gaze left her and went to the snakes that writhed around her feet. "Children, it is time!" Her next words were spoken in a sing-song tone that was surprisingly soothing, almost mesmerizing.

In one swift strike you must kill
so those below may know my rage.
Power glutted, you drink your fill
now create for me a perfect cage.

Lynette felt the power build with every sentence the vampyre spoke and she, along with the sixty people who were frozen with their arms raised, could do nothing but wait for what would happen next.

For me to make the world anew
my Temple must be divine—strong.
To me you shall always be true
show Tulsa a righteous Goddess song!

For as long as she lived, Lynette would not be able to wipe the vision of what happened next from her memory. With the words "Goddess song," Neferet lifted her arms, and, as if that was the signal they had been waiting for, sixty of the snakes shot away from her and rocketed toward the unknowing backs of the people. Lynette held her breath, expecting the serpents to slither up their legs and possess them, but her expectations were so, so wrong. Instead of possessing the people, the snakes—as one—hit the each of the sixty in the middle of their backs, bursting through them with such force that blood and gore spouted like scarlet rain flowing with the snakes over the stone balustrade. Disbelieving, Lynette watched as the creatures slithered down the sides of the Mayo, washing it with blackness and blood, as if unfurling a dark, dripping curtain.

A sound brought her attention back to Neferet. Numbly, she saw that the vampyre still had her arms raised. Her head had lolled back, and her body was jerking in spasms as she moaned in terrible pleasure. Lynette was certain she saw a dark glow shimmering and expanding around her. Suddenly she understood. *It's the people dying—somehow she's feeding off their souls, just like her creatures are feeding off their bodies.*

And they were feeding off the newly dead—all the snakes that had remained on the rooftop. Lynette felt her head shaking back and forth. There were so many of them, still so many of them.

Lynette was still shaking her head and staring at the creatures who seethed over and around the dead, attaching to them like giant leeches, draining what was left of their limp bodies, when Neferet's arms went down. She straightened her robe and, without so much as a glance at any of the sixty, she turned and, smiling, approached Lynette.

"Kylee! Throw the bodies over the balustrade when the children are done feeding. Oh, and call Judson and the rest of my staff. There is no need for them to guard the door anymore. You are all safe. Nothing can penetrate my veil of Darkness. No one can enter or leave my Temple without me permitting it. So have the staff inform my remaining supplicants that they do not have to stay in that dismal basement. They may return to their rooms without fear. I have made sure they are protected—as long as they worship me. It is now time for them to begin worshipping me."

"Yes, Goddess," Kylee said, disappearing through the penthouse door.

Neferet's emerald gaze met Lynette's. "What did you think of my event?"

Lynette swallowed around the sick in her throat that threatened to choke her and answered with absolute honesty. "I have never seen anything like it."

"I have never seen anything like it, what?" Neferet asked expectantly.

"I have never seen anything like it, *Goddess*," Lynette said, dropping into a deep, trembling curtsy.

"And now you actually mean it. How delightful. Rise, Lynette, my dear, and pour us both a glass of wine while we discuss what type of worship events you intend to plan for me."

Lynette stood and did exactly as her Goddess commanded.

CHAPTER SIX

Detective Marx

Ever since that dark, snowy night Zoey Redbird had called him to the old depot, where she and a teenage boy had narrowly escaped being killed, Detective Marx had had questions about Neferet, who was then High Priestess of the Tulsa House of Night. The vampyre has seemed *off* to him. Zoey had obviously been leery of her when he'd returned the fledgling to the House of Night and Neferet had welcomed her with what seemed like real warmth. Zoey had remained guarded. She'd even made a show of revealing new tattooing their Goddess had gifted her with that night, which, to the Detective's trained eye, said the fledgling had successfully told the high-ranking, most powerful vampyre at the school to back off.

Marx supposed he should have taken the vampyre's side and questioned the fledgling's veracity. But instead Marx had felt an itch under his skin around Neferet, the same itch that had saved his ass more times than he could count out on the street. He'd liked Zoey just fine. There'd been no itch under his skin around her. Neferet, he hadn't liked *at all*.

He'd asked his sister, who had been Marked almost two decades ago, about Neferet. Anne had been unusually short in her response to him: *Neferet is a powerful High Priestess. Steer clear of her.* When he'd asked her for details, Anne had totally shut down the conversation. She'd even avoided his calls for almost a week. That had been more than weird. He and Anne were twins, and they'd stayed close even after she'd been Marked and then Changed. Currently, she taught Spells and Rituals at the San Francisco House of Night. Marx vacationed there at least once a year. He'd even stayed on the school grounds as her guest several times. Anne was usually open and honest with him about her vampyre world. She knew she could trust her brother. But one mention of Neferet, and Anne had thrown up a wall between them.

Marx had hated that, hated not having his sister's confidence. So he'd never asked about Neferet again.

Not even when the High Priestess had left the Tulsa House of Night and given a press conference, condemning mainstream vampyres in general and her old House of Night in particular.

Not even when Neferet had disappeared after her penthouse had been vandalized.

Not even when the Tulsa House of Night's new High Priestess, Thanatos, had accused Neferet of the murder of Mayor LaFont.

Not even when an anonymous tip had come in through their Crime Stoppers line saying that a naked vampyre fitting Neferet's description had been seen entering the Boston Avenue Church.

The last twenty-plus minutes had changed his mind about not questioning his sister.

"Here! Officer, down over here!" Marx waved his arms at the ambulance that had screamed up to the makeshift blockade he and the other officers were crouched behind. He glanced at Jamison. The guy was obviously a goner. The six bullets that had ricocheted from the invisible shield Neferet had erected had somehow conveniently hit him everywhere *except* the parts of his body covered by his Kevlar vest. *How the hell had she done that?* Marx added another to the long list of questions he was absolutely going to ask his sister.

More marked cars than he could count skidded up, parking in the middle of the streets surrounding the Mayo. The officers not running to back up Marx's ground were hurrying to evacuate all the buildings adjacent to them. Marx had radioed officer down *and* a major hostage situation.

It was with a mixture of relief and regret that he saw Chief Connors leading the group of SWAT officers.

Chief Connors was not known for his diplomatic skills.

"Detective, bring me up to speed," the chief said.

"Neferet confessed to the Boston Avenue killing. She's in there with hostages. She has them under her control. I can't tell if it's a spell, or if she's just got them so damn scared they're willing to do anything for her. But you wouldn't believe the terrible things she's got those people doing."

"After seeing what she did at Boston Avenue, I don't think there's anything she can do that'll surprise me," the chief said grimly.

"See that body? That girl ripped her own throat open for Neferet while she said, 'Thank you, Goddess.'" Marx nodded at the bloody mess that used to be a young woman.

"Any idea how many people are in there with her?"

Marx shook his head. "It has to be around a hundred, but best guess is all we have. She's closed the restaurant and locked the building up tight. As far as we can tell, she's not letting anyone out."

"Well, she's going to have to let us in."

"Chief, I think we'd better get some kind of intel on the hostage situation. We don't want a repeat of what happened at the church. She slaughtered those people, but the bodies didn't look like anything I've ever seen a vampyre do before. They were sliced up and chewed up and drained. Neferet's power is like nothing we've ever dealt with."

"Yeah, I saw them." The chief shook his head. "How the fuck could a vampyre do that? I've heard of High Priestesses who can mess with people's minds—do some control and even memory wiping. And I know they're physically powerful, though not as powerful as their Warriors. But the slaughter in the church . . ." He shook his head. "That I've never heard of. What about you? Isn't your sister a vampyre?"

"She is, and I'll give her a call, but there's something you should know. Neferet isn't saying she's a vampyre. She's calling herself a goddess, specifically the Goddess of Darkness and Queen Tsi Sgili, whatever that is. She said she's made the Mayo her Temple and she wants Tulsa to worship her."

The chief made a derisive grunt. "Fat fucking chance. As soon as we've got the hostage situation pinpointed, we're going in. Let's see what our sniper's fifty-caliber can do against her delusions of divinity."

Marx nodded in agreement, but the familiar warning itch was back under his skin, giving him a bad feeling about how this thing was going to play out.

"Goddamned vampyres have lost their heathen minds lately. First killing the mayor, then those two men in the park, the church slaughter, and now this. I'm thinking we need to do more than just lock down the House of Night. I think we need to round them up and kick them the hell outta Tulsa!"

"Chief, about those two men in the park." Marx frowned. He knew the anti-vampyre sentiment was running high, but he hated to hear such racist crap coming from the chief of police.

"Yeah, what about them? Wasn't it you who brought in that fledgling who confessed to their killing? Hell, she could've killed LaFont, too!"

"Actually, sir, Neferet just confessed to the killing of the mayor and those two men. She bragged of it, as well as the massacre at the church."

The chief blinked in surprise. "Well, then, what the hell was that fledgling doing giving herself up as a killer? Is she in league with Neferet?"

"I sincerely doubt it. Zoey Redbird and Neferet have a history of bad blood between them. It's more likely that Zoey had a run-in with the men, she protected herself, and when she heard they were dead thought she *must have* killed them. She's a good kid, Chief. I think she turned herself in because she was consumed by remorse. She didn't even want any adult vampyre near her."

The chief gave him a blank look. Marx stifled a sigh and explained. "If a fledgling isn't around adult vampyres, there's a one hundred percent chance her body will reject the Change and she'll die. Zoey had tried and judged herself—and decided her sentence was death."

"I forget how much you know about vampyres." The chief shook his head in disgust. "Guess it doesn't matter whether they're human or fledgling—teenagers have no damn sense."

Marx had opened his mouth to protest—respectfully—that he actually knew some teenagers who had some damn sense, and that would include Zoey Redbird, when the cry of a uniformed cop interrupted him.

"Oh my God! Look up!"

Marx's head jerked and his gaze shot skyward in time to see creatures, grotesque black creatures that appeared to be snakelike, except they had no eyes—only gaping mouths framed with teeth that glistened wet and red—being hurled by some invisible force over the stone railing of the Mayo's penthouse. The creatures carried with them an explosion of blood and guts, body fragments and gore. And as they fell, they expanded, changing from eyeless snakes to a dark, pulsing curtain, stained scarlet. The curtain clung to the stone façade of the Mayo, swathing it in darkness and blood as it unfurled downward.

"Fire! Kill them!" shouted the chief of police.

Marx tried to stop him. Tried to remind him that there were innocent citizens inside who could easily be wounded or even killed. Tried to tell him that the attack would only serve to antagonize the vampyre who held those citizens hostage and who was already so insane she believed she'd become immortal. But panicked gunfire erupted all around him, and his words were lost in the frenzy.

At first Marx didn't want to look up. He didn't want to see the gunfire-ravaged Mayo and start dealing with the aftermath of the chief's rash command. But Marx wasn't the kind of man who avoided the hard things in life; he'd made a career out of dealing with them. Resolutely, he looked up.

The snakes-turned-curtain had expanded so that it looked like the building had grown a crimson and black skin, a skin so tough that not even the Glocks the uniforms carried had penetrated it.

They all watched the darkness continue to spread down the building to street level and pool there with a rustling sound that reminded Marx of the time he'd visited New York City and stayed at the Plaza—and made the mistake of going out for a smoke at 3:00 A.M. Rats. He'd walked to a row of neatly trimmed hedges in front of the Plaza's grand entrance and heard a rustling. He'd looked down, shocked to see dozens of fat rats scurrying among the hedges. That's what the shroud of darkness Neferet had created sounded like as it settled where the building met the ground and washed, restlessly, against the 1920s stone.

"Fire on the doors. Break through that damn thing and get ready to rush inside!" the chief shouted.

"No!" Marx cried as the uniforms around them jumped to obey their chief.

Determined to survive to fight another day, Marx ducked down behind a squad car.

It was over in seconds. The officers ran toward the double doors, firing at the glass that now was covered in slick gore-stained black. His heart broke when the screams began. Marx was already calling into his radio, "Multiple officers down! We need more buses at the Mayo! And backup! More backup! Get every uniform in Tulsa here now!"

When the chief staggered back and fell heavily to the pavement, a friendly fire bullet causing a bloom of red in the middle of his forehead, eyes rolled back, milky, sightless, and undoubtedly dead, Marx did the only thing he knew to do—he took charge.

"Cease fire and fall back! Fall back!" he shouted, and the men responded with obvious relief.

A young uniformed cop crouched down next to him, breathing heavily, his hands trembling. Marx thought the kid couldn't be much older than twenty-one.

"Mother of God, that black stuff didn't even chip! It ricocheted the bullets back at us, like it was actually aiming. What the hell is that?" he said, voice shaking as hard as his hands.

"Magick," Marx said. "Dark, evil magick."

"How the hell do we fight it?"

Marx met the young man's eyes. "*We* don't. We need help. Thankfully, I know where to get it."

Zoey

"I wish I knew what the hell was going on!" Stark paced back and forth in front of her cell.

"Go see if Grandma's still in the waiting room. She can find out what's happening. She brought cookies. No one can resist Grandma's cookies," I said.

"Good idea. I'll be back in a sec."

Stark shot down the hall, leaving me to take up his pacing for him.

Neferet. If something crazy was happening at the Mayo, Neferet had to be responsible. I wanted to grab the bars of my cell and shake them like a hysterical person and scream, *Let me out let me out let me out!* If Neferet was out there causing goddess only knew what, *I* should be out there, too, trying to figure out how to stop her.

And I would be if I hadn't lost my mind and killed two men.

Stark jogged back to me and wrapped his hands over mine, which really had been holding onto the bars of my cell like I could bend the stupid things.

"They must have kicked your grandma out with Thanatos and the rest of them. No one's here except a front desk cop. The fucking place is deserted! If I had a key I could break you outta here with no problem." His brows raised and, with his hands still pressed over mine, he gave a little shake to the metal bars (which did *not* budge). Then he smiled his cute cocky grin. "But since I don't have a key, do you happen to know someone who could, say, summon a few elements to, I dunno, blow this door down?"

"Stark, I'm in here for a reason. I did something really, really bad. Breaking out is *not* going to help anything."

"It might help if Neferet is on the rampage, eating the unsuspecting citizens of Tulsa. Actually, they might forget about your accident at the park and thank you if you help bring down Ms. Batshit Crazy."

I smiled sadly. "They might forget about it, but I wouldn't. And Stark, I can't stop Neferet."

"You have before."

"Not for good, and not without help."

"Well . . ." He threw his arms wide. "You have help!"

I snorted. "Not enough. If we were enough, we would have been able to make sure Neferet couldn't come back from when we kicked her butt last time." Then my shoulders slumped and I shrugged. "It's probably not her at all. It could be bank robbers."

"At the Mayo? Uh, Z, that's a hotel, not a bank."

"Well, it could be—"

The door to our hallway opened, banging metallically against the wall, and Detective Marx hurried toward us. He looked crappy. I mean, really crappy. His suit was smudged with dirt and one knee of his pants was torn. I could smell blood, which I totally made myself ignore. Actually, it wasn't that hard to do because the look on his face was so disturbing.

He looked scared.

"What happened at Woodward Park?" he demanded as he came up beside Stark.

"I already told you."

"Tell him again," Stark said.

"Why, what's going on?"

"Answer my question first."

"Okay, like I said before, the two men made me mad and I threw my anger at them."

"What did they do that made you so mad?" he asked.

"Not enough to make killing them okay," I said.

"Just answer my question!" Marx snapped.

Surprised at his tone, I heard myself saying, "They were hanging out in the park looking for girls to scare into giving them money. They didn't see my tattoos until after they'd already started messing with me. Then when they realized I wasn't just some helpless little teenager, they changed their minds about trying to scare me. They basically said they were just gonna look for some other girl to victimize. It really pissed me off." I paused and added, "But there's more to it than that. I was already pissed when I got to the park. That was why I was there. I was trying to cool off. I—I couldn't get a handle on my temper."

"Tell him the rest. Tell him why you gave Aphrodite the Seer Stone when you gave yourself up to him," Stark insisted.

"I didn't realize it then, but now I can see that the Seer Stone, a kind of talisman I'd been given on the Isle of Skye, had been doing something to my emotions—amplifying them, or causing them, or maybe just feeding off my stress. It gets hot when it works, and at the park it was super hot. That had to have been how I lifted those guys off their feet and smacked them against the wall by the grotto."

"You can't do that, say, right now, can you?" Marx asked, watching me closely.

"I don't think so. At least, not by myself, no. I'd have to call one or all of the elements, and they're most powerful if my circle is with me and all five of us are channeling them."

Marx nodded thoughtfully. "Did you know that the two men were dead when you left the park?"

"No. I mean, I knew I'd smacked them against the wall, but it was like a crazy explosion from me. It, well, it surprised me," I said. Absently, I rubbed the palm of my right hand on my jeans and then glanced down at it. In the center of the latticework tattoos a perfect circle had been branded there. I held my palm out so the detective could see it. "That mark in the center—the circle—that's from the Seer Stone. It happened when I threw my anger at those men. It was like power came from it through me. When I realized what I'd done, I walked over to look at them." I swallowed hard, remembering.

"And exactly what did you see?" Marx prompted impatiently.

"They were laying there, at the base of the wall that makes the stone ridge over on the Twenty-first Street side of the park. I—I remember that I heard one of them moan, and I saw the other one twitch. It was obvious that I'd hurt them—maybe even badly—so I got scared, and I ran away. They must have been dying when I took off. I'm so sorry. I really am. I know that doesn't make any difference. And I know it also doesn't make any difference about the fact that they were in the park messing with girls, *or* that the Seer Stone gave me the power to do what I did. My anger is what killed those guys. I'm responsible." I bit my lip hard. I was *not* going to start crying.

"No, Zoey. The truth is that you didn't do it, and no, you're not responsible for their deaths." He swiped a key card over the pad on my cell door, and the steel lock sprung open with a click.

"Huh?" I blinked at him, feeling like I must be dreaming. I looked at Stark, who was staring at the detective.

"This has something to do with Neferet," Stark said.

"This has everything to do with Neferet," Marx agreed. "She confessed to killing those two men. No, that's not totally accurate. Neferet *gloated* about killing those two men."

Stark whooped and scooped me up into his arms. "Z, you didn't kill anyone!"

"I didn't kill anyone!" I echoed Stark's shout as he held me, laughing. I was feeling light-headed, almost dizzy. *I hadn't killed anybody!* Holy crap—I'd almost rejected the Change. I'd almost died. Because of Neferet.

It always came back to Neferet.

I thumped Stark's shoulder, and he put me down (but I did keep hold of his hand).

I faced Detective Marx. "What else has she done?"

"You and your friends were right. Neferet did kill the mayor. He and the two men at the park were her warm-ups. She slaughtered a church full of people, and right now she's declared that she's a goddess. She's made the Mayo her Temple, and she's barricaded in there with a bunch of people who are under her spell."

"Shit!" Stark said.

"Ohmygoddess!" Neferet had finally done it. She'd finally outed herself and shown *everyone* what she really was.

"You're free, Zoey. You've been cleared of all charges. But before you go, I do have a favor to ask."

I met his gaze. "You don't have to ask. I'll help you. I'll do everything I can to stop her."

Marx's shoulders slumped in relief. "Thank you. I'm not going to lie to you, Zoey. What's going on at the Mayo is bad, really bad. Neferet is powerful and dangerous."

"And absolutely batshit crazy," I finished for him. "I know. I've known for months."

"Then you know what you're up against."

"We all do," Stark said. "Because we've been the only ones fighting the crazy bitch."

"All right, then. Do you need to get that Seer Stone thing before I take you to the Mayo and—"

"Wait, no, you don't understand, Detective Marx. When I said *I'll* do everything I can to stop Neferet, that doesn't mean me alone." I squeezed Stark's hand. "One thing I've learned for sure is that I'm stronger with my friends."

"Just tell me what you need, and I'll make it so," Marx said.

"Everything I need is at the House of Night," I said.

"Then come with me, Zoey. I'll take you home."

CHAPTER SEVEN

Zoey

I'd barely gotten out of Detective Marx's shot-up town car when Grandma rushed out of the front of the school building and wrapped me in her arms.

"*U-we-tsi-a-ge-ya!* It is you! I knew it—I knew you were coming home."

I hugged her quickly, then linked my arms with hers and guided her back into the House of Night, with Detective Marx and Stark close behind me. The sun was in the process of setting, but I was hyperaware that it could still cause Stark pain. As we hurried into the building, I smiled at Grandma and said, "I didn't kill anybody!" Then I remembered who had—and what else she'd done—and my smile slipped from my face. "Neferet killed them."

"Neferet?" I looked up from Grandma's happy face to see Thanatos, Aphrodite, and Darius coming out of the High Priestess's office.

"Zoey, Detective Marx, please explain what has happened." Thanatos said.

"Neferet has confessed to killing the two men in the park—" Detective Marx began to explain, but I interrupted him. "Wait, there's way more to it than that, and I need my circle to hear all of it." I looked at Thanatos. "Neferet's revealed herself. We have to hurry."

"Darius, Stark, gather Zoey's circle. Bring them to the school Council Chamber. Get Lenobia as well. She is the oldest Priestess at this house—we can use her wisdom. Go, now!" Thanatos said.

Stark and Darius took off.

"Detective, let me show you the way to our Council Chamber. Sylvia,

I would appreciate it if you lent your wisdom to whatever it is we're now facing with Neferet. Would you join us?"

"Of course," Grandma said wryly. "I know more than a little about Neferet and her unique brand of evil." Grandma kissed me softly on the cheek and began walking with Thanatos and Detective Marx toward the stairwell that led upstairs to the Council Chamber.

That left me alone with Aphrodite.

"I'm not asking whether you want me to or not. I *am* coming to this meeting," she said before she started to follow the three adults.

I touched her arm and her head jerked around so that she could look at me. I couldn't tell if I saw more fear or anger in her eyes—both made me feel terrible.

"I'm sorry," I said simply. "I was wrong. You were right all along. You were right to go to Shaylin. You were right to have her watch me. You were right to keep your vision from me. I should have listened to you, but I didn't, and I wouldn't have, even if you'd told me about your vision. I was out of control. I was selfish. I was stupid. I'm sorry," I repeated. "Please forgive me."

While I'd been talking, Aphrodite had gone very still. She didn't put her hand on her hip, sneer, or flip her hair. She listened to me and watched me with intent, bright eyes. She didn't say anything for what felt like a really long time, and when she finally spoke, her voice wasn't snide or bitchy or sarcastic. She was serious. Her manner was calm. She looked and sounded like the Prophetess of a Goddess.

"I thought you were my friend," she said.

"I am."

"You hurt my feelings."

"I know. I wish I could tell you that I didn't mean to, but I'm not going to lie to you. At the time, I did mean to hurt you because I was hurting so bad. Aphrodite, the Seer Stone did something to me. I'm not using that as an excuse for what I said or did. It was still *me*. I was still wrong. I'm just trying to explain to you that I realize what happened—or at least *how* it happened. And I give you my oath that I won't let it happen again."

She kept studying me silently.

"I'm going to apologize to Shaylin, too," I added.

Aphrodite nodded. "You should. You totally freaked her out."

"It won't happen again," I repeated solemnly. "I swear it."

"Do you want the stone back?"

"Hell no!" I said, taking a little step from her. "I want you to keep it away from me."

"That's my plan," she said. "I just wondered what yours was."

"I haven't really got one past saying I'm sorry and asking you and Shaylin and, well, everyone else, to forgive me."

"Well, that figures," Aphrodite said, sounding more like herself. "You tend to be underprepared. And underdressed. Do they have no flat irons in jail?" She gave my bedhead hair an appraising look.

"No. Good hair isn't a priority in jail."

"Well, up until now I'd only heard that Oklahoma's prison system sucked. Now I'm sure of it."

That made me grin. "So, do you forgive me?"

"I suppose I have to. You look like crap. I'd hate to add insult to the fashion injury your short incarceration has already committed against you."

I laughed and linked my arm with hers. "Is there anything you can't simplify down to fashion?"

"No, and you are welcome."

I laughed again and we headed to the stairway. I felt light and happy, and for a few moments I let Neferet slip from my mind. I focused my thoughts on a single, silent prayer to Nyx: *Thank you, Goddess, for giving me such a good friend!*

"Hey, don't think that you can start hugging me and shit. I am *not* the hugging type. Let's still consider this"—she waved her free hand in front of herself—"a no-touch zone. Darius, of course, has a zone waiver."

"Got it," I said, but I kept my arm linked with hers as we climbed the stairs in tandem. "I wouldn't think of crossing the no-touch zone."

"Good," she said, but she didn't pull her arm from mine until we were just outside the conference room. Then she paused and turned to face me. Serious again, she said, "I forgive you, Zoey."

"Thank you." I blinked fast, surprised by the sudden tears in my eyes.

"Well, shit," she said and, after glancing around to be sure we were alone, opened up her arms and hugged me, whispering, "I love you, Z." I sniffed and hugged her back. "I love you, too."

The sound of the stairwell door opening had her springing away from me. "Don't cry," she said sternly. "Snot will not help the fashion disaster you have going on."

"'Kay." I sniffed some more.

"Zo! I heard they unjailed you! Whoohoo!" Aurox yelled jubilantly, sounding weirdly and wonderfully like Heath. He jogged toward me, clearly intending on crossing *my* no-touch zone. I took a few skittering steps backward and then froze when he flinched and staggered to a halt. I didn't know what the hell to do. I mean, we'd decided to be friends. Friends hugged. But then again, we'd decided to *just* be friends. Well, actually, *I'd* decided we'd just be friends and—

"Oh, for shit's sake, throw the bull a bone. Without you he's been bereft." Aphrodite shook her head in disgust. "And I'm using alliteration. If I start rhyming, I'm going to hurl myself off a tall building. Suck face or whatever quickly, and then get your butt into the Council Chamber. Sadly, we don't have time for boy drama." She flipped her hair, opened the door, and twitched inside.

Aurox and I stared at each other.

"Suck face?" he asked.

My cheeks felt like they were on fire. "She means kiss."

His brows lifted. "Would you like to kiss me?"

Thankfully, nothing he'd said after *whoohoo* sounded the least little bit like Heath. I cleared my throat. "I don't think that would be a good idea, but thanks for asking."

"Well, I am glad you're back," he said, smiling tentatively.

"Me, too." I returned his smile. "And even though it's confusing, I'm glad you're back also."

I'd meant it to be a compliment—and maybe even an inside joke (wouldn't the whole situation be better if we could laugh about it??), but Aurox's tentative smile instantly faded.

"You don't mean *me*. You mean Heath. And Heath's not me. Excuse me. Darius said he thought I should be in this meeting." I moved aside and let him open the door. He didn't hold it for me but let it swing shut in my face, leaving me standing in the hallway alone, feeling like poop.

Okay, I told myself, *it would make my life easier if Aurox stayed pissed at me—or at least annoyed and uninterested.* Aphrodite was proving to be right too damn often. I didn't have time for boy drama (though I didn't think that was very sad).

I combed my fingers through my really messy hair, squared my shoulders, and entered the School Council Chamber.

The room was big, but it always appeared to be small because of the giant round table that dominated it. I'm pretty sure the idea had been to mimic King Arthur (who had, of course, been the High Priestess, Mogan le Fay's, consort), so that it had no real head, but what had ended up happening was that wherever the school's current High Priestess sat, well, that automatically became the table's head.

Speaking of the current High Priestess, I was surprised to see her enter the room from the rear door, just as I closed the front door behind me. Thanatos nodded to Aurox, who took a guard-like position standing beside that door. Then she glanced at me and gestured to the empty seat between Grandma and Aphrodite. Thanatos sat to Grandma's left, beside Detective Marx. As I settled myself and tried not to fidget, Thanatos leaned forward and spoke around Grandma.

"It is officially good to have you home, Zoey," said the High Priestess of Death.

"I can't tell you how glad I am to be here—and to know I didn't kill anyone," I said.

"But you have learned a valuable lesson from the experience," Grandma said.

"Yeah. Neferet has to be stopped no matter what," Aphrodite said.

"Well, yeah, she does. But I think the lesson Grandma's talking about is when in doubt, choose kindness," I said.

"Don't think that one is going to do us much good with Neferet," Aphrodite muttered.

"You may be surprised, child," Grandma said softly, smiling wisely at her.

The door opened then, and Stevie Rae burst in, followed by Stark, Damien, and Shaunee.

"Z! Ohmygood*ness* it's so good to see you free!" Stevie Rae ran to me and enveloped me in a giant bear hug. "I knew you couldn't have killed those guys."

I gave her a quick hug back before disentangling myself. I met her gaze. "I have something to say about that, but I want to wait until everyone gets here."

"Wait is over. Handsome is here," Aphrodite said, smiling as Darius entered the room with Lenobia and Shaylin. Darius and Stark took their places on either side of the main door. Stark sent me a quick wink, and I was glad to see that he wasn't as pale and his eyes had lost their bruised look. For him to be looking so much better, the sun must have set, and I figured Rephaim would probably be showing up any second, too.

Lenobia sat beside Detective Marx, nodding cordially to him. Shaylin chose a seat as far as she could away from me and wouldn't meet my gaze. I stood up and cleared my throat.

"I know an emergency with Neferet is going on downtown, but I need to say something before we start dealing with that—and I'll make it quick. As you guys know, I found out today that I didn't kill those two men in the park. But even though I didn't actually cause their deaths, I know that I could have. I was out of control. It had something to do with the Seer Stone, but it was also *me. I* was wrong. Aphrodite was doing exactly what Nyx would expect from one of her Prophetesses—she was letting Shaylin know that there was something going on with me, something bad." I looked at Shaylin until she reluctantly met my gaze. "Shaylin, I've already apologized to Aphrodite, but I owe you a major apology, too. You were right to follow me. You were right to talk to Aphrodite about the changes you were seeing in my aura. I was very, very wrong to push you and lose my temper like that, and I'm not just asking if you'd accept my apology. I'm also giving you"—I paused and looked around the room at my friends—"and everyone else here my oath that I'm going to do whatever it takes to be sure it never happens again."

"I forgive you," Shaylin said with no hesitation, though her smile was hesitant, and she still seemed scared. "By the way, your colors are back to normal now."

"Thank you," I said. "And please let me, or anyone else here, know if you see my colors messing up again. I was wrong when I told you that you should keep that kind of stuff to yourself. It's not an invasion of privacy. It's using a gift given to you by Nyx."

"Zoey, where is the Seer Stone right now?" Thanatos asked.

"I have it," Aphrodite spoke up before I could.

"And I don't want it back," I added.

"If it's as powerful as you all are saying it is, Zoey may have no choice but to take it back," Detective Marx said. "Because it's going to take a whole lot of power—magickal power—to fight Neferet."

"Detective, it's your turn. Explain exactly what Neferet has done," Thanatos said.

I sat down and listened with a clenching stomach and a terrible premonition that Marx was right.

Zoey

There had been a long, sickening silence after Detective Marx described, in awful detail, Neferet's slaughter at the church, and then what had happened at the Mayo.

"I felt the deaths," Thanatos said, shaking her head sadly. "I knew it was some type of mass human tragedy that had to have occurred very close to Tulsa. I've been watching the news, expecting to hear that a commuter plane had gone down, or maybe there had been one of those tragic school shootings again. I hadn't expected this. I truly hadn't expected that Neferet was responsible for all of this."

"We have been unable to predict her behavior, but we may be able to learn something of what to expect from her in the future by retracing Neferet's crimes," Grandma said. "She killed the mayor, and that death fueled her as far as Woodward Park." Grandma paused and smiled sadly at Aphrodite. "I am sorry to speak about your father's death in such a clinical manner, child."

"I understand. I want you to," Aphrodite said earnestly. "If Dad's death helps us figure out how to take down Neferet, then at least it'll mean he died for *something*."

Grandma nodded and continued. "She must have hidden at the park until Zoey had her altercation with the two men."

"I was sitting on that bench by the grotto when they started messing with me," I said, trying to help put the pieces together. "Neferet could have been hiding in the grotto."

"I'll have some uniforms check it out," Detective Marx said, taking notes on his little black spiral pad.

"The deaths of the two men in the park must have given Neferet the power to get to the Boston Avenue Church," Grandma said.

"And there she found another, greater source of power," Lenobia added. "We must remember that power is always what is most important to Neferet."

"She uses power to control those snake-like creatures—the things that killed the people on the roof of the Mayo and created that . . . I don't even know what you'd call it." Marx hesitated, thinking. "It's a protective skin, or a barrier. But whatever it is, it's filled with power."

"Those snake-creatures are made of Darkness. Think of them like hateful, horrible, evil thoughts that have taken physical form," I explained to Detective Marx. "They do what she wants them to do because she makes sacrifices to them. I promise you Neferet didn't eat all of those people at the church. She sacrificed them to those creatures so that they'd keep doing what she wants them to do."

"A Tsi Sgili requires much more than blood for power," Grandma said.

"Tsi Sgili—Queen Tsi Sgili," Marx said, "that's what Neferet called herself when she named herself a Goddess."

"Tsi Sgili is an ancient name my people have for witches who have chosen Darkness over Light. They live apart, shunned by everyone." Grandma shuddered. "Our legends say they feed from souls."

"Death," Thanatos said. "I should have understood it before now. Neferet feeds from the energy that is released from a person's spirit at the instant of death."

"Oh Goddess!" Lenobia looked horrified and pressed a hand against her chest. "I have known Neferet for more than a century. She was always nearby when a fledgling rejected the Change. We thought—the

Priestesses thought—that Neferet's healing gift comforted the young ones' passings."

"She didn't comfort them. She used them," I said.

"Neferet had something to do with us dying and undying," Stevie Rae said. "I can't remember—maybe 'cause I can't make myself. I dunno." She shivered. "But I know it felt like something inside me was being torn apart." Her gaze found Stark, the only other red vampyre in the room. "What do you remember?"

"Pain. Darkness. Terror. Anger." His words were clipped, though his voice remained low and we strained to hear him. "And when I came out of it, I wasn't me anymore. Not until Zoey said she believed in me and trusted me."

"And I didn't really come out of it, either, until Aphrodite believed in me and trusted me," Stevie Rae said.

Aphrodite snorted. "That's not exactly how I remember it. What I remember is that you tried to eat me and then you took my fledgling-ness from me."

"Because you let me. Because you sacrificed your humanity for me," Stevie Rae said.

"The eating part was not cool," Aphrodite muttered.

"Love is stronger than hate. That is the only absolute in the universe. Love can conquer Darkness," Grandma said. "We simply need to discover how love can conquer Neferet."

I heard a bunch of sighs echoing mine.

"Okay, I'm all for love winning," Detective Marx said, "but we have to contend with whatever is going on with those snake-things, too."

"Neferet's feeding them," I said, feeling the truth of my words as I spoke them. "She gives them what they want—fresh blood sacrifices— and they obey her. If we can get to Neferet, make her weaker—or at least contain her and keep her from killing more people—she won't be able to feed them, and they will leave her."

"I agree, but I think there is more to it than that, Zoey. The tendrils of Darkness are changing—evolving—along with Neferet," Thanatos said. "I have never, in the more than five centuries I have been a vampyre, heard of anyone creating the kind of barrier Detective Marx described." She turned to Marx. "And you said it seems sentient, that it actually directed those bullets back to specific officers?"

"No doubt about it. I was there. I saw it up close and way too personal. The first shots fired at her *all* hit the officer who had offended Neferet—but only in places on his body that his Kevlar vest didn't protect. The next shots wounded several other uniforms, but killed the chief of police—the man responsible for giving the order to storm the building," Marx said.

"Lenobia, have you ever heard of such a thing?" Thanatos asked.

"Never."

"Then call in the cavalry," Marx said. "Get the Vamp High Council involved. Maybe they can help us figure out how to stop Neferet."

"The High Council has refused to aid us," Thanatos said. "We *are* the cavalry." She stood. "So, Detective Marx, let's go to the Mayo and see exactly what we're up against."

The rear door to the Council Chamber opened and Kalona, barechested, with amber eyes flashing in anger, strode to Thanatos. "It is time you call in the full cavalry. I am Death's Warrior—so where you go, I go. Humans and consequences be damned." His black wings unfurled and seemed to encase the entire room.

Detective Marx's jaw dropped open. Literally.

"Holy shit," Aphrodite whispered.

"Ditto," I said, wondering what the hell would happen next.

CHAPTER EIGHT

Detective Marx

The guy was huge. *And he had wings.* Gi-fucking-gantic wings. Marx was glad he was already sitting because just looking at the . . . whateverthehellhewas . . . made his knees feel like rubber.

First the crazy-assed vampyre/goddess and the bloody black curtain at the Mayo. Now a winged giant who said he was Death's Warrior.

Was he fucking dreaming?

Well, if he was, the dream kept on going and going, because Thanatos was talking to the winged giant and Marx damn sure wasn't waking up.

"Go with me? To downtown Tulsa in full view of the—"

"What will you do if Neferet's threads of Darkness attack you? I understand this manifestation of Darkness. I battled it over and over again in the Otherworld." The giant's powerful voice shot out: "Which would the humans fear more, the incarnation of evil, or the presence of a god battling it in the streets of Tulsa?"

"Humans don't believe the gods walk the earth anymore," Thanatos said.

"My point exactly!" said the winged giant. "Neferet's actions have negated the norm. It is past time humans take their heads from the sand and realize this world is filled with magick and mystery and danger. It is also time I do what I was created to do—be a Warrior and battle Darkness."

The High Priestess bowed her head ever so slightly in acquiescence to the winged man. Then she turned to Marx. "Detective, I would like to introduce you to my Oath Bound Warrior, Kalona. He is my protector, as well as this House of Night's Sword Master. He will be accompanying us to the Mayo."

Marx hesitated a moment and then did the only thing he could think to do—he held out his hand to the big guy. "Good to meet you, Kalona."

Kalona gripped his forearm in the traditional vampyre greeting. "And you as well, Detective."

"You aren't a vampyre, are you?" Marx couldn't help asking.

Kalona's smile was sardonic. "No. I am not."

Marx glanced at the guy's wings, which now were tucked against his back. The damn things were so long they actually brushed the floor. "What *are* you?"

Kalona's smile widened and seemed to turn genuine. "There is a complicated answer to that, one I promise to give you *after* we have dealt with Neferet."

"I'll hold you to that promise," Marx said, trying not to look directly into the guy's eyes because doing so made his head feel woozy and thick, like it was filled with cotton balls.

"You won't have to, Detective. I've learned the hard way that it is best that I hold myself to my promises."

"So we're actually *all* going to the Mayo?" Aphrodite asked.

"No. Kalona and I are going, as well as Zoey, Stark, and her circle. Darius, Aurox, and Aphrodite—you will remain here with Lenobia. The two of you will call a school assembly. Fill in the professors, Warriors, and the student body. Give them the basics and no more. And put the school on high alert. We have no idea what Neferet's next move may be."

"Do ya really think everyone should know what's goin' on?" Stevie Rae said, echoing Marx's thoughts.

Zoey spoke up before Thanatos could. "I'm thinking that Darkness hates to have light shined on it, so let's shine a big ol' spotlight on what Neferet's up to."

"That's damn sure one way to find out who wants to slither back under the rocks with Neferet and who wants to stand up and fight her with us," Stark said.

"The two of you have echoed my thoughts exactly," Thanatos said.

"Well, all right, then. But I'm calling in Kramisha to help me. She always knows who's up to what," Aphrodite said.

"It is a wise Prophetess who gathers to her others gifted by her Goddess," Thanatos said, giving her approval.

"It's also a wise Prophetess who keeps her cell phone close by. Call if all hell breaks loose—literally or figuratively," Aphrodite said.

"Will do," Zoey told her.

"We'll follow you, Detective Marx," Thanatos said.

Marx drew a deep breath and totally turned off his sanity switch. "All right. Let's do this."

Lynette

"Lynette, I do adore a surprise . . ." Neferet hesitated before continuing, lifting one slender finger, "*if* the surprise is pleasant. If it is not, then a surprise is nothing more than an irritating interruption. I loathe interruptions almost as much as I loathe being irritated." Her gaze left Lynette's, and she glanced at what appeared to be her bare legs. "Speaking of irritations—why are you milling aimlessly about? I am perfectly safe, and you have all been perfectly satiated. Go amuse yourselves elsewhere and cease tugging at me. Go on now, shoo!" Neferet fluttered her fingers dismissively before turning her attention back to Lynette.

Lynette didn't see the snake-things, but she could feel the cold brush of *something* slithering past her. She suppressed a shudder of revulsion.

"Dear Lynette, where were we? Ah, yes, I remember. You announced that you have planned a little surprise for me. Please continue to explain yourself."

Lynette met the Goddess's gaze without flinching. The panic that was gathered somewhere under her breastbone shivered and shied, but she tightened the mental reins she'd tethered it with and let only the joy of planning a spectacular event fill her mind. Lynette's smile was full of confidence, as was her voice. "Goddess, I am very good at my job. Even though I was working under unusual circumstances with limited means, I absolutely believe you will find my surprise pleasant."

"Limited means—that sounds so tawdry, so cheap." Neferet frowned. "I certainly never meant for you to feel as if your Goddess is miserly."

"Oh, I don't feel that at all!" Lynette assured her, hoping she hadn't tripped Neferet's crazy trigger. "I put myself under a time and means constraint because I wanted to prove my worth to you. But of course this is just a small sample of the events I could plan for you daily—had I more time and money with which to work."

Neferet's brow unfurled. "You are a wise woman, Lynette. Show me what you have concocted for me. If it pleases me, you may be assured that you will be allowed to move forward with limitless means, though I cannot promise I will be patiently allotting you too much time. I waited far too long to begin my reign. I am restless for the worship of my supplicants."

"That is very understandable, Goddess," Lynette said. "I have never been as concerned about time as I have money when it comes to event planning."

Neferet studied her.

Lynette concentrated on business. She excelled at business. She was confident about business. Business did not terrify or repulse her.

Neferet smiled. "You are being absolutely honest. Your business and the acquisition of money have long been your main concern. Lead on, my supplicant! Reveal my surprise."

Lynette curtsied and led Neferet from the penthouse suite to the elevator, stopping it on the mezzanine. "Please wait just a moment, Goddess."

Neferet smiled and made a gesture of acquiescence. Lynette punched the hold button on the elevator and then tapped the almost invisible earbud, speaking quickly and quietly. "Kylee, wait ten seconds and then cue the quartet to begin."

"Yes, Lynette," came Kylee's robotic response.

Lynette glanced to her right and made a *come-here* gesture. Judson, the handsome bellman, stepped from the shadows. He was dressed impeccably in a freshly pressed uniform, and he was carrying a shining silver platter on which rested one perfect crystal flute filled with bubbling pink champagne. He bowed perfectly, mechanically, to Neferet and said, "May I offer you champagne, Goddess?"

"Why, yes. Thank you, Judson."

The music began the instant Neferet lifted the flute from the tray. Lynette was pleased to see a smile lift the corners of the Goddess's lips.

"Strauss's 'Blue Danube'—one of my favorite waltzes. Ah, Vienna—it was so lovely and decadent in the past."

"Please, follow me, Goddess," Lynette said formally, leading Neferet around the mezzanine to the spot she'd had her temporary throne moved to—just above the landing from which she'd addressed her new "supplicants" a mere three hours before, and where, now, the string quartet from last night's wedding was nervously, but beautifully, playing.

Neferet sat gracefully, peering down at the quartet. "They play well, though I would prefer a full orchestra."

"Time and means," Lynette said with a wry smile.

The Goddess's lips twitched. "I am taking note of that."

Lynette bowed her head to Neferet and surreptitiously tapped her earpiece again. "Send them at the beginning of the next six count." Then she held her breath and hoped the twelve performers managed to keep themselves together.

The heavy velvet drapes that enclosed the ballroom below parted, and from opposite sides of the room, six couples moved quickly to the center of the marble floor. The women were all wearing dresses that were as close to the same shade of scarlet as Lynette could find. The men were in tuxedos she'd managed to piece together from whatever was left over from the wedding, was clean enough, and could be made to fit.

Fit! That had been only part of this wretched event's problems. It had been a horrendous job to find six men and six women from what Lynette had already silently named the prisoner pool, who were relatively attractive, relatively graceful, and relatively able to learn and perform the simple steps of a basic waltz. Yes, she could have used all of the snake-infested staff members—they'd certainly obey anything she told them to do as long as she didn't try to escape the Mayo. But Lynette's instinct had told her that people already under her control going through a performance by rote wouldn't impress Neferet.

No, Lynette believed Neferet wanted, *needed,* the illusion of being worshipped. So she'd threatened, nagged, and cajoled twelve decent-looking people into working for her.

Lynette could see that they were nervous—two of the women were trembling so badly she could she their arms shaking—but just as she'd instructed, the couples positioned themselves in a large circle and managed to be in place at the end of the first six count. At the beginning of the second set of notes, all twelve people looked up at Neferet, paused for three counts, and then as one, each man bowed and each woman curtsied to the Goddess.

Lynette saw their mistakes. Saw that the woman named Cindi almost fell over, and only her partner's quick hand under her elbow saved her. Camden, the tall kid who had been best man at the wedding last night—and unlucky enough to have been too hungover to have made the dawn flight the bride and groom had caught to Dallas—held his bow far too long. Lynette gritted her teeth. If that spoiled frat boy messed this up, he was going to be sorrier than she was.

Lynette glanced at Neferet. Obviously pleased, the Goddess smiled and nodded her head regally in response to the performers.

Now just dance and don't look too awkward! Lynette thought.

They danced. All twelve of them actually began on the same note and moved around the room in an almost circular pattern. They were far from perfect, but the music was lovely, and if some of the dancers faltered, "Blue Danube" remained true. When the final note ended, the six couples curtsied and bowed again to Neferet, this time holding their poses in a freeze frame that even Lynette had to admit was actually rather beautiful.

Neferet stood and, to Lynette's immense relief, applauded and laughed.

"Well done, all of you! That was quite nice. Judson, open fresh bottles of champagne for these lovely supplicants."

"Goddess, they are waiting for you to allow them to rise," Lynette whispered to Neferet.

"Of course they are, and thank you for reminding me, dear Lynette. You may rise!" Neferet called down to them. "Enjoy your champagne and your Goddess's gratitude for your worship."

Lynette tapped her earpiece. "Kylee, tell the quartet to begin the next piece." Within just a few moments, music filled the ballroom again.

"'Waltz of the Flowers' from *The Nutcracker*. Two lovely pieces and excellent choices," Neferet said.

"So my surprise was pleasant?"

"It was. The candelabrum, the flowers, the tuxedos, and the red dresses—they were all thoughtfully chosen. Lynette, you have made a very good beginning as my event planner. I approve of your theme— exquisite music, a beautifully appointed space, and respectful homage being paid to me."

"Then is it safe for me to assume you would like more events planned as such?"

"Yes, it would be, but next time choose to set the event in a theme of my favorite era—the 1920s. That was a decade worth reliving. Can you Charleston, Lynette?"

"Do I have access to the Internet?"

"Yes, you do, as well as a very generous event account," Neferet said, smiling knowingly at Lynette.

"Then I can Charleston, and so can your supplicants."

"We will need more musicians," Neferet said.

"Yes, Goddess. I will make it so," Lynette said, already tapping notes into her smartphone.

"And costumes. We will need many more costumes."

"Of course, Goddess," Lynette agreed.

"And I need more than just dancing, though that is a nice beginning."

Lynette glanced from her notes to Neferet. The Goddess wasn't looking at her. She was stroking the crystal champagne flute and staring down at the ballroom and the six couples who were milling in a little group, nervously accepting the champagne Judson was offering them. Lynette followed her gaze. The spoiled frat boy was downing what appeared to be his second glass of champagne. Neferet was devouring him with her eyes.

"It pleases me that my supplicants are so attractive," she said.

Lynette's sarcastic snort was automatic, but when the Goddess's gaze snapped to her, she was instantly sorry she'd allowed her composure to slip.

Neferet raised an auburn brow. "Ah, I see. You chose the twelve of them carefully, because not all of my supplicants are so attractive—and that's that truth, isn't it."

She didn't frame the words as a question, but Lynette felt compelled to answer. "Yes, that is the truth." She shifted her shoulders restlessly. "I'm sorry, Goddess. I just wanted to be sure that you were happy with this first, small event."

"That is very understandable, dear Lynette. Actually, I appreciate your efforts, and while I appreciate all of my subjects, I also appreciate things—and people—that are pleasing to my senses." Neferet leaned forward in her throne and spoke to Lynette in a conspirator's voice. "You could add that to your duties as my event planner."

"I'm willing to serve you in any way you require, Goddess." Lynette tried to understand her meaning. "But what duties do you mean by 'that'?"

"Making certain my supplicants always appear as attractive as possible, of course. Yes, I am quite sure you will have a talent for makeovers."

"Makeovers." Lynette repeated the word, feeling utterly overwhelmed as snapshots of some of Neferet's less-than-attractive supplicants flashed through her memory. *The fifty-something woman who needed to lose fifty-something pounds . . . the scrawny redheaded preteen whose face was already blotched with acne . . . the businessman who was bald and had a bulging gut and a triple chin that looked like a goiter . . .*

Neferet's mocking laughter ended the slide show in her mind. "Stop fretting, dear Lynette. Between the two of us we shall cull the herd. After all, I can control everything they eat, everything they do. Don't you agree that diet and exercise are very important?"

Lynette felt her head nod and tried to keep her mind completely focused on Neferet's emerald gaze.

"So besides putting some of them on a diet and making sure they spend time in my Temple's gymnasium, I'm confident you can give hair, makeup, and clothing tips. Correct?"

"Yes, Goddess," she said automatically.

"Excellent. I am glad you brought this to my attention. It is important my supplicants always look their best. They are, in some small manner, a reflection of myself." As if that settled the subject, Neferet's gaze moved back to the group below them, halting predatorily on Camden.

"You made an excellent choice in that one, Lynette. He's tall, young, and blond. That is how I prefer my men," Neferet said. "His name?"

"Camden," Lynette said. "He was best man in the wedding that brought me to the Mayo."

"*Best* man? Really?" Neferet's emerald eyes gleamed with a dangerous intensity, and Lynette was thankful that intensity wasn't focused on her. "Perhaps I will put that title to a test and see if Camden is, indeed, the *best* man here."

Lynette repressed her shiver of fear. "Would you like me to send for him?"

"No, dear Lynette. I can summon best man Camden with ease. Perhaps he would like to visit the balcony of my penthouse." Her jeweled gaze turned to Lynette and the feral gleam in them hardened. "My staff has gotten rid of those unsightly remains, have they not?"

Shit! I was too busy pulling off this performance to worry about being sure all the pieces of people were thrown off the balcony. Lynette's mind scrambled and she let out a relived sigh when she found the answer. "Goddess, I believe Kylee was in charge of seeing to your balcony."

"That girl," Neferet muttered, sipping her champagne. "She's good at some things, but she needs so much supervision. Could you use your useful little ear machine to remind her of my command?"

"Of course, Goddess," Lynette said.

"And while you supervise Kylee, I believe I shall mingle with my adoring, attractive supplicants. Can you imagine how honored best man Camden would be if I allowed him to ask me for a dance?"

Thankfully, Neferet's question was rhetorical, and instead of focusing on Lynette for a response, the Goddess turned her back to her and, sipping her champagne, she walked toward the large double staircase that led down to the ballroom.

Lynette noted Neferet didn't glide. *It's because she sent the snake-things out to play,* Lynette thought. Somehow they must carry her—or channel power to lift her—or something equally insane.

She shook her head, as if clearing cobwebs away. She couldn't afford to overthink. She couldn't afford to do anything except survive.

Lynette tapped her earbud. "Kylee, Neferet is going to inspect her balcony. Soon. She's holding you responsible for it being clean."

"I understand and will obey," came Kylee's robotic response.

Lynette sighed heavily. She took a few stumbling steps back and leaned against one of the marble pillars, doing nothing for just a moment except breathing.

She'd made it through Neferet's first test. She was still alive, and still not possessed by anything that slithered. But if she was going to stay that way, she couldn't afford to relax. There would be time for relaxation after she got through this. And Lynette would get through it—she always got through whatever bullshit life shoveled on her.

To begin, Lynette had a list to make.

She had to check out every single person in the building. They needed to be categorized as either attractive and acceptable, or needs work. Under the **needs work** category she'd subcategorize as fat, fashion impaired, or just plain ugly. The first two could be fixed—maybe. The third, well, just plain ugly would have to learn some skills that kept them behind the scenes.

"Here's hoping they can cook or sew . . ."

Lynette was mumbling to herself as she tapped her smartphone notes list when she heard a scream coming from the ballroom. *What now? What more could Neferet be doing?* Her mind was heavy with fear and exhaustion, but she made her feet carry her to the mezzanine railing.

Neferet was standing beside Camden. He was staring at the plunging neckline of the Goddess's short velvet dress. The other eleven people were staring at the slithering snakes that were coiling around Neferet's bare ankles.

"Oh, do be quiet," Neferet snapped at the girl who had screamed. "You need to get used to my children. They're never far from my side, just as you, my loyal supplicants, are never far from my side."

"I-I'm s-sorry, Goddess. Th-they look like snakes. I-I'm afraid of snakes," the girl stammered.

"They are not snakes. They are much more dangerous. And I'm not asking that you get over your fear of them. I'm commanding that you not voice it." Neferet shifted her gaze downward to the snake-things that were writhing with what seemed like excitement around her feet. "What is it, my darlings?"

"Goddess, the detective has returned," Judson called from the front of the foyer. "He's brought more people with him."

"That means nothing. He can bring an entire Oklahoma National Guard armory with him. They cannot penetrate my protective curtain."

"He hasn't brought an army, Goddess. He's brought a vampyre who is making the air around her glow while a large man who appears to have wings hidden under his trench coat paces nearby."

"*Why did you wait until now to tell me?*" Neferet shrieked. "Children! Come with me!" Lifted by the fully visible nest of slithering vipers, the Goddess glided to the front doors.

Lynette's body went cold. She slipped out of her chic heels so that she could sprint quietly around the mezzanine, heading for the large picture windows that overlooked the front of the building, trying not to think at all, but especially trying not to hope.

CHAPTER NINE

Zoey

"Holy crap, the Mayo looks awful!" I blurted.

"Like it's dripping with death." Damien sounded as horrified as I felt.

"Not with death," Thanatos said. "Death is inevitable for all mortals. It is neither good nor evil; it is simply part of the great spiral of life. What Neferet has coated that building in is pain and fear, blood and despair."

Her voice sounded weird. Grandma, Stark, Shaylin, and I were all smushed into the middle row of seats of the school's Hummer, and Thanatos was sitting up front with Marx. I'd noticed that the closer we'd gotten to the Mayo, the more restless the High Priestess had appeared. She was literally fidgeting, which was super strange for her—Thanatos was usually like a mountain of calm.

Her obvious nervousness had my stomach clenching like crazy.

"Chaos," Kalona said. I glanced over my shoulder where he was sitting with Damien and Shaunee (they were super smushed because his wings were taking up way too much room) to see him shaking his head in disgust. "Neferet has used the threads of Darkness to create chaos, and that is protecting her."

"Well, chaos smells bad," I said, wrinkling my nose.

"Fetid and horrible," Damien agreed. "And we don't even have a window cracked."

"Sorry," Marx said. "I meant to warn you about the stink."

"No need to be sorry, Detective," Grandma said. "I don't believe there is any way you could have prepared us for this."

"You're probably right, but I better mention that we can't be sure if all the body parts have been cleared from the area," Marx added. "So watch where you step."

"Body parts?" My voice squeaked.

Marx nodded. "The snake-things killed a lot of people when they came over the edge of the balcony and spread blackness and guts down the building. All evening Neferet's been tossing pieces of people, drained of blood, off the penthouse balcony."

"I can feel the spell she has bound in blood and death and Darkness," Thanatos said. "She used the deaths of those poor people to make a barrier."

"Neferet cast the spell, but she wouldn't dirty her hands with the cleanup," Kalona said grimly. "Which means she has people in there who are still alive and doing whatever she tells them to do."

"Does it really matter who's doing the tossing? Especially if Neferet's holding them all hostage?" Shaunee said.

"What truly matters is that everyone remember if we stop Neferet, we stop all this madness," Thanatos said.

We nodded in grim agreement.

Marx had driven through the police barricade areas and pulled up over the curb, parking across the street from the Mayo on the wide sidewalk in front of the ONEOK building, where we sat and gawked.

"We've set up two command posts inside the ONEOK. The one on the third floor has all the audiovisual equipment. The one on the roof has the snipers," Marx explained as we sat stared at the gore-coated building across the street.

"Snipers can't kill Neferet," Kalona said.

"Yeah, we've figured that out," Marx said dryly. "But they can kill people, even people who are under her spell."

"You can't shoot those people! They're victims," Grandma said, shifting beside me in agitation. "They're not responsible for their actions—Neferet is."

"Yes, ma'am, I know that and I don't want to shoot anybody, but if Neferet commands a group of her minions, or whatever you want to call them, to attack us or any of Tulsa's citizens, we're going to be forced to stop them."

"She would like that," Thanatos said as she stared at the building. She sounded pissed. I thought she looked paler than usual, but she'd been a vampyre for, like, a gabillion years. She always looked white, so I couldn't be sure. "It would give her power from their deaths, as well as the satisfaction that she had forced you to kill innocents." Thanatos shifted her gaze to Kalona. "We can't allow that."

"Agreed," Kalona said.

"Good," she said. "Enough sitting and speculating. I need to be out there. I need to understand exactly what it is we're dealing with."

Thanatos exited the Hummer, slamming the door behind her and leaving the rest of us to follow—reluctantly.

Kalona moved quickly to her side. In the distance I could hear calls of, "Hey, there're some vampyres!" and "Focus the camera in—something's going on in front of the Mayo!"

The winged immortal had pulled on a long black trench coat over his typically naked chest in a fairly successful attempt to hide his ginormous wings. I saw him shift his body, trying his best to tuck up the huge feathered things. He gave the crowd behind the barricade an annoyed look before his gaze found Detective Marx. "I believe it would be wise if you removed all of the civilians from this area of town. No one is safe here."

"Yeah, try telling that to the media. We've managed to corral them back there, but a free press is a bitch to deal with."

Kalona shrugged. "Then they will have to learn the lesson them-selves." On that ominous note, he turned his attention to the Mayo. Thanatos was staring at the building, almost as if it mesmerized her. I swallowed my fear and stood beside her, grateful for Stark's strong presence.

"I should have known it before now." Thanatos's voice was strained. She took several steps toward the building. "But I have rarely been called to the site of a human's death, and never to a human death site of this magnitude." She moved closer to the building, standing within the circular driveway that fed into the grand entrance. Thanatos lifted her hands, palms out, and shuddered. "The terror used to make this barrier lingers."

"Priestess, I advise that you do not approach the building," Kalona said, moving swiftly to her side, gently taking her elbow and trying to guide her back to the street.

"I must help them," she said, shaking off his hand.

"Them?" Marx asked.

"Not all of the dead have moved on. Their end was too violent, too terrifying, too far beyond the realm of anything these poor people had ever imagined. I sense spirits so panicked that they are endlessly circling, unable to find their way from this realm to the next."

"Can you help them?" Grandma called from over by the Hummer.

"Yes, I believe I can."

"Try to do so quickly," Kalona said.

"Should I cast a circle?" I asked.

"No, Zoey. You and everyone except Kalona stay safely back. This is something I must do on my own. Our Goddess has gifted me with everything I need"—she paused and smiled her appreciation at Kalona—"including a mighty protector. I must trust in the strength I draw from Nyx."

"Do like Thanatos says, move back to the Hummer," Stark said, pulling me back with him. Marx backed up more slowly, his eyes focused on Thanatos.

"Damien! Hey, Damien!" A young, handsome human suddenly rushed up.

Damien turned in time to get caught in a giant hug.

"Adam! You shouldn't be here, it's too dangerous," Damien scolded him.

"Hey, I'm a journalist. I'm all about danger," he said, grinning.

Finally, I recognized him. It was Adam Paluka, a newsman from Fox—the guy who had interviewed us after Neferet gave her ridiculous news conference. I knew he and Damien had been dating, and from the way they smiled at each other, I guessed things were going well. Jeesh, I'd been so wrapped up in what was going on with me that I hadn't even thought to ask Damien how he was dealing with dating someone so soon after Jack—

"You need to get back behind the barrier," Marx said, approaching Adam with a thundercloud look.

But just then Thanatos began her spellwork, drawing all of our attention to her.

The High Priestess raised her hands and closed her eyes. When she spoke, her restlessness was gone. Her words were rhythmic, mesmerizing; her voice was calm. She was strong and wise and beautiful—and I was proud to be a fledgling in a House of Night under her reign.

> *Spirits who still suffer here, come to me*
> *My voice for you let it a lifeline be*
> *Calmly, sweetly, my Goddess Gift sooths thee*

All around Thanatos, the air began to sparkle, as if someone had tossed magickal, floating snow globes filled with glitter toward her.

"Oh my God! What's happening? What's that vampyre doing?" I was so focused on the spell Thanatos was casting that I barely acknowledged the background noise from the pressing crowd. I felt more than saw Adam lift his iPhone and I heard the little *ping* that meant he was recording. Stark squeezed my hand before he whispered, "Marx looks like he's going to kick all of the reporters out. I'm gonna see what I can do to help him. Be sure you, your circle, and Grandma stay close to the Hummer."

I nodded and vaguely understood Stark was arguing with Damien about making Adam leave while Marx began walking purposefully toward the barricade. But I never took my eyes from the High Priestess. I couldn't. Thanatos commanded all of my focus.

> *I am your guide from this world's pain to flee*
> *Your terror is done; love has heard your plea*
> *Calmly, sweetly, your spirits shall now be free!*

The glowing orbs completely surrounded Thanatos. When she spoke the last line of her spell, she spread her arms wide and every one of the shining things rushed to her. Laughing in absolute joy, Thanatos, face illuminated with love, tossed her arms up. The sparkling orbs shot into the night sky like Fourth of July fireworks—only instead of leaving behind a foggy smoke, the disappearing globs left behind a ripple of relief and happiness that had me forgetting the stress of the situation—the horror of the blood and stench and Darkness-covered Mayo—had me forgetting everything except the fact that human or vampyre there was one constant among us all: love. Always love.

And then Neferet burst from the front of the building totally spoiling my happy moment. I thought she'd looked like Crazy Town before, but I'd been wrong. What she was now made all the earlier Neferet craziness look no more eccentric than an old cat lady who smelled vaguely of urine and catnip. She was wearing a short green dress. For a second I was almost relieved. I mean, she wasn't naked. Okay, she didn't have shoes on, but I thought that wasn't that big a deal—until I actually looked at her feet. They were resting on a writhing nest of black tendrils that coiled and pulsed around her, wrapping up her ankles and calves, and actually lifting her off the sidewalk.

But that wasn't even the most insane thing about Neferet. It was her eyes that gave away her crazy. Something had happened to her pupils—they were gone. They were like creepy marbles, completely emerald green.

"What's wrong with her ey—" Adam began, but Neferet's shriek cut him off.

"Death's crone, you have no dominion over my Temple!" Neferet pointed at Thanatos, and two of the tendrils raced toward her.

Kalona moved so fast everything blurred. Suddenly he was there, between Thanatos and the attacking creatures. He'd shrugged off his coat and pulled free the ebony spear he'd strapped across his back. His wings unfurled as he met the tendrils, skewering one, and while it writhed in a death agony, he spun and sliced the other in half.

Neferet screamed, as if she could feel the pain of the severed tendrils. "Ignore Kalona! Kill Thanatos and then the others!"

Everything exploded.

Tendrils of Darkness, like poison spewing from a viper's mouth, shot from around Neferet's feet, attempting to swerve around Kalona to get to Thanatos and the rest of us. Stark sprinted back to me, pushing Grandma and me behind him and yelling for Damien, Adam, Shaunee, and Shaylin to get into the Hummer.

I stumbled backward, sure that I was going to watch Thanatos be sliced apart by Neferet's creatures, probably only seconds before they attacked Stark and then devoured the rest of us.

But none of that happened. Darkness didn't win this battle—the winged immortal did.

Kalona was everywhere. His spear moved so fast it made a thrumming noise in the air.

"Light saber," Damien gasped. "For real and not *Star Wars* make-believe."

"Get them to safety!" Kalona shouted at Marx.

Marx rushed to the High Priestess, and as Kalona used his body, his wings, and his spear to shield us, we piled into the Hummer.

"Hang on, everyone. I'm jumping the curb and getting him out of there!" Marx told us as the Hummer roared to life.

"Wait," Thanatos said. "He's coming to us. Watch the tendrils. Their strength dissipates as they get farther from Neferet."

The High Priestess was right. Kalona, battered and bleeding, was still fighting the creatures, but he was working his way to us and away from the Mayo. And the threads weren't following him.

As Kalona reached the rear of the Hummer, Neferet lifted her arms and commanded, "Return to me, children! I will succor you!" The snake-things slithered to her, wrapping themselves around her arms and legs. She stroked them, as if to comfort them, and just before she disappeared inside the Mayo, her blazing emerald gaze focused on us. "Thank you for the lesson. Next time *I* will win."

Zoey

"No, truly, I do not need to go to your hospital," Kalona repeated for like the zillionth time to Marx. "As I already said, bring me water—or, better yet, wine. I will go to the rooftop of this building and heal myself."

We'd driven around the back of the ONEOK building and entered through the rear to join the Tulsa task force on the third floor. I could see why Marx was stressing over Kalona—he was a bloody mess. Everyone in the room was staring while they tried not to stare at him. Seriously, if he hadn't been immortal, he'd have been in a body bag.

Marx blew out a breath and ran his fingers through his hair. "All right, I get it, I get it. You're fine. Carter!" he yelled at a uniformed cop, who instantly stopped pretending to study his computer screen and gave the detective his full attention. "Find the CEO's boardroom. There'll be booze there." Marx looked back at Kalona. "Will whiskey do? These corporate types seem to prefer it."

"It will do," Kalona said.

"Get on it," Marx told Carter. "All right, while Kalona is recouping on the roof, let's do damage control. Paluka, give me that phone and get out of here."

"You can't just take my phone! That's illegal!"

"It's evidence in an ongoing multiple homicide investigation. I'm not taking it. I'm impounding it," Marx said.

"A moment, please, Detective," Grandma said.

"Ma'am?" Marx and everyone looked at Grandma, perplexed.

Grandma smiled serenely. "Adam, correct me if I'm wrong, but I believe you are far from the only newsman who witnessed what just happened outside."

"You aren't wrong," Adam said.

"Ah, as I thought. Which means there were probably multiple camera crews filming from behind that police barricade, not to mention random cell phone recordings, much like the one you made."

I heard Marx sigh as Adam said, "Right again, ma'am."

Grandma and Thanatos exchanged a look, and then the High Priestess took up where Grandma had led. "Mr. Paluka, how would you like an exclusive interview with Kalona and me?"

Adam's eyes sparkled with excitement, but otherwise he remained completely professional. "I would like that very much, High Priestess."

"Then you shall have it." Thanatos glanced at Marx. "Sometimes it's easier to give up control and let fate handle whatever comes next."

"At least clean off some of his blood first," Marx muttered. "And get me a fistful of Tylenol."

Zoey

Kalona did attempt to clean off the blood that had been seeping from long whip-like wounds, and smaller, deeper bite-sized gouges that crisscrossed and dotted his body. I thought he still looked pretty beat up, and he was still bleeding some, but he was acting totally normal— strong, silent, intimidating. Thanatos did make him put on the long coat. She said that his wings made a big enough appearance in the battle clip Adam was going to show during the interview. Silently, I agreed with her, but I also thought the coat was good cover for the wounded mess underneath it. For once I managed to keep my mouth shut and let others deal with the Neferet aftermath while I got to sit out of the spotlight. It was a little moment of relaxation for me as I curled up beside Stark while Grandma, Damien, Shaylin, Shaunee, and I watched what I couldn't even have imagined a couple of months ago— Kalona being interviewed on Tulsa TV.

Adam had called in a lighting crew and a cameraman. I thought they were doing a really good job of not gawking too continuously at Kalona. Adam explained to everyone that he was going to upload and play a clip of the battle, and then he'd begin the interview. He also explained that it would be airing live as breaking news.

"Man, I'm glad that's not us over there," I whispered.

"Adam is doing an excellent job." Damien spoke softly, his eyes smiling at the newsman.

"I like him," I said.

Damien met my gaze. "Do you think Jack would like him?"

I reached past Stark and squeezed Damien's hand. "I know he would."

Damien nodded and blinked back tears. "Somehow that makes it easier, only a little easier, but I'm grateful for that little."

Then our attention was on Adam as the blinking red light on the camera went solid and we watched the footage of Kalona's battle play on the portable prompter.

"This is Adam Paluka, live, with the vampyre and the Warrior we just saw in that amazing footage taken moments ago in front of the

Mayo Hotel, downtown Tulsa, when the High Priestess known as Neferet attacked several innocent citizens, including me." Adam paused, then smiled warmly at Kalona. "I haven't thanked you for saving my life. Thank you!"

Kalona looked surprised, almost shy. He nodded once and said, "You are welcome."

"Kalona was doing his duty. He is my Oath Bound Warrior. Neferet, who is no longer recognized by any vampyre authority as a Priestess of Nyx, attacked me and those with me. It was Kalona's duty to protect us," Thanatos said.

"Thanatos, it is good to be speaking with you again. Many of our viewers will recognize you as the new High Priestess of Tulsa's House of Night. Could you explain what you were doing in front of the Mayo?"

The High Priestess drew a deep breath and then spoke slowly and clearly, as if she wanted to be sure everyone understood her. "By now you will know what we had only suspected before now, that Neferet is utterly mad and has gone rogue. She has admitted to a killing spree. She murdered Tulsa's mayor. She murdered two men in Woodward Park. From there her killing spread to the innocents at the Boston Avenue Church Sunday morning, and then to the Mayo Hotel, where she has barricaded herself. The deaths she caused at the Mayo have allowed her to create a protective shield over the building. I was drawn there because of my Goddess-given affinity, which is to aid souls as they pass from this world to the next."

"Those glowing lights! They were souls?"

Thanatos nodded. "They were indeed. They had been trapped on this realm because of the violent manner of their deaths. I simply helped them to become untrapped."

"Wow, that's incredible!"

Thanatos's smile was beautiful. "The circle of life is, indeed, incredible."

"Yes, it sure is—Hang on, Thanatos. That means those were *human* souls you helped pass on."

"Yes," she said serenely.

"But you're a *vampyre*."

The High Priestess's smile widened. "I thought we had already established that."

"Yeah." Adam ran his hand through his perfect hair. "But one of your own kind attacked you because you were helping *human* souls."

"Adam, I have lived for more than five hundred years, and in that time I have learned that humanity is defined by choice and not by genetics. Quite simply, humans and vampyres are more alike than different."

"Obviously Neferet doesn't think the way you do," Adam said.

"Neferet is mad. Her thoughts are erratic and dangerous."

"What were those things she sent after us?" Adam asked.

"Evil that has taken tangible form. They follow Neferet's commands—as long as she sacrifices to keep them loyal to her." Thanatos turned her gaze directly to the camera. "I cannot stress too much that it is imperative that no matter what Neferet threatens, no humans go near the Mayo. Neferet gets power from death. Stay away from the Mayo, and her power source will, eventually, end."

Adam paused, looked shocked, and then glanced off camera. "Detective Marx, do you agree with Thanatos's request regarding the Mayo?"

The cameraman turned toward an annoyed-looking Detective Marx. Unflappable, he answered without hesitation, "I do. TPD has set up roadblocks around the Mayo. No one, not even police or military personnel, is allowed near the building."

"Isn't it true that Neferet has hostages inside the Mayo?" Adam asked.

"It is, but at this time we don't know names or numbers," Marx said. "I understand that people will be missing their loved ones. TPD has opened a 1-800 line for inquiries and missing person calls. The public should address their questions through that line."

"Which Fox 23 will scroll across the bottom of the screen," Adam said.

"Thank you," Marx said, though he didn't look particularly thankful.

"Detective Marx, I must ask—if you won't allow anyone near the Mayo, how will Neferet be stopped?" Adam said.

"She will be stopped by me, and by those vampyres and fledglings who fight beside me. Neferet is of our kind—and it is our kind who must defeat her," Kalona said.

All of us, including the cameraman, focused on the winged immortal.

"Kalona, you are not a vampyre, correct?" Adam said.

"Correct."

"Then what are you?"

He didn't even hesitate—he said it as if he was talking about what he'd had for dinner the night before. "I am Kalona, immortal brother of Erebus. Once, when the earth was younger, I was Warrior and companion to the Goddess, Nyx, but I chose poorly and because of that I Fell from the side of my Goddess in the Otherworld to this realm."

There was a long, breathless silence, and then Adam asked, "What are you doing here?"

Kalona's broad shoulders straightened and he looked directly into the camera. "I am trying to atone for my past mistakes and gain the forgiveness of Nyx."

"Well"—Adam swallowed audibly—"it seems to me like you're doing a pretty good job of atonement. You saved your High Priestess, a bunch of vampyres and fledglings, a detective, and me. If you can manage to stop Neferet, I'll start calling you Superman."

Kalona's full lips turned up. "If you see Nyx, I would appreciate you telling her that."

"Consider it done," Adam said. Then he turned to Thanatos. "Is there anything you'd like to add, High Priestess? Any way the public can help?"

"There is," she said. "They can pray and send positive thoughts and energy to us. The House of Night will do its best to protect the people of Tulsa, but we appreciate divine intervention."

"Pray? To whom, God or Goddess?" Adam said.

"Why, to either or both, of course. I like to believe prayers aren't tethered to semantics."

Adam smiled. "I like to believe that, too." He turned to the camera. "Let's all pray for an end to Neferet's insanity and the violence that has erupted because of it in Tulsa. And that's the latest from the standoff at the Mayo. This is Adam Paluka reminding you to stay tuned to Fox 23 for all the breaking news."

"The brother of Erebus. Isn't that interesting?" Grandma said as Adam shook Thanatos's hand and thanked her and Kalona for the interview.

"Did you know he was Erebus's brother?" Damien whispered to me.

"Well, uh, yeah," I said. "He did mention it a few days ago."

"But we've been kinda busy since then," Stark said.

Damien rubbed his forehead. "I vaguely remember in an anthology of ancient vampyre poetry a few mentions of the Son of the Moon and Warrior of Night, along with the usual descriptions of Erebus as Son of the Sun and Consort of Nyx. Initially, I assumed they were just different names for Erebus, but in retrospect it makes more sense that they were talking about two different immortals."

"It makes Kalona's centuries of rage more understandable," Grandma said.

"Yeah, to have gone from the Warrior and companion of Nyx to not even being allowed entrance to the Otherworld. That must really hurt," Damien said, watching Kalona with big, sad eyes.

"He raped and murdered people. Who knows what he did in the Otherworld before he Fell. Don't feel too sorry for him," Stark said.

"Everyone deserves a second chance, *Tsi-ta-ga-a-s-ha-ya*," Grandma said, using Rooster, the Cherokee nickname she'd given him. "I remember not long ago, *you* were given a second chance."

Stark looked at his feet.

I drew a deep breath and said, "So was I."

Grandma raised her brows in a question.

"Today I was given a second chance," I explained. I looked from Grandma to my friends, one at a time, and finally my gaze found Stark's. "We're a whole team of people who have needed second chances. I'm glad Kalona's getting his with us."

Grandma touched my arm. "Someday you should tell him that, *u-we-tsi-a-ge-ya*. I think you will be surprised at what a difference your words could make."

CHAPTER TEN

Aphrodite

"Holy crap! You will not effing believe what's just gone viral on You-Tube!" Nicole ran up the stairs from the auditorium to the stage, waving her iPad like a crazy person.

Aphrodite glared at her and brushed the iPad away. "Seriously? The assembly *just* ended. You were on YouTube when I was speaking?"

"Seriously." Nicole rolled her eyes. "Get over it. Everyone was on YouTube. You have to check this out." She shoved the iPad at Aphrodite.

"Being a teacher is a pain in the ass. Teenagers suck," Aphrodite said, still ignoring the iPad.

"Ohmygood*ness*, is that Kalona? On YouTube?" Stevie Rae pushed around Aphrodite to peek at the screen.

"What? Kalona?" Lenobia hurried to join Stevie Rae, with Darius and Rephaim close behind.

"Fine. I'll look. Now that I'm done telling the entire student body that we're going to have to save the world. Again." Aphrodite glanced at the screen and her eyes went huge and round. "Oh, for shit's sake! What took you so long to tell us? Turn that damn thing up!" She grabbed the iPad, tapped the replay button, and turned the volume up all the way.

The video wasn't professional, but the beginning of it was super clear. First, it focused on Thanatos. She was standing in front of a seriously messed up-looking building that appeared to be covered with a slimy black curtain. They watched as the High Priestess finished her spellwork, raising her arms and cradling a bunch of beautiful glowing orbs. When they whooshed off into the sky, the video was still focused on Thanatos, but in the background they could hear Neferet yelling.

"Death's crone, you have no dominion over my Temple!"

The video shifted so that they could see Neferet standing in front of what had to be the Mayo.

"She's a bunch of fries short of a Happy Meal," Stevie Rae said.

Aphrodite didn't take her eyes off the screen. "That's all you got, bumpkin?"

"I'd say crazier than a shit house rat," Nicole said.

"No one asked—" Aphrodite began, but the explosion on the video cut off her words.

"Oh, Goddess, no!" Lenobia gasped as they watched Neferet blast a wave of Darkness after Thanatos and the rest of them.

"Father's saving them!" Rephaim said.

"Look at him move." Darius's voice was hushed, respectful. "His speed and strength are incredible."

Aphrodite didn't get a chance to agree. The video ended with whoever was taking it jostling around to get inside the school's Hummer, though he still managed to film Neferet and her bloody tentacles of Darkness slithering back inside the Mayo.

Then the interview began, and Aphrodite had to tell herself to close her unattractively gaping mouth because there sat Kalona, next to Thanatos—wings and all—on Fox 23.

"I am Kalona, immortal brother of Erebus. Once, when the earth was younger, I was Warrior and companion to the Goddess Nyx, but I chose poorly and because of that I Fell from the side of my Goddess in the Otherworld to this realm."

"Erebus's brother? You've got to fucking be kidding!" Aphrodite felt like her brain was going to explode.

"It is the truth," Darius said quietly as the video concluded.

The screen went dark and Aphrodite stared at him. "You *knew*?"

"Yes, Kalona told us—Zoey, Stark, me," Darius admitted.

"And none of you thought that was important enough to tell any of the rest of us?" Lenobia asked, looking almost as annoyed as Aphrodite felt.

Darius's wide shoulders shrugged. "Honestly, I didn't give the truth of it much thought. Kalona's veracity has been more than questionable since the moment he appeared here."

"But now you believe him," Rephaim said.

Darius met his gaze. "I do."

"Rephaim, did you know your daddy was Erebus's brother?" Stevie Rae asked.

Bird Boy's eyes looked sad. "Father never speaks of *before*."

"Which means no, you did not?" Aphrodite asked.

"Correct," Rephaim said, sounding eerily like his father.

"This changes things," Lenobia said.

"Yeah, in an awesome way." Nicole nodded like a bobblehead. "It means we have Nyx's Warrior on our team."

"No, it doesn't," Aphrodite said dryly. "It means we have Nyx's ex-Warrior who screwed up so badly he got kicked out of the Otherworld on our team. And *that* isn't so awesome."

"He said he's trying to atone," Rephaim said.

"And he saved Thanatos and the rest of them," Darius said.

"Sorry, but I'm not ready to jump blindly on Team Kalona," Aphrodite said.

"I think it is blind to ignore what is in front of our eyes," Rephaim said, gesturing at the dark iPad screen.

"And I think there's a whole bunch of stuff about Kalona we don't know." She paused and gave Darius a hard look. "Or at least *most of us* don't know. Now, if there isn't something you'd rather do, I'd appreciate it if you'd round up all of the fledglings you think might have some Warrior talent. I'm pretty sure Thanatos is going to want a battle-ready head count. After watching Crazy on YouTube, I have a feeling Neferet's not going to give a shit about Team Kalona." Aphrodite slapped her forehead and then added sarcastically, "Wait! Effing Neferet probably already knows about the Kalona slash Erebus connection like practically *everyone else except me*." She flipped back her hair and twitched away.

It wasn't until Aphrodite got outside the auditorium that she slowed down and let her thoughts catch up with her emotions. Her heart was thundering and her stomach felt sick. She was pissed. Super pissed.

No, that's not true. I'm not pissed. I'm freaked out and upset.

With a giant sigh, Aphrodite moved from the sidewalk to one of the benches under a budding oak. The hand that brushed the thick blond hair from her face was shaky.

Darius had kept something from her, something important. Until that moment she'd thought he was different from all the other guys on this earth. *He* was supposed to be honest. *He* was supposed to be loyal. And, most of all, *he was supposed to love her enough never to lie to her or keep anything from her.*

A lie count was the real gauge of how much someone loved you. Aphrodite knew that because she'd grown up watching an ongoing lie count grow and grow. Her parents had pretended to be the perfect couple, but the truth was they had hated each other almost as much as they hated her. Except for when they were in public, they'd lived totally separate lives—they hadn't even shared a bedroom for more than a decade, let alone shared secrets.

They'd lied to each other on a daily basis.

When she'd been only eight years old, Aphrodite had sworn to herself that she'd never, ever get herself into anything like her parents' marriage. Hell, until she'd met Darius, she hadn't let any guy get close enough to her for it to matter whether he lied to her or not. She'd been sure she'd lied to them *first*. Cheated on them *first*. Broken up with them *first*.

"I can feel your sadness, my beauty. Please talk to me."

Aphrodite looked up at the sound of Darius's voice, but she didn't meet his eyes. She stared over his shoulder. "What do you want to talk about?"

He sat beside her and used the back of his hand to gently wipe a tear from her cheek. She jerked away from him, hastily brushing at her other cheek. She hadn't even known she'd been crying!

"I want to talk about us," he said.

"Really? Wouldn't it just be easier to keep on going like we have been? Pretending to be all 'in love forever and ever'?" she air-quoted sarcastically.

"That has never been a pretense for me. You know that, Aphrodite." He spoke calmly, earnestly.

She wanted to slap him—hurt him—make him feel even a little of the fear she was feeling. But she didn't do anything violent. That would mean she'd lost control. That would mean she'd become her mother. Instead, Aphrodite struck him with words.

"And how the hell would I know that? I can't be inside your head. I can't even share your feelings like a real Priestess would. But, whatever. Don't worry about it. Everything's fine, and we both have a bunch of shit to do because, as per usual, Darkness is about to try to take over our world."

"Darkness will have to wait, because you *are* my world, and if I lose you, I lose myself."

Aphrodite meant to stand up and walk away and not look back. She was going to make her heart hard, like it used to be when it had actually protected her. Before the shit storm that was Zoey and her Nerd Herd and Darius had happened to her.

She was going to, but somehow Darius had said exactly the right thing so that her legs suddenly decided to listen to her heart instead of her head.

Aphrodite met his gaze. "You lied to me."

"No, my beauty. I simply didn't tell you something."

"Why? Why did you keep that from me? Kalona being Erebus's brother is a pretty big fucking deal!"

"I don't care about Kalona or what he did or didn't say. I care about you and what you say."

"Me?" Aphrodite frowned at him. "What the hell are you talking about? Not once have I mentioned anything remotely like the possibility of Kalona and Erebus being brothers."

Darius's smile was slow and sweet. "Exactly. And if you, my beautiful, wise, gifted Prophetess, don't have any insight into Kalona's true past, then why would I care to mention an offhand comment the winged immortal made? Aphrodite, if it was important for us to know Kalona was Erebus's brother, then I believe *you* would have told *me*."

Aphrodite shook her head, feeling a little dizzy as she realized what Darius was actually saying to her.

He took her hand. "Have I told you how much I love you today?"

"N-no," she whispered, thinking, *Please don't say it if you don't mean it—please, please don't.*

"With all my being," he said.

Tears leaked down her cheeks, but she didn't look away from him.

"Don't be afraid," he said.

"I am. It still scares me," she admitted.

"It scares me, too, but being with you—really with you and not just pretending so that my heart stays safe—is worth facing and conquering that fear."

"But you're a Warrior. I'm nothing, not really. I'm just . . ." Her voice faded. She couldn't say it, but the words filled her mind: *I'm just the daughter of an awful woman who taught me how to hate, and to never, ever trust love.*

"You are the bravest person I know," Darius said solemnly. "And you are not, nor will you ever be, your mother."

"And you won't ever lie to me."

She didn't speak it as a question, but he dropped from the bench to his knee and pressed her hand against his heart, saying, "Aphrodite, Prophetess of Nyx, I give you my oath that I will never lie to you. Should I not always speak to you the truth, may the earth swallow me whole so that my spirit never finds its way to the Otherworld."

A terrible shiver passed through Aphrodite and she grabbed Darius and pulled him into her arms. "No, stop it! Anyone can accidentally tell a lie, anyone! I don't accept that oath!"

Darius leaned back, holding her gently by her trembling shoulders and smiled. "But I am not *anyone.* I am yours. Your Warrior. Your lover. Your mate. I swear never to lie to you because that would wound you beyond bearing, and I would rather the earth swallow me forever than do that to you."

As she stared at Darius and saw the truth in his eyes, something broke free inside Aphrodite—something small and sharp that had been lodged deep within her for a very, very long time. She gasped, drew a breath, then let it out slowly.

"It's gone," she whispered.

"What is gone, my beauty?"

"My fear. It's gone, Darius. You chased it away." Aphrodite knew she sounded young and silly. She didn't care. For the first time in her life, she wasn't afraid of losing love. "I can't lose you!" she blurted.

"No," he said, smiling again. "You cannot ever lose me. And I did not chase away your fear. You released it."

"Oh," she said softly, finally understanding. "Sorry that I took so long."

"You took exactly as long as was necessary, and I don't regret one moment of the wait."

Darius kissed her then, and Aphrodite knew complete happiness.

Until Aurox's voice interrupted. "Darius! There you are. Come quickly. They are at the gate!"

Aphrodite leaned on Darius's shoulder and frowned up at Aurox. "Oh, for shit's sake, if you messed up this moment because Zoey and the Nerd Herd are back, I am going to smack the crap right outta—"

"Not Zoey!" Aurox said. "Humans! There are humans at the gate asking to be let inside because they want us to protect them from Neferet!"

"Well, in that case, I suppose we should let them in," Darius said, standing and offering Aphrodite his hand. "Don't you think so, my beauty?"

She sighed and muttered, "Fine. Whatever. As long as there are no politicians with them."

CHAPTER ELEVEN

Zoey

"Ah, hell! A mob? That's all we need right now." I sighed in frustration as we went through the Twenty-first Street light at Utica and got within sight of the school. It was a super-weird scene. By now it was after midnight, and the street was dark. It should have been empty, too, but the big iron school gates were open, and a whole bunch of people were crowded at least ten deep in front of them. The two gas-lights encased inside weathered copper sconces threw flickering shadows in a semi-circle over the group. People also stretched down both sides of the street. Outside the reach of the school's flames, I could see the dark shapes of the cars that were parked up on the sidewalk, looking abandoned and totally out of place.

"Do you see anything burning except our lanterns? Like a ginormous cross?" Shaunee's head poked between Stark's and mine as she tried to get a better view from the backseat.

"Stop and let me out of here. I shall deal with this!" Kalona said.

"No!" Thanatos and Marx and Grandma shouted together.

"They don't appear angry," Thanatos said.

Detective Marx braked and rolled down his window. We all strained to listen, then he said, "It's hard to see, but I don't hear any yelling."

"My night vision is better than yours and I can see no shoving or panicked milling. Everything looks remarkably calm," Thanatos said.

"Yeah, well, I'd rather be safe than sorry, so let's be sure they know which side of the law the House of Night is on."

The detective grabbed the portable cop light he'd brought from ONEOK and slapped it on his side of the roof of the Hummer. He flipped a switch and it started to rotate the blue and red strobe that was all too familiar to any of us who might have not *fully* stopped at the four-way down the street from South Intermediate High School on 101st and Lynn Lane. Not that I had any *personal* experience with that. I'm just sayin' it was weird to be inside the cop car when the thing lit up.

Marx tapped at it again and an even more obnoxious siren shrieked twice. The light and the sound worked together perfectly. The crowd rippled and turned toward us and, recognizing the presence of the TPD, parted so that the Hummer was able to turn into the school's entrance.

Standing where sturdy iron should have been safely closed, Aphrodite, Darius, Stevie Rae, Rephaim, Lenobia, and Aurox were lined across the driveway, making a human gate.

"What are they doing?" Stark asked the question we all had to be thinking.

"I hope they are making wise decisions," Thanatos said.

Silently I agreed as my eyes went to Aphrodite first. If she looked pissed and/or had a drink in her hand, I'd know whatever was going on was bad—burning cross and shouting townsfolk or not. All she looked was confused. I mean, obviously confused. She had one hand on her hip and was shrugging her shoulders. At the same time Lenobia was nodding and speaking to someone in the crowd I couldn't quite see.

"Aphrodite looks confused, but not freaked," I spoke my surprised observation aloud. "And Lenobia looks like she's okay with whatever is going on. It must not be that horrible, whatever it is."

"There's Sister Mary Angela and Sister Emily. Oh, now I can see! There's a group of the nuns in the forefront." Grandma pointed and waved. "All is well if they're part of the crowd."

"That's a good theory, but I'm pulling inside the school grounds before any of you get out. And I want you to stay on the House of Night side of the gate—no matter who might be calling you outside," Marx said.

I could see that Grandma had her scolding face on, but Thanatos's hasty, "Agreed, Detective," silenced her.

I was glad. Okay, maybe it was because I hadn't been out of jail for twenty-four hours, but a crowd of humans milling around at the school's gate—even familiar humans who appeared to be milling peacefully—made my stomach clench with stress. Not to mention that it was past midnight not long after Neferet had been tossing exploded people parts from the balcony of the Mayo. I had no desire to scold or disobey Marx and Thanatos. Actually, I hoped I'd done enough disobeying for the rest of what would, hopefully, become my long and boring life.

And then Kalona got out of the Hummer.

"Hey, is that the winged guy?" someone from the crowd shouted.

"Wow! Son of Erebus!" someone else called out the misinformation *and* mispronounced Erebus so that it sounded like airbus, which had Stark covering a laugh with a cough.

I elbowed Stark and he shot me his cute, cocky grin, mouthing *airbus!* I rolled my eyes.

"Okay, okay," Detective Marx was saying while he raised his hands in a calming gesture. "There's nothing to see here. You folks need to move along and not block this entryway."

"Oh, do not worry, Detective. We don't wish to block the school's entrance. We only wish to enter the school." The tall, wimpled nun strode forward purposefully, smiling with motherly warmth. "It is so nice to see you again, Kevin."

"Sister Mary Angela, ma'am." Detective Marx tipped an invisible hat to her in an old-time gesture of respect. "It's awful late for you and the other ladies to be paying a social call."

"Oh, Kevin, we aren't here to socialize," she said cryptically.

Before Marx could start to question her, Grandma spoke up, walking past him to meet the nun at the boundary of the school. "Mary Angela, I was just thinking of you earlier." They embraced quickly.

The nun laughed and said loudly enough for a good part of the watching crowd to overhear, "And when did you think of me? Before or after you were being attacked by Darkness? You do lead such an interesting life, Sylvia."

Aphrodite, who had come over to stand by me, snorted, saying, "Old people should have less interesting lives."

"*We* should have less interesting lives," I said under my breath.

Grandma smiled as if she could hear us. "It was afterward, when Thanatos called for the prayers of Tulsa to aid us."

"Ah, that is a lovely coincidence, because prayer is what brought us here."

"Please explain, good Sister," Thanatos said. I noticed she didn't join Grandma. I glanced at Kalona, who was sticking to her side like he expected more tendrils of Darkness to appear at any moment.

"Oh, for shit's sake, enough with this procrastinating," Aphrodite muttered, and then strode forward. "They want protection."

I followed her, though Stark's hand on my elbow slowed me down.

"I believe the correct word for what they want is 'sanctuary,'" said Lenobia.

"You mean the politically correct word," Aphrodite said.

"If any of us were politically correct, we would not be here." From the middle of the flickering lamplight, a petite woman, followed by a slender man, walked to stand beside Sister Mary Angela. She nodded politely to Thanatos. "Shalom, High Priestess."

"I greet you with peace, Rabbi Margaret," Thanatos said. Now that they were closer to the light, the couple looked kinda familiar to me. "I greet you with peace as well, Rabbi Steven. It is always a pleasure to see our neighbors from Temple Israel."

I realized that's why the woman and the man looked familiar. They were the married rabbis, Margaret and Steven Bernstein, who had recently become the rabbinic leadership at Temple Israel, which literally backed to the Utica Square side of the House of Night. I remembered that they'd raved about Grandma's chocolate chip cookies at our open house before that night had, of course, ended in disaster and death.

"So it is indeed sanctuary you seek here tonight?" Thanatos asked the couple, but her voice carried throughout the crowd.

"We do," said Rabbi Margaret, as she and her husband, as well as a bunch of people standing behind them, nodded their heads.

"The Benedictine Sisterhood seeks sanctuary as well," said Sister Mary Angela.

"As does the congregation of All Souls," said an older woman, moving forward out of the shadows. She had long, faded blond hair but eyes so brilliantly blue that even in the dim light they sparkled like little aquamarines. She walked straight up to Thanatos, ignoring Detective Marx's glower, and stuck out her hand. "It's about time we met. I'm Suzanne Grimms, leader of *The Point* ministry at All Souls. Like I said, we're asking you for sanctuary, too."

Thanatos hesitated. She glanced at Lenobia, who smiled. She glanced at Kalona, who frowned. And then she surprised me by glancing over her shoulder at me. I met her eyes and did what my gut told me to do—I smiled and nodded.

Thanatos turned to Suzanne, grasped her forearm in the traditional vampyre greeting, and raised her voice so that it was filled with the power of Nyx: "As High Priestess of Tulsa's House of Night, I welcome you and grant sanctuary to all who seek it!"

Beside me, I heard Stark sigh and whisper, "*Ah, hell . . .*"

Zoey

"No, Bobby! How many times does Mommy have to tell you? You *cannot* touch the tall man's wings!" A frazzled-looking woman plucked a toddler from where he was teetering on the field house's sandy floor, arms stretched out, reaching for the tip of Kalona's wing.

I bit my cheek to keep from giggling as the winged immortal grunted in annoyance and sidestepped to avoid sticky reaching fingers. The toddler tried to lurch out of his mom's tired arms. Kalona dodged around her the other way. As usual, whenever Kalona appeared, all the humans focused their attention on him, which seemed to be wearing on him. He looked tired. Weirdly, his wounds hadn't totally healed yet but were painful-looking pink lines and puckered gouges. I was thinking that he must not have spent enough time on the roof of the ONEOK building when Aphrodite's "Psst!" took my attention.

"Z, bumpkin—over here with me, now!" Aphrodite called to us. Stevie Rae and I let go of the case of water we'd been carrying into the field house and followed Aphrodite to the shadowy far wall and a little alcove that held a statue of Nyx.

"Man, I'm beat," Stevie Rae said.

"Seriously," I agreed.

"We're overdue for a break," Aphrodite said, tossing cans of brown pop to Stevie Rae and me. Then she totally surprised me by cracking open her own can.

"Pop? You? I thought you hated it."

"I do, and this isn't pop. It's Sophia champagne," she said, sipping happily through a little pink straw that she'd unwrapped from the side of the slender pink can.

"Champagne in a can—who knew?" Stevie Rae said.

"Anyone civilized."

"I didn't know," I said.

"My point exactly," Aphrodite said. Then she cut her eyes to Kalona, who was standing in the middle of the field house, obviously looking for someone and just as obviously trying to ignore the people who were staring at him.

"Kalona and humans, especially little humans, equals apocalyptic train wreck," Aphrodite said.

"In total agreement with you," I said. "Does he look tired to you guys?"

Aphrodite snorted. "We *all* look tired."

"I think he looks like he always does, except beat up, which makes it kinda mean that I was rootin' for that baby to grab a feather," Stevie Rae said.

"Kalona's an immortal. He's fine, and a baby yanking on his feathers would be beyond awesome," Aphrodite said. "I wonder what I could bribe a toddler with to do that—or, better yet, his mom to allow him do that. Do you think she likes mimosas?"

"That mom sure looks like she needs a mimosa, *without* the orange juice. She'd probably like one of your pink cans," Stevie Rae said.

"I don't say this often because it isn't often true, but I think you're right, Stevie Rae," Aphrodite said. "I'll need more than one of these little cans, though. Looks like a job for the Widow Clicquot."

"Widow Clicquot? Is she from Temple Israel?"

"Oh, you poor, ignorant peasant," Aphrodite said, shaking her head sadly at Stevie Rae.

Kalona had made it past the toddler, and he was moving again. Ugh, it seemed he was heading in our direction. "Tell me he isn't coming our way."

"Wish I could," Aphrodite said.

"He's like a ginormic homing pigeon," Stevie Rae said.

"Should we meet him halfway?" I asked, yawning. I glanced at the school clock. It read 5:30 A.M. There was a little over an hour left before sunrise, and for once I totally understood red fledgling exhaustion.

"Save Kalona from the humans? Not no, but hell no," Aphrodite said.

"Ditto on that," Stevie Rae said.

I shrugged and yawned again. "Okay by me. I'm too tired to move anyway."

Thanatos had decided that the best place to put all the humans—and there really was a bunch of them—was in the biggest building on campus, our field house. I thought it was a good idea. The place was huge, and with them all together in here they'd be easy to keep track of. Of course the majority of the field house floor was sand because it was used for Warrior training, and the sand sucked. Sand, sleeping bags, and tired, scared, grumpy, gawking humans don't mix well together, so we'd all (meaning almost everyone on campus except for Thanatos, Grandma, Detective Marx, and the religious leaders) spent the past several hours struggling to spread tarps and transform the Warrior training grounds into a what was finally starting to look like a temporary tornado shelter. Not that that was much better, but at least it was less sandy and was more or less neatly sectioned off in family sleeping areas.

"Check it out." Aphrodite bumped me with her shoulder. "The guy Rabbi Steven Bernstein has Kalona cornered. I'll bet he's asking him all sorts of crazy Torah questions."

"It's Kalona's own fault," I said. "It wouldn't kill him to wear a shirt."

"Right? What's with his constantly naked chest?" Aphrodite agreed.

"Hey, guys, check it out." Stevie Rae pointed. "I think Nicole and Shaylin are gettin' to be real good friends. I'm glad. Nicole's done a lot of changin', and, well, Shaylin needs a BFF, especially after you went all psycho on her, Z," Stevie Rae said, then quickly added, "Sorry, Z. Not to be mean or anything."

I sighed. "No problem. I did go psycho on her, and I'm glad she has a nice BFF, too."

Aphrodite and I swiveled our gazes to watch the two dark-haired girls. They were making up sleeping bags together. They did look super buddy-buddy. Actually, as I kept watching them, I saw their shoulders touch and their heads tilt toward each other. My brows went up. Nicole reached out and brushed Shaylin's hair back from her face, caressing her cheek as she did so, weirdly reminding me of something Stark would do to flirt with me. I cleared my throat. "Hmm, they do seem *close*."

"Everybody should have a BFF!" Stevie Rae beamed at me.

"Uh, Stevie Rae," I began, still watching the touches and looks that Nicole and Shaylin passed back and forth. "I think they might—"

"Oh, for shit's sake, Z. You scared Shaylin gay!" Aphrodite said.

I frowned at Aphrodite. "Be nice."

"Ohmygood*ness!*" Stevie Rae's eyes looked twice their size as we saw Nicole sneak a quick kiss on Shaylin's neck. "I didn't know you could scare somebody gay."

"Seriously, bumpkin, I ask again—are you retarded?"

"You know how I feel 'bout the r-word," Stevie Rae said.

"And you know how little I care."

"And you both know how bad you make my head hurt when you bicker. Aphrodite, don't be mean about Shaylin and Nicole. They can love whoever they want to love. Stevie Rae—no, you can't scare someone gay. Jeesh."

"Hey, I don't care who she loves *or* who she sleeps with, but I am going to enjoy watching the shit storm that's brewing." Aphrodite pointed a little way from the bed Shaylin and Nicole were making. "Here comes Clark Kent, right on cue. And I think he just saw the kiss."

"Yepper," Stevie Rae said. "He musta. Look at him."

"Befuddled. That's what Grandma would say about how he looks. Totally befuddled," I said. "I know I shouldn't, but I'm going to enjoy watching this."

"Are you kidding? I want to record it and watch over and over," Aphrodite said.

Erik had already started talking to Shaylin. Even from how far away we were, I could see he was using his hundred-watt movie star smile on her.

"I know he can be a douche sometimes, but you have to admit he is a cutie patootie," Stevie Rae said. "Not like Rephaim, but still."

Aphrodite made a gagging sound.

Nicole didn't hesitate, and she didn't back off. She stuck to Shaylin's side, reached out, and wrapped her arm intimately around the girl's slender waist, staring straight at Erik with obvious possessiveness.

"I knew Nicole would be the guy," Aphrodite said.

"Erik looks like his head is gonna explode through that cleft in his chin," I said.

"Zoey, Thanatos has summoned you, Stevie Rae, and Aphrodite. She asks that the three of you join her in the Council Chamber. That is, if you are finished watching the *humans*," Kalona said sarcastically, jerking his head toward the *non*-humans we had actually been watching.

The three of us jumped guiltily at the sound of his voice. As usual, Aphrodite recovered first.

"Well, thank Nyx *and* the little baby Jesus for getting us out of here before sunrise," Aphrodite said. "It'll take me days to get the sand out of my sparkly Jimmy Choo flats. I'm way better at Prophetess-ing than I am at schlepping." She flipped her hair and twitched toward the door. I could hear her sucking up the last of the champagne through her straw.

"Okay, uh, thanks," I said lamely. "Should we get Stark and Darius and Rephaim, too?"

"The males are busy." Kalona cut his eyes to where our three males were struggling with the end of a ginormous tarp.

"Well, okie dokie, then. We're outta here," Stevie Rae said, waving at Rephaim. I blew Stark a quick kiss before following her out.

CHAPTER TWELVE

Zoey

We passed Sister Mary Angela, the girl Rabbi Bernstein, and the All Souls minister as we entered the hallway to the Council Chamber.

"Zoey, Aphrodite, Stevie Rae," the nun greeted us, gesturing to the women standing beside her. "Let me introduce the three of you to Rabbi Margaret Bernstein and Suzanne Grimms."

"Merry meet," we chimed, semi-together.

The women looked tired, but they smiled. "We're happy to meet you and to be welcome here," said Rabbi Bernstein.

"Yes, and thank you for all the hard work you must have done helping everyone get settled in," said Suzanne.

We nodded our *you're welcomes,* and as the women moved away, Sister Mary Angela caught my eye. "Good luck, Zoey."

"She knows something we don't," Aphrodite whispered.

I signed in agreement, headed to the Council Chamber door, then almost crashed into Shaunee, who burst around the corner looking everywhere except right in front of her.

"Jeeze, be careful," I said, grabbing her so that neither of us fell over.

"What in the world are you doin' running around up here?" Stevie Rae asked. "My mamma would say you're actin' like your hair's on fire."

Shaunee raised a brow. "I'd rather have my hair on fire than have a lost cat. I can't find Beelzebub anywhere."

I'd been super happy to have discovered that while I was locked up, Shaunee and Kramisha had gone to the depot and brought all of our cats—and Duchess, of course—back to the House of Night. Nala had launched herself at me when I'd gone up to my dorm room to change, and I'd squeezed her so hard she'd been super disgruntled and sneezed in my face.

"Why are you stressing? You know how cats are—they come when then want and they go when they want. I have no clue where Maleficent is right now," Aphrodite said.

"I just hope she's not around here," Stevie Rae said under her breath.

I jumped in before Aphrodite could start hissing. "I gotta agree with Aphrodite. Beelzebub is probably just glad to be out of those tunnels and he's stretching his paws."

"That's what I'd think, too, but Beelzebub never misses dinnertime. *Never.* And I always feed him right before sunrise. I shook his Whiskas bag and he didn't come running as usual. So I started checking things out. Have you guys noticed that the cats are being super stealthy?"

I thought about it. I'd seen Nala before we'd gone to the Mayo, but since we'd been back she hadn't made an appearance. Actually, now that I was thinking about it, I hadn't seen any of the cats recently. "Huh, now that you mention it, no. I haven't seen any of the cats. Duchess was in the field house with Damien and Stark, but Cammy wasn't with him, and neither was Nala."

"Like that surprises you? Please. Don't be asstards. The field house is swarming with humans. I'm not a cat, but that makes me want to be super stealthy. I sure as shit can't blame them for disappearing."

"Makes sense," Stevie Rae said. "Cats are weird like that. No offense," she added, glancing at Aphrodite.

"I embrace weird. As I've said before, normal is overrated."

"Okay, well, I'll try not to worry about him. Sorry I crashed into you guys. See you later."

"Join us in the Council Chamber, young fledgling." Kalona's voice surprised all of us.

"He lives in super stealth mode," Stevie Rae whispered to me.

"Thanks for asking, Kalona, but no thanks," Shaunee told him. "No one ever leaves a Council Meeting saying, 'Wow! That was fun! I can't wait to do it again!'"

I started to laugh and wave Shaunee away, but then my gut kicked in, making my mouth say, "Actually, I'd appreciate it if you did join us."

Shaunee stopped, sighed, and shrugged. "All right. I guess it's better than making beds in the field house."

I smiled my thanks to her and the five of us entered the Council Chamber.

Thanatos and Grandma were sitting beside each other. Lenobia was there as well. I was surprised to see Detective Marx standing, arms crossed, behind Thanatos. I thought there wasn't anyone else in the room, but a movement in the darkness by the rear door caught my eye, and I saw Aurox was there again, as if stationed on guard. He didn't look at me.

"Zoey, Aphrodite, Stevie Rae, Kalona, please come in—sit," Thanatos said. "Shaunee, I don't believe I called for you."

"I asked her to join us," I said.

"Then she is welcome as well," Thanatos said, gesturing for us to take our seats.

It wasn't until I got to the table that I saw that the big, flat screen of the computer was lit up. I blinked in surprise and then smiled and hurried the last few feet to the table.

"Sgiach! Hi, it's super awesome to see you!" I blurted.

The queen smiled and responded much more regally (and appropriately), "Merry meet, Zoey. It pleases me to see you as well."

"We called Queen Sgiach, thinking to speak with one of her Warriors who could relay the message to her that we would like to confer," Thanatos explained.

"And then were surprised—and pleased—when the queen herself answered our call," Grandma added.

I quickly added in my head: if it was almost 6:00 A.M. in Tulsa, it had to be almost noon in Scotland. What the heck was Sgiach doing awake? I took a closer look at the queen. She was seated at the huge wooden desk in her private library—that all seemed normal. But Sgiach wasn't looking normal. Her hair was crazy messy. Her face was smudged with dirt and, I leaned closer to the screen to get a better look . . . "Blood! Why is there blood and dirt on you? Are you okay?"

"I live," Sgiach said, which I didn't think really answered my question.

"Where's *Shawnus*?" Aphrodite asked, mispronouncing Sgiach's Guardian's name on purpose.

"*Seoras*," the queen said, enunciating it correctly and giving Aphrodite a narrow-eyed look, "is leading the daylight guard and protecting the island."

"Wait, protecting during the *day*?" I shook my head in confusion. "But your island protects itself, especially during the day."

"That was true as long as Light and Darkness were in balance," Sgiach said.

"Zoeybird." Grandma touched my hand, as if lending me strength. "Neferet has unbalanced the world. Ancient Darkness has begun to extinguish Light."

My knees gave out and I sank down in the chair. Stevie Rae sat heavily beside me. Aphrodite paced back and forth behind us, almost colliding into Detective Marx, and Shaunee chose a chair close to Lenobia. "But Neferet has been crazy for a really long time. I don't understand why she's suddenly messed everything up," I said.

"Oh, child," Thanatos said sadly. "This is not a sudden thing. It is a culmination of a terrible tide that has been rising since Neferet released Kalona from his imprisonment."

I frowned at the winged immortal who was standing across the room by the main doorway, bare chested, stone faced, and silent.

"He's on our side now. That should help, not hurt, the balance," I said.

"This isn't a game. These forces can't be tallied," Sgiach said. "It is the act of release that caused the flood to begin. Kalona was simply the first chink in a failing dam."

"Then let's plug the stupid thing back up!" Aphrodite said.

"Indeed," Thanatos agreed. "That is why we called on Sgiach."

"So, what do we do?" I asked.

"You harken to the wisdom of a different time, a different world. Ancient forces are at work. It is with ancient knowledge that you must stem the tide and repair the balance."

"Can you be less cryptic than one of my damn visions?" Aphrodite said.

"Absolutely, arrogant young Prophetess." I thought Sgiach was going to give Aphrodite a serious butt kicking via Skype, but instead she turned her gaze on me, and even across the thousands of miles that separated us, what she said had the little hairs on my arms standing up. "Detective Marx has explained what happened between you and the humans in the park. Thanatos and your grandmother tell me your violence against them wasn't an isolated incident, and that it involved your Seer Stone."

"Yeah, but I don't even have it anymore," I assured her quickly. "I'm not using it at all."

"Child, you were never using it. *It* was using *you*," she said.

I swallowed around a terrible dryness in my throat. "I know. That's why I gave it to Aphrodite when I gave myself up to Detective Marx."

"Tell me what you were feeling the day of and the days leading up to the incident in the park," Sgiach said.

I hesitated and tried to order my thoughts. Finally, I began. "I was mad. Frustrated. Annoyed. It seemed like I felt pissed off all the time."

"Did it get worse after you used the Seer Stone to reveal the mirror that reflected Neferet's broken past to her?"

My eyes widened. "I haven't thought about it, but yeah, it did get worse after that." Instinctively I rubbed the raised scar on my palm. "It got hot a lot more often. And I lost time." I blurted this last part quickly, not looking at my friends, who I *hadn't* told about that.

"Did you see things during the time you lost?" she asked.

"Yes," I admitted slowly, not liking the look on her face.

"Things like the Fey, the elemental sprites you saw on Skye when you were with me?"

"No." I shuddered. "They might have been Fey, but they weren't like the elementals on Skye. They were horrible."

"Some of the Fey are horrible. As with the rest of us, not all of them choose Light. What you saw when you lost time, was that before or after you used the stone to save your Grandmother?"

"Before," I said.

"Zoey, here is a truth you must hear: Old Magick can set the balance of Light and Darkness to right again, which means your Seer Stone is key to winning the battle."

"Then I need to give it to someone else because what I was doing with it didn't work. Everything got worse, not better," I said.

"I wish it were that simple," Thanatos said. She and Grandma and Sgiach shared a look, and I knew they'd been talking about the stone and me before I'd gotten there.

Sure enough, Grandma patted my hand and said, "No one else may wield the Seer Stone, *u-we-tsi-a-ge-ya*. The stone warms for you. That means it has chosen you, and you alone can wield Old Magick through it."

"Okay, well, how do I do that?" I asked, hating how my stomach clenched just at the thought of touching the Seer Stone again.

"I'm with Zoey," Aphrodite said. "Simple or not, tell her what she has to do."

"Yeah, Z's kicked Darkness and Neferet in the butt before—we all have," Stevie Rae agreed.

"Because of the volatile nature of Old Magick, I can only tell you what I know *not* to do," Sgiach said. "In order for its power to work to balance and not corrupt, it must be commanded by a Priestess who is neither aggressor nor victim. Her intent must be pure. It cannot be vindictive or defensive."

"But Zoey has to use it defensively!" Marx shouted. "Neferet is a sociopathic killer, bent on enslaving Tulsa, maybe even the world."

"It is not a maybe," Kalona said. "Neferet wishes to do more than force a few unlucky humans into worshipping her. She wishes to rule as the one and only Goddess in this world, and to make us all her slaves."

"So how the hell is this stone thing supposed to be a key to stopping her if Zoey can't use it defensively?" Marx asked.

"Detective, Old Magick is neutral—it is power at it rawest. And it is shaped by the intent of the Priestess who wields it. If her motives are not completely altruistic, chaos will be the result." She shifted her gaze to me. "You have evidence of that before you. From what we know of Neferet's past, in light of what she has done in the present, I believe there are clear indications that she has been wielding Old Magick for a very long time, perhaps even before she was Marked."

"But I've never seen her wearing a Seer Stone," I said.

"A Seer Stone is only one conduit for Old Magick. Consider the tendrils of Darkness that shadow her everywhere. They are too base, too raw, to be anything but connected to the Ancient Powers of Light and Darkness. I know. In the Otherworld I battled Darkness in different forms for ages. It can be seductive and cunning. Darkness wears many faces, and some of those faces can seem, at first, like allies."

"I don't see how those disgustin' snake-things could ever seem good," Stevie Rae said.

"Neferet rarely speaks of it, but she was raped by her father on the night she was Marked," Lenobia said. "Something helped her get through that terrible ordeal, and it wasn't another fledgling or even her Mentor. The records at the Chicago House of Night clearly state that she returned to her family home and strangled her father to death before she had even completed the Change. The coroner recorded that the assailant was so strong that her father's head was almost severed from his body."

"And she got away with that?" Marx asked.

"The crime happened in the late 1800s in a far bigger world, Detective. The Chicago House of Night Council, together with those of us on the Vampyre High Council, decided it would be best to secrete her from the state and allow her to start over on a new path whereby Neferet had the opportunity to heal from her tragedy," Thanatos said.

Lenobia said, "And please remember, Detective, that this man raped and brutalized his sixteen-year-old daughter."

"The High Council's records reported that there were numerous bite marks—human bite marks—on Neferet, and that she had been horribly beaten and violated the night the Tracker found her," Thanatos added in agreement with Lenobia.

I felt a shock of remembrance. "Right after I was Marked, Neferet mentioned something to me about being hurt by her parents."

"Her mother died in childbirth. Her father was a monster," Lenobia said. "All of us who knew Neferet from her youth knew the rumors about what had happened to her the night she'd been Marked."

"I'm sorry about her past, but that doesn't change the fact that Neferet is an unstable immortal who must be stopped," Marx said.

"We do not mention Neferet's past to excuse her present," Sgiach said. "We mention it as a lesson for Zoey." Sgiach's gaze burned into mine. "Old Magick was drawn to Neferet, and Neferet discovered that she could wield it. Just as it has been drawn to you, and has been wielded by you."

"Okay, yeah, but I don't like being compared to Neferet," I said.

"And yet what has been happening to you ever since you began using the Seer Stone is very like what happened to Neferet. *It uses you, and as it does so, it corrupts you.*"

I felt like she'd punched me in the gut. "I'd never be like Neferet!"

"Have you ever thought that if you could simply control everyone around you, then you could make everything better for your friends—for yourself?" Sgiach shot the question at me.

"Yeah, but I didn't want anything bad to happen! I just wished I could make everyone act right so that all this craziness would stop."

"Act right according to whom?" Thanatos asked.

"Well, me, I guess, since I was the one doing the wishing," I protested, feeling trapped.

"Intent!" Sgiach blasted back at me. "Old Magick is neutral—it is shaped by the intent of the Priestess who wields it! And the Priestess's intent cannot be revenge or frustration or anything self-serving. Your intent must be pure and entirely for the greater good—whether that means you survive being the vessel the magick uses or not."

"I'm scared," I admitted, and Grandma squeezed my hand, lending me strength. "And I don't know how to do what you're asking me to do. I need you to help me!"

"Only you can help yourself. Grow up, young Priestess. Show all of us why Nyx has chosen to gift you so greatly," Sgiach said. "But do it quickly. You need to command the Seer Stone if we are to have a chance of stopping Neferet and setting the balance of Light and Darkness to right."

The queen's sharp gaze went to Thanatos. "High Priestess, understand that Neferet must be contained so that the contagion of evil is slowed."

"What is your advice on containing her without using Old Magick?" Thanatos asked, making my cheeks feel warm. I knew she shouldn't have had to ask Sgiach that question—I should be grown enough to use the Seer Stone to help her.

"Look to the most ancient rituals and spells," Sgiach said. "Do not think to defeat Neferet—you cannot do that without Old Magick. Think to isolate her, distract her, annoy her—anything you can do that forces her to rethink her plots and plans, anything that is a stumbling block slows Neferet, thus aiding you."

"And giving Zoey more time to discover the path to commanding Old Magick," Grandma said.

I sent her a nervous smile, wishing I had the confidence in myself she had in me.

"I'll try as hard as I can, I promise," I said.

"You cannot *try,* Zoey. *Trying* is far too dangerous. You can do nothing until you *know* you have banished from yourself all negatives: fear and anger, selfishness, vindictiveness, hatred, and even annoyance and frustration. Only then will you command *and* control Old Magick. Until then Aphrodite is to keep the Seer Stone far from you. We do not need to be battling two immortals who once were gifted Priestess of our Goddess."

I couldn't believe what she'd just said! She was actually sounding like she believed I could turn out like Neferet!

"I'm not immortal! I'm just a kid who doesn't want anything to do with Old Magick or that damn Seer Stone!"

"I would imagine a young Neferet would have said much the same thing, and she was far from 'just a kid' as well," Sgiach said.

Before I could even begin to recover from that horrid statement, Thanatos added, "I have only known one other fledgling who was as gifted as you are, Zoey Redbird. Her name was Neferet."

I held tight to Grandma's hand, feeling like my world was falling away from me.

"And now I must tend to my own flood," Sgiach said. "I trust you, Zoey. I believe you will find a way to bring the forces of Old Magick into our battle on the side of Light. Until I see you again, may you blessed be."

Then the Skype connection clicked off, leaving the room in utter silence.

Zoey

"Obviously, this is your fault," Aphrodite told Kalona before turning to me and adding, "If you start calling me Frodo I'm going to be pissed."

"Not to be mean or anything, Aphrodite, but you are Frodo-ing for Z," Stevie Rae said.

"If that's true, then that would make you a short, fat Samwise Gamgee," Aphrodite said.

"A teenager?" Marx's voice grumbled from behind us. "Why would the power to balance good and evil be given to a teenager?"

I frowned at him.

"I have been wondering that for months," Kalona said.

"I must insist on productive discussion only!" Thanatos's voice cut through the room, making even Marx and Kalona look sheepish.

"Actually," I said hesitantly, "Detective Marx's comment got me thinking."

"I didn't mean it to sound so rude," Marx insisted.

"Oh, I know," I said. "What you said wasn't rude—it was just the truth. Why *would* the balance of good and evil be dependent on me?" I hurried on, not wanting my thoughts to get interrupted. "Maybe it's not me, or even us, that's so important. Sgiach says Old Magick is what's important. Basically, I'm just along for the ride because for some reason that none of us gets, it works through me. So, like I said, it's not *me* who's important. It's the magick."

"What are you getting at, Zoeybird?" Grandma asked.

"Well, Old Magick responds to Sgiach, too. Thanatos, Lenobia, please correct me if I'm wrong, but isn't Sgiach the personification of her island?"

"She is," Thanatos said, and Lenobia nodded her agreement.

"Old Magick is in the land," Grandma said, sitting up straighter in her chair. "Just as our Cherokee ancestors believed."

"Oklahoma holds ancient power within its red dirt," Kalona said. "I know. It drew me here not long after I was created, and again after I Fell."

"And it entrapped you for centuries," Thanatos said.

Kalona's jaw tightened, but he nodded. "It did."

"The day I was Marked, I ran away to your farm, remember, Grandma?" My voice was getting less hesitant as my thoughts discovered a path to follow. "I passed out trying to find you."

"I remember," Grandma said. "That was the first time Nyx appeared to you."

"Yes! She told me that I was supposed to be her eyes and ears in a world that was struggling to find the balance of good and evil."

"Even then the Goddess was warning us through you," Thanatos said.

"Seems like it took way too long for us to listen," Stevie Rae said.

"Not just you guys," I said, "but me, too. I don't think I really understood what Nyx was warning me about until now. I mostly just paid attention to the part she said about Light not always being good, and Darkness not always equating to evil. I thought Nyx was telling me to beware of Neferet, because Neferet's so gorgeous to look at, but she's totally rotten inside."

"Makes sense," Aphrodite said.

"Totally true," Stevie Rae said.

"Yeah, but check out what else Nyx said. I remember she told me that I was special, her first *U-we-tsi-a-ge-ya V-hna-I Sv-no-yi.*"

"Daughter of Night," Grandma translated for me.

"That's not all she said, though. Nyx said I was special *because* of my ancient blood combined with my understanding of the modern world."

"And your blood holds within it the power of ancient Cherokee Wise Women," Grandma said. "Women who drew strength from the land."

"*This* land," Thanatos said.

"Oklahoma is where the Trail of Tears ended," Grandma said.

"And where I was drawn, as well as Neferet," Kalona said. "Let us not forget that Zoey holds within her a piece of the soul of A-ya, the maiden formed from this land."

I didn't want to think too long about that, so I hastily added, "It's also where Aurox was created by the blood sacrifice of my mother with power taken from the land of my grandmother."

Marx frowned. "Aurox?"

"I am Aurox," he said, moving forward out of the shadows.

"Hang on," Marx said. "You don't even have a crescent on your forehead. I thought you were just some guy who was the Consort of the High Priestess."

The thought of Aurox being Thanatos's Consort made me feel hot with embarrassment.

Aurox ignored me and looked questioningly at Thanatos. She nodded slightly. He turned to meet Marx's gaze. Sounding strong and sure, he said, "I am not human, nor am I vampyre. I am a vessel created by Old Magick whose purpose was vengeance and destruction."

"But who was also created with a soul, and given the ability to choose to turn from vengeance and destruction, which is what you have done," Grandma said.

"Hell, that almost sounds good!" Marx said, studying Aurox carefully. "If he has these Old Magick powers, can't he help us fight against Neferet?"

"The fighting part isn't important," I said, not looking at Aurox. "It's the creation part—how he, like me, came from this land and the blood that goes back generations on this land."

"We need to use the power of the land to fight Neferet, at least until Zoey gets a handle on the Seer Stone," Aphrodite said.

"Ohmygoddess! I have it!" Shaunee's hand shot up. "Sorry, sorry, I don't mean to interrupt, but I think I know what you need to do!"

"What is it, Shaunee?" Thanatos said.

She put down her hand, speaking rapidly. "Sgiach told us to look to the most ancient spells and rituals to mess with Neferet. You said we need to stop her from spreading. It's been right in front of our faces! Thanatos, you even taught a lesson on it just the other day."

"Shaunee, please be clear," Thanatos said.

"We use Cleopatra's Protection Ritual! We can make like Tulsa is Alexandria!" Shaunee said excitedly.

"I have no idea what she's talking about," Marx said.

"I do," Lenobia said.

"As should all of us," Thanatos said. "But as we all should also know, Cleopatra's spell calls for the High Priestess who casts it to seclude herself, fasting and praying, for three days."

"At the rate Neferet's killing, we don't have three days," Marx said grimly.

"We do have ancient power in the land, though," I said. "Can't we use it to boost the spell and make it work?"

"Interesting idea," Thanatos said. "The spell would have to be cast from a place of exceptional power as close to the Mayo as possible. And the Priestess who casts the spell and sets the ritual would have to remain in seclusion at that site in meditation and prayer, keeping her intent set and true."

"That won't be me," I said. "And I don't mean that because I'm whining about not being grown enough or High Priestess enough. I mean that because I have to figure out this Seer Stone thing and be free to use it against Neferet as soon as I do."

"Agreed, Zoey. I am High Priestess of the Tulsa House of Night. It is my duty to cast the spell and to maintain it for as long as my will holds," Thanatos said.

"Fire is the basis of Cleopatra's spell. I'll stay with you," Shaunee said. "As long as it takes."

Thanatos bowed her head respectfully to Shaunee. "I will appreciate your company and the power you lend to the spell, daughter."

"Oh, thank the great Earth Mother! I know the place of power you must use!" Grandma said, slapping her hand on the top of the table to punctuate her words. "The Council Oak Tree—its ancient power has reigned over that Busk Ground for centuries, and it is within walking distance of the Mayo Hotel."

"Lenobia, Aphrodite, Zoey, Stevie Rae, Shaunee—what say you? Are you in agreement with Sylvia Redbird?" Thanatos asked.

"I am," Lenobia said.

"Yes," Shaunee said.

"Yep," Stevie Rae said.

"Sounds like a plan," Aphrodite said.

I met Grandma's gaze and saw wisdom and love and truth. "Absolutely," I said.

"Then let us all rest. At dusk, Zoey's circle will go to the place of power, and as the sun sets I will set the protective ritual and cast the spell, and may Nyx lend us strength. Thus we have chosen; so mote it be."

CHAPTER THIRTEEN

Zoey

"Stark, have you seen Nala?"

"No. Come to bed. She's probably busy with the other cats letting the local mice know they're back," he said sleepily, patting the spot on the bed next to him. The sun had risen a little over an hour ago, and he was fading fast.

"But Nala always sleeps with me."

"No she doesn't. Sometimes she sleeps with Stevie Rae." He yawned giantly. "Stop worrying and come here. You've been a big ball of stress ever since the Council meeting. You're going to figure out how to use the Seer Stone—I know you will. Worrying all the time won't help. Lay down and I'll rub your shoulders."

I looked at him and smiled. Not only did I love love love it when he rubbed my shoulders, but he was totally cute and sexy with his rumpled hair and his sleepy eyes. Plus, he was right. Me worrying wouldn't help me figure out how to use the stupid Seer Stone. Giving in, I curled up in bed with my back to him and then moaned in pure bliss when his strong thumbs began kneading the stress knot that always bunched between by shoulder blades.

"I think you might be perfect," I said.

"See, the less you worry, the smarter you get," he said, yawning again.

"Hey, I'm fine. Go ahead and go to sleep."

"I know you're fine, but you'll be finer if you be quiet and let me take care of your shoulders." He kissed the back of my neck.

"Okay, but you can quit whenever you want," I said, relaxing into his massage.

"Z, I'll never quit you—you know that." He kissed the back of my neck again.

I sighed happily. "I love you."

"Love you, too," he said. By the time his hands had stilled, I felt all limp and warm and tired. I closed my eyes and, smiling, fell sound asleep.

For about two point five minutes. Then my eyes popped open and I sat up, listening.

"Did you hear something?" I asked Stark.

He mumbled something that sounded like, "Cat . . . okay . . . stop wor . . . ," rolled over, pulled up the blanket around his ears, and started to snore softly.

"Jeesh, no Warrior on duty," I grumbled. Then I yawned and stretched. I seriously needed to go back to sleep. My alarm was set. We had to be up and piled into the windowless school van and on our way to the Council Oak Tree before dusk. Who knew what kind of craziness a protective spell would cause Neferet to unleash. Hell, she was already—

Then I heard it again and knew exactly what had woken me up. It was faint, but it was definitely the sound of a cat yowling.

And there was no Dr. Nal curled up in a disgruntled orange ball at the foot of my bed!

As quietly as possible I pulled on my jeans and grabbed my shoes, tiptoeing in my socks to the door. Not making a sound, and concentrating on happy thoughts, I opened the door and slipped into the hallway. I hurried downstairs and through the deserted common room of the dorm, and went outside, blinking as the morning sunlight stung my eyes. No darn way could I go back upstairs and get my sunglasses, so I shielded my eyes and called, "Nala! Kitty kitty kitty kitty! Come here, Nal!" Then I held my breath, listening.

I heard it again! It was definitely a cat's yowl. And it definitely sounded like it was in trouble. I couldn't tell if it was Nal or not, but I could tell that it was coming from somewhere over by the east wall of the school.

Bad stuff always happens over there! I took off, jogging around behind the dorms, heading toward the wall, and calling, "Kitty kitty kitty kitty! Nala!"

The cat kept yowling. I realized that was good and bad. Good, because I could follow the sound of its voice. Bad, because as the closer I got, the more pitiful the cat sounded.

The next yowl had my stomach clenching. I was close enough to the old broken oak to know the cat was definitely somewhere up in that tree. *Ah, hell! Why did it have to be that tree?* The tree Kalona had split in two when he'd escaped his earth prison, the tree where Jack had died, the tree where I'd seen the disgusting Old Magick creatures.

I slowed down as I approached the creepy-looking thing. Okay, I like trees. I really do. I mean, I loved the Goddess Grove in the Otherworld. I love my earth affinity, even though I'm not as in tune to it as I am to spirit, but still. Normally, I don't have a problem with trees.

This tree was different.

Kalona's cave opened beneath it, and the way it had split apart made it look like it was the bones of a beast, frozen in death, crouched over the opening. All the other trees on campus were budding up, flushed with green. Not this one. It was black and leafless, malevolent and broken. Its branches making more claws than I could count.

"Mee-uf-ow!"

"Nala!" I scooped her up in my arms and kissed her wet nose. She, of course, sneezed on me.

"Rorw?"

I was still hugging squirming Nala when I heard the second cat and looked down. "Cammy?" He padded up to me and rubbed against my legs, leaving blond fur everywhere. "I'll bet Damien doesn't know you're out here. You should be curled up with Duchess and him sound asleep."

"Meeeeeow!"

That meow I knew without seeing the white beast who owned it. I looked over at the shattered base of the tree and, sure enough, there sat a giant white, smushed-face ball of fur and attitude. "Maleficent, Aphrodite would definitely not be happy that you're out here terrorizing the other cats." I paused. "Well, that's probably a lie, but still. You should try not to be so much like her. Jeesh, what the heck do you think—" Then the shadows around the tree moved, and I realized that the creepy old oak was completely surrounded by House of Night cats.

I hugged Nala as an ice cube made its way down my spine. "What is going on out here?"

"That is what I was wondering."

Aurox's voice startled me into squeezing Nal too hard, and with a pissed-off grunt, she wriggled from my arms and padded to join the other cats around the tree.

"Did you make these cats come out here?"

"Me?" I shook my head at him. "Of course not. And if you knew anything about cats you'd know that you can't *make* them go any-where."

"I do not know very much about cats," he said.

"Well, all I did was follow the terrible yowl. Actually, it woke me up. I thought it was Nala, but she seems to be okay."

"Yowl? What yowl? All I heard was you talking to the cats."

I frowned at him and opened my mouth to explain the obvious— that *something* had brought me out here and that *something* was up with the cats, and also up with him. I mean, he didn't have to sound so cold and rude whenever he bothered to talk to me, but the cat inter-rupted me.

"Wroooowwwwwwwwww!" The pathetic yowl seemed to go on for-ever.

"It's coming from up there, in the tree." I shielded my eyes and squinted up into the nest of broken branches.

"There!" Aurox pointed. "I see it!"

I followed his finger and saw it, too. Way, way up, in the topmost branches, clung a really big cat. It was a long-haired orange and white tabby. Not the color of Nala's bright orange. This cat was a softer color, like the orange had been diluted with cream. It looked familiar, and I squinted, trying to figure out whose cat it was, when I got a glimpse of his eyes. They were a startling greenish-yellow color, bright with intel-ligence.

"Holy crap! That's Skylar! Neferet's cat," I said.

"Neferet's cat? But why would he be here? He should be with her."

"Wroooowwwwwwwww!" Skylar shrieked his yowl as the wind made the branches shudder beneath him and he scrambled to claw into his shifting perch.

"He's going to fall," Aurox said, moving so quickly that cats scattered in his wake.

"Hey, be careful. Skylar is a known biter. Seriously, Aurox. Cats pretty much reflect the fledgling or vampyre they choose, and we all know Neferet is—"

"Zo, I can't just let him fall!"

And that shut me up. Not only did he sound like Heath, but he was doing a very stupid, very sweet, very Heath-like thing. Of course he was probably going to mess up as badly as Heath would have, but there didn't seem to be much I could do about it except to wait to clean up the mess. And think. Hmm . . .

"Hey!" I called as he scrambled up the tree, monkey-like. "I've never heard of this, but maybe if a cat's vampyre goes bad, it, well, commits suicide or something. He might be up there because Neferet is batshit crazy and he can't deal with it."

"I'm not going to let anyone commit suicide on my watch, not a fledgling or vampyre or annoying human—or even a cat. Known biter or not."

"Okay, well, I hope Nyx is with you."

"As do I."

"Wroooowwwwwwwww!" Skylar shrieked as Aurox grabbed onto the group of branches that held him, adding a nasty sounding, low-voiced growl while he scrambled backward.

"Try to talk to him. Kitty-kitty him nicely."

"Kitty-kitty him? What is that?"

"Oh, boy. He's doomed," I told Nala. She sneezed and seemed to agree with me. The other cats were all staring up at Skylar, like they were there to witness something. I had no clue what to tell Aurox. "Um, well, try talking to him. I remember that he's super smart."

"All right. I will try." Aurox hefted himself up so that he was sitting almost even with Skylar. I heard him clear his throat, and then in a completely normal, conversational voice, he started talking to the cat. "Merry meet, Skylar. I understand that you have been connected to

Neferet. I, too, have been connected to her, so I can imagine some of what you may be feeling. She hurt me as well. She continues to hurt others. I cannot allow you to hurt yourself, though. I have chosen to protect this school, and you are part of this school."

What happened next was one of the craziest things I'd ever seen—and I have definitely seen some serious crazy. Skylar cocked his head to one side as if he was listening to Aurox.

"Skylar," Aurox continued solemnly, "I will protect you, even if it must be from yourself."

Then Aurox held out his hand.

Slowly, Skylar stretched himself forward until he was within touching distance of Aurox's hand. I held my breath, expecting the big cat to growl again and slap him with his claws. But he didn't do that. Instead, Skylar sniffed him, paused, and then began rubbing his chin against Aurox's hand. Even from where I was standing down below them, I could see the smile that lit Aurox's face as he tentatively started to pet the cat. Skylar paused for a moment and cocked his head, studying Aurox again.

"You can choose not to let Neferet's Darkness destroy your life," Aurox told the cat earnestly as he stroked Skylar under his chin.

With no more hesitation, Skylar trotted nimbly forward into Aurox's arms.

And every cat sitting around the broken tree began to purr.

When Aurox dropped to the ground, he was cradling Skylar tightly to him. The cat looked like he was hugging him and had his fluffy head tucked under Aurox's chin. As Aurox got close to me, I could hear Skylar purring.

"Something happened up there," Aurox said, moonstone eyes shining.

"Yeah." I sniffed and wiped my face with the back of my sleeve. "Skylar chose you. You guys belong to each other now."

Aurox gazed down at Skylar, petting the cat in long, loving strokes. Skylar never opened his eyes. Except for the fact that he was purring like crazy, he looked like he'd fallen asleep.

"Zo, he's awesome!"

I smiled through my tears. "Yep, he sure is."

Aurox glanced at me. Then he automatically reached into his jeans pocket and handed me the Kleenex. "You're snotting again."

"Yep, I sure am," I said.

His eyes met mine. He looked away fast, but not before I saw the rawness of his expression.

"I am sorry. I should not call you Zo."

"You can call me that if you want to," I said.

His gaze met mine then, and I saw anger flash through his expression. "Do not be nice to me because you think I'm Heath."

"Damn it, Aurox, I'm being nice to you because I like you! You saved my grandma. You're cuddling a super-mean cat you just saved. YOU ARE A NICE GUY!" I paused, getting my voice under control before I finished. "That's why I'm nice to you."

"I wish that was the truth," he said.

"Aurox, I promise you that I am only going to tell you the truth. I have way too much personal crap to deal with to add lying to the list."

"You mean that, don't you?"

"Yeah, I do." I wiped my face and sniffled. "Thanks for the Kleenex."

"You are welcome."

"Do you have cat stuff in your room?"

He hesitated and then said softly, "I don't really have a room."

"Where've you been sleeping?"

"I don't sleep."

Goddess! He's not even human! I felt the shock of it, and the memory of what he looked like when he morphed into the bull creature played through my mind. Purposefully, I pushed the image away.

"Well, you're gonna need a room now. That cat needs a place to sleep and eat and, um, do you know anything about litter boxes?"

"What's litter?"

I smiled at him. "Come on. Kalona doesn't sleep either. Let's find him. He can set you up with a room, cat food, and a litter box." I kitty-kittyed Nala, and she actually came to me, jumping up into my arms. I noticed then that all the other cats had disappeared.

"Do you think Kalona knows things about cats?" Aurox asked me as we walked side by side.

"I'd bet on it. He used to be Nyx's Warrior, and cats are a big part of the Otherworld. The Goddess loves them."

Aurox's expression went blank and he said, "Zo, do you think Skylar choosing me might mean Nyx cares about me? Just a little?"

"I'd bet on it," was all I could say before my throat closed with tears and Aurox had to hand me another Kleenex.

CHAPTER FOURTEEN

Kalona

"Okay, I have to tell ya, that seemed really strange to me. Did it seem strange to you, too?" Detective Marx asked Kalona. He'd fallen in to step beside the winged immortal as they left the boys' dormitory and walked out into the bright, beautiful midday sunshine.

Kalona raised his brows and gave a sideways glance at the detective. He was unused to conversing easily with anyone—especially anyone human. But Marx wasn't awed by him. Nor did he judge him a monster because of his past. *He treats me as if we are comrades-in-arms,* Kalona realized with a small, unusual start of surprise.

It was with another start of surprise that the winged immortal realized he actually enjoyed the detective's company.

"Strange? Having a mad, immortal vampyre's cat choose a creature created out of Old Magick to be a weapon of Darkness, and then have to explain to the creature, who looks exactly like a confused boy, how to feed it and clean its litter box?" Kalona snorted. "Detective, I believe strange isn't a strong enough descriptive word."

"Glad to hear you say it!"

The detective smacked Kalona's shoulder in a gesture that was filled with esprit de corps. Kalona had to grit his teeth against the stab of pain that shot through his body as Marx's innocent gesture opened an unhealed wound. Kalona made certain his grunt reflected agreement and not discomfort.

Unaware of anything except their conversation, Marx chuckled and continued, "Yeah, there was a moment in there when the kid was scratching that damn giant cat under its chin that I was sure his eyes started to glow."

"The cat's or the kid's?" Kalona joked mildly, ignoring the lingering pain.

"The kid's. Can the cat's eyes glow, too?" Marx shook his head. "No, don't tell me. Now I understand why my sister says some vampyre things are off-limits to humans. It's not good for our minds—might make us lose them."

Kalona chuckled. "I think that has more to do with the strangeness of our times than the ability of humans to comprehend the abnormal."

"You may have a point. These are definitely some weird-assed times."

They walked on together without speaking, though Kalona didn't feel the silence was awkward. They were just two men going about the business of protecting those who were important to them.

This is what it feels like to be part of a family. I like the way it feels! The thought came unbidden to Kalona's mind, and he didn't know what to do with it. *How had the House of Night become his family?* Kalona had no idea, but even Zoey Redbird, the fledgling he'd first tried to seduce and then destroy, had come to trust him enough that she sought him out to advise and aid Aurox when Neferet's feline chose the vessel as his familiar.

Thus came Kalona's third start of surprise.

"Hey, never mind. I didn't mean to pry. My sister keeps telling me it's a bad habit I've developed since I made detective."

Kalona mentally shook himself. "I am sorry, my mind was elsewhere. Did you ask something?"

"Yeah, but it was too personal, especially because of who you were. Forget about it—I need to grab a few hours of shuteye before all hell breaks loose again," Marx said quickly.

"You may ask me what you will. We battle Darkness together. There should be trust between us."

They'd reached the girls' dormitory building and Marx paused, leaning against the wide porch stairs. "All right, then. I was just wondering why Nyx doesn't come down from heaven and stop Neferet herself. She's the Goddess's ex–High Priestess. I'd think it would really piss Nyx off that she's misused her power."

"First, Nyx doesn't reside in heaven, or at least not the traditional heaven of modern Western civilization."

"Right, sorry. I forgot. My sister explained that part to me years ago. Nyx lives in the Otherworld, correct?"

"The Otherworld is Nyx's realm, that is correct."

"And you've been there?"

"For eons it was my realm as well," Kalona said slowly, unused to talking about the Goddess or the Otherworld.

"If I'm prying, I'll shut up, and—"

"I do not mind speaking of it," Kalona said, and realized only after he'd spoken the words that he was telling the truth.

"Then you know Nyx pretty well."

Kalona drew in and breathed out several long, slow, breaths. The answer to the detective's question was as simple as it was heartrending.

"I *knew* the Goddess well. Very well."

"I see, past tense." Marx seemed to be musing aloud. "That could explain what's going on. Nyx has changed since you knew her. Maybe she's lost interest in the modern world. Who could blame her? That's why she's letting Neferet get away with corrupting her Goddess-given power and hurting not just humans, but fledglings and vampyres as well."

"That's not true. Our Goddess hasn't lost interest in us."

Kalona looked from Marx to see Shaunee walking down the sidewalk toward them, carrying a gray cat in her arms. She had on dark sunglasses and a hoodie pulled over her face, but it was clear that the sunlight was making her uncomfortable. *She must be close to completing the Change,* Kalona thought, and then realized that the idea of Shaunee making the Change and becoming a vampyre Priestess gave him a feeling that was very close to pride.

The realization had his voice turning gruff. "Shaunee, you should be in your room asleep. Sunlight is not healthy for you."

She brushed his words off with a shooing motion, but she did move past them and into the shadows that the dormitory's overhanging roof provided.

"I'm going to bed. I just had to find Beelzebub. But before I go I wanna make something real clear to Detective Marx." She focused her guileless brown eyes on the detective. "Nyx hasn't lost interest in us," she repeated.

Marx's gaze flicked to Kalona and then back to Shaunee. Before he could respond, the fledgling was already speaking. "Don't go to Kalona for answers about Nyx." She sent an apologetic look to Kalona. "This is going to sound mean, but I'm not being cruel on purpose." She refocused on Marx and continued. "Kalona *Fell*. That makes him *not* a good expert witness on Nyx, Detective. If you have questions about our Goddess, ask me. I talk to her every day, and sometimes she even answers."

"Okay, then. Can you explain why Nyx would let Neferet cause so much pain and suffering, and just stand by and do nothing about it? She gave Neferet the gifts that allowed her to accumulate so much power. Why doesn't Nyx *at least* revoke her gifts? That would make sense. Doing nothing doesn't make any sense to me. I say this with respect for your Goddess, but hers don't seem the actions of a loving deity."

"Nyx won't take away Neferet's gifts, or the gifts she's given any of us, because she loves us unconditionally and she always keeps her word, even if we don't keep ours and betray her," Shaunee explained as Kalona crossed his arms and pretended nonchalance while he did not move—did not breathe—but only listened.

"And she doesn't swoop in and save the day *because* she loves us so much that she will always allow us free will." She paused and then asked, "Do you have kids, Detective Marx?"

"Yes, two daughters, nine and eleven."

"What if you never let them make any mistakes? Or, better yet, what if you let them make mistakes, but then you swooped in and took all the consequences from them?"

"I suppose I'd be raising a couple of spoiled brats," he said.

"What kind of women do you think they'd grow up to be?" Shaunee asked.

"Selfish and irresponsible ones. *If* they grew up at all."

"Exactly!" Shaunee smiled. "How would we learn and grow and

evolve if Nyx rescued us from our bad decisions—or stopped allowing us to make our own decisions, good or bad?"

Kalona couldn't keep silent another moment. "It would be easier if Nyx took over! I still know her well enough that I can promise you the Goddess would be benevolent and kind—and that's more than any of us can promise about the general public, vampyres or humans."

"If Nyx took over, the powers of Light and Darkness would be out of balance forever," Shaunee said.

"Light would win! Is that not the point?" Kalona said.

"Ohmygoddess! Don't you see what you're asking for?"

"Yes! I'm asking for peace! An end to bloodlust and bloodshed, betrayal and destruction."

"No!" Shaunee countered with, "You're asking for an end to free will. We'd be like those fat, floating people on *WALL•E,* or worse."

"What language are you speaking?"

"I know what she's talking about. It's from a Pixar movie. She means we'd turn in to lazy, unmotivated idiots." Marx scratched his chin. "Actually, she might be right. Have you been to the state fair recently?" Then the detective chuckled at his own joke, which made no sense at all to Kalona.

Shaunee didn't blink. She didn't so much as smile at Marx. Soberly, she met Kalona's gaze. "You're not going to get close to Nyx that way. You gotta let go of your control issues and choose to really trust— really believe—really love." Then she kissed the sleeping gray cat on top of its head. "So, does that answer your questions, Detective Marx?"

"Not all of them, but it'll do for now," he said.

"Awesome! I'm going to bed. See you guys at dusk." She skipped up the rest of the stairs and disappeared inside the girls' dorm.

"I'm hitting the hay myself. Thanatos said I could bunk in the professors' residence. You look beat. Are you coming?"

"No. I'll take Aurox's shift and sweep the perimeter," he said.

"A double shift—those are tough. You want company?"

Kalona looked at the detective. The skin under his eyes was bruised, and his steps were dragging. "Maybe next time. Thank you for the offer, though."

"No problem. Be safe out there and, like the kid said, see you at dusk."

Kalona nodded and began walking toward the far wall of the school trying, unsuccessfully, not to replay Shaunee's words over and over again in his mind.

Lynette

"The costumes are lacking!" Neferet said as she shook her head and glared at the group of trembling people Lynette had chosen to wear what were supposed to be 1920s-era clothing.

Had everything, or even *anything* been normal, Lynette would have said her latest event was experiencing a few roadblocks. In the insanity that her world had become, Lynette had decided her latest event was a suicide bomber's vest filled with explosives and set to detonate—and she was wearing the damn thing.

"Goddess, remember the two things I need? Time and means?"

"I remember *everything.*"

Lynette clasped her hands in front of her so that Neferet would not see how badly they were trembling. She cleared her mind and concentrated on what she did best—handling the client so the event was successful.

"And that is just one reason why it is so refreshing to be planning events for a Goddess and not a human or a vampyre," Lynette said.

Neferet's slit-eyed glare softened with the flattery. "What is it you need that I have not provided? We decided on my next worship event last night. It is almost dusk, and all I asked was that I preview the costumes of my supplicants while they practice the Charleston. I am quite sure Tulsa has costume shops aplenty, and you have an unlimited access to my *means.* So explain to me why not one of these costumes remotely resembles the era of the 1920s."

"Tulsa has two decent costume shops, Ehrle's and Top Hat," Lynette began.

"Only two?" Neferet sighed. "I should have begun my Temple in Chicago. Chicago is *filled* with exquisite shops. Kylee! My goblet is empty!"

The Kybot, which is what Lynette had silently renamed the robotic receptionist, scurried up the stairs to where Neferet lounged on her throne, instantly refilling the scarlet liquid the Goddess couldn't ever seem to get enough of.

"But I interrupted you, dear Lynette. Please, continue to explain this travesty." She fluttered her long red-tipped fingers at the ballroom below them and the group of mismatched people waiting there.

"I contacted the owners of both shops. They refused to deliver to us." Lynette gave Neferet the news quickly and then braced herself for insanity.

Instead of exploding, Neferet got very still. In a voice that was soft and contemplative, she asked, "And why did they refuse me?"

"They said the police have the block around the Mayo cordoned off and that they are not allowing anyone to approach us."

Neferet tapped her goblet with the tip of one sharp fingernail. She cocked her head contemplatively. Then her expression cleared and she smiled. "The solution is simple. The police are keeping humans from entering. Their attention is turned outward. They won't expect anyone to be sneaking out."

"Sneaking out?"

"Yes, well, it wouldn't be just *anyone* who will be doing the sneaking. It will be you."

Lynette leaned against the wrought-iron railing. "Me?"

"My dear, are you having a problem with your hearing?"

"N no," Lynette hastily assured her.

"Kylee, pour Lynette a glass of wine. She's looking pale." Gratefully, Lynette chugged the wine as Neferet began the insane explanation. "It will be quite easy for you. You'll go out the back way, around where they pile the horrid refuse. Climbing the fence shouldn't pose a problem for you—you appear to have kept yourself in decent physical condition. And, of course, you'll have Judson with you to help with any problems that arise. Judson, you'll be sure dear Lynette returns safely *and* you'll carry her shopping bags for her, won't you?"

Judson nodded automatically and, blank faced, said, "Yes, Goddess."

"Excellent! I will have Kylee call a cab to meet you at, um, let's say in front of the Central Library at Fourth and Denver. That's far enough away that it won't be within the police barricade, and close enough so as not to be too taxing when you are dropped back off. Judson will do all the heavy lifting for you."

Lynette's mind was racing. *She's making Judson come with me to force me to return. But he's really not more than a robot when Neferet's not pulling his strings. Maybe I can give him the slip, especially when we get to the library. Someone there will be able to—*

"Let me be clear, Lynette. Judson and you won't be alone. I wouldn't think of allowing you to be so vulnerable. Several of my children will be escorting you." The Goddess reached down and stroked the black snake-thing that was wrapped around her leg. "They will also be eager to get *closer* to you should you falter. Then you and Judson will have more in common than you do now—much more."

Lynette snapped her thoughts into order. *The job! I will concentrate on the job!*

"Is something amiss, my dear? Surely you don't have a problem with my solution."

"Honestly, I agree with you about sneaking out." Lynette focused on the one normal thing left in her world, being concerned with completing her job. "The police won't be expecting anyone to do that. But I am worried about getting back in. Even you said that's what they're focused on—keeping people out."

"You are so right to be concerned. I forget that you cannot read my mind because I can so easily read yours. The answer to that problem is simple as well. We shall wait until after the sun has set for you to begin your trek. Night and the inattention of the police will hide you on your way out. On your return, my children will call mist and magick, shadows and fog, so that Darkness will conceal you."

Lynette gaped at her, keeping her thoughts carefully blank, not knowing what to say.

"You needn't look so concerned. Being concealed by Darkness won't hurt at all. Well, I should more correctly say, it won't hurt *you* at all. My children will have to be fed. Tonight one taxi driver will get rather more than he expected as a tip!" Neferet's laughter was cruel and utterly mad.

Lynette upended her goblet and drank deeply.

"Now, send these poorly clad supplicants to their rooms. The next time I see them I want to be dazzled." Neferet clapped her hands with her command, as if she was a pharaoh dismissing slaves. "Lynette, you should probably change that dress for slacks and a dark top. I would hate for you to accidentally be overexposed. You are dismissed until after the sun has set."

"Yes, Goddess," Lynette curtsied and backed shakily away, heading to the elevator that would take her to the fourth-floor loft Neferet had given her. When the doors closed, she covered her mouth with both of her hands, muffling the scream she couldn't stop. For the first time, Lynette understood that there really was no way to survive Neferet's madness, that the question wasn't if she was going to die, but how and when.

CHAPTER FIFTEEN

Zoey

"That is one ginormous tree! I'm glad the stupid icepocylapse didn't kill it. I saw somethin' online about how many Bradford pear trees were killed this winter in T-Town, and it was a crazily high number," Stevie Rae said. She was huddled next to me in the van looking like a bad Halloween ghost costume with a white blanket covering her except for where she'd poked two little eyeholes. The sun had almost set, and the van was windowless, but Thanatos said we weren't going to take any chances. Stevie Rae and Shaylin were totally covered up, and they were the only red vampyre and fledgling allowed to go with us— much to the pissed-off-ness of Stark.

"We cannot take chances with our most powerful assets," Thanatos had told Stark when he'd protested that he damn sure was coming with me. "And you, young Warrior, have proved yourself to be powerful and an asset."

I would rather have had Stark with me, but I'd agreed with Thanatos. Plus, I'd said, we wouldn't be far from the school. As soon as the sun had set, he could come to us.

Thanatos had totally messed that plan up by deciding no, Stark didn't need to come to us. It was more reasonable that Stark and Aurox would change positions for a little while. Stark was going to protect the school. Aurox was going to protect the circle—and me.

I would have protested and overridden Thanatos's command. I mean, Stark was *my* Warrior. Not even the school's High Priestess could boss him around. But Kalona had to be at the Mayo while Thanatos was casting the spell to be sure that if, for some horrible reason, it didn't work as well as she'd planned, he'd be there to battle whatever awful things Neferet did. So Thanatos was sending away her Warrior because that was what was best for everyone. It would be childish and selfish of me not to do the same.

Stark knew that—I could see it in his eyes as we drove away from the school, leaving him behind. And that didn't make any of it even one tiny bit easier.

"Z, you're not even listenin' to me," Stevie Rae said, butting against me when she'd failed to get my attention.

"Yeah, I'm listening to you. The tree's big."

I could see her frown through her eye peepholes. "I said way more than that, but never mind, now you're listenin'. Have you ever been here before? It's way cooler than I thought it was gonna be."

"I've been here before with Grandma," I said, trying to shake off the unease I felt at leaving Stark behind. "She likes to come for the New Year's Busk, even though that's a Creek ceremony, not Chero-kee. Grandma says the tribe doesn't matter as much as the positive energy."

"Your grandmother is a wise woman," Thanatos said.

"What is a Busk?" Shaylin asked from where she was hunkered down next to Stevie Rae. She was holding as tightly to her blue water element candle as she was to the blanket that protected her from the setting sun. I didn't blame her for being nervous. I had practically picked off all my fingernails because of my nerves.

"I looked it up," Damien answered her because I was busy inner-babbling. "It's a sacred and lovely ritual—the most important yearly ritual of the ancient Creek peoples. Tribes would come together to do everything from cleansing themselves to settling disputes and debts. It was established here in Tulsa in 1836 by the Loachapoka clan of the Alabama Creek Nation. They had been forced to leave their homes. It was a terrible ordeal for them, not unlike the tragic Trail of Tears. The survivors held a Busk Ceremony around the tree where they deposited ashes from their home fires in Alabama, proclaiming that they were Tulsa-Loachapoka, and this was their new home."

We were all quiet, peering through the front window of the van, studying the tree and thinking about what Damien had said. I'd known the story. Grandma had told it to me the first time I'd come to the little park that now surrounded the Council Oak Tree.

"Sounds like a place filled with energy," Aurox said from behind me.

"Yes, and let's be certain that energy is positive," Thanatos said.

"You're going to have to tell me what I should and shouldn't do," Detective Marx said. He'd driven us. Thanatos had decided that he and Aurox would be the perfect guardians for this ritual. The detective could deal with any problems with the locals, and Aurox could deal with anything supernatural. Neither of them looked particularly frightening. Marx was tall and in good shape. Actually, he kinda reminded me of John Reese from *Person of Interest*. (All he needed was the black suit!) And Aurox, well, Aurox looked like a cute boy. Tall, blond, built. The only weird thing about him, unless he morphed into a hideous beast, was his eyes, and they weren't that bad. Unless you really stared at him, they just looked baby blue and—

"Zoey Redbird! You must focus!"

Thanatos's voice cut through my mental fog and I jumped. "I am focusing," I said automatically.

"Then what did I just tell Detective Marx?" she asked, turning around in her seat to give me a stern look.

I sighed. "Sorry. You're right. I wasn't focusing. I'll try harder."

"Don't try! Do!" she commanded.

Damien lightened the mood when his whispered, "Yoda?" carried through the Hummer. Stevie Rae giggled and Shaylin whispered back, "You're such a nerd!"

Thanatos sighed deeply and her expression relaxed. "We are all nervous. We are all on edge, and it does no good for any of us to snap at one another. I apologize for my harsh words. So, let me begin anew."

"Thank you," I said. "You have all of my attention."

"Mine as well," Damien said.

"Yep, I'm listenin'," Stevie Rae said.

"Me, too!" Shaunee and Shaylin said together.

Aurox and Marx didn't say anything, their attention had been focused on Thanatos the entire ride.

"Well done, all of you," Thanatos said. "As I was saying to Detective

Marx, I appreciate that he visited the site earlier to unlock the gate so that we can access the sacred tree."

"You're welcome," Marx said. "I also brought the wrought-iron table you asked for. I placed it under the tree, a few paces south of its base, like you said. Does it look good to you?"

We'd parked where the sidewalk fed into stairs leading up to the little Council Oak Park. The plot of land the tree sat on was a raised knoll, now in the middle of a neighborhood. It had been fenced in for protection but the gate was open and there was a finely built wrought-iron table placed under the tree.

"It looks excellent," Thanatos said. She lifted the basket she'd brought with her and continued to explain. "Beginning at this moment, it is of the utmost importance that each of you focus on what it is you wish to protect—Tulsa from Neferet's Darkness. And why it is you wish to protect it—because you want to restore the balance of Light and Darkness."

"Even Aurox and me?" the detective asked.

"Absolutely," Thanatos said. "You will not be within the circle, but your energy will affect it. Why do you think I chose the two of you as our Guardians?"

Aurox spoke up, "You're using us because we're expendable."

Marx's brows shot up. He started to speak, but Thanatos responded too quickly. "You are *not* expendable," she said sternly. "I chose the two of you because your ethos is one of guardianship. That is exactly the energy this ritual needs surrounding it. And, young Aurox, let me assure you—I do not use people."

Aurox nodded slowly. "Thank you for explaining that to me, High Priestess."

"Yeah, it's good to know," Marx said.

"Now, Shaunee, as you know, the element that is most important in this ritual is fire."

"Yes," Shaunee said.

"I would ask that you carry the sacred chalice, the ritual matches, and the oil-and-cinnamon mixture I've brought in this bull bladder to the iron table." Thanatos passed a large crystal chalice, beautifully made with the image of Nyx etched around it, a floppy brown bag-thing full of sloshy liquid, and a long box of ritual matches to Shaunee. "Before you take your place in the south, pour the cinnamon oil into the chalice and leave the matches on the table."

"I can do that," Shaunee said. "And I reread the ritual in my *Fledgling Handbook*. I'm ready to do the rest of my part, too."

"Good. I am counting on the support of you and your element."

"You'll have it. I promise."

"Thank you, daughter," Thanatos said. "Other than that, I ask only that the five of you set and keep your intention strong, no matter what happens outside—or inside—the circle. I shall do the rest."

My intuition was like an itch I couldn't scratch, and I couldn't help asking, "Is something weird going to happen inside the circle?"

"Weird, no? It isn't weird for a Major Ritual to drain the High Priestess casting the spell. But you should be prepared for what might happen to me."

"You're gonna be okay, right?" Stevie Rae said.

"I believe I will be, but perhaps not until after I no longer need to maintain the spell."

"Until then, what can we expect?" Damien asked. "I've studied Cleopatra's protective spell. Nothing happened to her when she cast it."

"Cleopatra had time to fast and prepare. I do not have that luxury. Just know that even after I tell you to close the circle, you cannot move me. I must remain at this place of power, channeling protective energy from the land, if the spell is to remain effective."

"But we can't just leave you here by yourself," Damien said.

A movement outside the van caught my gaze, and my eyes widened in happy surprise. "I don't think Thanatos is going to be all by herself," I said, pointing to my little blue Bug that had just pulled up across the street from us. While we watched, Grandma, Sister Mary Angela, Rabbi Margaret Bernstein and Suzanne Grimms piled out of my car.

Grandma led them to the passenger's side of the van, where she waited, patiently, for Thanatos to crack the window.

"Merry meet, High Priestess," Grandma said, smiling broadly.

"Sylvia? Whatever are you and these ladies doing here?" Thanatos asked.

"My spirit told me you would need to be watched over. We are here to do so," Grandma said simply. "I have smudged each of us and set our intent to protect Tulsa. We are ready to proceed when you are."

Thanatos reached through the open window to grasp Grandma's hand. "Thank you, my friend—my friends," she said, her voice husky with emotion.

"The sun just set!" Stevie Rae said, pulling off her blanket.

"Perfectly timed now that we are all here," said Sister Mary Angela.

"Then let us proceed," Thanatos said. "Zoey, as spirit, please lead your elements into the space around the tree. Position yourself at the head of the table, facing away from Stevie Rae. You will turn with me as I invoke each element."

"Okay, I got it," I said.

"Does everyone have their candles?" The five of us held up our ritual pillars. Thanatos smiled. "I see my circle is ready. Zoey, proceed, and may Nyx be with us."

Automatically, I whispered, *"May Nyx be with us"* in response— and so did every person gathered there, so that the blessing seemed to echo around and through us with magickal intensity.

That's good, I thought. *That's really good.*

I drew a deep breath and slid open the van door. I waited on the sidewalk until my five friends fell into step behind me, and then, like a Pied Piper, I led them up the stairs and through the gate to the tree.

The ancient burr oak seemed to grow bigger as I approached it. Its branches spread high, wide, and low. I could see that it was budding up, but no leaves had formed yet. Even so, some of its massive boughs brushed the ground. I moved around them, making my way to the iron table placed beneath it. Shaunee stayed with me, but Damien, Shaylin, and Stevie Rae silently took their places, forming a circle around me. I could see that Grandma and the other ladies came inside the fence but were careful to stay outside the circumference of the circle Thanatos would soon cast. Detective Marx and Aurox remained outside the fence. Keeping their attention turned outward, they began walking around the area, vigilant and ready to act.

Shaunee poured the thick liquid into the crystal chalice. I inhaled deeply the familiar scent of cinnamon. She met my gaze briefly when she was done.

"Blessed be," I said softly.

"And blessed be to thee," she responded before moving to her position at the southernmost part of the circle.

A movement by the gate caught my attention. Thanatos was taking off the cloak she'd been wearing. My breath caught as she stepped forward. The High Priestess was dressed in a long scarlet dress that seemed alive. As she moved, the silk train of the dress lifted and rippled. Except for that train, the dress was formfitting—high necked and long sleeved—so that it looked as if she had been dipped in fresh, shining blood. She wore no jewelry. The only adornment on her was a slender woven leather belt that wrapped low around her hips. From it hung a sheath. The hilt of the athame, a ritual dagger, that rested there was covered with rubies that twinkled even in the fading light.

She began immediately, picking up the box of ritual matches and going to Damien. I faced east with her. Thanatos lit the candle and touched the flame to Damien's yellow air candle. "Air, in Nyx's name I summon thee to this circle."

Damien's hair lifted as his element rushed to join him.

Thanatos moved deosil to where Shaunee waited expectantly with her red candle raised.

"Fire, in Nyx's name I summon thee to this circle."

Thanatos didn't even have to touch the match to Shaunee's candle. It burst into flame all on its own and Shaunee's smile was as bright as her element.

Thanatos continued to the west and Shaylin. "Water, in Nyx's name I summon thee to this circle."

I smelled the salt of the ocean on the fire-lit breeze that swirled around the circle.

The High Priestess moved to stand in front of Stevie Rae, touching her green candle with her match and saying, "Earth, in Nyx's name I summon thee to this circle."

The scent of Grandma's lavender field drifted through the circle. I heard Grandma's joyous laughter, and I knew our elements were filling the sacred space.

Then Thanatos was standing before me.

"Spirit, in Nyx's name I summon thee to this circle." She lit my purple candle and I felt a rush of happiness as spirit completed the casting.

"Oh, that's so beautiful!" Rabbi Bernstein exclaimed, and I looked up from my candle to see that a shining silver thread floated around the circumference of the circle, connecting each of the elements.

"Thank you, Goddess. Please continue to be with me and to strengthen me. Whatever comes, I accept it willingly as my fate. So I have spoken; so mote it be," Thanatos spoke softly, reverently. She closed her eyes and drew in and let out three deep breaths. Then with no further hesitation, she took the sacred chalice in her left hand and, scooping the liquid with her right hand, she moved to Damien and began walking slowly around the circle, sprinkling the oil onto the ground. As she moved, she cast the spell:

> *I call upon the element fire to watch, bless, and guide this Ritual. To honor fire I anoint the circle with cinnamon oil poured into the goblet by the fledgling Shaunee, beloved of the fire element. I proclaim my Intent to seek fire's protection over Tulsa. To show my Intent is pure, I proclaim these ancient truths first spoken long ago when Cleopatra, another child of Nyx, called upon you.*

In a loud, clear, power-filled voice, Thanatos cried out the ancient Egyptian proclamation:

> *Hail, Nyx-Strider! Coming forth to cast this spell I do no wrong!*
> *Hail, She-Whose-Two-Eyes-Are-on-Fire! I have not defiled the things of the Goddess in thought or deed!*
> *Hail, Disposer-of-False-Speech! I have not inflamed myself with rage!*
> *Hail, All-Seeing-Goddess-Provider-of-Her-Children! I have not cursed using Your name!*

By this time Thanatos was back in the center of the circle, which was filled with the scent of cinnamon and the wonderful, electric sense I'd learned that powerful magick brought with it.

Thanatos lit the oil that was left in the chalice, and it blazed with a bright flame as red as her dress—as red as Shaunee's candle. She lifted the flaming chalice over her head, saying:

With pure Ritual Intent I hold fire to this oath of protection. Its strength is in me, and through me its flame will be lasting, consuming with fierceness any who wish ill or violence to Tulsa. I ask especially that flame protect the heart of the city, where Darkness dwells. Entomb all there with ill intent and do not allow evil to escape this flame!

While Thanatos's words still echoed around us, she grasped the hilt of her athame, pulling it free of its sheath. Still holding the flaming chalice, she approached Shaunee, who offered her pillar to the High Priestess. Thanatos bowed her head respectfully, saying, "I thank you, Child of Fire, for the gift of your element." Then she took the pillar from Shaunee and dropped it into the chalice. As the flame ate the candle, growing higher and hotter, Thanatos didn't flinch. She held the chalice up and slowly passed the blade of the dagger through the flame three times, speaking power-filled words:

I am one with the flame. Even in the midst of sunshine, I enter into the protective fire. I come forth from the fire, the sunshine has not pierced me, thou who knows my pure intent has not burned me, but thy fire will keep this city safe, cutting like this knife through wax any who dare defile this Ritual!

With the blade of the athame hot and glowing, Thanatos carved TULSA into the skin of the flaming red candle. Then she walked to me. She glistened with sweat. Her long silver-streaked hair was slick with it. She was breathing heavily, but she didn't look burned—she just looked hot and tired.

"*Thank you, spirit, you may depart. Blessed be,*" she said, and I blew out my candle, sad, as always, to say good-bye to my favorite element.

Thanatos then went to Stevie Rae, Shaylin, Shaunee, and Damien— thanking and blessing each element, until the silver thread disappeared in a poof of glitter. Thanatos rejoined me at the table at the center of the circle, placing the still flaming chalice on the table, watching it carefully until the entire candle was consumed by fire. As the flame went out, Thanatos lifted her athame and drove it into the earth at her feet, crying, *"And so I have set the protective spell for thee, what Nyx decrees next, so mote it be!"*

As the dagger buried itself to its hilt, the sky north of us, in the heart of downtown Tulsa, flashed red with an explosion of blood-colored light. It was followed by a shriek filled with madness and rage that echoed across the night sky.

"Oh, blessed Goddess, thank you. The spell is set," Thanatos said, and then she collapsed, falling lifelessly to the ground.

"Thanatos!" I meant to hurry to her, but all of a sudden my legs wouldn't work. In one step they turned to jelly and I dropped to my knees. Dazed, I could see that Shaunee had toppled over, too. I turned to call out to Damien in time to see his eyes roll in the back of his head as he fainted. And then the power-filled earth beneath me seemed to spin, and somehow I was flat on my back with a weird ringing sound in my ears, looking up through the limbs of the Council Oak at the clear night sky. I saw specks of light as my vision tunneled, and then everything went silent and black.

CHAPTER SIXTEEN

Neferet

"Lynette, my dear, you look lovely in black, and the classic lines of those slacks suit you. I think slacks are so much more feminine and attractive than jeans, don't you?"

"Yes, I do. Wearing jeans denigrates women's fashion." Lynette shuddered. "I especially dislike the so-called boyfriend jean. Do those girls not own mirrors? Where are their mothers? It's shameful."

Neferet beamed at her supplicant. It was this frankness and bigotry toward her own kind that the Goddess found so refreshing about Lynette. Even now, when Neferet could feel the waves of fear and nervousness flowing through the woman, Lynette was able to engage in an honest, interesting conversation with her.

"When I was a girl, it was unheard of for women to wear them. There were many things that needed to change as we entered the twentieth century, but the acceptance of those horrid waist overalls as fashion for women was not one of them," Neferet said.

"I could not agree with you more. I'm not a goddess, so I wasn't alive in the 1800s"—Lynette paused to curtsy gracefully to Neferet, which never failed to please the Goddess—"but I know the fashion was more appropriate then."

"You are so wise, my dear. And that is why I look forward to beholding the spectacular worship event you will produce after you return with the new costumes. Are you prepared for your adventure?"

Lynette paled just a little, but she bowed her head slightly and said exactly what Neferet wanted to hear: "If you believe I am prepared, then I am prepared."

"Judson, be sure you take good care of Lynette. She is my favorite supplicant and I would be highly displeased if anything untoward happened to her."

"Yes, Goddess," Judson responded automatically.

Her command to Judson was for Lynette's benefit alone. Neferet expected no other reply from the possessed bellman. The tendril of Darkness that nested within him would ensure his complete cooperation and loyalty, but dear Lynette needed to be reminded that, even though she was out of Neferet's eyesight, she was not out of her control. The Goddess adored her human pet; that did not mean she trusted her.

Neferet looked down at the threads of Darkness that writhed in constant motion around her. "You, you, and you." She stroked three of the thickest, longest tendrils with her finger, appreciating the cold, pliant feel of their flesh. "I command you to accompany Lynette and Judson. Remain hidden from human eyes. You may each consume one human apiece as sacrifice, *after* Lynette makes her purchases and is safely out of the costume store. And if you eat the cabdriver, be sure he has driven Lynette and Judson back to the library. Then, this is my demand: *With night and mist and magick made real, Lynette and Judson you shall conceal. Return them to me, whole and safely, then I shall welcome you joyously!*"

The tendrils she'd chosen quivered with pleasure as she stroked them and spoke the rhythmic words that made her command into a binding spell. Neferet felt Lynette's fear and disgust. The Goddess knew her children repulsed the human, and that Lynette's greatest terror was not about her death but about being possessed by one of them. But the human never allowed her revulsion to show. She wore a pleasing mask at all times, and Neferet appreciated the talent and tenacity it took Lynette to do so.

She also appreciated the fact that Lynette would do anything for Neferet so that she would *not* be possessed. That was the kind of loyalty Neferet understood and could control. She smiled at her favorite supplicant. "Lynette, to show my appreciation for you, I have decided to cloak you myself as you leave my Temple. I have considered it carefully, and it is simply not right that you should have to scramble over rubbish and slink about to do my bidding."

"Why, thank you, Goddess," Lynette said, with true surprise.

Neferet laughed and gestured for Lynette to accompany her through the ballroom to the grand foyer and the glass and brass front doors.

"Shouldn't we wait a little longer?" Lynette said, trying valiantly to mask her fear. "The sun just set a little while ago. It doesn't even look like it's fully dark outside yet."

"That is nothing for you to worry over," Neferet assured her, draping her arm familiarly around Lynette's shoulders. "It does not need to be fully dark for me to call the powers of night to cloak you." She paused as they passed the receptionist's desk. Kylee was, of course, alert and at her station. "Are there any humans lurking outside my Temple?"

"Not that I have seen, Goddess. Even the police are keeping their distance."

"Excellent, though I only ask for amusement's sake. Lynette, be assured I can hide you so fully that the entire police force could be watching and they would see nothing but shadows and mist."

"That's good to know," Lynette said.

"Kylee, call Lynette and Judson a cab. Tell the driver to meet this lovely couple at the Central Library's main entrance."

"Yes, Goddess."

"Now, Lynette, I need you join me at the doors. I will call mist and shadows from within, and when I motion to you thus"—Neferet swept her hand regally toward the doors—"then you and Judson may exit. Make your way quickly to Denver Street. We wouldn't want the cab to leave and have you stranded there, alone with my hungry children."

"No, we wouldn't want that," Lynette agreed hastily. Then she added, "Goddess, may I ask a question?"

"Of course, my dear."

"How am I going to walk through your . . ." The human hesitated, obviously struggling to find the correct word. "Your protective curtain?" she finally settled on.

"It will part easily with my command." Neferet could see that Lynette was still struggling with a question. "If something is worrying you, simply tell me and I will see to it that it is a worry no more."

"It's the blood and the stench. I'm worried about it getting on my clothes," Lynette said quickly.

"Of course that would worry you. That would be so inappropriate as you're shopping, and draw entirely too much attention your direction. Worry no more, my dear. You and Judson shall pass through my barrier untouched."

"Thank you, Goddess," she said with genuine relief.

"You are most welcome. And now, I will send you off to do my bidding." Neferet faced the doors and raised her arms, looking through the Darkness-covered glass to the night beyond.

> Hear me, shadows and Darkness beyond,
> to my command you must respond.
> Cloak my servants with blackness and night
> Hidden by will, conceived by my might.
> No eyes but Darkness and mine shall see
> Shadows they become, so I mote it be!

Neferet could feel the power of the night pulsing beyond her Temple. The things that came out at night—the deepest shadows, the blackness that not even a full moon could penetrate—those were the things that hearkened to her call. Their response thrummed through her body with her heartbeat. She gathered them, focusing them on her will, and readied herself to let loose those dark, secret things so that they could conceal Lynette and Judson, just as they often concealed beings who chose to embrace them.

It was an instant before Neferet released her spell that she felt it. It seemed as if the skin of her Temple shivered. The thought flitted through her mind that something odd had occurred, but Neferet was too focused on shadow and night to give it much attention. Instead she swept her arms toward the doors and the waiting concealment of her night, while she willed her bound and blood-filled children to part for Lynette and Judson.

As Neferet expected, Lynette did not allow herself to hesitate. The Goddess had read in the human's mind that she equated hesitation with weakness, and Lynette did not intend to show any weakness. So she strode to the doors, flung them open, and walked purposefully through the parted blood curtain and into a concealing shadow.

"Well, why are you waiting?" Neferet gave Judson and the three tendrils an annoyed glance. "Follow her!"

Judson walked mechanically forward with the three tendrils of Darkness clinging to his legs, but instead of stepping through her Temple's curtain and into the concealment Neferet had summoned, they collided with a wall of scarlet fire.

For an instant, Neferet was too shocked to respond. She only stared at Judson, who was screaming and beating the flames from his clothing. The three tendrils left him the instant fire had appeared, slithering back to her.

"Concealment begone!" A sound like a thunderclap followed the command, and a burst of moon-colored light shot through Neferet's cloaking shadows, exposing a wide-eyed Lynette, frozen in terror in the middle of the sidewalk.

It also exposed the immortal, who strode to the middle of the street, wings spread and spear raised in battle stance. That was all the goad Neferet needed.

"Children! Cripple Kalona and I shall let you gorge yourselves with his immortal blood!" She snarled the command.

From all around her, tendrils of Darkness shot from the shadows, rocketing toward Kalona. When the first wave of them breached her protective curtain, the wall of flames roared to life, swallowing them whole.

"No! Children! Come back—come back to me!" The tendrils not consumed by flame crawled back to wrap around her body. "What have you done?" she screamed at Kalona.

"Changed sides. Were you not so self-absorbed, you would have noticed before now," he said. Then he held out his hand to Lynette. "Come with me and you will be free of her."

"She is my Goddess. I cannot."

Incredulous, Neferet realized Lynette sounded resigned, even disgusted, and not the least bit worshipful. That made her furious. "Return to me, Lynette! I command you!"

Kalona ignored Neferet. Hand still extended to the human, he said, "We've imprisoned her. Nothing of ill intent can leave or enter her Temple. And Neferet is incapable of ridding herself of ill intent. Come with me and you will be safe from her."

Lynette hesitated. She looked back at Neferet, obviously appraising the situation.

"You are my supplicant! You must do as I command!" Unable to help herself, Neferet began moving forward, determined to force Lynette's loyalty—until the wall of fire exploded with an intensity that seared her. The Goddess staggered back, shrieking in rage and pain so loudly that her divine cries echoed throughout the night.

Lynette turned her back to Neferet and grasped Kalona's hand. "Get me out of here!"

"That I shall do," he said.

"Lynette, hear me!" Neferet shouted at her departing back. "I will break this spell and free myself from this bondage, and when I do there will be no place in this realm or any other that you can hide from me. I will find you and I will possess you as my own!"

Lynette stumbled, but Kalona's strong hand held her upright. He kept walking, ignoring Neferet.

"Kalona, hear me! When I free myself I will come after you, too. Never forget that I held you bound, doing my bidding, once before. I shall do so again!"

The winged immortal didn't even bother to turn to look at her. He called back over his shoulder, "Yes, I remember. I also remember that you could not keep me bound to you."

"The next time I will not be so magnanimous. *The next time we meet, I give you my oath I will destroy you as Nyx should have done when you betrayed her!*"

That halted the winged immortal. He turned to meet her gaze, and in a voice that seemed to share the power of the fiery wall, Kalona blasted back at her, "Do you know why Nyx didn't destroy me when I chose to Fall? Because Nyx is a *true* Goddess—loving, benevolent, loyal, and kind. You? You are a petulant child, a pretender, and a usurper. No matter how much vengeance you spew or how much chaos you cause, you will *never be a Goddess!*"

As he and Lynette disappeared into the night, Neferet shrieked her fury to the sky.

Zoey

When I woke up I smelled the delicious, familiar scent of roasting sweet corn and warm salted butter. Still not quite awake, I smiled. I was at Grandma's house. Grandma grilled the best sweet corn in the universe.

Then I made the mistake of opening my eyes. I was lying on one of Grandma's quilts, but I was definitely not at Grandma's house. I was looking up at the night sky through the drooping boughs of a giant oak tree. Then my memory caught up with the rest of my senses and I sat straight up.

"Slowly, Zoey. You shouldn't try to stand yet," said Sister Mary Angela. As she hurried over to me, the nun called, "Zoey's awake," over her shoulder.

"Here, drink this." She handed me a plastic cup. I could smell that it was filled with blood-laced wine, and my mouth started to water. I hesitated to take it from her, though. It just felt too awkward, maybe even disrespectful, to take blood and wine from a nun.

She patted my shoulder. "It will ground you. Take, drink, and be nourished."

"Thank you. I haven't told you this recently, but I really appreciate how great you are. You—you mean a lot to me." I sniffled, feeling tears in the back of my throat.

Sister Mary Angela smiled. "Well, thank you, Zoey. I know you mean what you just said, but I promise you won't feel so emotional after you drink that."

"Okay." I sniffled again and upended the cup. I don't really like wine, especially not red wine, but as disturbing as it sounds, *I love blood.* The blood in the wine made it taste like liquid chocolate, dark and smooth. My taste buds registered immediate deliciousness, and then an instant later power zipped through my body, clearing the impending tears from my eyes and the cobwebs from my brain. I looked around and right away saw Stevie Rae, Damien, and Shaylin. They were awake, standing by the park's outdoor charcoal grill, munching away on grilled sweet corn. *Well, at least I hadn't imagined that.* Smiling, Grandma was coming toward me with an ear of corn on a paper plate and another plastic cup in her hand. I started to smile at her and then realized who I *hadn't* seen.

"Where are Thanatos and Shaunee?"

Grandma handed me the plate, saying, "Eat and finish grounding yourself, *u-we-tsi-a-ge-ya*. Thanatos is within, being well cared for." She nodded her head toward a place behind me, and I swiveled around so that I was looking at the base of the ginormous tree.

White canvas had been draped over and through the lower boughs, forming a small tent above the wrought-iron ritual table. Suzanne Grimms and Rabbi Bernstein were seated on either side of the open front flap of the tent. The ladies had their eyes closed and their hands folded in silent, meditative prayer. Through the opening in the tent I could see that all five pillar candles had been placed on the table and lit. They sent a warm, flickering glow over the mound of blankets at the base of the table and the still figure that lay on the makeshift pallet. I could also see that Shaunee was sitting on the ground near the pallet. She was sipping from her own cup. There were two nibbled ears of corn on a paper plate beside her. She caught my gaze and gave me a grim smile.

I started to get up, but Grandma pressed my shoulder down, sitting beside me. "Eat and drink first. Besides Thanatos, you are the last to awaken."

"So, she's okay? She's just sleeping?" I asked around a mouthful of corn.

"She seems well, though she doesn't wake. Tell me, Zoeybird, do you remember your dreams?"

I shook my head. "I only remember seeing everyone passing out, and then I fainted. Then I smelled your corn and thought I was at your house."

She smiled again. "I brought supplies with me. Corn is always eaten after a Busk Ceremony. I thought it would be appropriate after this ceremony as well."

"It's perfect, Grandma. And yummy, too. As usual." I chewed quickly and swallowed, then asked, "Did it really work? Is Tulsa protected from the Mayo?"

"Well, I don't know about the Mayo, but Tulsa is protected from the rest of the world."

I looked up to see Detective Marx approaching me. He had his phone in his hand and a super-shocked look on his face.

"What does that mean?" I asked.

"It means this ancient spell Thanatos cast is working exactly like the spell Cleopatra cast around Alexandria. The 911 lines are flooded. Apparently, there is a selective wall of fire stranding some people inside the city limits and stopping others from entering Tulsa—and that includes the FBI team that was supposed to be providing our backup."

"Thanatos's spell asked that no one with ill intent enter or leave Tulsa," I said. "Wow, it did work!"

"The FBI can be a pain in the ass, but they don't wish us ill," Marx said.

"They intend violence. Do you think violence is a positive or negative thing, Detective?" Aurox asked, joining us.

Marx frowned. "If I had to make a blanket categorization, I'd have to say violence is negative, but there's way more to it than that. Violence can be used in a positive way, to protect and serve. I'd know a little something about that."

Grandma nodded in acknowledgment. "We are all quite sure you do, Detective. It has been your life's work."

"And mine," Aurox said. "That is why I understand it so intimately. Be it good or ill willed, there should be choices made that do not include violence. Thanatos has seen enough death to understand that, too. She cast a spell as raw and basic as Old Magick, and as Zoey can tell you, Old Magick works on intent more than anything else."

"Thanatos's intent wasn't just to stop Neferet. It also was to stop the violence and chaos that are going on in our unbalanced world," I said.

"You do understand," Aurox said.

I started to tell him I understood and agreed, when the phone I'd stuck in my pocket started vibrating like crazy. "Sorry, I thought I turned this off," I said, pulling it out of my pocket to see Aphrodite's picture lighting up the screen.

"Speak to your Prophetess," Grandma said.

I tapped the phone. "Hey," I said.

"Get back here. Now," Aphrodite said.

"What's going on?"

"Kalona's back. The spell worked. One of Neferet's hostages got out. And to say Neferet's pissed is like saying Louis Vuitton makes cute purses. Hello, understatement of the decade."

"Okay, we're on our way." I clicked off and faced my audience, which now included Stevie Rae, Damien, and Shaylin. "It worked. Totally. And Kalona got one of Neferet's hostages out. They're waiting for us at the House of Night."

"Neferet will be furious," Grandma said.

"And hard to contain," Damien said.

I glanced at the tent that held Thanatos in time to see Shaunee coming out to join us. She looked tired, but she seemed to be okay. "The spell worked," I told her.

Shaunee nodded. "I know. I can feel it whenever the protective wall flames on."

"You should eat more," Damien said. "You don't look grounded yet."

"I'll unwrap the sandwiches I brought and get more corn," Grandma said, reaching into her bottomless picnic basket.

"You do look really tired. Are you okay?" I asked Shaunee.

She didn't answer for long enough that I started to worry. Finally she said, "I'm not bad, but I'm not okay, either. And I can say the same for Thanatos."

"Did she wake up?" I peered around Shaunee, but all I saw was the High Priestess's motionless form.

"She's not asleep," Shaunee said. "She's meditating. It's only the power of her intent, mixed with the power of my element, that is holding the spell in place."

"How long can you two keep this up?" Detective Marx asked.

Shaunee's shoulders slumped. "I don't know. It's hard—really hard—and draining. It's like I'm running a marathon without moving. I don't understand how Cleopatra kept her spell up for all those years."

"She wielded Old Magick." I felt guilty as hell. "I wish I could help you!"

"'Course ya do, Z. We all know that. And we all believe you'll figure it out," Stevie Rae said.

"Go back to the school, Z. Meditate, pray, do whatever you have to do to find a way to use your Seer Stone," Shaunee said. "Thanatos and I can't hold on for the years Cleopatra did."

"Wait, you're not coming back to the school with us?" I asked.

"I'm staying here as long as Thanatos needs me. I promised her."

Instantly I wondered: *What am I supposed to do if I have to cast a spell and my fire is missing?* But I didn't get a chance to ask my question aloud because a car roared up and screeched to a stop, parking street side of the park. We all gawked.

"It's a 1968 fastback Mustang, might even be a Bullitt. Silver with a black stripe, just like Eleanor in *Gone in 60 Seconds*. That old girl is a monster," said Detective Marx with that weird guy appreciation they seem to all have for muscle cars.

Erik got out of the driver's side.

"I thought Erik had a new red Mustang," Shaylin said.

"He did. He sold it and bought this one," Damien said.

"Of course he did," Stevie Rae and I said at the same time.

"Girls, be kind. Erik is a nice young man," Grandma said.

"His colors *are* getting better," Shaylin said. "But he's not really my type."

I was super glad Aphrodite wasn't with us, but the comments I could imagine her saying had me biting my cheek to keep from giggling.

"Hi, guys. Nice job on the spellwork," Erik said. His gaze went to the tent. "Is Thanatos okay?"

"For right now," Shaunee said.

"Meaning she or the spell isn't going to be okay for much longer?" he asked.

Shaunee blew out a frustrated breath. "Look, Erik, we're doing our best!"

"No, no, that came out all wrong. I didn't mean to sound negative. What you've all done here is incredible. It's just that Kalona sent me here to relieve Marx and Aurox because he's calling all of you back to the House of Night, and I just wondered how long I'm going to be here."

I frowned at him. "Like you *mind* being here?"

He ran his hand through his hair in frustration. "No! *That* came out wrong, too. I'm going to start over." He turned around and the Erik that faced us again was totally the actor—charming, smiling, concerned. "Hey, guys! Great job on the spell! Kalona has called you back to the House of Night. I'm going to stay here, though, and take care of Thanatos and Shaunee, *for as long as you need me to.*"

I still frowned at him, saying, "No one knows how long the spell can last. Thanatos is meditating too hard to talk. Shaunee is helping her with the fire part, but that's about all anyone can do."

"And four Wise Women are watching over them both as they struggle to maintain the spell," Grandma said.

"The rest of us are ready to go back to the school," I said, standing up and brushing off my jeans. "Right, guys?"

Everyone nodded except Aurox, who was studying Erik thoughtfully. He said, "Did Kalona request by name that I return?"

"Yeah, Kalona said you and Marx were needed back at school, and I'm going to take your place protecting Thanatos."

Aurox looked from Erik to me, clearly not happy. "What's up?" I asked.

"Well, Zo, Erik isn't exactly a Warrior," Aurox said, having one of his I-sound-freakishly-like-Heath moments.

"Hey, kiss my ass!" Erik said, puffing up like a blowfish. "I don't have to be a Warrior to keep nosy humans from messing with Thanatos and the rest of the women."

"I meant no disrespect to the vampyre," Aurox said, ignoring Erik completely (which only made the situation worse) and addressing me. "I simply wish to be sure our people are protected."

"*Our* people?" Erik said sarcastically. "You don't *have* any people, Bull Boy."

"Okay, that's enough," I said as Marx stepped between them because idiot Erik looked like he actually might throw a punch at Aurox. "You're not going to fight on this sacred ground."

"It would be a sacrilege," Grandma said, shaking her head sadly at Erik. "Erik Night, I would have thought you would know better by now."

He stepped back, unable to meet Grandma's eyes. "I'm sorry. You're right."

"It is Aurox who deserves your apology, not me," Grandma told him.

"I was wrong. I'm sorry," Erik said, offering his hand to Aurox.

"Apology accepted." Aurox shook his hand in a forearm grip. "I truly meant you no disrespect."

"Well, I truly meant some to you," Erik said. "You touched a nerve with that whole Warrior thing."

"Understood," Aurox said. "I will choose my words more carefully in the future."

"There, *that* energy is what this sacred ground represents—the joining of peoples and the clearing of enmity," Grandma said with satisfaction. Then she turned to me. "Return to the school with the rest of your circle, *u-we-tsi-a-ge-ya*. We will look after Shaunee and the High Priestess. Let your mind be free of worry for them." Grandma hugged me tightly. "Take my love with you and let it give you strength and wisdom."

I clung to her, wishing with all my might that at least a little of the Wise Woman my grandma is would rub off on me *and* my friends.

CHAPTER SEVENTEEN

Aphrodite

"I don't trust her. At all," were the first words Aphrodite said to Zoey as she led her group through the main entrance of the House of Night. She'd stopped her pacing and stood in front of Zoey, hands on hips, frowning at all of them and feeling a ball of stress stabbing between her shoulder blades. "And the next time you try to leave me behind to deal with a group of humans, I am going to quit. I'd rather face Neferet alone with no damn powers at all than explain to one more paranoid mommy that *No, fledglings and vampyres are not all salivating at the thought of so many humans sleeping under their roof, no one is going to eat you or your snot-nosed offspring!* Talk about annoying! Why would anyone want to eat any of them? Most of them are fat anyway. Eesh!"

"Aphrodite, you're gonna have to slow down. I have no clue who the 'her' is, or why mommies would be asking you crazy questions," Zoey said.

"The *her* is Lynette Witherspoon, supposed ex-minion of Neferet. And mommies are asking me questions because I am the only non-threatening, non-fledgling slash vampyre in sight."

"They don't know her very dang well if they think Aphrodite is non-threatening," Stevie Rae said.

Aphrodite skewered her with her eyes. "Zip it, bumpkin."

"Did you say Lynette Witherspoon? As in the owner of Everlasting Expressions?" Damien asked.

"Yes and yes," Aphrodite said. "And how the hell do you know that?"

Damien grinned. "I simply adore *Brides of Oklahoma* magazine, and Everlasting Expressions is the event planner for the most spectacular of the magnificent weddings."

"You are *so gay*," Aphrodite told him.

"Good, you have finally returned," Kalona said, striding into the foyer.

"That's what I was saying. Are you going to fill them in or am I?" Aphrodite said.

"I am going to relieve Darius and Stark at the perimeter. You brief Zoey and the rest of them." Kalona hesitated. "I will bring our Warriors up to date. Detective Marx and Aurox, would you join me?"

The guys nodded and moved off with Kalona.

Aphrodite sighed, wishing *she* were going to meet Darius, even if that would mean she'd have to put up with Aurox and Kalona and Marx. It seemed like forever since she and her gorgeous Warrior had had one stress-free day.

"Earth to Aphrodite—hello? Anybody home?" Damien said.

"Yeah, you're supposed to be briefin' us, remember?" Stevie Rae said.

"Stand down, Herd of Nerds. I'm getting to it. Follow me to the infirmary. Lenobia is tucking Witherspoon away in one of the rooms there. I think she should be in the dungeon, but Lenobia and, shockingly, Kalona, outvoted me. Apparently, dealing with Neferet has the woman on the edge of a nervous breakdown. Whatever. Like we haven't all been there before?" Aphrodite started marching away while we scrambled to keep up with her.

"Do we have a dungeon?" Shaylin asked.

"No, we don't," Damien assured her. "Don't let Aphrodite get to you." Then he reached out and plucked at Aphrodite's sleeve. "Slow down, we're all exhausted from the Protection Ritual."

Aphrodite narrowed her eyes at Damien, but Z stepped in. "Damien's right. Plus, none of us need to hear whatever Crazy Town you're going to tell us about while we're chasing after you. And there's no point in updating us in front of the woman you're talking about, especially if you don't trust her. Let's go to the cafeteria, get some more to eat so that we can start to feel normal again, and you can tell us about this Lynette Witherspoon person there."

Aphrodite clued Z in, saying, "The cafeteria is full of humans. Loud, nervous, stress-eating, annoying humans."

"All righty, then, let's make it the professors' dining hall instead," Z said.

"Oooooh! I've never been up there! Are you sure it's okay?" Stevie Rae chirped.

"I'm sure it is," Zoey said before Aphrodite could answer her.

Aphrodite raised one brow, stepped aside, and motioned for Z to take over. "Well, then, lead on with your big girl panties."

And Zoey did.

Zoey

A long, shocked silence followed Aphrodite's retelling of everything the Witherspoon woman had reported.

Shaylin brushed a trembling hand over her face and said, "Dead Fish Eyes—that isn't just the color of Neferet's aura; it's what she really is—dead inside."

"All those people," Damien said in a hushed voice. "She's going to kill them all eventually."

Aphrodite nodded. "When Lynette described everything that had happened, the puzzle pieces fell into place from my last vision. Goddess, I hate figurative language." She looked at me and raised her brow. "You were too busy being a raving bitch, so I haven't had a chance to tell you, but a pain-in-the-ass poem was my bonus prize." She closed her eyes and recited:

> With great power comes great responsibilities
> Weigh the pleasure of leadership and luxury with the sword
>   Damocles
> When she believes the ancient is the key to all her needs
> Then is when all will tumble down; then is when Light bleeds
>   and bleeds.

Aphrodite opened her eyes and met my gaze. "I thought it was talking about you." She held up her fingers, ticking off her points. "First, you have way more power than makes sense. Second, you sometimes do actually act like a leader, and we do actually follow you, which means you have access to all of this—" Aphrodite paused and gestured at the beautiful dining hall. "Then there's the end part about 'she' believing the ancient is the key and Light bleeding because of it. Well, that sounds like you using your Seer Stone and messing up the balance of Light and Darkness."

"That analysis does sound reasonable," Damien said.

"Thank you, Queen Damien. Reasonable, yes. Correct, apparently not. I skipped the whole sword Damocles part because I didn't want to look it up and because I seriously hate trying to figure out symbolism. But then we found out you didn't kill those men, and Neferet slaughtered a shit ton of people and proclaimed the Mayo her Temple and herself Goddess. So I read the stupid story of Damocles."

"That's about, like, waiting for something awful to happen, right?" Stevie Rae said.

"Most people think so," Damien said in his teacher voice. "Actually, the story is an ancient parable. Damocles was a courtier whose job was, basically, to do nothing but lie around and amuse and flatter his king. One day Damocles made some comment about how fabulous it would be to be king. Basically, his king said, 'Hey, if you think it's so great to be king, then go ahead, try out my throne.' Naturally, Damocles took him up on the offer. He was having a gay old time—" Here Damien stopped to giggle and say, "Gay! Heehees!"

"Oh, for shit's sake, tell the rest of the story or I will," Aphrodite said.

Damien got himself under control and continued. "*Anyway,* Damocles was having such a good time that it took him awhile to notice it, but hanging above him, on a thread as thin as a horse hair, was a sword. All of a sudden being king didn't seem so awesome to Damocles and he begged the king to let him go back to his own life."

"Oh, so the moral isn't that doom and gloom is lurking," I said as my mental lightbulb lit up. "It's that you should be happy with what you've been given."

"Yeah, and—as the guy in the NPR story explained so that I could effing understand the metaphor—not covet what you haven't been given because that other oh-so-awesome life has it's own bad shit, usually in proportion to how much responsibility and luxury you have. In conclusion, I think the prophecy was more about Neferet than you," Aphrodite finished.

"Which means we're super screwed because it's *not* Zoey," Shaylin said.

"Huh?" I said.

"Zoey, if it was about you, you'd listen to the warning," she continued. "You really already have. You know Old Magick is important, but you realize the key to that power is you and your intent, and not just hooking into the power. Right?"

"Absolutely," I agreed, and my mental lightbulb got brighter. "Oh, I get it! It *is* a warning about what Neferet is up to. She's messed up the balance of Light and Darkness by waking up Old Magick."

"And she's not going to stop," Damien said.

"True," I said. "So the answer is simple. We're going to have to stop her. For good."

"I'm hoping you have a plan for that," Aphrodite said.

"Thanks to you guys, I have the beginning of one. We need to find Neferet's Damocles sword," I said.

Kalona

"At least the protective wall contains her." Darius was the first to speak after Kalona had explained to him, Stark, Aurox, and the detective the full extent of the macabre charade Neferet was playing out in her "Temple."

"Only temporarily," Aurox said.

Marx nodded. "Yeah, Thanatos and Shaunee are giving it all they've got, but it's taking a terrible toll on them. Even they don't have any idea how long they can keep the spell going—especially since it's not confined just to the Mayo. It's got all of Tulsa in a protective bubble."

"You realize that's good, right?" Stark said. When the detective looked at him questioningly, the boy continued. "The last thing we need right now is national involvement. Look at it like this—the fewer people who actually witness Neferet's insanity, the easier our cleanup is going to be once we stop her."

"Do you still believe she can be stopped?" Marx asked.

"I do," Kalona said, and he did believe it. "I fought Darkness in one form or another for eons in the Otherworld. The war against it was never won because there must be Darkness as long as there is also Light. But Light does win individual battles. Neferet is simply another individual battle in which Light must vanquish this one particularly tenacious and evil form of Darkness."

"But the whole balance and battle versus war thing means that you lost sometimes, too," Marx said.

"I did," Kalona said grimly. "But the biggest losses I experienced were internal. I allowed Darkness to corrupt something that was pure and honest and true, and when that happened, Darkness won a battle."

"What makes you think Darkness won't get to you again and you'll lose another battle? This time at our expense," Stark said.

"You've lost a battle to Darkness yourself, boy," Kalona shot at the arrogant youth. "What makes you think Darkness won't get to you again and you'll lose another battle?"

Stark bristled, but he answered with no hesitation, "Because I love Zoey and I've pledged myself to the path of Nyx."

"And that is how I can assure you, and myself, that I will not lose this battle—because of love and because of the oath I have given. I know what it's like to be forsworn. I will not do that again. Ever," Kalona said. He ran his hand across his brow. It was still damp with sweat, the only outward evidence he couldn't control that showed the wounds he'd received the night before had not yet fully healed and continued to pain him. *I need to climb high—perhaps to the roof of Nyx's Temple. There the immortal magick in my blood can call healing to it—I must make time . . . I must make time.*

"Hey, big guy, are you sure you don't need some rest?" Marx was asking him.

Kalona waved away his inquiry, avoiding the question with one of his own. "Detective, I'd like to ask a favor of you."

"Sure, anything, especially if it'll help get rid of Neferet."

"I'd like you to interrogate Lynette. She appears to be no more than an utterly terrified human, who has just been through the most traumatic experience in her life. She has answered all of our questions readily—explained how Neferet's creatures are possessing humans, given us precise counts of how many humans are trapped in the Mayo, what Neferet is doing with them, and how many of them are under her control."

"Sounds like she's cooperating well," Marx said.

"Yes, it does appear that way. But two things about her bother me. First, she keeps asking questions about Neferet."

"Questions, like what?" Marx asked.

"Like what happened to Neferet to make her insane, how did she attain her power, is she really a goddess, and if she is, how are we going to stop her."

"I can't blame her for asking any of those questions," Stark said. "If Neferet had just held me hostage, I'd want some info about her, too."

"Agreed," Kalona said. "And it wouldn't worry me as much except for the second thing: she hesitated when I asked her to escape and come with me."

"She absolutely refused to come with me," Marx said, and then added, "Which was understandable. There was no protective shield up and Neferet would never have allowed her to walk out of there."

"Very true, but my intuition says there is more to Lynette than she's presenting. She claims that tonight she was being forced to go on an errand for Neferet, and that she was being accompanied by the threads of Darkness and a possessed servant to ensure her compliance and return. Yet she was outside the Temple, cloaked in Neferet's concealment, well before anyone else joined her."

"What's her explanation for that?" Marx asked.

"That Neferet was showing all the other hostages she was her favorite by allowing her to leave the building unaccompanied," Kalona said.

"Actually, that's not good. Could be Lynette is harboring some Stockholm syndrome symptoms."

"What is that?" Stark asked.

"It's a survival mechanism for hostages fighting for their lives," Darius said.

"I'm impressed," Marx told him.

Darius's lips twitched up. "Detective, Warrior training includes much more than swords and knives and guns. It also includes psychology—both human and vampyre."

"I didn't have any Warrior training," Aurox said.

"Neither did I. I was born a Warrior." Kalona paused and glanced at Stark, adding, "And the boy hasn't had enough training to know much of anything. Please explain the syndrome to us."

"Basically, certain conditions must be met. Let's see, it's been awhile since the academy. First, there has to be a perceived threat to the hostage's survival and the belief that the captor is willing to act on that threat," Marx said.

"The Witherspoon woman meets that condition," Kalona said.

"The next step is that the hostage's perceptions of small kindnesses from the captor must come within an atmosphere of terror," Darius added.

"I would definitely call watching tendrils of Darkness burst through sixty human bodies while Neferet gave her a nice glass of wine and then discussed event planning afterward meeting that criterion," Stark said.

"Yeah, you can check that box off," Marx said. "And the last step is that she has to have been isolated from everyone's perspectives other than those of her captor, and have the perceived inability to escape."

"Check and check," Stark said.

"That could explain her curiosity about Neferet. She isn't asking because she's worried. She's asking because she's obsessed," Darius said.

"I'll talk to her," Marx said grimly. "Keep her on lockdown, only be sure you do so in an unthreatening manner. And your gut is right, Kalona. Don't trust her."

Kalona

By the Goddess he was tired! Now that he was finally alone, Kalona could allow the extent of his weariness to show. His wings drooped, brushing the ground. His shoulders ached. Actually, his entire body ached!

The winged immortal looked up at the rooftop of Nyx's Temple and blew out a long, exhausted breath. *Just do it. Do not think it. Stark has to be relieved before dawn, so I must find a way to shake off the lingering pain of my wounds.* He put his head down, took several long strides and, with a groan, leaped, forcing his wings to beat against the air and lift him far enough off the ground that he was able to grab the lip of the Temple's pitched roof. He pulled himself up and lay on his stomach, trying to catch his breath.

When the blast of sunlight hit him, Kalona couldn't control his weakened body's automatic response to turn away and cringe. Gruffly, he said, "Dim your light, Erebus! You'll draw the entire campus."

The garish sunlight faded to the soft glow of the gloaming of twilight. "Brother, you do not look well."

Kalona used the peak of the Temple's roof to pull himself to a sitting position, leaning against the stone chimney with what he hoped was nonchalance. "And you look exactly as you look every time you appear near me—unwelcome."

Instead of responding in anger, Erebus studied his brother and then said, "Something has happened to you."

"Yes. I have changed sides. Though I have not changed the level of my patience. This is the second time today I have had to explain myself, which is two times too many. Why are you here, Erebus?"

"Nyx sent me to check on you. It appears she was right to be concerned."

Kalona's heartbeat increased. *Nyx is concerned about me!* But he was careful to keep his expression bland. Erebus might exploit any weakness he showed—emotional or physical. "Tell the Goddess that I appreciate her concern, but I am simply following her edict. Nyx commanded that I protect those in need from Neferet, and that is what I am doing. Nyx commanded that I take responsibility for my role in

Neferet's descent into madness, and that is what I am doing. As my human friend, Detective Marx would say, *There's nothing to see here—move along.*"

"I remember well Nyx's edict," Erebus said. "I carried it to you. So I also remember that the Goddess proclaimed"—he made a sweeping gesture, and the night sky lit up with words burning with sunlight— "*IF HIS HEART DOTH OPEN, BARED AGAIN, FORGIVENESS MAY CONQUER HATE AND LOVE WIN . . . WIN . . .*"

Once more, the Goddess's edict blazed into Kalona's eyes and heart. He looked away from the glowing words and they disappeared.

"Like you, I remember well Nyx's words," Kalona said.

"And?"

"And my heart as well as Nyx's forgiveness are none of your business, Erebus!"

Erebus shrugged. "I am just here in the place of a concerned Goddess."

"Tell the Goddess if she is really so concerned, the next time she should check on me herself," Kalona couldn't stop himself from saying.

Erebus laughed. "As you would say, that is between you and Nyx, and none of my business. Tell her yourself—if you think she will hear you."

"I'll do that, after I win the battle against Neferet," Kalona said. *Surely Nyx will hear me then. Surely she will forgive me then.*

"You sound quite certain of yourself, but you don't look as if you're ready to battle Darkness," Erebus teased.

Kalona straightened and glared at his brother. "I look as if I just battled Darkness and won! Little wonder you don't recognize a Warrior after battle. You have never been in a battle, have you?"

Erebus's bantering tone turned serious. "You Fell, but I remained by her side. Who do you think has kept her safe for all these long, lonely years?"

Kalona almost responded with an insult and a retort, but the words died before they were given voice. Instead the winged immortal nodded his head wearily. "Yes, I know who has kept the Goddess safe. Has Darkness been difficult to battle?"

Erebus was visibly surprised, so much so that he took several moments to collect himself to answer. "It has. I am no true Warrior. That was your role, not mine. I think I have been a poor substitute for you."

Kalona met his brother's golden gaze. "And yet Nyx is safe."

"She is."

"Then you *have* been a true Warrior."

Erebus blinked several times. "You leave me speechless with your compliment."

Kalona's smile was wry. "Then I accomplished my goal. I have shut you up. Now, go back to the Otherworld and continue to try to hold the spot I mistakenly vacated."

"Always so arrogant. You barely have the strength to cling to the roof of this Temple, and yet still you order me about as if it was your right. Take heed, Kalona! Someday your arrogance will cost you dearly."

"Brother, it already has. I lost my Goddess because of it," Kalona said.

"Then why haven't you learned to temper your arrogance? What are you doing here, Kalona? Why must you lord your power over these mortals?"

"You call me arrogant? Well, I call you a blind fool! What I do here isn't because of arrogance or a desire to lord power over mortals. What I do here is my duty! And for some of us, that entails more than frolicking about in the sunshine with nothing more than lovemaking and butterflies on our minds. For me it means I will battle Neferet, and not just because my Goddess commands it, but because my Oath Sworn duty requires it of me."

Erebus stared at him, with an expression Kalona couldn't read. "Apparently, Brother, you have changed more than sides. Still, I am compelled to remind you that Nyx trusts you will be the means by which Neferet is vanquished, so have care. Your actions affect others than just yourself."

"Yes, yes, I know. I am the Warrior. I will eternally be the Warrior. Begone, Sunshine. You make my head ache." Kalona was gathering his waning strength to slap Erebus with a clap of moonshine, when his brother jumped from the rooftop. Showing off his untaxed strength and agility, he hovered in the air for a moment before disappearing in a burst of glittering gold.

Kalona shook his head and used the chimney as a handhold to pull himself to his feet, muttering, "How can we be twins? He is like a yapping dog who eternally makes so much noise protecting his bone that no one notices his lack of teeth." Finally standing, Kalona sent an apologetic look upward. "Not that I meant to compare you to a bone, Goddess."

As Kalona threw open his arms and back his head, embracing the immortal magick that hummed through the ether of the night sky, calling healing and power to his body, he was almost sure he heard her laughter in the wind.

Erebus

Invisible to Kalona, Erebus watched his brother call the divine energy from which they both had been formed. *He looks tired. He looks lonely. But he also looks determined. Kalona has changed—he truly has.*

Yes, Kalona was still insufferably arrogant, no matter what his brother said, but he had also paid him a compliment, given Erebus a measure of respect for the role he had been fulfilling in Kalona's absence for many, many years.

Erebus smiled. He'd always believed there was a hero buried beneath that obnoxious and prickly exterior. He could not, would not, change the events that were playing out in the mortal realm. Nyx would never allow that, and Erebus understood all too well why, but he could well-wish his brother:

> *A brother's blessing from me to thee*
> *Allow the hidden hero to be free*
> *Accept what should have been your destiny*
> *Forsworn no more shall you ever be.*

Erebus spoke the well-wish into the wind so that it was carried away from his brother's ears. Kalona hadn't changed so much that he would welcome his brother's blessing—their past was too filled with misunderstanding, jealousy, and conflict. No, Kalona must not hear the blessing, but Nyx must hear it. And Darkness must hear it. Nyx should know that Kalona, her fallen Warrior, had taken one more step into the Light. And Darkness—Erebus smiled grimly—Darkness should know to beware the power of a winged hero.

CHAPTER EIGHTEEN

Shaunee

Shaunee was so tired her hair actually felt heavy. She was glad Grandma Redbird and the other women were there with her and Thanatos—really glad. She might have been able to watch over the High Priestess, and keep her element focused for a little while, but she absolutely could not have set up a tent, fed and nurtured everyone, and turned the little park into a sanctuary. Grandma Redbird and the other women had done all of that, and they kept on doing it. All Shaunee was able to do was to wander a few feet from Thanatos's side to the fire pit Grandma Redbird had built for her, plop her butt down on the ground, and stare into the dancing flames, trying to draw even a little strength from it to keep for herself.

"Uggh," she moaned. The rush of power hit her again and she bent over, hugging herself around the waist.

"Hey, are you okay?"

Not able to speak yet, Shaunee nodded. Without looking at Erik, she focused on the campfire—on its heat and beauty and familiarity, on channeling it and encouraging it to blaze brighter and brighter. As her element roared through her, she snagged just a tiny bit of its strength for herself so that she didn't pass out. She'd learned that trick a few hours ago, after passing out—again. Shaunee breathed slowly in and then out, in and then out, in and then out . . . until her element dissipated and she was able to sit up straight again.

Erik was at her side looking helpless and freaked-out. "Are you going to pass out? Should I get Grandma Redbird?"

"No." Her voice sounded like sandpaper, and she cleared her throat. "And no, but I would like something to eat and drink."

"Oh, sorry. Here." He picked up the plate and the cup he'd put on the ground beside them. "I was bringing this to you."

Shaunee took the plate, smiling wearily. "I think I'm becoming addicted to Grandma's chocolate chip and lavender cookies. Seriously, I love them so much I feel like we're in a relationship." She took a big bite of soft, sweet cookie and a giant gulp from the glass. "Cookies and sweet tea. Does it get more Okie than that?"

Erik smiled, obviously relieved that she wasn't doubled over in pain anymore or unconscious. "I think the only way you can get more Okie is to make it cookies and Dr Pepper."

Shaunee screwed up her face. "That's not Okie. That's redneck. I'm not a native, but I'm pretty sure of those boundaries."

"So, you're feeling better," Erik said.

Shaunee took another bite of cookie and talked around it. "Better than when I was bent over? Yes. Better better? No."

"Why were you bent over like that anyway?"

"Someone of ill intent tried to enter or leave Tulsa, and the protective wall flamed on. When it does that, fire goes through me and I concentrate to intensify it," she explained.

"That hurts?"

"Yeah, like trying to add one more set to a circuit workout that has already kicked your ass. Only I'm doing it over and over again and I don't feel like I'm getting a break between circuits."

Erik didn't say anything for a little while. He just nibbled his own cookie and stared into the fire. Shaunee was okay with that. Silence and fire staring were good with her.

"You're strong," he eventually said, "a lot stronger than I realized before."

"Before?"

"When you and Erin, well, you know," he finished awkwardly.

"When we were Twins," she said.

He nodded. "Yeah, but it was stupid of me to bring it up. The last thing you need is to feel sad right now. Sorry, sometimes I'm a douche and I don't even mean to be."

Shaunee felt herself smiling at him. "Hey, that's a talent—being a douche without meaning to be."

He sent a tentative smile back to her. "A crappy talent."

"True, but still, not everybody has even a crappy talent," she said. "Plus, you can act. *Really* act. So that accidental douche thing will probably come in handy when you head to Hollywood."

"I don't think I'm going to go to Hollywood," he said.

Shaunee saw the shocked expression that fixed his face into frozen lines the instant he'd spoken the words.

"Is that the first time you've said that out loud?" she asked him gently.

"That's the first time I've even thought it," he said. His face had unfrozen, but now he was looking pale and unsure of himself. "I don't know why I said it at all."

Shaunee downed the rest of the sweet tea and then said, "Well, why did you want to go to Hollywood to begin with?"

"To be a star," he answered quickly—automatically.

"Why?" she asked.

"Because I want to be famous," he said.

"Why?" she prompted again.

This time he took longer to respond. "So that people think I'm important."

"Why do you care what people think?"

He turned his gaze into the fire. "Because I'm tired of people thinking I'm nothing but a great smile and awesome bone structure."

Shaunee studied his profile. Had she ever looked beyond Erik's famous hotness?

No. He'd always been the hottest guy on campus, and all she really knew about him was that lots of girls wanted him, and the most popular girls on campus had had him. She didn't actually know anything about the guy under the famous Erik Night suit.

"If you could change what people think, what would want them to think of you?"

He turned from the fire and looked at her, and she realized that in those gorgeous blue eyes she could see honesty and vulnerability. "I wish they would think that I'm strong like Aurox, or brave like

Darius, or faithful like Stark. Instead everyone thinks I'm a useless, conceited pretty boy."

The raw honesty of what Erik had said had shocked her silent, and Shaunee was trying to figure out what to say next to him, when her body convulsed and flame blazed through her, using her as a super-conductor on its way to reinforce Thanatos's spell.

"Argh," she moaned, holding herself tightly again and focusing . . . focusing . . . trying to strengthen her element as it roared through her.

But she was so tired! This had been going on for hours and hours. Why were so many people filled with ill intent? They were draining her! And probably killing Thanatos. No way could she keep this up. No way could she—

A strong arm went around her shoulders and Erik's deep, beautiful voice spoke soothingly to her. "Breathe through it. It's okay. You can do this. You've got this. Remember, flame is your element. It's part of you. Don't fight it—go with it. You can do it. You're strong and smart. That's why fire chose you. You can do it. I'm right here, and I believe in you, Shaunee. I know you can do this."

His voice was a lifeline and Shaunee grabbed onto it and clung, following it back to herself, back to the familiar campfire.

"Here, drink my tea." He shoved his cup into her hands and she drained it.

"I'll get you some more cookies."

He started to get up, started to take his arm from around her shoulders. "No, not yet," she said, still panting. "Could you stay here, like this, for a few seconds?"

Erik smiled at her. Not his oh-so-perfect movie star bazillion-watt smile. He *really* smiled at her, and within his vulnerability, Shaunee saw kindness and true compassion. "I'll stay like this for as long as you want me to," he said, tightening his arm around her.

"Shaunee, I thought you might like another sandwich and some more tea," Grandma Redbird said. Her smile grew as her gaze took in Erik sitting there with his arm around her. "Well, I'll get a sandwich for you, too, Erik."

"Thank you, Grandma Redbird," he said.

"That'd be awesome, thank you," Shaunee said.

"You are most welcome," Grandma Redbird said, and just before she turned away she added, "Well done, Erik Night. I am proud of you, son."

Shaunee looked up at Erik and saw that he was actually blushing, but when his eyes met hers his gaze didn't falter. "I'm starting to think I'm proud of myself, too," he said, and squeezed her shoulders again.

Shaunee leaned against him, borrowing strength and comfort from him, thinking, *Now I know what they mean when they say "when you're not looking for it, it'll find you."*

Lynette

"You've been very helpful, Ms. Witherspoon," Detective Marx said, closing his little notebook and hooking his pen back in his jacket pocket. "I apologize if my questions have tired you. You have been through a terrible ordeal."

"There's nothing to apologize for, Detective," Lynette assured him, though she felt as if there was sand under her eyelids, and she was pretty sure the shot the vampyre healer had added to her IV was a lovely anti-stress, pro-sleep pharmaceutical cocktail. "I want to do anything I can to help you stop Neferet." Lynette paused and tried to order her thoughts. The damn drugs had her words slurring and her mind turning foggy. "Detective, may I ask you a few questions now?"

"If you feel up to it."

"I do, though please pardon me if I get some of my words mixed up." She gestured to the IV bag. "This is definitely not blood they're giving me."

The tall detective smiled. "Just a little something so that you rest easily. The nurse said your system has been through a terrible shock. You need sleep to recover."

"Yes, that's my first question. Why am I here, at a vampyre infirmary, rather than at St. John's Hospital just down the street?"

"Well, Kalona brought you straight here after he rescued you. I don't believe a hospital for humans is anywhere on the immortals' radar."

"He didn't rescue me. The High Priestess who put up that wall of fire did."

"I suppose you could say that Kalona was at the right place at the right time," the detective agreed. "Would you rather I call an ambulance from St. John's and have you transported there?"

"Maybe in the morning. It was the High Priestess who made the wall of fire, wasn't it?"

"It was teamwork that created the spell."

The detective seemed determined to evade her question, so Lynette got to the point. "Did the High Priestess and her team kill people to make the spell work?"

Marx looked genuinely shocked. "Of course not! Ma'am, I was there when Thanatos cast the spell. Elemental magick was used, not human lives. Neferet has gone mad. She kills without remorse because she's a sociopath, not because she's a vampyre."

"Has Neferet tried to get to the House of Night? Has she tried to contact anyone here at all?"

"Not that I know of—not that any of the school officials or fledgling leadership knows of. Neferet cannot leave the Mayo as long as the spell holds and her intent is to cause harm."

"What if she just wants another case of her expensive wine? Or a new outfit or two from Miss Jackson's? She might go out for those things, especially now that I'm gone. And her intent would only be to shop." Lynette could feel her heart rate increasing as she spoke.

"No matter what Neferet's reason to leave the Mayo would be, her true intent will always be to do violence, which the spell interprets as ill intent. She swore to kill both you and Kalona. That oath alone is enough to keep her trapped."

"She won't kill me. She'll command one of those black snakes to go into my mouth and wrap itself around my brain and posses me!" As Lynette's body began to tremble in renewed fear, the detective called from the room, "Hey, I need some help in here!"

The vampyre healer with the tattoo that looked like geometrical figures hurried into the room, frowning at the detective as she checked Lynette's vital signs and made some adjustments on the IV.

"Detective, you have questioned my patient enough. It is time you left," the healer told him sternly.

"No problem. I can see Ms. Witherspoon needs her rest. If you have any more questions, or think of any details you missed, here's my card." He put it on her bedside table. "Just give me a call."

"Ms. Witherspoon will be resting. Not calling," said the vampyre.

"Right, well then, good night, Ms. Witherspoon."

After the detective had left the room, the healer offered her a glass of ice water, holding it for Lynette while she sipped gratefully from a straw.

"You are safe here, Lynette," the healer spoke calmly, soothingly. "You are among friends and allies. Our campus is filled to overflowing with humans who have come to the House of Night so that they are out of Neferet's reach. Have no fear. Rest and recover. We will watch over you."

Lynette's mouth couldn't seem to form the word to thank her, so she just nodded and tried to smile. The vampyre understood because she patted her hand gently and, before she left, extinguished all except one of the gaslights that had been softly illuminating the room. Finally alone, Lynette leaned back against her mound of pillows and allowed herself to close her eyes and relax into the drugs.

"Ah, hell! She's asleep."

Lynette kept her eyes closed, careful not to move or change her breathing. She'd told the vampyres and the detective all she knew—and she had absolutely had enough questioning for one day. This new voice was going to have to wait.

"I told you we should have come straight here. She was fading fast last time I saw her."

Lynette recognized the second voice as that of the mayor's fledgling daughter, Aphrodite. Though it seemed the girl had somehow exchanged her fledgling status for that of a Prophetess.

"Zoey, Aphrodite, Stevie Rae, you may not disturb the human," came the no-nonsense voice of the vampyre healer. "I have drugged her to ensure she is not bothered for the remainder of the night."

Lynette could hear the soft squeak of the healer's rubber-soled shoes fading away.

"Drugged to the gills," said Aphrodite after a brief pause. "Lucky her."

"Lucky? No dang way would I call that woman lucky," said a voice with a thick Oklahoma twang. "Neferet is gonna hunt her down and skin her alive."

"We're not going to let her."

Lynette recognized Aphrodite's sarcastic snort. "Then you better get to Old Magicking and stop her, Z. From what you described, Thanatos and Shaunee aren't going to be able to keep that spell up for long. But you're right, bumpkin. I shouldn't have called her lucky. It's us that are lucky because of her and Kalona."

"What do ya mean?"

"Simple. Those two have pissed Neferet off badly enough that she's going to go after them first. It's good luck to be moved down on Neferet's who-I'm-going-to-kill-and-torture list."

"I have a feeling we're always close to the top of that list," said the girl who must be Zoey.

"Yeah, no shit," said Aphrodite. "Okay, I'm outta here. And I'm *not* going back to the field house. Did I mention that even more humans flocked here while you guys were off having a good time spell casting?"

"Yes, Aphrodite, you've mentioned that."

"Only about a gabillion times. Jeesh, you're definitely our *whine* expert."

"I'm going to go find Stark while he's still conscious. I don't care if I have to stand guard with him, he and I need some alone time."

"I hear you on that, Z. I need to find Rephaim before dawn."

"Why don't you marry him and put a GPS chip in the ring. Then you could track him. It'd be like a National Geographic reality show . . ."

Bickering, the girls' voices faded away, leaving Lynette alone and paralyzed by fear and drugs.

CHAPTER NINETEEN

Neferet

"Sometimes I cannot help but wonder why I have the desire to be worshipped by humans at all." Neferet lifted her lip in a sneer as she looked down from the mezzanine at the herd of people Kylee had commanded to gather in the ballroom. "Fat, ugly, and unimpressively dressed. I wager their blood tastes like sloth. Kylee, are you quite certain this is all of them?"

"Goddess, these are all of the people Lynette had on her list under the column headed UNATTRACTIVE AND NO SKILLS."

Neferet rounded on the girl, backing her against the marble pillar and lifting her by her neck so that she gasped for air and twitched like a fish out of water. "I told you I never want to hear that woman's name uttered in my company again!"

Kylee's eyes grew wide and her face began turning colors. Neferet watched, enrapt by approaching death, when the head of the thread of Darkness that possessed the human began emerging from her mouth. The Goddess let loose her hold on the girl, allowing her to slide to the floor while she gulped air and the tendril, which disappeared within her again.

"You are right, my child. It wouldn't do to lose one of you because of a human's mistake." She looked down at Kylee. "I forgive you. Do not let it happen again. Now, get me another bottle of wine while my children and I cull our herd."

Neferet ignored Kylee as she crawled away. She crouched and stroked the tendrils that still clung to her, weak and wounded from being scorched by the wall of flame.

"They have dared to imprison me. They will pay—I vow it. For every one of you they harmed, I will sacrifice one hundred of them. And you may choose whether those hecatomb are human, fledgling, or vampyre." Neferet stroked the injured tendrils and crooned to them. "And when I destroy the winged immortal, you shall all feast on his blood." She stood and pointed at the group of nervous humans huddled together in the middle of the ballroom. "Until then, those of you who have been wounded, feed from this herd and restore yourselves."

The scorched tendrils moved slowly. Their kills were awkward. They lacked the beautiful razor edges—the neatly severed limbs—with which her healthy children killed. Annoyingly, the screaming went on and on.

Quivering around her, eager to be loosed and join the feeding frenzy, her unharmed children pulsed and throbbed.

"Be patient, as am I. You shall all be fed." Then the first of the humans died, and Neferet closed her eyes, concentrating on the rush of power she felt as she absorbed the humans' energy, thinking, *Sloth-like or not, they feed and renew us. They are not worthy sacrifices; they are necessary sacrifices.*

Kylee returned with a new bottle of wine as the last of the herd stopped breathing. "Ah, excellent timing. I am going to retire to my penthouse."

"Yes, Goddess."

"Well, then, give me the bottle and go back to your receptionist's station and await my next command."

Kylee obeyed her instantly, and as Neferet entered her penthouse elevator alone, the Goddess shook her head in disgust. She wouldn't tolerate hearing Lynette's name spoken, but that didn't change the fact that none of these humans could take her place.

Irritated, Neferet strode from the elevator, through her spotless penthouse, and out to the wide stone balcony.

The night was clear and cold. She approached the stone balustrade cautiously. Slowly, Neferet extended her hand. As it neared the edge of the railing, the air began to glow red, singeing her fingers.

Shrieking in anger, she hurled her glass of wine at the abomination.

"Traitors! Betrayers! You will not cage me!" Unhindered, it flew through the barrier to shatter far below on the street.

Enraged, Neferet stalked around the balcony, careful to stay away from the balustrade. Power swirled around and through Neferet. What an irony it was! She was at her most powerful, and yet she was trapped.

There must be a way out of this prison, she reasoned as she returned inside her penthouse to replace her absent goblet and pour herself another glass of wine. *Even the betrayer Kalona found a way out of the oath that bound him to do my bidding. Breaking this wall must be simpler than breaking an oath.*

Kalona's voice mocked her as the scene echoed from her memory. *The winged immortal hadn't even bothered to turn to look at her. He'd called over his shoulder, "Yes, I remember. I also remember that you could not keep me bound to you."*

Traitorous, forsworn bastard! Neferet's memory shifted, replaying the night she'd discover him, too badly wounded from Zoey's tantrum to protect himself, yet still selfish and ambitious enough to agree do her bidding and be bound by the oath she'd conjured: *"If you, Kalona, Fallen Warrior of Nyx, break this oath and fail in my sworn quest to destroy Zoey Redbird, fledgling High Priestess of Nyx, I shall hold dominion over your spirit for as long as you are an immortal."*

Kalona had failed to destroy the fledgling, though he had somehow broken his bondage to her. Trying to drown the indignity of the memory, Neferet lifted the goblet to her lips—and realization hit her with such force that her hand convulsed and she snapped the stem, sending wine and crystal shards all over her marble floor. *Kalona hadn't broken his oath. The oath could not bind him because the conditions of it no longer applied.*

"That fool! He has shown me the path to his destruction." Neferet ignored the glass that cut her feet and the tendrils of Darkness that lapped at her pooling blood. *She* was immortal—cuts and blood meant little to her.

She lifted the telephone and punched reception's number.

Kylee answered on the first ring. "How may I do your bidding, Goddess?"

"Send Judson to me. I believe he can help me with a small matter, and you can help me with another. Do I remember correctly that *that woman* made special annotations regarding the personalities of the more attractive of my worshippers, their likes and dislikes and such?"

"Yes, Goddess. *That woman* took notes on everyone she thought you might value."

"Excellent! Go over the lists and find the nicest of my supplicants."

"The *nicest,* Goddess?"

"Yes, Kylee. Are you having difficulty understanding English?"

"No—no, Goddess."

"Good. Then do as I command. Bring me my supplicants who *that woman* noted as the most kindhearted, those whose intentions are always good."

"It will be as you command, Goddess."

"Of course it will be," she said. "But don't bring those people to me yet. I need to speak with Judson first. He will let you know when I am ready to receive my most loving supplicants. At that time, I want you and all of the male members of my staff to escort the group to my penthouse."

"Yes, Goddess."

Neferet hung up the telephone. Her victorious laughter mixed with the scent and taste of her blood, and her children rejoiced.

Aphrodite

"Seriously, Z, you've got to stop the whole coitus interruptus thing. It's getting on my nerves." Aphrodite untangled herself from Darius, straightening her clothes but not getting off his lap.

"You weren't doing it. Yet. So it's not technically coitus interruptus," Stark said.

"How do you even know what she's talking about?" Z asked him.

"*Big Bang Theory.*" Stark grinned his ridiculous, cocky smile at Zoey. "Now who's the dork?"

"Oh, for shit's sake, *you're both dorks.*"

"Oh, I think I get it," Zoey said, and her cheeks turned pink. "Uh, sorry. Stark and I just wanted to grab a few minutes by ourselves. We didn't think anybody would be over in this part of campus. You know, too close to Nyx's Temple for the humans to wander over here, too far from the wall for Aurox or Kalona to patrol."

"And too near dawn for noisy fledglings to be wandering around. Yeah, exactly what Darius and I thought, too," Aphrodite said.

"Great minds think alike, my beauty," Darius said, scooting both of them over so that there was room on the blanket. "Would you sit with us?"

"Being as you already interrupted our plans," Aphrodite muttered.

"That'd be great," Zoey said, sitting beside Stark, hand in hand. "I don't feel like I've had a break since we ate after the ritual."

"Humans are a lot of work," Darius said.

"And there are so many of them." Aphrodite shuddered delicately.

"I wish Grandma was here. She knows how to deal with large groups of people. She'd have them all weaving herbs and beating drums," Z said.

"Well, I heard Lenobia say something about beating, but I'm pretty damn sure it wasn't drums she had in mind," Aphrodite said, rubbing at a headache that had just begun in her forehead.

"Yeah, she's pissed that they're so close to the horses. She and Travis are doing double duty to keep those kids out of the stables," Stark said.

"I should never have told those mommies that the House of Night vampyres didn't want to eat them. I should have told them we *all* wanted to eat them, so they'd better take their Valiums and stay quiet," Aphrodite said, wishing the damn headache would go away. "I even heard Damien almost lose his temper when some brat asked if he could see his fangs—six times after Queen Damien had already explained, patiently, that real vampyres don't have fangs."

Zoey was laughing when Aphrodite realized her headache was causing her vision to blur and narrow. She only had time to reach for Darius when the vision crashed over her.

Aphrodite was in the sky, looking down at a wall of clouds rolling into Tulsa. It was night, but sky lightning was flashing so often that it was illuminating the entire skyline. *Nyx, I don't mean to be a bitch, but T-Town can watch Travis Meyer and* The News on 6 *for a weather*

report. It doesn't take a vision to clue Okies in about wicked weather—
we're down with that.

The scene shifted, focused on downtown, and something fell out of the sky. Suddenly Aphrodite wasn't an outside observer anymore. She was inside the body as it tumbled, end over end, hurtling toward the earth below. She tried to make her wings work (wings?), but they wouldn't obey her. She tried to brace herself, but the shock of hitting the ground reverberated throughout her body, breaking her bones. Gasping but unable to draw in air, her fading gaze found her body. There was a bloody hole where her heart should have been and her broken wings lay useless, their raven black color turning red as her life's blood seeped from her body.

No, she thought as the mind she'd inhabited lost consciousness. *Not* my *body. Kalona's body!*

Warn him, so that he may choose freely . . . The Goddess's voice pulled her from Kalona's dying body and was her conduit to return to herself.

"Aphrodite! Talk to us! Aphrodite!" Zoey was holding her hand. She couldn't see her, of course, because her eyes were filled with blood, but she knew Z was there. Just like she knew Darius's arms were around her and Stark was standing protectively over them.

"Kalona," she gasped. "You have to take me to Kalona."

"You need water and your bed," Zoey said, her voice sounding shaky. "And we need to get all this blood cleaned up."

Aphrodite knew it was bad. She could feel the warm wetness that had washed down her face and soaked through her shirt. She ignored it and squeezed Z's hand—hard. "Afterward. Get me to Kalona *now.*"

"He's somewhere walking the perimeter. I'll find him," Stark said.

"I'll carry her to Nyx's Temple. That's the closest building to here," Darius said.

"And I'll stay with her," Z said, still holding her hand even though Darius had stood and was already moving.

"And I'll just lay here and dream about the Xanax and wine that wait for me," Aphrodite said, resting her head against Darius's strong shoulder, keeping her eyes shut tightly against the pounding pain.

Kalona

"Kalona! You have to come with me. Aphrodite needs you right now!" Shouting, Stark ran up to Kalona as he and Detective Marx were making a perimeter sweep and discussing options for housing the increasing number of humans who were seeking sanctuary at the House of Night. Kalona had been enjoying Marx's company and his sense of humor, and feeling renewed and well-rested after spending time on the roof of Nyx's Temple. Stark's appearance changed everything.

"Has there been a breach in campus security?" Marx shot out the question.

"No, Aphrodite's had a vision. She says she has to talk to Kalona."

"I will go to her." Kalona sprinted off.

"Wait!" Stark called after him. "She's not in her dorm. She's in Nyx's Temple."

That news didn't serve to dissipate the foreboding Kalona was beginning to feel, though he changed direction and raced toward Nyx's Temple, with Stark and the detective doing their best to follow.

He tried not to hesitate at the door of the Goddess's Temple. He wanted to stride in, confident that Nyx would allow him, but his hand trembled as he touched the handle of the arched wooden door. He paused.

Stark almost ran over the top of him. "What're you waiting for?" The boy flung the door wide and hurried within. Kalona held his breath and followed him.

The opening did not turn to stone, nor did the door close against him. Nyx allowed him entrance.

Now on Stark's heels, Kalona passed through the foyer and entered the heart of the Goddess's Temple. The sweetness of vanilla and lavender candles mixed with the metallic scent of fresh blood. Aphrodite lay on the ancient table that held an exquisite statue of Nyx. Darius sat on the table, cradling her head in his lap. Zoey was arranging a wet T-shirt over Aphrodite's eyes, which still wept blood.

"Oh my God!" Marx rushed into the room. "She's crying blood tears."

"I'm not crying. I'm visioning. Big difference." Blind Aphrodite turned her head as if she were listening. "Kalona? Are you in here?"

Aphrodite tended to alternately amuse and annoy Kalona. He'd never understood why Nyx tolerated her attitude, which always seemed to border on blaspheming. But as he approached her, a profound sense of reverence came over him. *This girl is a true Prophetess of Nyx and thus worthy of my respect.*

"Yes, Prophetess, I am here in answer to your summons," he said, kneeling beside the table.

"Good. My vision was about you. Actually, in my vision I was you. And you died," she said, wincing and rearranging the wet shirt that covered her bloody eyes.

"Kalona is immortal. He cannot die," Darius said.

"I know you hate this kind of stuff, but could this vision be one of your symbolic ones?" Zoey asked.

"It didn't feel symbolic. It felt dead. Real dead," Aphrodite said.

"How was I killed?" Kalona asked.

"You fell from the sky and you had a big bloody hole where your heart should have been. I'm not sure which killed you—the hole or the fall. Your wings were all broken up, too. Either way, you were totally, not symbolically, dead."

"Man, that sounds bad," Marx said. "Do her visions always come true?"

"*She's* right here, and no, they don't," Aphrodite said. "Which brings me to the rest of the vision. Nyx told me to tell you"—she paused—"the you being Kalona and not you, Marx, that I was supposed to warn you about what I saw so that you could choose freely."

Kalona's gaze went from Aphrodite to the statue of Nyx. "You are sure it was the Goddess who spoke to you of me?"

"That's what I said."

"And you are certain Nyx said that you were given the vision so that I might choose freely?"

"One hundred percent. It's not like this is the first time. I do know a little something about Nyx," Aphrodite said with her usual sarcasm.

"Do you know why there are always vanilla and lavender candles burning in Nyx's Temples?" Kalona asked the Prophetess.

Aphrodite shrugged. "My guess is because they smell good."

"It is because they carry the same scent as her skin," Kalona told her. "You see, Prophetess, I know a little something about Nyx, too."

"Fine, you trump me. But I do know her voice, and I'm sure it was Nyx who said to tell you about my vision so that you could choose freely."

Kalona stared at the statue as the most painful of his memories flashed through his mind. For the first time in uncountable eons he embraced the memory and relived it honestly.

He was on his knees before Nyx, and he was weeping. His Goddess watched him, not with a stone-like expression that lacked compassion but with equal measures of sadness and resignation.

Don't do this! You are mine!

I do nothing, Kalona. You have a choice in this. I have given even my Warriors free will, though I don't require them to use it wisely.

Instead of painting Nyx as the villain, as he had in his memory for so many self-deluded centuries, Kalona forced himself to relive the scene truthfully. This time, he acknowledged the tears that had begun to spill down Nyx's face—and the fact that it was his own expression that had hardened, his own voice that had become spiteful, and not hers.

I cannot help myself. I was created to feel this. It is not free will. It is preordination.

Yet as your Goddess I tell you what you are is not preordained. Your will has fashioned you.

I cannot help how I feel! I cannot help what I am! Remembering the scene honestly, Kalona cringed at how like a petulant child he had sounded.

He had stopped weeping, but Nyx's sadness could not be contained. Tears spilled from her eyes to wash down her cheeks. In a choked voice, his Goddess had said, *You, my Warrior, are mistaken; therefore, you must pay the consequences of your mistake.* Then it was not with a thoughtless flick of her fingers that she cast him from her; it was with regret and tears and despair that she gathered her divine energy and hurled the consequences of his own choice at him.

The memory faded, leaving him in the present, looking up at the beautiful statue of Nyx.

"I believe you, Aphrodite. This is not the first time Nyx has bade me make a choice," he said as the finality of her vision settled within him.

"Was there anything else in your vision that might help us figure out how Kalona is going to be attacked?" Darius asked her.

Aphrodite hesitated, then said, "It's always harder when I'm inside the person the awful thing is happening to. Everything gets jumbled because time is passing so fast and, well, awful things are happening. I know he was in Tulsa. I think downtown because I remember seeing the skyline below me. Oh, and a big storm was rolling into town."

In the distance thunder rumbled and the stained-glass windows of Nyx's Temple quivered as the wind shifted and increased.

"Ah, hell!" Zoey said.

Kalona's newly awakened memory flashed several other scenes through his mind: his trespass into the Otherworld . . . his battle with Stark . . . Stark's death in the pit . . . Nyx's intervention and that the price of her intervention had been a piece of his immortality.

Kalona silently agreed with Zoey.

CHAPTER TWENTY

Neferet

"Thank you, Judson. I knew you would find exactly what I needed. You may leave it on the table there, beside the door to the balcony. Oh, but please don't go. My need for you is not finished. As you can see, here comes Kylee, right on time with the little group I asked her to fetch for me." Neferet's smile included the frightened-looking group of humans who were reluctantly entering her penthouse, as well as her male staff members, though she truly smiled only at her children who possessed the men. "I do appreciate punctuality, Kylee. Pour me a glass of wine."

Neferet counted the humans. Twelve of them. Out of more than two hundred worshippers, *twelve* were genuinely kind enough for Lynette to make note of them. The Goddess wasn't upset by that low number, she simply had to be sure her math was accurate and that there were enough of them. "Yes," she spoke aloud as she ran the numbers in her head. "One every five minutes should suffice. It's a short distance from here to the House of Night. That will give him plenty of time and incentive."

"Goddess? Is there something you'd like us to do? A dance you'd like us to learn?" an attractive young woman asked, curtsying gracefully.

"You were one of the waltzers, were you not?" Neferet said.

"Yes, Goddess. My name is Taylor."

Neferet sighed in disgust. "Oh, no matter. I'll let you keep that name."

"Th-thank you, Goddess," Taylor said hesitantly.

"And yes, Taylor, there is something monumental I want the twelve of you to do before sunrise, which is only a little more than an hour away. In celebration of such an extraordinary event, I shall break my own decree and speak her name. *Lynette*"—Neferet spoke the name carefully; to her it tasted of betrayal—"noted that each of you is especially kind."

Taylor's smile was hesitant but genuine. "That was nice of her." The woman glanced around the penthouse. "Where is Lynette?"

Reminding herself that she might need all twelve of them, Neferet did not strike Taylor down. Instead, with enormous patience she said, "Taylor, I said that *I* shall break my decree and speak her name. I did not say anyone else could."

"Oh, I'm sorry, Goddess," Taylor said quickly, bobbing another curtsy.

"That is quite all right, and quite understandable. I should have made myself clearer. Think nothing of it, Taylor. So, as I was saying, *Lynette* made note of each of you. I wanted to be sure you understood that you are here because of her." A shiver of fear began to move through the group. Neferet felt it with them and smiled. "Why don't you sit in the living room? I prefer you to be comfortable. Kylee, would you pour champagne for my supplicants, please. Judson, go to that clever little writing desk that is in my bedchamber and bring me one of those lovely Tulsa postcards and a pen."

While her servants did her bidding, Neferet opened the glass door that led to the balcony. Wind whipped inside, carrying the scent of rain with it. Neferet opened her arms, reveling in the power in the atmosphere that foretold a storm. As if she'd drawn it through her desire, thunder rolled in the distance and lightning followed it, gleeful and bright, across the sky. "This is a truly magnificent night! A predawn storm is my absolute favorite. I do adore Oklahoma in the springtime."

"Goddess, your postcard and pen."

"Thank you, Judson." Neferet took the card, and in her flowing script she wrote four words on it. When she was finished, she looked up, smiling at the frightened group. "Now, who shall be first?" Neferet tapped her chin, as if considering. "Taylor! It will be you!"

"What can I do for you, Goddess?" Taylor asked nervously, though she added her honest, kindhearted smile to the question.

"Come here, my dear. First I want to give you this."

Taylor trembled as she approached Neferet. "Let's see, yes, I think the front pocket of those slacks will do. They are made of such a fine-quality material with nice deep pockets. Lynette was right, I am going to ban the wearing of jeans. Let us hope she was just as right about this little group." She smiled at Taylor and handed her the postcard. "Put this in your pocket, please."

Taylor glanced at the card, put it in her pocket, and asked, "What does 'one every five minutes' mean?"

"Well, Taylor, if my calculations are correct, it means one of you is going to die every five minutes. Judson and Tony, bring Taylor along."

Neferet strode onto the balcony, glad the wind carried away Taylor's pathetic screams. "There"—she pointed to the front of the balcony—"throw her from there. Swing her several times so that you give her a good toss. If I understand the intent behind the wretched spell that binds me here, kindhearted Taylor should pass through the barrier untouched so that she can fall, shrieking, to the pavement below."

With no emotion, the two men swung the hysterical girl once, twice, thrice, and then heaved her up and over the balcony. Curious, Neferet watched her windmill her arms and legs until she landed almost exactly where Neferet had imagined.

"Next time aim a little more to the right," she commanded the men. Then she returned to the penthouse door and the screaming, panicked people within. "The loudest of you will go next!" Like snuffing a candle, they muffled their own screams. "Kylee, set the kitchen timer for five minutes," she said, then she shut the door to the penthouse, took the Glock that Judson had found in pharmaceutical representative's room, and sat at the wrought-iron bistro table she'd chosen earlier for its height and stability.

"Come to me, children," Neferet commanded.

The tendrils obeyed her immediately, swarming to her and circling around her bare feet. She studied them carefully, finally bending to pick up an especially fat one. Neferet placed it on the top of the little table before her.

"This will be over swiftly," she told the waiting tendril. "I will honor your sacrifice with my own blood." Though it trembled, the creature did not struggle or try to escape. Neferet smiled. "You are brave and strong—exactly what my spell needs. And so it begins!" She pierced the black, rubbery flesh near the tendril's open mouth, and then, in one swift motion, Neferet ripped a thin thread of skin from her child.

Precious flesh filled with magick power
Obey my command; fulfill my will
Kalona's end I prophesy within this hour
The masquerading immortal I shall kill!

Neferet lifted the Glock and wrapped the bloody thread of skin around its muzzle, covering the weapon in Darkness. Then she pursed her full lips and blew on it. As her breath touched the tendril, it rippled and then disappeared, having been fully absorbed.

"If I am right, and I am rarely wrong, that should do very, very well." Absently, Neferet slit the inside of her forearm and offered the scarlet slash to the wounded tendril, who eagerly began to feed and heal itself.

Then Neferet sipped her wine and waited.

Kalona

"Do her eyes always bleed like that when she has a vision?" Marx asked him.

Before he could respond, his son answered for him. "Yes. The visions cause her a lot of pain. Stevie Rae and Zoey worry about her, especially because the intensity of them seems to be getting worse."

Kalona and Marx hadn't left Nyx's Temple, but they had moved to one of the candlelit meditation alcoves, along with Rephaim, making way for Stevie Rae and Damien, whom Zoey had called to bring wet washcloths, fresh clothing and, after much discussion, a bottle of red wine. Aphrodite had gotten sick when Darius had tried to move her, so Darius had announced it was in the Goddess's Temple his Priestess would remain until she was recovered.

Truth be told, Kalona had been glad for the excuse to stay within Nyx's Temple. After so long being absent, he couldn't seem to get enough of the Goddess's presence, even if it was only through the blessed energy that, as surely as vanilla and lavender, permeated the air.

"Father, the vision troubles me." The worry in Rephaim's voice brought Kalona's attention from the ethereal to the tangible.

He smiled at his son, enjoying the warm feeling it gave him to accept the boy's affection. "It is no more than symbolism. You know how much Aphrodite dislikes symbolism. That is why she prefers a literal interpretation."

"But she saw you fall and die."

"And she said it was a real death, not a symbol," Marx added.

Kalona shrugged. "Yet here I am, two feet solidly on the ground, very much alive."

"But not completely immortal." Rephaim spoke the words so softly that Marx said, "What was that, Rephaim? Your father isn't what?"

"My son worries too much." Kalona cut Rephaim off, giving him a look that stopped whatever else he might have said. "The truth is, Aphrodite has seen Zoey's death twice, as well as her grandmother's death. There stands Zoey. And you know Sylvia Redbird is alive and well." Kalona put his hand on his son's shoulder, pleased by his concern but also wanting to alleviate it. "It is less than an hour until dawn. Should you not be—"

The detective's phone rang. Marx glanced at it and excused himself to take the call.

"I won't be silenced about this, Father," Rephaim said.

"About what?" he prevaricated.

Rephaim frowned at him. "Your impending death."

Kalona chuckled. "Immortals do not die. Or did you forget why Neferet is causing us such problems? Were it otherwise, Stark could simply direct an arrow to kill her and we would be done with it."

"You changed in the Otherworld, enough that an oath you swore on your immortality was no longer binding."

"Son, I have battled Darkness since then and survived what would surely kill any mortal. I appreciate your concern, but your worry is needless."

Marx rushed into the Temple. "Neferet is throwing live hostages from the balcony of the Mayo—one every five minutes. Two are already dead. We have four minutes until a third is added to that number."

A sense of calm came over Kalona. "She must be trying to break the protective spell." He turned to Zoey. "Get your circle to the Council Oak Tree. Strengthen Thanatos and the protective spell. No matter what happens, do not let that spell fail."

"I'll drive," Stark said. Already they were all running for the door.

"Go with them!" Aphrodite said, pushing Darius away from her. "If Neferet gets out, we're all dead."

"Rephaim, go with Stevie Rae. Be sure your Priestess is safe," Kalona told his son.

"You riding with me?" Marx asked him as they jogged toward the parking lot.

"No," Kalona said. "I'm flying. It's faster. I'll meet you there."

"Be careful up there," Marx said, offering his hand.

Kalona grasped it. "You stay safe as well, my friend."

Then he turned to Rephaim and pulled his son roughly into an embrace. "You are the part of my life of which I am most proud." He released Rephaim, but before he could launch himself skyborne, Kalona felt a soft hand touch his arm. He looked down to see Zoey Redbird watching him with wide, knowing eyes.

"I'm glad you got your second chance with us," she said. "I'm glad you're on our side."

He smiled at her, surprised by how much her words meant to him. He touched her cheek. "As am I." Then he took to the sky, beating the air powerfully with sweeps of his mighty wings.

Kalona streaked across the billowing thunderclouds almost in time with the lightning. The storm's winds buffeted him, but Kalona took no heed of it. He had one duty, one responsibility, one edict from his Goddess. He would protect the people in need. No matter the cost, he chose to stand between Neferet and those he had come to value, even to love.

Suddenly, the clouds before him began to boil and change form until Kalona was staring into the glowing eyes of the White Bull.

His body was an enormous cloud, his horns dripping with a rain of blood.

Though it has been eons since last we met, you are as predictable now as you were then. The voice blasted through Kalona's mind. *What mutually beneficial deal shall we make this time, Kalona?*

"None, bull. Last time we met I rejected you in words, but not in my heart, nor in my deeds. Last time we met I allowed your Darkness to feed that which was weak within me and poison my life. This time I am different. This time I reject you in words, in heart, and in deeds."

Really, Son of the Moon? Would you still reject me if I told you I had the power to restore to you everything you lost during the eons you have wandered the mortal realm?

"There is nothing you can give me that would be worth the price."

But you haven't even heard my price. It would be so very little in comparison to that which you have lost.

"Hear me, and hear me well, bull, though you will never truly understand what I say because your spirit is diseased. Even if I do not get everything I desire—even if I cannot control everything around me—the end does *not* justify the means. It is impossible to capture love with evil. Once and for all, I choose Light!" Kalona lifted his arm and his onyx spear appeared. "Now, begone and leave me to the consequences of my choice!" He hurled the spear into the bull-shaped thundercloud. With a roar of pain and anger, the creature disappeared.

Kalona fisted his hands to control the tremors that cascaded through his body. "I have no time for fear. I have my duty to complete." Resolutely, he flew on.

Kalona landed on the rooftop of the taller ONEOK building in time to see two men dragging a struggling girl across the Mayo's balcony. Neferet was seated at a small table in the middle of the balcony, sipping from a crystal goblet.

What is she doing? Why is she throwing people from the balcony? Kalona tried to puzzle it through as the men holding the girl watched Neferet expectantly, obviously awaiting her sign. Kalona could see nothing but madness behind Neferet's actions. *It is not unlike her to torture humans. And death gives her power. Perhaps this is an amusement* and *an energy gain for her. Perhaps she is simply bored and playing her macabre version of a game.*

Neferet nodded. One man took the girl's arms. Another took her legs, and they began to swing the girl so that she could be tossed over the edge. Even above the howling wind and the rumbling thunder Kalona could hear her screams.

Kalona stood, spread his wings, and readied himself to dive—to catch the girl.

Neferet's goblet shattered on the stone floor as she saw him. She picked up a handgun and sighted it at him.

Then Kalona understood her game.

He also understood Aphrodite's vision. The Prophetess had been correct. It had been literal rather than symbolic.

Thank you, Nyx, for allowing me a choice. But this time, I will uphold my duty. This time, I choose Light, no matter the cost.

Kalona leaped from the rooftop of the ONEOK building, arms and wings spread, a clear target as he hurled forward to save one more human from the consequences of Neferet's madness.

But the men didn't throw the girl. Instead they ducked down, giving Neferet a clear line of sight. The red laser lit up the center of Kalona's chest instants before Neferet began to pull the trigger over and over and over again, emptying the weapon into his body.

Darkness-coated bullets slammed into Kalona, piercing him and sending poison to scorch his heart. He tried to remain upright, but his body, driven back by the force of the bullets, tumbled head over feet, disorienting him. He commanded his wings to catch the sky and hold him aloft, but all control over his body and its preternatural strength had been severed.

For the second time in his eons of existence, Kalona fell.

Detective Marx

"He's down! The winged guy is down! We need a bus to the Mayo—now!" The radio in Marx's unmarked car blared the news and he floored the accelerator, turning left down Seventh Street. He picked up the mike and shouted, "This is Detective Marx, clear the blockade on Seventh and Boulder—I'm coming through." As his car fishtailed, he prayed silently, *Let your warning have saved him, Nyx . . . Let your warning have saved him . . .*

As he sped through the roadblock and the street in front of the Mayo came into view, Marx tightened his grip on the steering wheel. A sickness gripped his stomach. Kalona lay crumpled in a heap in the middle of the street. Heedless of his own safety, Marx maneuvered his car between the Mayo and Kalona, forming a shield. He ran to Kalona's side and knelt. The big guy was still breathing, but it was bad. Worse than bad. He didn't seem to have any broken bones, and his head hadn't split open. But the center of his chest was a jagged burned and bloody wound, obviously made by multiple gunshots. The brunt of the fall had been absorbed by Kalona's enormous wings. They lay around him in pieces, shattered as if they had been made of black porcelain. Blood seeped from the broken bones that protruded through the raven-colored feathers. Marx did the only thing he knew—he pressed both of his palms to the chest wound an applied pressure.

"Hang on, Kalona. There's an ambulance coming."

His amber eyes opened and he focused on Marx. "Tell Aphrodite she was right." He had to force the words, and the effort made him cough and moan.

"Save it. Tell her yourself. Just stay with me. I'll get you to the hospital."

"No hospital. Take me to Thanatos." Then he closed his eyes and didn't speak again.

Marx kept talking to him, though, and kept pressure on the wound, even as Kalona's blood pooled around them in an ever-widening tide.

The ambulance finally got there. The EMTs who got out looked confused and afraid, hesitant to approach.

"What the fuck is your problem? Get him on the gurney!" Marx exploded on them.

"Detective, he's too big. He won't fit on the gurney," said one of the EMTs.

"We'll lift him with you, Detective." Marx looked up to see young Officer Carter and a dozen or so uniforms.

Marx nodded a grim thank-you. "Get the gurney out of the back. We're gonna put him in there, and then we're taking the bus." Not giving the EMTs a choice, he said to Carter, "Let's get him in there. On three, lift him."

The officers circled Kalona and lifted him, leaving broken pieces of his wings in the blood pool. Kalona didn't make a sound as they slid him into the back of the ambulance. Marx would've thought he was dead had he not climbed in beside him and saw that his heart was still pumping fresh blood from the terrible wound. Marx ripped open HemCon pads, pressing them against Kalona's chest while he shouted through the open window at Carter, who had taken the driver's seat. "Get us to the Council Oak Tree, stat!"

Neferet

"Up, children! Lift me so that I may witness my plan come to fruition!" The threads of Darkness swarmed to her, swirling, lifting her high enough that she could see over the balcony to the street below while being careful to keep her far enough away from the edge not to be singed.

"How magnificent! He landed perfectly in the center of the street. Almost in the same spot from which he so recently and arrogantly mocked me, disrespected me, and stole my favorite servant from me. Well, my children, he will not do that again. *No man will ever betray me again.*" The girl Judson and Tony had baited Kalona with was sobbing hysterically, still collapsed where the two men had dropped her. Neferet sighed and motioned for her children to lower her. "You are safe now," she told the crying girl. "What I did was to keep all of us protected. Kalona was my enemy, thus he was also yours. You should rejoice in my victory."

The girl wiped at her eyes with trembling hands, but she was unable to stop crying. "Kylee!" Neferet called, and the servant hurried from inside the penthouse to her. "They simply cannot grasp the fact that what I do is to protect us all. Get rid of them. Immediately. They're giving me a headache. Judson will help you."

"Would you have us throw them off the balcony together?" Judson asked.

"No, no, no! There is no need to waste them. Just escort them back to their rooms."

"Yes, Goddess," Judson and Kylee intoned together before Judson dragged the hysterical girl from the balcony and herded the remainder of the weeping mortals from her penthouse.

"There. That is so much better," she said as blissful silence returned to her domain. She addressed the chef who had been standing there, obediently waiting for her next command. "Tony, you may return to the kitchen. In celebration of my victory, I'd like cake. Chocolate cake with night-blooming jasmine flowers decorating it. Can you do that for me?"

"It will be as you command, Goddess," he said woodenly. Neferet smiled. Tony's possession had definitely improved his personality.

Still smiling, Neferet strolled leisurely back to the little bistro table to retrieve her glass of wine, and then frowned in annoyance. She'd forgotten that in her haste to shoot Kalona she'd broken the goblet. "Kylee is never here when I need her," she said and sighed. She considered commanding one of her children to bring her a new goblet. "If only you had opposable thumbs," she muttered, more to herself than the snake-things that were never far from her. Neferet stood, and the atmosphere of the balcony utterly changed.

The balmy wind turned frigid. The scent of the spring thunderstorm was lost in the reek of a grave. Her children swarmed to her, coiling around her body fretfully.

"You have nothing about which to worry," she told them. Neferet moved gracefully to the middle of her balcony. Straight and proud, she waited for him to materialize.

The White Bull took form before her. She shivered as his massive body solidified. His opal horns were wet at their tips, touched ever so slightly with the scarlet of fresh blood. His coat was luminous in the predawn light. Each spike of lightning that speared the sky glistened across him. White was too simple a description for his magnificence. The longer Neferet gazed at him, the more iridescent colors she saw within him—and the more she longed to stroke him.

"My lord," she said, curtsying ever so slightly to him. "Welcome to my temple."

Thank you, my heartless one. I have been watching. His voice rumbled through her mind, putting to shame the power of the impending thunderstorm. *You have surprised me—twice since last we met.*

"I am so glad to hear it, my lord." Neferet moved closer to him. She reached one slender finger out and touched it to the point of a razor-tipped horn. Delicately, she took her finger into her mouth and tasted the blood. "Vampyre, old vampyre. Very old and powerful. So that is what has been keeping you from me, though I cannot believe this ancient vampyre gave himself to you as freely as do I."

The bull's laughter echoed around them. *The Scots never give themselves easily. Though when I pluck them from the Isle of Skye, they are especially succulent and worth the effort.*

Neferet showed no outward sign of the inward shock his words made her feel. She smiled and dipped her finger once more in the blood. "The Isle of Skye," she began contemplatively, pausing to lick her finger. "If you have been hunting on Sgiach's island, it must mean that the balance of Light and Darkness is truly shifting."

You are as wise as you are heartless—and surprising. He licked the soft flesh inside her arm.

Neferet shivered in pleasure. "Thank you, my lord. And that is twice you have mentioned surprise. Tell me, what have I done that is worthy of your divine notice?"

The first time was at the church. I have long wondered whether you would truly embrace your nature as you embrace your immortality. Watching you do both in such a spectacular display of carnage impressed even me.

Neferet smiled seductively. "You flatter me."

You surprise me, and so I enjoy flattering you.

"And the second of the surprises?" she coaxed when he seemed more interested in tasting her skin than continuing to flatter her.

You know very well that the second just happened.

"Kalona's death." Neferet said the words reverently, as if praying to herself. "I haven't enjoyed anything so much . . . well, so much since last I worshipped you."

Ah, now you flatter me, my heartless one.

"Always, my lord. I choose to always flatter you," Neferet said.

Would you truly choose to always worship me? The voice inside her head intensified so that it was on the edge of causing her pain.

"What is it you propose?" she asked, stroking his muscular neck and enjoying the frigid feel of his coat.

I can take you from this cage in which they have imprisoned you. You could roam all of the realms with me. I would call you Consort, as you once desired.

"A tempting proposition, my lord," Neferet said, dipping her finger in the blood on his horn again and buying time as she tasted it. *Why should I be Consort when I have already proclaimed myself Goddess? Why should I be bound to serving a god when I am immortal?* "Might I have time to consider?"

Of course you may, and I would like to give you a gift while you are considering my proposal. I would free you from the protective spell that entraps you.

"My lord, that is very generous of you," Neferet said, thinking, *and binding of you, as that would put me in your debt once more.* "But I would rather break free myself. It would be another opportunity to surprise you."

Instantly Neferet felt the bull's displeasure. *Ah, a third surprise.*

"I hope not an unpleasant one." Neferet stroked his neck again.

Think nothing of it, my heartless one. Throughout eternity I have found that the more something is desired, the dearer the sacrifice must be to attain it.

Then he drove his hoof into the stone balcony, causing the rooftop to shake. And with the sound of a deafening thunderclap, the White Bull disappeared into the roiling clouds, leaving his cloven imprint behind.

Thanatos

"Zoeybird?"

Thanatos heard the worry in Sylvia Redbird's voice. She opened her eyes. Shaunee was already peering through the tent flap. The wind had increased and thunder rumbled in the distance. The women had been working to secure their makeshift shelter against the upcoming storm while she and Shaunee rested within.

"What is it?" Thanatos asked tiredly.

Erik, who hadn't been far from Shaunee all night, called back from just outside the tent, "Zoey's here. So's the rest of her circle plus Stark, Darius, and Rephaim. I'd better—"

"Hurry!" Zoey shouted above the wind. "Neferet is trying to break the spell. We have to circle and channel more energy to you."

Thanatos sat, grasping the table to steady herself. She was dizzy and weak, but she felt no new drain against the spell. "Zoey, circle if you believe you must, but I sense no disturbance in the barrier."

"Neither do I," Shaunee said. "Actually, it's gotten better since it's so late and there's obviously a bad storm brewing. People are finally staying home."

"We're circling," Zoey told Thanatos decisively. "You don't have to cast it. I'll take the spirit candle and channel the elements to you." As Damien, Shaylin, and Stevie Rae took their places, Zoey entered the tent for the spirit candle. "Sorry about this, Shaunee. I know you're tired, so sit just outside the tent. I'll do my best to channel as much of fire as I can for you."

"Come on, I'll help you." Erik offered his hand to Shaunee. She leaned on him for a few feet, and then she sank to the ground, facing the tent.

"Zoey, explain to me what has happened. Why are you so frantic?" Thanatos asked.

"Neferet's throwing hostages from the roof of the Mayo. She's trying to break the barrier," Zoey explained quickly as her circle took their places and she retrieved the long wooden matches from the altar table.

Struggling to clear her thoughts, Thanatos stood, leaning heavily on the table. "No, as Shaunee said, the barrier is secure. There is no disruption within it. Neferet must have other motives. She—" Thanatos gasped with shock and fell to her knees.

"Darius! Stark! Help me! Something's wrong with Thanatos. She passed out."

"No," Thanatos fought to speak. "Not me—Kalona!"

"What did she say?" Stark asked as he and Darius tried to make her comfortable.

"She said Kalona's name." Zoey's voice was hushed, as if she already had guessed what Thanatos knew.

The scream of an ambulance siren drew closer and closer. "Help me stand. Help me stand!" Thanatos said. "Zoey, ready your circle. I am going to need its borrowed power, though not for the barrier."

"I'm really sorry," Zoey said, and grasped her hands, squeezing them briefly before she took the ritual matches and moved to stand before Damien in the east.

Thanatos grounded herself and made ready. Zoey returned to the center to face her, called spirit, and invoked, "Air, fire, water, earth, and spirit! Please fill our High Priestess, Thanatos, and lend her strength for what is to come."

Thanatos straightened, drawing a deep breath and feeling the power of five elements flowing through her veins as if replacing her blood. She stepped free of Stark and Darius and their helping hands. The ambulance lurched to a stop in the middle of Cheyenne Avenue.

"Rephaim, come here to me, please." The boy had been standing close to Stevie Rae, just outside the circle.

"You want me to enter the circle?"

"You must. And quickly, too."

With a worried look at Stevie Rae, Rephaim approached the glowing silver thread that joined the elements and drew the circumference of the circle. The thread of light rippled and drew back on itself, opening just wide enough for Rephaim to step within before closing once more.

"Something is very wrong," Rephaim said to her.

Thanatos held the boy's gaze. "It is your father. Be strong for him."

Rephaim's face drained of color as the wide rear door of the ambulance opened, and police officers, led by Detective Marx, carried Kalona from within.

"Father!"

Thanatos put a restraining hand on his arm. "He needs to come to us. The circle will welcome him as it did you." Thanatos raised her voice and called, "Detective Marx, bring my Warrior to me."

There was a terrible crack of thunder, and lightning flashed across the sky, making the torches that Sylvia had lit throughout the park seem as insignificant as fireflies.

"I can't carry him alone," Marx said from just outside the glowing circumference of the circle.

"All who bear Kalona are welcome within," Thanatos said.

Marx didn't hesitate. He stepped forward. His men moved with him, bringing Kalona to her and laying him gently on the ground at her feet.

Rephaim was weeping. Thanatos looked from Kalona's shattered wings to the scarlet soaked pads that did little stop the blood that seeped down the sides of his chest. Finally, her gaze rested on his colorless face. Still not looking away from her Warrior, she said, "Detective Marx, thank you for bringing him to me."

"She shot him while he was in the air! Emptied a Glock into him. He was trying to save the people she was throwing from the balcony. There was not a damn thing I could do."

"You have done what he needed. You were a good friend to him."

"Wish I could have been one longer," the detective said, wiping the tears from his face.

"He's *dying*?" Rephaim's eyes were glazed with shock and grief.

"Yes," said Kalona, opening his eyes. "Come here, son." His hand lifted weakly.

Rephaim dropped to his knees beside his father, clutching his hand. "No! You can't die! You're immortal!"

Kalona coughed, and foam flaked with blood came from his lips. His voice weakened as he spoke. "Knew this could happen. My choice, Rephaim. Remember, *my* choice." Kalona's gaze left his son for a moment to go to Stark, who stood silently beside Thanatos. "Use the piece of immortality I gave you for Light. Protect your Priestess." His eyes seemed to be losing focus. He blinked, struggling to look around, then he found Zoey. "Forgive me—the pain I caused."

"With my whole heart I forgive you," Zoey said.

Kalona coughed more blood and grimaced, then he touched his son's face. "You are the best of me. Find your brothers. Care for them. And watch over Stevie Rae. If you lose her, you will lose yourself."

"I will do as you say, Father," Rephaim said, sobbing. "I love you."

"I will always love you. Always," Kalona said. Finally, his fading gaze met Thanatos's. "Thank you for trusting me."

Thanatos's chest felt heavy with grief, but she smiled at him. "I have never accepted a Warrior's Oath before you, and there will be none to come after you. You have been a fine and worthy Guardian."

Kalona's red-flecked lips lifted in a satisfied smile. "I did not break my oath . . ." He drew a gasping half breath, and then his bloody chest did not rise again, his amber eyes lost their light, and Kalona died.

CHAPTER TWENTY-ONE

Kalona

Dying was more painful than Kalona had imagined it would be—though during his eons of life, he had rarely imagined it. He had been familiar with death in an abstract sort of way. He had, of course, killed countless times. Some of the killings had been justified; some had not. Since he had left the Otherworld, most of the deaths he had been responsible for had fallen into the latter category.

It was a thing he regretted as he died—those unjust deaths he had caused. That, plus the time he had squandered before he accepted the love of his son as well as the loss of Nyx. Those were his three greatest regrets, though even as he died he could hardly bear to think of the loss of his Goddess.

When he could draw no more breath, his vision began to gray, to blacken—and then, finally, the shards of pain from what remained of his wings dissipated, and the blaze of agony that was his chest slowly cooled. Kalona had only an instant to ready himself for the unimaginable to come, and then everything went black.

"Reach out, Kalona. Take my hand."

Thanatos's voice drifted through the blackness that was smothering Kalona. He tried to draw breath. He could not breathe. He tried to open his eyes. He could not see. Kalona's spirit battered against the walls that entrapped him.

"Kalona! You must take my hand."

I cannot see your hand!

"You need not see it. Just have faith that it is there. Kalona, take my hand."

Blindly, Kalona reached. And Thanatos was there! He could not see her, but he could feel her warm, steady hand. With all his might, he held that grip as she pulled. With a *whoosh!* of light and sound, Kalona's vision returned. He staggered, but Thanatos held tightly to him.

"All is well, Warrior. You are free of the body that bound you," Thanatos said.

Kalona glanced down and had the unexpectedly vertigo-like experience of seeing his own battered corpse. His gaze moved quickly away from the body and returned to Thanatos.

I am dead.

"You are."

I can only see you and feel you because of your affinity.

"Yes and no. You can feel nothing on this realm except my grip that has freed you. You can see others, though they probably cannot see you." Thanatos gestured around them.

Kalona blinked. His eyesight was strange, as if he were viewing everything except Thanatos through a thick, cloudy lens. He looked around. He could see the tree and the circle. He glanced quickly back at his body, and this time he saw Rephaim, kneeling at his side, weeping brokenly.

Tell him to stop grieving. Tell him I stand here, beside him.

"If that is what you truly wish, I will do so. But you should know that I will only be able to communicate with you for a limited time. Even my gift has limits."

What am I supposed to do? How do I help him?

"You can no longer help him, or anyone else, on this realm. It is time you moved on."

Kalona stared at Thanatos. *You mean to the Otherworld—to Nyx's realm.*

"Yes."

Kalona felt some of the panic he'd experienced when he had been trapped in his body return. *She banished me. She will not admit me.*

"How can you be so certain Nyx will not admit you?"

His mind flailed, remembering what had happened when he'd trespassed and asked her forgiveness. Nyx's response had been unwavering: "If you are ever worthy of forgiving, you may ask it of me. Not until then . . . your spirit, as well as your body, is forbidden entrance to my realm."

I asked it of her. Nyx would not forgive me. She forbade me entrance.

"Had you earned her forgiveness then?"

No, of course I hadn't! But have I earned it now? How could I possibly atone for the centuries of pain I caused the Goddess and her children because I chose anger and jealousy over trust and love?

"That is a question you must have the courage to pose to our Goddess," Thanatos said.

What if she refuses to forgive me? What will happen to me?

Thanatos's eyes suddenly seemed ancient with the knowledge of too much pain, too much suffering. "If Nyx does not allow you entrance to the Otherworld, you will wander the realm on which you died."

Without being able to be heard or seen? Thanatos nodded. *For how long?*

"How long is an eternity?"

A terrible shiver went through Kalona, and his gaze returned to his son. *Will you know whether Nyx accepts me or not?*

"Yes, but I will lose the ability to communicate with you," she said sadly.

If she rejects me, I will watch over my son.

"He will not know it," Thanatos said.

He will if you tell him.

"I will do so, if that is your request."

It is. He met her gaze again. *I am ready. What must I do?*

"I am all that anchors you to this world right now. Simply release my hand and ascend."

Thank you, Thanatos. For everything.

"Kalona, I wish eternally for you to blessed be." As the High Priestess of Death lifted her arm, he released her hand, and his spirit soared up . . . up . . .

Kalona was intimately familiar with flying. He'd taken to the skies of this realm as well as the Otherworld. And, if he had the time and inclination, he could recount other realms in which he'd flown, always on the Goddess's business.

This ascent was like nothing he'd ever before experienced.

At first the blackness was complete, so much so that he could only hope he continued to rise. As he was beginning to despair—to think that Nyx had already judged and found him lacking—the blackness before him rippled, shimmered, and took on an iridescence that reminded him of the color of the sea surrounding the ancient island of Capri.

The topaz sky rippled again, and then, like a curtain, it parted to reveal a round patch of familiar rust-colored ground. Behind the ground were two trees, a hawthorn and a rowan. Kalona recognized them. He and Nyx had often visited the spot—this entrance to her Sacred Grove. Strips of brightly colored cloth were knotted together within the gnarled limbs of the trees, tied there with well-wishes by Nyx, as well as those who passed through the Goddess's realm. The strips of cloth lifted lazily in the wind, changing colors so that an infinite number of wishes were represented. Behind the wishing tree stretched acres and acres of Nyx's most sacred land. Kalona knew every path, every tree, every crystal stream and moss-carpeted glen.

Even if he could not be by her side, Kalona longed to walk there again and to have the peace of the grove fill him once more.

His ascent concluded, Kalona stepped onto the rust-colored ground and waited.

Zoey

Kalona was dead! It was unbelievable but undeniable. I'd been standing next to Thanatos, holding the spirit candle, when he'd died— smiling and saying he hadn't broken his oath.

Rephaim lost it. He was bending over his dad's body, sobbing so hard it seemed like he was going to shake his body apart. Stevie Rae was behind me, still in the northern position of earth, but I could feel her restlessness. She was going to break the circle and go to Rephaim. I couldn't blame her. I was just about to blow out my spirit candle and close the circle when Thanatos held out her hand, like she was offering it to Kalona as if he was going to reach up and take it. And I remembered what Thanatos had said as she told me to cast the circle, *Zoey, ready your circle. I am going to need its borrowed power* . . .

Thanatos had known Kalona was dying. She needs the circle for him!

"Stevie Rae, you have to stay there," I said, looking over my shoulder at my BFF, who was bawling her eyes out. "We can't close the circle. Thanatos needs it, and that means Kalona needs it, too."

"But he's dead!" Stevie Rae sobbed. "And Rephaim needs me now."

"Stevie Rae, Thanatos *is* Death. Just like you're Earth," I said. "She asked us to cast this circle. Trust her to let us know when we can close it."

Stevie Rae's candle was trembling with her heaving shoulders, but she nodded and didn't break the circle.

I turned my attention back to Thanatos. It looked like she was frozen with her outstretched hand. Her expressions changed, like she was having a psychic conversation with someone, but nothing else changed about her.

"Do you know what's going on?" Detective Marx asked me. He looked pale and sad, and he was covered with Kalona's blood.

I didn't know for sure, but I took a chance and spoke from my heart. "Thanatos is helping Kalona's soul. Remember, like in front of the Mayo."

Marx squinted and lowered his voice to a whisper. "I don't see any glowing lights."

"Those were human souls. No matter what happened today, Kalona has been immortal for centuries and centuries. His soul probably looks way different."

But I was wrong. Thanatos suddenly unfroze and threw up her arm as if she was slinging a Frisbee off into space, and a glowing silver orb—a whole lot like what she'd gathered in front of the Mayo—shot up into the thunderclouds of the predawn sky.

"Thanatos must have been right. We're more alike than different," Marx said.

"Ohmygoddess! Look up there!" Shaylin was pointing up.

We all looked, and the sky over the Arkansas River rippled and parted. Kalona was standing on a round space of red dirt in a place I remembered very well.

"It's the entrance to the Otherworld and the hanging tree!" Stark said from his position just outside our circle.

"And Nyx's Sacred Grove," I added. My gaze met his and we shared a smile. We knew the place well. Stark had almost died there so that I could live.

"Son, turn your eyes from the shell that was your father and see what he has truly become," Thanatos said, resting her hand on Rephaim's shoulder.

He looked up in time to see Nyx step from her grove and approach Kalona. A winged immortal walked at her side. He looked almost exactly like Kalona except that his wings were gold and he seemed smaller, more delicately made.

"That has to be Erebus," Damien said.

Then Kalona dropped to his knees and bowed his head, and we were too mesmerized by the scene unfolding to speak.

Nyx, I kneel before you and ask for your forgiveness. Kalona's voice traveled easily between realms. I could even hear how vulnerable and unsure he sounded.

Do you truly ask her, or are you simply terrified that you might be forced to eternally wander the mortal realm? Erebus asked. He didn't sound hateful. He sounded curious. But I could feel my hackles starting to rise. Why was he suddenly speaking for Nyx?

Kalona's head remained bowed, as if he couldn't bear to look at the Goddess, but he spoke again, this time with more confidence. *Goddess, I am here only to ask for your forgiveness, and I fully accept whatever consequence I must face for the mistakes I have made.*

As Erebus opened his mouth to say something else, Rephaim jumped to his feet, shouting, "Leave him alone! He's not even talking to you!"

It didn't seem like Kalona could hear him. But Erebus was silenced.

"That's right!" Stevie Rae said with a little hiccup. "Leave Rephaim's daddy alone. He's asking for Nyx's forgiveness, not yours."

I held my breath as Nyx's beautiful, loving eyes turned from Kalona to us. She stepped forward. I could see Kalona tremble as her gossamer robes brushed his arm. She raised her hand and swept the sky in front of her and suddenly they weren't way up in the air anymore. They were right in front of us!

"Merry meet, beloveds," the Goddess said.

Our answering "Merry meet" drifted around the circle that was now shining with such intensity that it was hard to look at.

Nyx approached Thanatos, who bowed deeply to her. "There is no need for such formalities between us," Nyx said to her High Priestess, lifting her with a slight touch of her arm. "We have been acquainted too long for that."

"Thank you, my Goddess," Thanatos said.

"You are doing well here, Daughter," Nyx told her. "The spell is difficult, but your intent is pure."

"I will do my best to hold it firm," Thanatos said.

Nyx smiled. "I would expect no less from my Priestess of Death." Then she turned to Rephaim, who stood, sobbing, beside Kalona's body. He was staring at his dad—well, the spirit version of his dad, who was still kneeling. He didn't even seem to see Nyx, who reached across Kalona's body to touch his shoulder, gently saying, "Your grief be soothed, my son."

Rephaim jerked under her touch, and his focus shifted to the Goddess. Wide-eyed he said, "Thank you." And his sobs slowed, and then stopped as he stared at Nyx.

And then she was turning to me. Today her hair was so light it was almost white, like a full moon, and her eyes were lavender. It was hard to look at her straight on for very long. There was something incomprehensible in her beauty.

"Zoey Redbird, of all the mortals here, Kalona has caused you the most pain. He has lied to you, seduced you, and tried to kill you. Through spite and anger and jealousy, he has murdered those dear to you. Within you, there rests the spark of the maiden created by the ancient Wise Women and breathed to life by the Great Earth Mother to keep him captive for the crimes he committed against your peoples. Do you acknowledge all of this, Zoey?"

I swallowed hard. "Yes, I do."

"Then speak from your soul and tell me truly, Zoey Redbird, should I forgive Kalona?"

I was stunned silent by her question. *Me? I'm supposed to judge him?*

While I struggled with an answer, I felt Grandma's hand slip into mine. "Consider wisely and speak only the truth, *u-we-tsi-a-ge-ya.*"

I looked at Kalona. Nyx was right. He'd done terrible things—not just to me, but to people I loved, and to the Cherokee people. He'd created a whole breed of monsters, the Raven Mockers, who had terrorized the old and sick for centuries. My gaze went from him to Rephaim. He used to be one of those monsters, but love had saved him. Nyx had forgiven him, even when Rephaim could barely find a way to forgive himself.

And I knew the right answer to my Goddess's question.

"Goddess, I believe you have already forgiven Kalona. You just wanted him to be worthy of your forgiveness."

"And is he, young Priestess? Is he worthy? Can you forgive him?"

I squeezed Grandma's hand. "Yes, and yes." I said with certainty. "He's earned his second chance."

Kalona

From his knees, Kalona watched Nyx smile at Zoey, but instead of replying to her, the Goddess turned to Erebus. "It seems your duty has come to an end, my old friend."

Erebus's smile was a bright as summer sunshine. "It took him a long time, but I never doubted that he could do it."

The Goddess raised one slender brow. "Never doubted?"

"Well, almost never. I will miss tormenting him."

"You were not supposed to be tormenting him. You were supposed to be helping him to find his way back to us," the Goddess said.

"Well, we both know how stubborn Kalona can be." Erebus went to Kalona, who was staring at his brother, in shock. "Tell me, what would have happened if I had told you that during those uncountable years I was your greatest ally?"

"I would not have believed it," Kalona blurted.

Erebus laughed heartily. "Exactly! And yet, from the day we both were created, I have wanted only one thing—and that is for *our* Goddess to be happy. You, my errant brother, used to make her very happy."

Confused, Kalona shook his head. "But with me out of the way, you are her Consort!"

"No, Kalona. You have been wrong about that for eons. No matter what happened between Nyx and you, I have always been her friend and playmate. I have never been her Consort."

"Do not play games with me now," Kalona said. He wasn't angry, but he felt as if his heart would break if Erebus played one more trick on him.

His brother sighed and glanced at Nyx. "Shall I continue?"

"Yes, my friend," Nyx said. "Perhaps he is ready to listen with a brother's heart."

Erebus turned back to Kalona, saying, "Who is my father?"

Kalona's brow furrowed. "The sun, of course."

"And yours?"

"The moon."

"And what is our Goddess's most revered symbol? What illuminates her sky? What follows her, ever-changing, waning and waxing to her eternal delight?"

"The moon." Kalona's voice has gone hoarse.

"I am the friendly warmth of her spring and summer. You were created to spend eternity beside her, protecting and loving her. All you had to do was to choose to be worthy of her love. And that, you have finally done. Blessed be, Brother." Erebus held out his hand to Kalona.

But Kalona didn't take it. Instead he stared up at Erebus, finally understanding. "From the beginning I have been wrong about you. Can you ever forgive me?"

"Brother, I have been watching you suffer for eons. I willingly grant you forgiveness."

"Thank you, Erebus." Kalona stood then, and instead of grasping Erebus's hand, he pulled his brother roughly into his embrace. When they finally parted, Kalona made no attempt to wipe the tears from his face. He smiled at his brother, whose cheeks were also wet. Then a movement at the side of Erebus pulled his gaze away from his brother, and Nyx stood before him. Erebus took several steps back, leaving him to face his Goddess alone.

Kalona dropped to his knees.

"I have been so wrong about so many things," he said, gazing at Nyx fully, his body trembling at her nearness. "I chose anger and jealousy over love and trust. I betrayed you by allowing Darkness to enter your realm. I hated my brother because of my own insecurities. After I Fell, I committed atrocities." Tears flowed down Kalona's face. "I have no right to ask, but Nyx, my Goddess, my true and only love, will you forgive me?"

Nyx extended her hand to him and said softly, lovingly, "Oh, Kalona, how I have missed you!"

He stared at her slender hand, suddenly unable to move, unable to even look up at her. When he finally lifted his head he felt so filled with happiness that he was almost unable to speak.

"You forgive me," he said, with a voice that trembled.

"I do."

"You love me."

"I do, and I always have."

Kalona took her hand in his, but he did not rise. "Nyx, Goddess of Night, I pledge myself body, heart, and soul to love and protect you. I beg of you to accept my Warrior's Oath."

"I gladly accept your oath and will hold it binding for all of eternity." As Nyx spoke, the air around Kalona shimmered. Power washed through his wings, changing them from raven black to the luminous white of a full moon.

Laughing joyously, Kalona stood, and just before the curtain to the Otherworld closed, he took his Goddess into his arms and lost himself in her welcoming kiss.

CHAPTER TWENTY-TWO

Zoey

After the curtain to the Otherworld closed, no one said anything for several long minutes. Everyone was sniffling, even the cops. Detective Marx finally broke the silence. He went to Thanatos and, totally surprising everyone—including Thanatos by the look on her face—Marx pulled her into a giant bear hug.

"Even if I was immortal, I think what I just witnessed would be the most incredible thing I ever saw in my entire life. Thank you for including us," he said.

The other five officers nodded as they wiped their eyes.

Thanatos smiled and gently extracted herself from his embrace. "You are most welcome, Detective, though it was not me who allowed it. It was Nyx."

"Then I hope you don't mind if someday soon, after the business with Neferet is settled, I visit Nyx's Temple with a gift to leave on her altar. I know it sounds crazy, but after what happened today, I feel really close to your Goddess."

"It isn't crazy at all. Nyx and I would welcome your altar gift. You see, Detective Marx, Nyx isn't just *our* Goddess. She belongs to anyone who seeks her." Thanatos's gaze found me. "Zoey, you may close the circle now."

I'd almost forgotten that I was still holding the lit spirit candle. While I quickly backtracked, thanking each of the elements in its turn and sending them all away, Grandma took one of the blankets from the pallet inside Thanatos's tent and gently covered Kalona's body.

The instant I blew out Stevie Rae's candle, she went to Rephaim, wrapping her arms around him and holding him. And then Stark was there beside me, holding me and telling me how much he loved me.

"I'll never leave you. I promise," he said. "I don't care about Aurox or Heath or even stupid Erik." He paused as if he'd just noticed that Erik was standing a few yards away from us beside Shaunee. "Sorry, dude. I didn't mean anything."

Erik shrugged. "Not a problem," he said. But he didn't even glance at Stark or me. Erik was watching Shaunee with a cute, concerned look.

I took Stark's face between my hands, telling him, "Don't worry. I'll never let you leave me." Then I kissed him as if we'd just been reunited after an eon.

The wind chose that moment to blow the thunderclouds from the sky, and suddenly we were standing in the pinks and yellows of pre-dawn.

"Uh-oh," I said. "You and Stevie Rae and Shaylin have to get under cover."

"We still have seven minutes until dawn," Stark said. "But you're right."

Reluctantly, I stepped out of his arms and went to Thanatos, expecting to have to help her to the tent. But she didn't look nearly as tired as she had since she'd cast the protective spell. Actually, except for the shadows under her eyes, she looked rejuvenated.

"You look a lot better," I said.

Thanatos nodded and smiled. "It seems guiding Kalona's spirit home to the Otherworld had an energy-boosting side effect, for which I am grateful. I am afraid it will not last long, though, so let us be brief—especially as dawn is breaking and our red vampyres and fledgling need to be inside. Detective Marx has agreed to transport Kalona's body to the House of Night. May I count on you to build his pyre and preside over his immolation?"

"Of course," I said.

"Shaunee," Thanatos called her over to us. "I have strength lent to me by Kalona, so I believe it would be safe for you to leave me long enough to return to the House of Night and add your element to Kalona's pyre, if you can do so quickly. Would you do that for my Warrior?"

"It would be my honor to light Kalona's pyre," Shaunee said.

I thought she looked better, too, and I sent a silent but sincere thank-you to Kalona.

"And I will watch over my father's pyre, from sunrise to sunset," Rephaim said, wiping his eyes. "But we need to move fast. I'm going to change in six minutes, and that means Stevie Rae is going to burn."

"What are you going to—" Marx began, then stopped himself, shaking his head. "Never mind. Explain it to me later. My men and I will take care of the big guy's body. The rest of you can go ahead. We'll meet you at the House of Night."

I hugged Grandma. "You showed wisdom in your response to the Goddess," she said as she let me go. "I am proud of you, *u-we-tsi-a-ge-ya*."

"Sylvia, if you and the others need a break, I am quite sure I can manage on my own while you rest," Thanatos said.

Sister Mary Angela moved up beside Grandma, along with Rabbi Bernstein and Suzanna Grimms. The ladies' faces were radiant, as if the tears they had all just shed had washed years from them.

"We choose to stay with you on this sacred ground," said the nun while the ladies nodded their agreement.

"Who could rest after that, anyway?" said Rabbi Bernstein.

"I'll stay, too, and be sure no one bothers any of you," Erik said, then added, "If you want me to."

"We appreciate your protection very much, Erik," Grandma said.

"Indeed," Thanatos agreed. She bowed her head to Erik and to each of the four Wise Women. "You have my gratitude. Thank you, all."

Stevie Rae took Rephaim's hand, pulling him toward the van so that he couldn't stand there and watch Marx and his men lifting his dad's body. Stark, Shaylin, Damien, and I followed her, piling back into the vehicle, while Shaunee got in Erik's car.

No one spoke. I searched my mind for the right thing to say to Rephaim. Should I tell him I was sorry about his dad? Or congratulate him about his dad? Since everyone else was silent, too, I figured they were all, even Stevie Rae, having a similarly tough time with what to say.

Thankfully, Rephaim saved us all. "I'm happy for Father," he said softly. "He is back where he always longed to be. Even lately, after he decided to follow Light and swore his oath to Thanatos, there was a loneliness about him that didn't get any better. Actually, I think it got worse."

Stevie Rae said, "I think once your daddy was finally able to accept love—your love to start with and then Nyx's love—once he did that it was like shuttin' the barn door after the cows were already out."

"Cows?" Rephaim said. I could hear the smile in his voice.

I turned around, and from where I sat in the front passenger seat, I could see that he was smiling at her. "She means that once he realized he needed love, he didn't have any more excuses. He had to admit that he really did need Nyx's love to be happy, even though he was the one who had left her, and not her him."

Rephaim nodded. "He's happy now. I felt it. That's how Nyx soothed my grief. She let me feel his joy." He smiled and wiped at his eyes again. "And I know I will see him again someday."

"Are you sure you're not immortal?" Shaylin asked. "Your aura looks an awful lot like his did."

"I'm sure," he said, putting his arm around Stevie Rae. "I'm just a boy who is lucky enough to be a lot like his father." Rephaim met my gaze. "Zoey, do what Thanatos asked. Make Father's pyre quickly so that Shaunee can light it and return to the Council Oak Tree."

"You know it'll be hard for the school to gather, especially if today is as sunny as it looks like it's going to be," I said.

"The school doesn't need to bear witness. I will be there. I will watch over Father."

I nodded and blinked fast, keeping myself from bawling.

Stark pulled through the entrance of the House of Night and just had time to park the Hummer under the covered parking attached to the building, when Rephaim kissed Stevie Rae quickly and said, "I love you." He looked at the rest of us and said, "It really isn't as bad as it sounds." Then he pushed open the car door.

His feet didn't even hit the ground. His scream pierced our ears, making everyone except Stevie Rae jump. The scream changed to the cry of a raven, and a huge black bird exploded from inside Rephaim's clothes, big wings sweeping the air as he soared out of the covered parking and into the morning sky to circle the House of Night.

"That was awesome," Stark said, squinting and using his hand to shield his eyes against the dawn, but still trying to follow Rephaim's flight.

"Yeah, he tells me it doesn't hurt that bad," Stevie Rae said, squinting alongside Stark. "I don't believe it, but I love him for tryin' to make me believe it."

"Hey, you guys need to get inside and go to bed," I said, herding along Stark and Stevie Rae and Shaylin.

"Not unless you're coming, too," Stark protested around a giant yawn.

"I'm coming, but first I'm going to fill in Darius and Aphrodite, and have him get Travis and some of the other humans to start building Kalona's pyre. Shaunee needs to get back to Thanatos before her burst of energy runs out," I said.

"I'll help," Damien said. "I'll tell Travis and Lenobia what's happened."

"And I'll supervise the humans building the pyre," Shaunee said. "Well, first I'll go get a hoodie and some sunglasses."

"But I can—" I stopped Stark's protest with a kiss and then whispered against his lips, "Please sleep so that you can stay strong and be safe. I'm not as strong as Nyx. I couldn't lose you."

Stark paused, and then, pulling me into his arms, he gave in.

Lynette

"You should be resting," said the Asian healer with the geometrical tattoos whose name Lynette had learned was Margareta. "Are you in pain?"

"No, I'm fine. I'm just not used to sleeping during the day," Lynette assured the vampyre. She was standing at the window and had pushed aside the heavy black curtain so she could watch a group of people piling logs and wooden planks in the center of the campus green. "Margareta, do you know what they are building out there?"

The healer moved forward a little, glancing out the window, but she didn't get close enough to have the bright morning light actually touch her. "I do know," she said. "They are building a pyre."

"A pyre?" Lynette stomach heaved. "Did someone die?"

"Someone was killed," she said.

"Who?"

Margareta studied her and then shrugged. "I see no harm in telling you. Kalona was killed."

"By her?" Lynette could hardly force her voice above a whisper. "Did Neferet kill him?"

Margareta nodded.

"Oh, God! He was supposed to be immortal."

"Apparently not," the healer said.

Lynette stumbled to her bed, collapsing there as her knees gave way. "Did she break the spell? Is she out of the Mayo?"

"No, the spell holds. For now. Are you quite sure you don't want me to give you something to help you sleep?"

Numbly, Lynette shook her head. "No. I'm fine. Really. Fine. I—I just need some time alone to think." She met the healer's watchful gaze and added, "Kalona saved me. It's a shock to think that he's dead."

"It is for us all as well," Margareta said. "I will leave you to your thoughts, then. As you know, I will just be down the hall. If you have need of me, just press the red button on your bed."

"I will. Thank you, Margareta."

When the vampyre was gone, Lynette's mind began to race. *Neferet had managed to kill an immortal while she was trapped inside the Mayo! It would be worse, so much worse, if she escaped.* Lynette shook herself mentally and made the correction in her thoughts. *Not if she escaped. When she escaped.* LaFont's daughter and the other two girls had said it themselves: it was only a matter of time before the spell their High Priestess cast was broken. And then they would be the lucky ones because Neferet would come after Kalona and her first. *With Kalona gone, that leaves only me.* Fear made Lynette feel dizzy. An immortal Warrior couldn't stop her. A protective spell couldn't stop her. The stone walls of this school and a small group of teenagers and vampyre professors sure as hell couldn't stop her.

If Lynette remained where she was, she would be on the losing side, and she would be found and possessed by Neferet's hideous serpents.

No! Lynette forced her breathing to slow, drawing in and out long, strong breaths. She fought back the panic, just as she had every moment she'd spent as Neferet's captive. *No!* She corrected herself. *I wasn't Neferet's captive; I was her employee. Her favorite employee. Her event planner. I was of value to her then. I will be of value to her again.*

Quietly and quickly, Lynette went to the small closet where the vampyres had hung her clothes. She changed from the hospital smock into her slacks and sweater. She exchanged her slippers for the attractive black ballet flats she'd worn the night before.

And then she tiptoed down the hallway. She paused at the door to the healer's office. Lynette could see the back of Margareta's head. She was studying a large computer screen that was showing the local news. Lynette watched, silent and horrified, as someone's iPhone caught Kalona's death. First it had focused on the rooftop balcony, as if waiting for something to happen. The immortal came suddenly into view, hovering with his enormous wings spread, his arms opened wide as he faced the balcony, looking like he was positioning himself to catch something. *Or someone,* Lynette thought the first time the video played through. And then she heard several cracks, one right after another, and Kalona's body was hurled backward. *Shots,* Lynette realized. *Neferet shot him!* The camera followed Kalona's fall. He tumbled end over end, landing on his back—broken and bloody—in the middle of the street where not long before he had led her from the Mayo.

Lynette couldn't make herself move until she'd watched the video play again. Then, as Margareta tapped replay once more, Lynette made her legs move. She held her breath until she was through the exit door and had closed it quietly behind her.

Even then she didn't pause. She knew she was on the third floor of the building at the edge of campus. She knew the way off campus as she had been very much awake and aware when the detective and Kalona had driven her there. She'd also seen the long line of cars that filled the school's parking lot to overflowing, so that people had had to park over the curb up and down Utica Street.

Lynette reached the ground-level door and paused, solidifying her plan. If she was questioned on her way out, she would say that she had decided to go home, that her adult daughter needed her. People weren't being kept as prisoners at the House of Night. As long as Lynette was not recognized, she would be free to come and go.

If she was recognized and stopped—what then?

Then they will have to keep me prisoner, and they have no reason to do so. It's a House of Night, but it's still America. I'm still free!

But by the time Lynette reached the big iron gates, she realized she had no need to worry about being stopped or questioned. There was no one patrolling the walls of the school. All of their attention was turned inward.

It was a little over three miles from the House of Night to the Mayo Hotel. Lynette walked. As she walked, she cleared her mind and then ordered her thoughts, focusing only on what had been most important to her for more than twenty years—making her business successful.

I am going to finish the job I started. I am going to finish the job I started. I am going to finish the job I started . . .

By the time Lynette reached West Fifth Street, her intent was solidly set. She walked calmly, not hurrying, taking in the roadblock and the uniformed officers who leaned against their cars, drinking coffee and talking to one another. There were other civilians in the vicinity. They wore lanyards, and Lynette recognized a few of them as reporters from the local networks. She remained calm, and she kept walking, settling comfortably into the role she'd played countless times over the past two decades. Lynette faded into the background. It was a unique and important talent. She had learned years ago that if one was to be a success in the event-planning business, one must have the ability to blend with the decorations—to stay out of the pictures—to keep the focus on the bride and not on oneself.

It worked for Lynette then as it had so many times before—right up until the Mayo was in view and she slipped quietly past the final police car in the roadblock. A uniformed officer was standing beside the car obviously trying to calm down a plump blond woman who was crying hysterically and clutching the hand of a tall, balding man.

"We have to know if our daughter is okay!" the bald man was shouting at the officer over the woman's crying. "Kylee Jackson is her name. She's the Mayo's receptionist."

"Please let us go see her!" the woman sobbed.

"Mr. and Mrs. Jackson, you have to stay back. Please, I understand how upset you must be, but we have a task force at the downtown station that is handling all of the inquiries of the victims' families."

"They aren't telling us shit!" Mr. Jackson said.

"They're telling you everything—"

Holding her breath, Lynette began to sneak past the distracted officer.

"Hey, hang on there! You gotta stay back behind the cars," the officer called to her. "No one's allowed past here."

Lynette turned and smiled at him. "Oh, no problem officer. I just wanted to thank you. You're doing an excellent job in a very difficult situation. I appreciate your service, as do Mr. and Mrs. Jackson." He returned her smile. The moment his shoulders relaxed and he turned back to the couple, Lynette sprinted away. Her blood pumped so loudly in her ears she couldn't hear what the officer was shouting at her. *Just run. Run as if your life depends upon it,* she told herself.

The buildings seemed to whiz past her as Lynette ran, expecting any moment to be tackled—or even shot. Not expecting to make it.

When she reached the shrouded Mayo, Lynette was too shocked to hesitate. She hurled herself against the door, paying no heed to the fetid, bloody curtain that had become the building's skin.

"Goddess! Let me in! Neferet, please! I've come back to you!" She pounded her fists against the slick surface of the door.

"Lady, get back here!" The cop had caught up with her and lunged forward to grab her arm.

The wall of flame blazed, setting him afire.

Horrified, Lynette watched him stagger back, screaming in agony as other officers, who had been physically restraining the Jacksons from following her, took off their jackets and tried to smother the flames.

With the sound of a bandage being torn from a fresh wound, the black curtain parted and the door to the Mayo opened.

Lynette bolted inside, gasping and trying to catch her breath.

"How dare you leave me!"

Neferet was standing on the landing between the floor-level ballroom and the mezzanine. The black serpents writhed all around her feet, covering the white marble of the landing and making it look as if it were alive with them.

With the single-minded intensity she had been practicing for the two hours it had taken her to walk there, Lynette went to the middle of the ballroom and knelt, bowing her head.

"Forgive me, Goddess. I was wrong. I should have never left unless you said my job was finished and you no longer needed me."

"You let him take you away! You betrayed me!"

"Forgive me, Goddess. Not because I deserve it, but because you deserve better."

"I deserved your loyalty!" Neferet battered Lynette with words as she glided down from the landing.

"Yes," Lynette said. She didn't lift her head. She squeezed her eyes closed so that she couldn't see the serpents that slithered around her. "And you have it. I have returned to you of my own volition."

"And why would you do that?"

"I came back because I left a job undone, and in the entire time I have been in business I have never done that. I don't intend to start now," Lynette said truthfully.

"We shall see about that!"

Lynette felt the violation as Neferet's mind probed hers. She trembled, holding her breath until the Goddess's will departed, leaving a pounding ache in her temples.

"You did return of your own will. You do want to complete your job."

Lynette was relieved enough at the surprise in Neferet's voice that she opened her eyes, though she did not lift her head.

"Please forgive me and allow me to finish what I started for you," she said.

"Do not think you fool me! I feel your loyalty. I also feel that it is based in fear and is self-serving."

"I don't deny that, Goddess. Since the moment I offered my services to you, I have not denied that."

"No, you control your fear and use your selfish nature to my benefit. Or you did until you betrayed me." Neferet's voice had softened.

"I still do," Lynette said. "I passed through the wall of fire without being burned. I have no ill intent whatsoever."

Lynette could see that the Goddess was pacing because the terrible serpents crawled back and forth, shadowing her every movement.

Finally, Neferet halted, so close to Lynette that she could see her bare feet. "Look at me," she commanded.

Lynette lifted her head and met her Goddess's gaze without flinching.

"Everything you have said is true, but tell me why I shouldn't command one of my children to possess you. You would still have the ability to perform your duties for me, and I would not have to worry about you running off again. It seems a good solution to your recent history of questionable loyalty."

Lynette drew a deep breath, forcing down the panic that threatened to choke her. With the pretense of calm, she said not what she had intended, not what she had practiced over and over again until the thought consumed her. Instead Lynette spoke the small, silent thing that she had kept buried beneath her single-mindedness. "Because I believe you truly care about me and you know how badly I am frightened of being possessed by one of your children. Goddess, I can prove my loyalty to you with the information I bring. I've been inside the House of Night. I've listened to Zoey and Aphrodite and Stevie Rae. They said the protective barrier is draining Thanatos. That the more it has to work, the faster it will drain her, until finally she won't be able to keep it up at all."

Neferet's face went utterly blank. Then slowly, the Goddess bent and placed both of her hands on Lynette's cheeks, cupping her face.

Lynette froze, unable to think. Unable to move.

Neferet kissed her softly but fully on the mouth.

"Rise, Lynette, my dear one. And take your place by my side where you belong and where you will remain until your too-brief mortal life comes to an end. And know when that happens, your Goddess will eternally mourn your loss."

Neferet helped Lynette stand, and even steadied her as she stumbled.

"Kylee! My dear Lynette and I are going up to the balcony to enjoy the sunset. Bring us my favorite wine and something nourishing to eat." Neferet paused. "A fortifying stew? Would that replenish your strength?"

Feeling utterly detached from any reality she'd ever known before, Lynette nodded. "Yes, please, Goddess."

"You heard her, Kylee! Lynette wants stew! Get it for her. And check with Tony about my chocolate cake as well. Chocolate goes so well with my favorite red wine."

As Kybot scampered away, Neferet led Lynette up to her penthouse, speaking sweetly and softly to her the entire way.

"My dear, you said you were at the House of Night. Were they cruel to you?"

"No, they weren't cruel. They didn't trust me, though."

"Did you actually see Thanatos upholding the spell?"

"No, I just saw the mayor's daughter, Aphrodite, and the healers," she told the Goddess.

"Those wretched creatures aren't true vampyre healers. They are mere assistants. Did you know that one of my abilities is that of a healer?"

"No," Lynette said with genuine surprise. "I wasn't aware of that."

"Yes, my dear Lynette. Rest assured that if one of them dared harm you, I could heal you."

"Thank you, Goddess."

"I would imagine Detective Marx had many questions for you."

Lynette ignored the chill that began working its way down her spine and answered the Goddess with complete honesty. "He did. He wanted to know how many people were inside your Temple."

"And did you tell him, my dear?"

"Yes," Lynette said without hesitation. "I told him. I also told him how devoted your servants are to you."

The cloud that had been beginning to form in Neferet's emerald eyes cleared and she smiled fondly at Lynette. "And he didn't like hearing that."

"No. Neither did Aphrodite or Kalona."

That made Neferet laugh with wicked-sounding glee.

By this time, they had reached the penthouse balcony. Neferet motioned for Lynette to sit at one of two barstools placed around a tall bistro table. On the table was a handgun, one of those dangerous-looking things that people in the movies tended to wave around a lot. Lynette shivered. She was a native Oklahoman, but she hated guns.

The Goddess sat beside her and leaned toward her intimately. "Did you know that today I killed Kalona?"

Lynette nodded. "Yes, I saw it on the news."

Neferet's smile was radiant. "Someone filmed it? How fabulous! Oh, and that reminds me, Lynette, when we are free of this place, I want you to hire the best camera crew my endless money can buy. I simply must have an accurate video record of my reign."

"Yes, Goddess." Lynette said.

"Hmm, yes. Hire someone to film it, but I will want you to edit the film. It must be the correct version of accurate. Do you understand my meaning?"

"Of course I do," Lynette said as she gained confidence and slid back into her familiar role. "I wouldn't allow anything distasteful or unattractive to make the edit cut."

"Oh, speaking of distasteful and unattractive. I referred to your list while you were taking your small sabbatical. I'm afraid you'll find I have a few less supplicants than when you left. I think you'll be pleased to know that I began with those you listed as unattractive and untalented."

Lynette hesitated only a moment. Then she nodded her head. "Well, Goddess, if you had to begin somewhere, that is where I would have advised."

"You are so wise, my dear Lynette."

Kylee hurried in, carrying a silver tray holding two large slices of a delicious-looking chocolate cake decorated with delicate white flowers, a bottle of red wine, and two crystal goblets. Lynette noticed immediately that Kybot's usually expressionless face looked worried.

"Ah, there you are, Kylee. I was beginning to wonder if you'd lost your way. I trust Tony is busily preparing Lynette's stew?"

"Yes, Goddess, he is. But there is a problem with the wine."

Neferet frowned. She looked at the bottle and her frown deepened. "Kylee, this isn't my favorite."

"Goddess, we are out of your favorite," Kylee said in a rush.

"Out of my favorite? How can that be?"

"Goddess, you drank it all, and we cannot leave to go to the liquor store, nor are they allowing us to receive shipments. And Tony sends his sincere apologies, but he wanted you to know that we are running short of supplies in the kitchen as well." Kylee place the tray on the table and stood trembling, obviously waiting for Neferet to explode in rage. Lynette braced herself, expecting the same.

The Goddess proved them both wrong. Instead of exploding, she spoke calmly. "Pour this wine for Lynette and me. It will do for now. And then tell Tony that I have heard his concerns."

Kylee's hand trembled as she did as Neferet commanded. After the girl had left, Neferet lifted the goblet, swirling it and studying it as if it might contain the answer to a great mystery. The Goddess sniffed delicately and then took a sip. She grimaced only slightly.

"It is exceedingly average, but drinkable," she said. "Go on, my dear. Try it and give me your opinion."

Lynette went through the motions of swirling the wine, sniffing, and sipping. "I agree with you, Goddess. It isn't your usual, but it will do."

"Yes, it will do," Neferet said, staring down at a spot in the center of the balcony as she swirled the wine and continued to sip.

Lynette knew when to stay silent. She averted her eyes from the Goddess and drank her own wine. Which was, actually, very good.

"Lynette, my dear, if I said to you, *The more something is desired, the dearer the sacrifice must be made to attain it,* how would you interpret that?"

Lynette's lack of food mixed with the rich red wine, and she was just tipsy enough to blurt, "That's easy. It's why I'm here right now. Nothing and no one means more to me than being successful and surviving. I've sacrificed everything in my life for those two things. And it has been worth it."

"Nothing and no one . . ." the Goddess mused. Then a long, slow smile lifted Neferet's lush lips. "After listening to you and an *associate* of mine, I have just realized how I can break Thanatos's spell. Now, let us eat cake while we plan the most spectacular event Tulsa has ever witnessed!"

CHAPTER TWENTY-THREE

Zoey

Kalona's funeral was sad and happy at the same time, and it happened super fast. Travis and Shaunee worked together so well it sometimes seemed like they were reading each other's minds. Darius and Aurox put up an awning to shield her from the sunlight, and from there she gave directions to Aurox, Travis, and a team of humans, which included Detective Marx and the officers who'd put themselves in charge of Kalona's body, as well as a group of men they'd somehow talked into helping.

All the while a big raven, obviously Rephaim, perched on the edge of the awning roof, right above Shaunee, cocking his head with active interest and silently watching over everything.

It was mid-afternoon when Shaunee said the logs and planks were perfect and called for Kalona's body. Detective Marx and Darius carried the front of the litter. The TPD officers, in freshly pressed uniforms, and Aurox, dressed all in black, spread out around the rest of the litter, lifting it and walking slowing, in perfect step, to the pyre. I waited beside the pyre with Shaunee, Damien, Lenobia, and Erik. At the last minute, wearing round, heavily tinted Chanel sunglasses, Aphrodite joined us.

"You okay?" I asked her softly.

"No, but too many of the Nerd Herd are missing. Someone has to represent."

I smiled at her and gave her a quick hug. "Thanks from them."

"Stop. Seriously. There's only so much PDA I can take when I'm hungover. Or even when I'm not hungover."

Then everyone's attention focused on Kalona's body as they carried him across the center green. He was covered with a ginormous silver rectangle of cloth. The afternoon sunlight seemed to brighten as he got closer and closer to the pyre, and the material shined and fluttered as if it were made of liquid mercury.

"That's incredible," I said. "I've never seen anything like that cloth."

"I found it in the drama room and gave it to Damien for Kalona's shroud," Erik said. "But it didn't shine like that inside."

"It's Erebus," Damien said. "He's put magick in the sunlight for his brother."

I blinked fast, and was so focused on not crying that I didn't notice the people until Shaunee pointed them out.

"Wow, check out all the humans!"

Led by Travis, a long line of somber people were trailing out of the field house.

"They liked him," Lenobia said. When I gave her my question mark look, she explained, "Kalona fascinated the humans, but it seems they also truly liked him. He was patient with their questions and didn't get angry when children tugged on his feathers."

"So kids did actually grab his feathers," Aphrodite said. "Wish I'd seen that."

"And also you have to remember that interview made him look like a hero," Lenobia said. "And the YouTube thing went viral."

"Kalona was a hero," Shaunee said firmly. "He saved Rephaim. He tried his best to save Grandma Redbird. He saved a bunch of us in front of the Mayo. He even died trying to save someone he'd never met. He made terrible mistakes in his life, but at the end, he was on the right side—he did the right thing."

"And Nyx forgave him," I said, agreeing with her.

The raven, circling low over our heads, croaked as if agreeing with Shaunee, too. And then he landed in the oak tree nearest the pyre, perching on a thick branch that extended toward it.

"Zoey, I'll help Travis circle the people. You can start whenever you're ready." I nodded and then turned to Shaunee.

"I think you should speak. He and I had too much history." She started to protest, but I interrupted her. "I don't mean that I have any bad feelings about Kalona now. Actually, I haven't for a while. But that's different from being his friend. His friend should speak at his funeral, and I think you were his friend."

"I'm agreeing with Z," Aphrodite said.

"As am I," Damien said.

"But I don't know what to say," Shaunee said.

"Yes you do." Erik took her hand and smiled intimately at her. "You're good at saying what you feel. Just do that for Kalona one more time."

Huh! They've got something going on between them! I was honestly happy for them.

"Okay, I'll do it," Shaunee said.

"I'll follow you with the torch. Let me know when you want me to give it to you," I said.

Shaunee nodded, lifted her chin, and walked purposefully through the circle of people to stand in front of Kalona's pyre.

The already quiet crowd went absolutely silent. I heard Shaunee draw in a big breath, and then she began, "Kalona was our High Priest-ess's Warrior, and Protector of this House of Night. He was my friend. He was father to his son, Rephaim. Those things are important—Warrior, friend, and father—but Kalona was something more. He was an ancient walking this earth among us, for good or ill, a constant reminder that our world is filled with magickal forces. Kalona was tangible proof that those forces can be awe-inspiring and awesome, frightening and mesmerizing, wonderful and terrible—all at the same time. He was our superhero, and even a superhero sometimes makes mistakes. Ours did, but in the end he kept his oath and sacrificed himself to protect us. When I remember Kalona, I'll remember him with respect and love, always love."

Shaunee motioned to me, and I stepped forward, handing her the burning torch I carried.

"Now you should all move back three big paces. I'm going to light Kalona's pyre, and it's going to be bright and hot. But you don't need to be scared. Fire listens to me, and I give you my oath that I will only use it to protect and serve goodness and Light." I saw her exchange smiles with Detective Marx and the uniformed officers. When everyone had moved far enough back, Shaunee said, "Fire, I call you to me. Light a blaze that Kalona will see all the way from the Otherworld!"

She touched the torch to the pyre, and fire roared from it, like she had just turned on a flamethrower. At the same instant a beam of light speared from the west, intensifying Shaunee's already awesome blaze. We all shuffled back farther, though no one acted scared or panicked. Above us, Kalona's son, in the form of a raven, called mournfully over and over. As dark shapes circled far above us, throwing strange shadows over the pyre, Rephaim's cries echoed in the wind, and I realized that it wasn't just one raven I was hearing, but hundreds of them.

Zoey

With the help of fire and, we suspected, a major dose of sunlight, the pyre had burned faster than any I'd ever seen before. Aphrodite, Damien, Erik, and I hadn't left yet, even though we were all doing a lot of yawning. No one said it, but I guessed they felt a lot like I did—I didn't want to leave Rephaim perched up there by himself, cawing pathetically. Stevie Rae would want us to stay. Hell, Kalona would probably even want us to stay. So we stayed.

The humans had mostly wandered back inside, though some of the children had discovered a bunch of jump ropes in the Warriors' gym, and they were noisily skipping up and down the sidewalk.

Aphrodite looked over the black rim of her sunglasses at the kids. "I don't know why anyone would purposefully procreate."

I grimaced as one of the children laughed so shrilly that I was pretty sure I heard Duchess howl in response.

"And this is the perfect time for me to make my exit back to Thanatos," Shaunee said. "Even though I kinda like kids. I used to babysit for friends of my parents who were so rich their playroom was like a Toys R Us store."

Aphrodite shuddered delicately. "Why did your parents hate you so much?"

Detective Marx joined us. "It was a nice funeral. Shaunee, what you said was perfect."

"Thanks," she said, smiling at the tall detective.

"Hey, I'm going to take that ambulance back to St. John's, and the other officers are going off duty. I'll get my truck and come on back here for the night."

"Shouldn't you go home to your daughters? They gotta be missing you," Shaunee said.

Marx smiled. "My daughters and my wife are right over there." He pointed at the group of jump-roping girls.

"Of course they are," Aphrodite muttered.

We ignored her. "Want to hitch a ride with us?" Marx asked Shaunee. "I can swing you by the Council Oak Tree on my way back to the station."

Erik cleared his throat. "If it's okay with you guys, I'll take Shaunee back and hang out there for a while."

I shrugged. "Okay by me."

"Awesome!" Erik said, smiling at Shaunee. "And tell Aurox he doesn't need to worry about relieving me until sunrise tomorrow. I know the Warriors have a lot on their plate here with all these humans."

"I'll tell him," I said. And everyone except Aphrodite scattered.

"When did they become a thing?" Aphrodite asked.

"Right? I was wondering the same thing."

"Guess he needed a backup plan since Shaylin turned gay."

"Aphrodite, you do realize what you just said was full of stereotypes, don't you?"

"Yes. It's figurative language I hate, not English in general," she said, rolling her eyes.

I frowned at her and shook my head. "Shaunee is an awesome person—*and* gorgeous. Erik could want to be with her for those reasons and not just because he needs to be with someone to make up for Shaylin."

Aphrodite started to say something and then stopped herself, thought, and started again. "Actually, you might be right. Erik has changed since he was 'our Erik,'" she air-quoted. "He's turning out to be an okay guy. Just don't ever tell him I said that."

"I won't."

"Plus," she said as she watched the two of them walk down the sidewalk together, "they're reminding me of Olivia and the president in *Scandal*. I'm liking this whole black girl–white boy thing. It's attractive. Not to mention how it broadens the typical white boy point of view. Goddess knows they need it."

"That's the most politically correct thing I've ever heard you say."

"You are welcome, retard," she said. "Go get some sleep. I'll see you after sunset." But before she could twitch away, Kramisha ran up to us, teetering on six-inch over-the-knee patent-leather boots, holding her hoodie up over her head so it wouldn't mess up her flaming red wig. Even with the giant mirrored gold sunglasses she had on I could tell she was scowling.

"Your boots are crazy," Aphrodite told her.

"Don't start with me. I didn't get my sleep." Kramisha pulled out a piece of her purple notepaper from inside her giant tote and shoved it toward us.

"Oh, hell no!" Aphrodite took a step back. "That's for Z."

"Act like you've got some damn sense. It's not like I'm out here 'cause I wanna be. Here, Z." She handed me the paper. "It is for you."

I wanted to scream and drop it like it was a spider, but I was trying to be grown up *and* have some damn sense. So instead I sighed and took the paper, reading the poem aloud:

> *Inevitable as death*
> *Wield the Old Magick*
> *His sacrifice accepted.*

"Um, late much?" Aphrodite said. "Even I can tell that haiku's about Kalona, and he's already dead."

"Do. Not. Speak." Kramisha held her finger up at Aphrodite. Obviously thinking she had Aphrodite under control, she turned to me. "I got a strong feelin' that you gotta get that stone back from Frodo over there."

"I will beat you with my brush if you call me Frodo again."

"Shhh!" I told Aphrodite. Then faced Kramisha, "I can't wield it until I've figured out how *not to* turn into another Neferet."

"Neferet's broke. You ain't. Old Magick is the only chance we have at beatin' a goddess. So use it or you won't have to worry 'bout turnin' into a crazy bitch because we'll all be the slaves of a crazy bitch." Kramisha snapped her head around to glare at Aphrodite. "I'm leavin' before she makes some stupid-assed slave joke that'll make me have to go all Jackie Brown on her." And Kramisha tottered away.

"Who's Jackie Brown?"

"I have no clue," I said.

"Maybe we should ask Shaunee."

I sighed. "Maybe we should focus on how I can use the stupid stone!"

"You want my opinion?"

I stifled another sigh and said, "Yes."

"Wear the stone. You know what it's capable of now. Keep a check on yourself. We'll all keep a check on you—this time out in the open. If you start to snap, you'll be tackled by a Herd of Nerds. Literally and figuratively."

"I really don't have any choice, do I?"

"Not anymore you don't. Neferet figured out how to kill Kalona. She's going to figure out how to break the protective spell. Then she's going to come after us. Mostly you, but the fallout will include the rest of us."

"You're right. Give me back the stupid stone."

Aphrodite reached under the neck of her shirt and pulled out a delicate silver chain, long enough that she didn't have to unclasp it to take it off. From the chain dangled the deceptively innocent-looking Seer Stone.

"It always reminds me of a coconut Life Saver," I said, reluctant to touch it. "That's a pretty chain."

"It's platinum. Try not to fuck it up, because I want it back. The chain, not the stone. Stop stalling and take it." She held it out so I had to do exactly that. "You know, your first step in this whole wield-the-Old-Magick thing might have something to do with you working on your confidence. Z, if you don't believe you can do this, there's no damn way you're going to be able to do this."

"I know." I put the chain around my neck and tucked the stone under my T-shirt. Then I waited for something to happen.

Aphrodite snorted. "Seriously? You walked around with that thing for weeks before you went postal."

"Well, something could happen!" I said defensively.

"Yeah, sure, and Oklahoma could elect a female Democrat to the Senate, hell could freeze over, pigs could fly, blah, blah. Relax. Stressing over it can't help."

"Okay, yeah, you're right."

"I love hearing that twice in one conversation."

"Don't get used to it." Aphrodite rolled her eyes and started to twitch away. I called after her, "Hey, I'm sending a group text. We gotta have a serious brainstorming session. Everyone needs to meet in the professors' dining hall for breakfast. Fifteen minutes after sunset."

"Make it an hour and fifteen minutes after sunset and I'll send the text for you."

"Aphrodite, we really need to get a plan."

"Zoey, we really need to get some sleep."

I chewed my lip and thought about how tired she looked and how tired I felt. "Deal," I said.

"Oh, and by the way, I know you're using this whole end-of-the-world thing as an excuse to take over the vamps' cafeteria, and I like it!" She waggled her eyebrows at me and then off she twitched.

Shaking my head and yawning, I started toward the girls' dorms—and then made a sharp turn, backtracked, and took a giant circular detour when I noticed that some of the jump-roping kids were gawking at me like they were gearing up to pull my feathers.

"It's bad when Kalona seems nicer than me," I mumbled to myself.

"You're usually nice, Zo."

"Holy crap, Aurox! You can't just sneak up behind me and scare me like that."

"I was jogging the perimeter and not sneaking at all," he said. "You were talking to yourself so loud you didn't hear me, or Skylar." He nodded upward at the school's wall, where the giant orange cat was padding on his tiger-like paws, keeping up with Aurox. "Why do you think Kalona was nicer than you?"

I made a gesture in the general direction from where distant girl giggles could still be heard. "He let them pull his feathers. I detoured all the way over here to avoid them."

Aurox smiled. "That doesn't make you less nice. It makes you smart. Young humans hurt my ears, too."

I grinned back at him, glad things felt easier between us since we'd discovered Skylar together. "Young humans, especially young human girls, would like you. They'd think you're super hot," I teased. Then instantly wished I could take it back, because the easy, friendly feeling between us evaporated.

"I should get on with my patrol. Blessed be, Zoey."

He started to jog away and I snagged his wrist. "Hey, hang on. I didn't mean to say anything to make you mad."

His broad shoulders slumped. "I'm not mad. I just get tired of it."

"It?" I asked, clueless.

"*It*—the fact that I'm not what I seem. If those little girls knew what I could turn into, they would be terrified of me."

"Oh," I said, getting it. "But they don't know, and you aren't turning into anything right now. Why don't you do what Rephaim does? He lives every moment of his *human* life to the fullest. He doesn't let the fact that he has to be a bird every day ruin life for him."

I could see I'd given Aurox something to think about. At least he didn't jog away, or turn all cold and distant. We walked on for a while without saying anything. When he finally answered me, he did so in a voice that was barely above a whisper.

"I would like to be like that, but Rephaim has two things I don't have, two things I don't think I'll ever have."

When he didn't keep talking, I prompted, "What two things?"

"The forgiveness of Nyx and the love of a woman."

I started with the one that wasn't a ticking time bomb. "Why don't you think Nyx has forgiven you? Have you asked her?"

"Every day," he said. "I light a candle at the feet of her statue and ask for her forgiveness every day."

"Well, then, why would you think the Goddess hasn't forgiven you? You've chosen her path. You're only doing good. You even saved my grandma from Neferet."

"She's never spoken to me." The sadness in his voice made him sound like he was a zillion years old.

"Nyx hasn't spoken to a lot of us," I said.

"That's not true here. Nyx has appeared multiple times. She appeared today."

"Well, yeah, but—"

"The Goddess knows what I am. She doesn't want anything to do with me."

"Aurox, that can't be true. Nyx allowed Heath's spirit to enter you so that you could choose to be more than a vessel."

His gaze met mine. "She didn't do that for me. She did that for you."

I didn't know what to say to him. I'd spoken with Nyx's authority before, when I'd heard her voice, or felt that nudge in my gut that said I was on the right path. I didn't feel either of those things right now. I just felt bad for Aurox.

"And as for the second thing—you know why I'll never have that," he said.

"Aurox, I care about you, but I'm with Stark. It's just too complicated between us for that to change."

"No, Zoey. You don't care about *me*. You care about *Heath*. And that's why it's too complicated to change. Now I am going to finish my patrol." His smile was sad and sweet. "Blessed be."

It was after he'd walked away that I noticed the absence of the warmth that had been spreading from the small, circular stone that rested between my breasts.

"Old Magick," I whispered, staring after him. "Aurox is definitely hooked into Old Magick." *So how the hell could that help me?*

I had no clue. But I was going to figure it out. I pulled out my phone and sent a quick text to Aphrodite: *Include Aurox in your group text.* I waited until my phone wookie roared with her return text saying *Okay. Go to sleep* before I walked the rest of the way to the dorm.

My feet felt super heavy as I dragged them up the stairs and to my room. It was cool and dark and quiet inside. Stark was sound asleep. I was glad. I didn't want him to wake up and feel my sadness and stress. I'd have to explain about the Seer Stone soon enough. And I didn't want to explain about Aurox at all. I brushed my teeth and washed my face, and worried in silence.

I had to move Nala so that I could lie down next to Stark. She only grumbled for a second and then she circled the covers at my feet, making a little Nal nest, flopped her fatty body down, and started up her purr machine. I closed my eyes.

Go to sleep. Go to sleep. Go to sleep.

I sighed and fluffed my pillow and scooted away from Stark so that my restlessness wouldn't bother him.

"You're worrying again." Stark's voice was sleepy. He pulled me back against him, and his hand found my shoulder, which he started to knead gently.

"You don't have to do that. I know you're super tired," I said.

He moved my hair and kissed the back of my neck. "I know I don't have to. I want to."

"Thank you for taking care of me," I whispered.

"Always, Z. Always," he said. And his touch led me to sleep.

CHAPTER TWENTY-FOUR

Lynette

"Lynette, my dear, you look lovely!" Neferet smiled and walked a circle around her. "I knew my gown would suit you. You're much thinner than your old clothes make you appear."

"Well, lately I've lost weight," she said, smoothing down the silk dress. Lynette caught a glimpse of herself in Neferet's long mirror. *I do look good, even though the only way I could fit into this dress was to have the gathered waist completely ungathered.* "And you were correct. It is good for morale to dress up and look our best."

"Of course I am correct. I am Goddess!"

Lynette watched Neferet do a graceful twirl around the room. Her long golden dress swirled around her and her serpents wriggled enthusiastically about her ankles, like they were a perverted version of puppies.

Kylee entered the penthouse. "Goddess, your supplicants are gathered in the ballroom, awaiting the gift of your presence."

Lynette was nodding her approval to Kybot—the girl had addressed Neferet exactly as she had coached her—when Neferet whirled by, taking the dumbstruck receptionist in her arms and commanding, "Waltz with me!"

She's been like this ever since she figured out how to break the protective spell. It's like she's having a manic episode. Neferet's jubilance worried Lynette. She knew all too well that what went up had to come crashing down. *I'm not going to be in her path when she crashes,* Lynette promised herself. *My survival instinct is one of the things Neferet appreciates about me—she's told me so.*

"Lynette, do stop thinking of yourself and pay attention."

Immediately, Lynette focused on Neferet, expecting to have to handle one of her temper tantrums. But Neferet wasn't unpleasant at all. She gave Kylee a last twirl and then, smiling and fanning her flushed face, Neferet simply repeated herself—exhibiting no anger or irritation at all toward Lynette.

"I asked if you'd made sure Tony did as I commanded. You know he's little more than a child's windup toy."

"Oh, yes, Goddess. Of course I did." Lynette assured her. "I double-checked everything before I came to you. Tony did exactly as you commanded. He prepared a feast, using the last of the food, and serving the last of the wine and liquor, to all your supplicants."

"Even my staff?" Neferet sent Kylee a fond smile.

Lynette nodded. "Yes, even your staff."

"Did you enjoy your feast, Kylee?" Neferet asked her, as if she really cared about her answer.

"Yes, Goddess, I did."

"Excellent!" She laughed happily and made a shooing motion at Kylee. "Go ahead and precede us to the ballroom, Kylee. Have the quartet begin to play the music I chose from the final scene of the ballet *Giselle*."

"Yes, Goddess."

When they were alone, Neferet said, "Come, Lynette. Would you help me make sure my hair is perfect?"

"I'd be happy to, though I have to admit that I'm not very good with hair."

"Oh, just be certain none of the flowers the stylist wove into the back fell out as I was dancing. What was that stylist's name? She was very proficient."

"Allison," Lynette said, tucking a stray sprig of baby's breath back into Neferet's dark auburn mane.

"Yes, that's right—Allison. Such a nice name. I am pleased that she made it to the feast."

"As am I," Lynette agreed. Only one stylist of the four who had been hired for the wedding that had brought them all to the Mayo was still alive. Lynette thought that it seemed that night had happened an eternity ago.

"Lynette, I am sorry you missed the feast, but it pleased me that you and I were able to sup together earlier. I hope you don't mind that the stew was simple and the wine not my best."

"Our meal was wonderful. I enjoyed all of it, even the wine," Lynette said, marveling at how genuine Neferet seemed. It was as if a switch had been thrown within the Goddess. Her entire attitude had changed.

Lynette was afraid to hope it would last.

"And now it is almost midnight. Everyone is dressed in their best and sated with food and drink. The scene is set for the perfect exit event," Neferet said.

"That is my fondest wish," Lynette said. Then she took a chance and asked, "Goddess, are you sure there is nothing I can do to help you with our actual exit?"

"Ah, my dear Lynette, no. I have already explained to you that your duty is to get everyone ready for our spectacular exit. The rest of this event is my duty, as it requires the magick of a Goddess."

"As you wish, Goddess—after you." Lynette curtsied as Neferet and her swarm of Darkness swept past her. Obediently, she followed her into the elevator, ignoring the cold-skinned serpents as they slithered over her feet in their haste to stay close to Neferet. Actually, Lynette was proud of herself. It was getting easier and easier to suppress the revulsion Neferet's creatures made her feel. And Neferet appreciated that. Anything Neferet appreciated was a good thing.

Lynette was worried about how Neferet was going to break them free of the Mayo. She had no idea what the Goddess had planned. All she knew was that Neferet acted as if she had absolutely no doubt she could break the spell and lead them from the Mayo, and she was very happy about it. As with Neferet's appreciation, her happiness was definitely a good thing.

"Lynette, my dear, have you ever been to Italy?"

Lynette blinked in surprise at the unexpected question. "Yes, actually I have. I've been to Rome and Venice, Sorrento and Capri."

"Did you enjoy Italy?"

"Very much," she assured the Goddess. "Would you like me to begin researching a trip for you?"

"Oh, let's see how tonight goes, shall we? As you always say, you need time and means to plan the perfect event."

A little confused, Lynette nodded in agreement. Supposing it was a good sign that Neferet was quoting her, she smoothed the lovely dress the Goddess had given her and patted her hair into place. This was one event for which Lynette absolutely wanted to look her best.

Zoey

"So, because I have somehow been drafted into being secretary for the Herd of Nerds, let me recap your pathetic attempt at coming up with a plan," Aphrodite said, pausing to glance at the yellow legal pad I could see that she'd mostly just doodled Darius's name all over. "We have zip. Nada. Nothing. And we've been brainstorming for hours, though I am getting extremely attached to the professors' dining room." She nibbled on the edge of a fudge brownie the chef had brought us a plate of an hour or so ago. "But if I stay up here much longer, my butt is going to be the size of this cushy chair."

"That's not true," I said. "Well, the part about your butt is probably true. The zip, nada, nothing part isn't true. We know I have to use Old Magick to kill Neferet. I'm wearing this"—I lifted the Seer Stone as Exhibit A—"and I haven't freaked out or gotten pissed or anything. So I might be able to use it without turning into anything terrible. I mean, I don't know how yet, but still."

"The Seer Stone heats up around Aurox," Stark added, sending Aurox an annoyed look.

"But not all the time," Damien said.

"Z, is it hot right now?" Stevie Rae asked me.

I closed my fingers around it to be sure before I answered and shook my head. "Nope. It's just a stone. Not hot. Not cold."

"Neferet can't be killed," Aurox said. Everyone looked at him in surprise. He'd been sitting off to the side of our group, listening but hardly saying anything, for hours.

"Yeah, genius. We know that. She's immortal," Aphrodite said.

"But Zoey just said she needs to use Old Magick to kill Neferet. Damien said it an hour ago. You even said it forty-five minutes before that. Stevie Rae mentioned it as soon as we all sat—"

"Okay, we get it," I interrupted him, feeling the irritation level in the room rising with each of his comments. "We know she can't be killed."

"At least we think she can't be killed," Rephaim said. "Father was immortal, and he is dead."

There was a long, sad silence, so when Aurox spoke, it sounded extra loud and extra awkward.

"I believe that is the core of your problem. You're not asking yourselves the right question because of what happened to Kalona. You know Neferet is immortal, yet you believe if Zoey wields enough power, she can still be killed. I think that is a mistake that is keeping you from finding your plan." As if he was warming to the subject, Aurox leaned forward in his chair, studying Rephaim. "No one has explained it to me, but you all seem to know the answer unsaid. Forgive me if this brings you pain, but can you tell me how it is your father was killed, though he had been immortal for eons?"

Stark stood and put his hand on Rephaim's shoulder. "I'll answer that for you." He gave Aurox a hard look. "When Heath, the kid who's soul is inside you, was killed by Kalona, Zoey's soul shattered and she was trapped in the Otherworld. I followed her there to try to get her back. Kalona did, too, because Neferet got control over him and sent him to be sure Z never made it back. Kalona and I fought in the Otherworld. He won. I lost. He killed me. Nyx interceded because Kalona cheated. He should have never been there to begin with. He was banished from the Otherworld by the Goddess, and he slipped back in under a technicality."

I saw Aurox's confusion and I explained, "Nyx banished Kalona physically, but didn't specifically say his spirit wasn't allowed in the Otherworld, either. He came back as spirit, not body."

Aurox nodded. "I see."

"Because Father disobeyed the Goddess's edict, she commanded him to give Stark a piece of his immortality," Rephaim said.

"And because Kalona obeyed her command, I'm alive today," Stark said.

"But he's dead because of it," Aurox said. "I understand."

"Do ya also understand that's a pretty sore subject right now?" Stevie Rae said, taking Rephaim's hand and sliding closer to him.

"Of course I understand that. I did not mean to cause anyone pain. Rephaim, you have my apology," Aurox said.

"Accepted," Rephaim said. "We all know Father made many mistakes. It's just difficult to relive them right now."

"And yet we need all of the information we can get to *defeat* Neferet, and that includes understanding that her immortality is intact," Aurox said.

"So she doesn't have an Achilles' heel, like Kalona did," I said.

"She doesn't have a literal weakness, as did Kalona and Achilles," Damien said in his teacher voice. "But maybe we can find something from her past that we can use against her."

"We already tried that. The Seer Stone turned into a mirror that showed her past, when she'd been beaten up and raped by her dad," I said. "The reason that worked then was that she was shocked enough that Aurox had a chance to gore her and throw her off the balcony. She won't be surprised by that again."

"But she was weakened enough to be defeated—even temporarily," Aurox said.

"Talk about fighting creepy with creepy," Aphrodite said. "No offense, Bull Boy, but you can be as gross as those spiders when you do that change-up thing."

I shivered, not liking the memory that flashed in my mind of what lurked beneath Aurox's normal-looking façade.

"No offense taken," Aurox said.

"Aurox, can *you* kill her?" I asked.

He shook his head slowly. "I used all of my power against her at the penthouse, and that did not kill her. What we need is something like what you and I did to her, only more permanent. We need a prison fashioned to hold an immortal, not a weapon to slay one."

"Holy crap," I said, sitting up straighter. "A-ya!"

"What is A-ya?" Aurox asked.

"She's a who, not a what," I said, speaking fast, trying to keep up with my zooming thoughts. "A-ya was a maiden created from earth and breathed to life—"

"With Old Magick," Aphrodite finished.

I nodded. "Yeah, with Old Magick. She lured Kalona underground."

"Because unless they have ties to the earth, immortals are weakest underground," Damien said, his voice mirroring my excitement.

"Neferet has no ties with the earth. She steals her power from souls as they die," Shaylin said. "She is a soul leech."

"The maiden A-ya was able to imprison Father because she was created with the Old Magick of the Great Earth Mother and elemental power focused by Wise Women who were defending their people," Rephaim said. "He was trapped for centuries."

"Until Neferet freed him," I said.

"I don't think she was ever a vampyre," Stevie Rae said. "She's more like a sorceress, a super-crazy, super-manipulative, super-mean one."

"Ohmygoddess!" Damien exclaimed, his fingers flying across his iPad. "Nimue's imprisonment of Merlin in the crystal cave created from his own magic! It's more than a boring trope or a clichéd, overused parable. It's our answer!"

"Oh, for shit's sake, speak English. Modern English," Aphrodite said.

Damien didn't even take time to frown at her. "Merlin was King Arthur's adviser, remember?"

"Yeah," I said. "Wasn't he a vampyre?"

Damien shook his head. "No, no, no, though people tend to make that mistake pretty often. The Arthurian legends were based on a human king who lived in medieval times. They were romanticized by authors like Alfred Lord Tennyson, T. H. White, and Marion Zimmer Bradley, who really just fictionalized everything—including Merlin."

"I remember," Stark said. "I read the Merlin Trilogy by Mary Stewart. Merlin basically makes Arthur king, and then isn't there to help stop the downfall of Camelot because he's trapped by his own magick used by Nimue—the apprentice he fell in love with. At least I think that's how the story went. I read them when I was a kid."

"I saw the Disney *Sword in the Stone*," Stevie Rae said. "I liked it, but I don't remember Nimue."

"The specifics aren't important," Damien said. "It's the heart of the myth that has the clue we need."

"We use her own magick to trap Neferet," I said.

"Not *we*, Zo. You," Aurox said.

"Ah, hell," I said. I sighed and took a big gulp of my brown pop. It was going to be a long night.

Lynette

The elevator opened to the mezzanine level, and Neferet walked gracefully around the balcony-like hallway, drawing the entire ballroom's attention to her as she came to the wide marble stairway and descended to the level on which her throne sat. Lynette followed more slowly, her eyes automatically searching the crowd below for anything or anyone who could spoil the festive ambiance she had worked so hard to create.

She breathed a long, satisfied sigh as everything appeared as close to perfection as possible. *Well, at least the only people left alive are the most attractive ones.* That had definitely made her job easier. Studying them, Lynette had to admit that they were a pretty group—if one didn't look too closely at their pale, worried faces, or notice the nervous way they tended to cluster into little groups, as if they were trying to make themselves as small and unnoticeable as possible. Lynette thought that the lack of light probably helped them feel more secure. They were running out of candles, so Lynette had told Judson to be sure the majority of the candelabrum trees were placed around Neferet's landing, hoping she would be spotlighted and not take notice of the lack of illumination in the ballroom.

Apparently, Lynette's plan was working. There was just enough light on the crowd so that the women's jewelry flashed, leaving everyone except the Goddess washed in a soft sepia color.

Neferet lifted her arms. Lynette was standing in the corner of the landing behind her, so she couldn't see the Goddess's face, but Neferet's voice broadcasted joy.

"My loyal supplicants, a grateful Goddess stands before you!" Lynette brought her hands up, miming applause. Neferet's servants immediately mimicked her, and the rest of the people followed, though with less enthusiasm.

"Thank you, thank you, how lovely of you!" Neferet said. The applause trailed away and the Goddess continued. "We have been through much together. I want you, my first supplicants, to know that your Goddess will eternally remember that her reign on earth began here, in Tulsa, with you."

Lynette decided not to interrupt with any more applause, especially since it died away so quickly. She'd save it until Neferet's speech was finished, and then cue the finale ovation.

"I would like to show special appreciation for my staff. Judson, Kylee, could you and the rest of the staff come to the front of the ballroom, please?"

That's unexpected, Lynette thought. *She was just supposed to thank her supplicants with a rather long-winded speech, wait for the clock to strike midnight* . . . Lynette glanced at the large clock that hung over the foyer, suspended in its elaborate art deco frame. *Fifteen minutes until midnight. Neferet hadn't said anything about any special recognition. Shit! I hope she wasn't expecting me to have gifts to present to them.*

Stress began to churn Lynette's stomach. *It can't be good that Neferet's gone off script.* Lynette watched the staff members moving forward from their normal stations at the rear of the ballroom. She grimaced. They were so mechanical, with no will left of their own! She didn't like to imagine what the serpents inside of them were doing to the actual people who were still in there.

Lynette repressed a shudder, glancing down to where there should have been a nest of the disgusting things slithering around Neferet's ankles.

They were gone. There wasn't one serpent anywhere around the Goddess.

That's really strange. Maybe she told them to be invisible. But no, Lynette had been within hearing distance of Neferet since they left the penthouse. She hadn't said anything to the creatures.

"Ah, my loyal staff." Neferet was beaming down at the eighteen serpent-possessed people who were standing side by side just below the landing. "How nice you all look in your newly pressed uniforms. Your Goddess is pleased with you."

Lynette was paying only partial attention to what Neferet was saying because she'd found the serpents. They had formed a black circle around the ballroom floor that was undulating slowly around and around.

"I want to acknowledge your obedience. Yes, yes, I understand that because of being possessed by my children, you had no choice but to be obedient," Neferet spoke lovingly to them. "Yet still I acknowledge appreciation of you."

Lynette's stomach heaved. The people in the ballroom hadn't noticed that they were encircled by Neferet's serpents. Yet. The ballroom was too poorly lit, and all of their attention was on Neferet.

"Now, to show my appreciation, I have decided that I would give the eighteen of you the ultimate honor. You know how much I love my children, don't you?"

Each of the eighteen nodded robotically.

"Then you will understand how much I love you as well when I sacrifice each of you to my child resting within." Neferet's voice changed to a singsong rhythm.

Eighteen children I do now set thee free!
Take, eat, each loving sacrifice from me!

Bile rose in Lynette's throat as Neferet's staff began to shriek and writhe. Then their mouths opened, opened, until they could open no more. Until little Kylee, Judson, Tony, and the rest of them exploded in showers of blood and gore, and the enormous emerging serpents consumed each of them, from the inside out.

The ballroom erupted in screams. Neferet seemed to take no notice. She raised her arms and shuddered with pleasure as each of her staff members died. A movement along the walls caught Lynette's shocked gaze. A curtain of pulsing black was pouring down the ballroom's walls, moving toward the circle of serpents.

It's the curtain Neferet created with the sacrifices on the balcony.

Lynette's mind was spinning with panic, but her body had frozen her in place. *Somehow she's called those creatures back to her.*

Arms still raised, Neferet's voice was amplified by a terrible power so that her words echoed, drowning out the chaos and panic below her, and she began another spell:

> *The time has come.*
> *Create for me bedlam.*
> *Death brings me power,*
> *Glut me for the midnight hour.*
> *I lose you now.*
> *My supplicants to you will bow.*
> *Sate yourselves! Feed!*
> *This night fulfill your every need!*

Neferet hurled her arms wide. The horrid creatures she called children became a living noose that closed on the screaming, panicking people, slaughtering them, every single one.

Neferet turned to face Lynette. Waves of energy were flooding the Goddess. Her skin quivered and pulsed with it, as if her body was changing, growing, beneath it. Her eyes glowed a solid emerald green.

Lynette pressed herself against the wall, too terrified to speak.

"Ah, my dear Lynette. I have truly saved the best for last."

"Please! Don't let one of them possess me!" The words exploded from her.

Neferet looked shocked. "Of course I won't let one of my children possess you. That is your greatest fear. I know that. I have known it all along." The Goddess glided closer and closer to her, until she was able to reach out with spider-like fingers and caress Lynette's cheek. "You returned to me. For that I reward you. Your sacrifice will be made to me alone. You will never again be frightened. You will never again have to struggle to rise above what the past has done to you. And, my dear, I will remember you for all of eternity."

Lynette felt a tug along her neck. It wasn't painful. It was oddly pleasant and soothing to her panicked nerves. Then she felt the wet heat of something wash down her body, soaking the beautiful gown

Neferet had given her. Lynette's legs stopped working, and she collapsed, but the Goddess didn't let her fall. Neferet took Lynette in her arms and began to feed from her, and as her world went black, Lynette wept silent, bloody tears.

Neferet

Neferet didn't allow Lynette's body to fall to the floor after she'd drained her dry. Instead she gently lifted her, carefully placed her on the throne, arranging her lifeless limbs and straightening her dress so that anyone who saw her would know that her Goddess honored her sacrifice.

"I will miss you, my dear," Neferet told the corpse, smoothing her hair from her face and kissing her forehead reverently. "You were the first to understand that it is impossible to flee from me. There will be so many others who will come to that understanding after you, but you will always be my first and eternally my favorite." She caressed Lynette's cheek one last time before descending the marble stairs and entering the ballroom.

Dismembered body parts littered the white and black checkered marble, but there was very little blood left to stain the well cared for floor. Her children had done an excellent job, and no wonder. Those of them who had so valiantly covered her Temple with protection had had nothing to eat for days, poor dears. And yet still they had remained where she'd commanded—vigilant, protective, loving.

They will do this thing for me. I know they will. My children love me as I love them.

Neferet stopped in the foyer before the wide brass and crystal-paned door, directly under the beautiful clock that was so artfully suspended from the ceiling.

"Children, come to me," she called. They rushed to her. Bloated and throbbing with power gained from their feast, they filled the foyer, eager to respond to her next command. Neferet knelt, gathering them to her, stroking their familiar, beloved skin, marveling at their strength—at how they truly had become her children.

"I know how to break Thanatos's spell and free us," she told them. Their eyeless faces turned to her, their writhing bodies surrounded her. "But I cannot do it myself. You must help your Goddess, your Mother. Lynette made it clear, the crone Thanatos hasn't the power to hold the spell; even she believes it will eventually break. As you know, my darlings, I am not a patient Goddess. And why should we wait?" She petted those children closest to her fondly as she explained to them, "Well, we needn't wait at all. The White Bull's words inspired me, and I know the answer. He said, *Throughout eternity I have found that the more something is desired, the dearer the sacrifice must be to attain it.* I have never desired anything more than to be free of this imprisonment so that I may reign over this mortal realm as Goddess of Darkness, once and forever to be in complete control of my own destiny. And there is nothing dearer to me than you, my loyal children."

Neferet stood. "So I am going to *ask* you, not *command* you. Will you save me? Will you break this spell and free me? If your answer is yes, not all of you will survive this night, but those of you who do will go with me, first to the betraying House of Night, where we will feast on fledgling, vampyre, and human alike, and then we shall go forth together to rule the mortal realm! Know that:

I swear by my immortality,
beside me you forever shall be.

The air around Neferet rippled with the force of her oath. Her children stilled in their writhing. It was a listening stillness—a waiting stillness—and it filled Neferet with joy.

The Goddess whirled around and faced the doors. "Open them!" she cried.

Her children rushed to obey her, holding wide open the Mayo's double doors so that Neferet could see the quiet, dark night beyond. As she spoke, the power within her began to build, amplifying her words, lifting her hair, skittering under her skin, and pulsing with Dark magick all around her.

P. C. CAST and KRISTIN CAST

I charge you,
oh my children
be my blood
surge forth
to me always true.
I charge you,
oh my children
be my sword
strike forth
with me make the world anew.
I charge you,
oh my children
be my life
carried forth
so that finally, eternally, I receive what to me is due!

Neferet flung her arms wide, and like dark lightning bolts, her children shot forth. The wall of fire flamed, engulfing the first wave of her children. Neferet shrieked her loss as they died. But their deaths did not stop the others. Her children surged forth, battering the flames. Where one burned, another took its place, and though tears washed down Neferet's face, her shrieks of rage and loss turned to cries of victory as slowly, inevitably, the flames burned lower and lower, until finally, with a hiss of ice covering a candle, the protective wall was extinguished.

CHAPTER TWENTY-FIVE

Shaunee

"It's hard to stop thinking about it, isn't it?" Shaunee said, as she and Erik had fallen into another silence while they stared at the spot Grandma Redbird and the other women had covered with sage and lavender—the spot where Kalona had died.

"It was amazing. I know Zoey and the rest of you guys have seen Nyx a bunch of times, but it still has my head spinning."

"Hey, I totally understand. Yeah, I've seen Nyx before, but it's not like I've gotten used to it. I don't think I'll ever get used to it."

"Kalona and Erebus—wow!"

Shaunee nodded, agreeing with him, and happy that he was still so awestruck by what he'd witnessed. She watched him out of the corner of her eye. He'd changed, and she liked the change.

"Thanks for sitting here with me," she said, glancing at the four mounds the human women made in their sleeping bags, and then looking inside the tent at Thanatos, who had gone back into her silent meditation not long after everyone else had left. "It'd be lonely out here by myself if it wasn't for you."

"I'm glad I'm here," Erik said. "I like being with you and—"

Waves of heat and pain slammed through Shaunee, and she doubled over with a terrible cry. *Use me—channel through me—let me strengthen the spell,* Shaunee recited over and over to herself as she rocked back and forth, trying to get control of the heat and the chaos and the pain that had exploded through her.

"It's okay. You can do this, I know you can. Just focus and breathe. Try to relax, just like before," Erik was saying.

"No!" Shaunee gasped. "Different—from—before! Bad." She moaned and fell to her side. "Can't—control."

"Shaunee, listen to me!" Erik's voice had gone from calm to concerned. "You can do this. Fire is your element. Remember that. Focus on that."

Pain flooded Shaunee. It was like she was being torched from within. It was asking too much of her. She had no more to give. Suddenly she realized that, like Cleopatra, she was going to be engulfed by her own element.

Then, as quickly as it had torn through her, it was gone, leaving her gasping, lying in Erik's lap. His arms were around her and, with a hand that trembled, he was smoothing her hair back from her damp forehead, murmuring, "You can do it . . . you can do it . . ."

Grandma Redbird and Sister Mary Angela were kneeling beside him, each holding one of her hands.

"Sweetheart, have you come back to us?" Grandma Redbird asked her.

"Y-yes," Shaunee said. "It's—it's gone. Whatever happened, it's over."

"Shaunee!" Thanatos was standing at the entrance to her tent. Her face was completely white. She was weeping tears of blood. "Neferet has broken the spell. Warn Zoey." Then she collapsed.

Shaunee struggled to get up, to rush to Thanatos. They all did. But before they could reach her, a smoky mist lifted from the ground in front of the High Priestess. The mist rolled like it was bubbling water and then took the form of a woman. She was beautiful and ethereal, but frightening. She held out her hand. Thanatos opened her eyes and took it, smiling beatifically.

And so finally, it is my turn to take your hand, Thanatos said.

Come with me where this world will no longer bind you. I have lifted the burden you have borne for me so long and so well. For you, my beloved daughter, the cares of this realm at last, at last, are over.

Still smiling, Thanatos stepped into the woman's embrace, and both of them turned into smoke and then mist, which drifted slowly down until it was absorbed into the earth.

Sister Mary Angela crossed herself reverently. Shaunee heard her begin to recite the rosary.

"That was Death," Erik said. "She took Thanatos away—all of her!"
Shaunee looked at where the High Priestess's body had been. He was right. Her clothes lay flat and empty on the ground.

"Warn Zoey!" Grandma Redbird shook her shoulders. "Now!"

Shaunee pulled her thoughts together and met Grandma's worried gaze. "I will. We'll stop Neferet. Somehow we will." She grabbed Erik's hand. "Get me to the House of Night, fast!"

"We will pray for you," said Rabbi Bernstein. All the women knelt under the Council Oak circle.

"May you all blessed be!" Grandma Redbird called after them.

Zoey

"Okay, so you each have your assignments," Damien said as we stood and stretched and finally got ready to leave the dining room.

"Yes, Queen Damien, Shaylin and I are going to get with Kramisha and Lenobia. We'll put our Prophetess superpowers together with what Lenobia knows about Neferet's past, and see if we can figure out an Achilles' heel in Crazy Town. *After* I work out," Aphrodite said, and then stuffed another brownie in her face.

"*Before*," I said. "This is more important than your butt."

Aphrodite gave me a look that clearly said *nothing* was more important than her butt. Thankfully, she was too busy chewing to speak.

"I'm going ask Professor P to go to the media center with me to research old myths and legends. Hopefully, we can find something in them that will help us," Damien said.

"Aurox, Rephaim, and I are going to relieve Darius, Detective Marx, and the fledgling Warriors they've recruited to patrol the walls," Stark said.

"And we're going to discuss more about Father's past," Rephaim said.

"I hate that you have to do that," Stevie Rae said.

"He would want me to. He'd want anything that would help us stop Neferet," Rephaim said.

"And Stevie Rae and I are going to Skype Sgiach. Again." I lifted the yellow pad Aphrodite had given me. "Yes, I have the questions we all came up with to ask her."

"Excellent," Damien said, and I thought, not for the first time, that he was going to make a really good professor someday.

"It's a few minutes after midnight," I said. "Let's meet back here about four thirty–ish. That'll give us a chance to talk about what we've learned and have dinner before sunrise."

"Okay, see you in a few—" Stark said, bending to give me a good-bye kiss, when Nicole burst into the room, followed by Shaunee and Erik.

"Thanatos is dead—the spell is broken—Neferet is free!" Shaunee said, gasping for breath.

"What happened? Are you okay?" I asked as Stark and Erik helped her to sit.

"I'll be fine. And all I know about what happened is that a lot of something big and bad hit the wall at the same time. Fire couldn't handle it. The force of it killed Thanatos." Shaunee gulped the wine Aphrodite handed her.

"It almost killed Shaunee, too," Erik said.

Marx and Darius ran into the room. "It's Neferet. She's loose and heading this way," Darius said.

"I'm getting reports from the uniforms at the barricades. She's taking them all out," Marx said.

Inside of me, everything got calm. My thoughts were clear and focused. "Damien, Shaunee, Shaylin, Stevie Rae—come with me," I said.

"You're not going anywhere without me," Stark said. "And why the hell aren't we all staying here? At least there are walls around us."

"A wall won't protect us against Neferet. She'll go right over it. She'll kill everyone, starting with that big group of humans who came to us for protection," I told him. "No, we're not staying here. But yes, you are coming with me. So are you, Rephaim, and you, Aurox."

"You're out of your fucking mind if you think I'm staying here," Aphrodite said.

"You have to. If she gets past us, you and Darius and Marx have got to get the people out of here. Go to the Benedictine abbey. Hide in the tunnels. She'll be less powerful down there. Call the High Council.

Call Sgiach. Hell, start calling *all the House of Nights in the world.* If we can't stop Neferet, she's not just going to be Tulsa's problem. She's going to be the whole world's problem," I said, walking over to Aphrodite. I hugged her and she hugged me back. "Pray that Nyx helps us find a way to stop Neferet," I whispered to her.

Aphrodite took me by the shoulders and met my gaze. In a firm, loud voice she said, "I'm going to pray that you're as smart and strong as I've thought you were since the first day I met you. You can stop her. I know you can. Just believe in yourself."

"And us," Stevie Rae said. She and the rest of my circle were standing by the door. "Believe in all of us, Z. We won't let you down."

"Then let's go," I said. "Let's stop her for good."

"Where are we going?" Stark asked.

"To Woodward Park." I looked at Marx. "Get on your radio. Tell your men to pull back. And tell them while they're getting out of her way they need to shout to each other that Zoey and her vampyres are circling in the park, waiting to trap her."

"She'll come straight to you," Marx said.

"That's the plan," I said.

"Blessed be," Darius said.

"Merry meet, merry part, and we *will* merry meet again," I said. And then we sprinted to the parking lot and piled into the Hummer.

It only took a few minutes to get to Woodward Park. "Drive the Hummer over by the ridge, the one that faces downtown." As I gave Stark direction, I had a burst of realization. *Holy crap! That might be it!*

"Isn't that where you thought you killed those men?" Stark said.

"Yes!" Get us there, fast!"

Stark barreled over the curb and floored the Hummer, fishtailing to a stop under a blackened oak. We all rushed out of the vehicle.

"Okay, listen guys," I said. "I have a plan—it's a small one, but at least it's something. At the base of the ridge is the grotto Neferet hid in before she killed the two men I thought I'd killed."

"Want us to circle around it, Z?" Stevie Rae asked.

"No. I'm going to stand at the top of those stone stairs, right over there." I pointed. There was only one streetlight working in the park—the place had been pretty messed up by the fire the lightning had caused.

But that one light was enough for us to see the stone path that led between clumps of scorched azaleas and emptied into wide, rough stairs descending to street level and the grotto. "Get your direction set, fast."

"North's that way!" Stevie Rae pointed in front of us.

"The rest of you have your positions from there?"

Air, Fire, and Water nodded. "Okay, spread out. Call your elements to you. I'm not going to cast a circle, not until she's close enough to be caught inside it."

"You mean caught inside the grotto," Aurox said.

I nodded.

"Our crystal cave," Damien said.

"How are we gonna keep her in there once we manage to smush her inside?" Stevie Rae asked.

"Old Magick," I said, with lots more confidence than I felt.

"How are we going to get her close enough to the grotto?" Stark asked, watching me closely.

"Well, her Achilles' heel is going to stand at the top of the stairs and talk crap to her until she's pissed enough to get close," I said.

"You're Neferet's Achilles' heel," Damien said.

"Yep," I said. "She's gone after me since I was Marked. She's gonna keep going after me."

"I don't like you being bait," Stark said.

"Then keep me safe until she's close enough for me to cast a circle around her," I told him.

"She'll have to go through me to get you," Stark said.

"And me," Aurox said.

"Thank you," I told them. "I believe in both of you." I turned to Stevie Rae and Rephaim. "Rephaim, keep Stevie Rae safe. We're going to be trapping Neferet inside the earth—that means Stevie Rae's element is going to be the key to this."

Rephaim nodded. "I'll always keep her safe."

"Damien, Shaunee, Shaylin—get your elements to conceal you until I let you know you can call them to the circle. The three of you will be the least protected of all of us."

Damien took Shaunee and Shaylin's hands. "We understand. And we won't let you down."

I went to Shaunee and took her hand. Stevie Rae joined me, completing our circle. "I love you. All of you. No matter what happens to me, if our circle breaks, get the hell out of here. Go to our tunnels under the depot. Stevie Rae, get them there. Use earth to seal yourselves in until you can regroup."

"Not without—" Stevie Rae began.

"No!" my voice was filled with power, making the four of them jerk in surprise. "You have to listen to me. If the circle breaks, I'll be like Thanatos. It's my circle, my spell. It'll kill me." As I said it, I knew it was true. My gaze found Aurox. "If I'm dead, protect them."

Aurox said nothing, he only nodded once.

My eyes met my Stark's. "If you're still alive, help Aurox get them to safety."

"I will, my High Priestess, my Queen, and then I will follow you to the Otherworld," Stark said, bowing somberly to me.

"At least this time you'll know where to find me." I smiled at him. "At the entrance, under the wishing tree. I'll wait for you."

A shrill scream sounded in the distance.

"Neferet's coming," I said. "I'm your center. Circle around me, but hide! Now! And may all of you blessed be."

My circle scattered north, south, east, and west, leaving me alone with Aurox and Stark. I took the Seer Stone out from under my T-shirt and pulled the thin platinum chain over my head. Holding it securely in my hand, I looked from Stark to Aurox. "If this thing starts to change me, kill me before I'm like her."

"It will be as you say," Aurox said.

Stark looked pale, but he nodded. "I won't let it make a monster of you."

"Thank you," I said. "And now let's stop this bitch before she hurts anyone else we love."

Stark and Aurox followed me as I walked quickly down the stone path. I felt a weird sense of déjà vu. Had it only been a few days ago that I'd stomped down this path, pissed at the world? It seemed a century ago, and I seemed a totally different person.

I am a different person. What happened here changed me. What happened here made me grow up. I realized.

I came to the top of the wide stone stairs and stopped. Pointing down over the lip of the ridge, I said, "There, see it? Inside that rounded stone area over there is the grotto. That's where we're going to trap her."

We heard another scream, this one closer to the park.

"I'm going down." Aurox pointed. "I'll hide behind the stones at the base of the stairs. Neferet will expect to see Stark. She won't be looking for me." He looked at Stark. "I'm going to change. If I lose control and turn on any of you, do whatever you have to, but stop me."

"Aurox, you will not lose control." Words whispered through my mind and I repeated them aloud. My voice didn't even sound like my own—it was older, wiser, stronger, and utterly filled with love. "Your bull has changed. It is no longer a creature of Darkness. Your Old Magick is now that of Light."

"Who are you? How do you know this?"

The whispers left me, and in my own voice, I said, "Well, I'm a Priestess of your Goddess. She tells me things. This time she also told you."

"It will have all been worth it if that is true," Aurox said.

"Then it's been worth it, because our Goddess never lies," I said.

Stark extended his hand to Aurox. "Good luck. I'm glad you're here with us in the end. It's only right that you help me protect Zoey."

Aurox grasped his forearm. "When this is over, I'd like it if we could share a beer, or six."

Stark grinned. "It's a deal."

"Great," I said, shaking my head at them both. "Death—destruction— our Goddess speaking—and you guys want beer."

"Not right now, Zo. Afterward," Aurox said in Heath-speak, and then he went down the stairs, taking them three at a time.

I turned to Stark, but before I could say anything he pulled me into his arms and kissed me. "Just live," he said when he finally released me.

"I will if you will," I said.

"It's a deal," he repeated.

Then a movement over his shoulder caught my eye. Under the streetlight at the Twenty-first and Peoria Street intersection, tendrils of Darkness swarmed.

"She's here," I said. I gripped my Seer Stone, thinking . . . thinking . . .

And then I knew—at least part of what I needed to do. "It has to be like on Skye. The Fey are attached to Old Magick!"

"What can I do to help you?"

"I need something sharp."

"No worries. I got this handled." Stark sprinted to the Hummer, yanking open the door and taking out the duffel bag full of arrows he'd brought. Then he was running to me. He paused and took one of his arrows from the bag. "Be careful. It's real sharp." He kissed me quickly, pulled his bow from his back, and took a position three stairs down from me. He smiled grimly and said, "I can't kill her, but I sure as hell can hurt her."

"She's vain. Remember that. Aim for her face," I said. "That'll really piss her off."

Then all my attention was focused on her tendrils of Darkness. They were swarming into the park, like black oil spilling over the ocean's surface. In the center of them, being carried forward with their tide of evil, was Neferet.

I shouldn't have been surprised that she'd changed. We'd all changed since the last time I'd seen her. I just hadn't expected that the madness inside of her would eventually seep out so visibly.

Neferet was bigger than she had been before. Her arms and legs were out of proportion with the rest of her. They had elongated, especially her fingers. They moved continuously, restlessly, as if she couldn't keep herself still.

A spider! Oh, Goddess, she reminds me of a spider!

"Spirit, come to me," I said before fear overwhelmed me. Instantly, I felt the infilling of my favorite element, soothing my nerves, calming my fear.

Nyx, I'll do the rest if you just please help me to be wise and strong.

The Goddess's voice washed through my mind along with spirit, filling me and chasing away the last of my fear. *You have my blessing, Zoey Redbird. Remember, love is the strongest of them all . . .*

Confidently, I stepped to the edge of the stone stairs.

"Neferet! It's Zoey Redbird. I'm here because I've had enough of your bullshit. Your killing time is over. Now."

Neferet's emerald gaze focused on me right away. Her smile was reptilian. "Don't you mean you've had enough of my *bullpoopie,* you vapid, ridiculous child?"

"Actually, no," I said. "Unlike you, I mean what I say. Bullshit it is because bullshit you are."

"How very grown-up of you," she sneered. "And what a lovely surprise it is to find you so quickly and easily. I thought I'd have to pry you from the middle of your circle after each of your friends willingly and stupidly sacrificed themselves for you."

"Well, Neferet, you are wrong. Again."

While she laughed at me and glided over the sidewalk and into the park, I drew a deep breath.

I can do this. I know that there is Old Magick in Tulsa, and where there is the most ancient of magicks, there is also the Fey.

I lifted the Seer Stone, and thinking about what Sgiach had taught me, as well as what Nyx had reminded me of, I sliced the arrowhead across my palm. I cupped my hand, welling the blood, then lifted my Seer Stone, saying, "Sprites of spirit! Come to me!" I blew a big puff of breath over my palm, shooting a cascade of blood at the Seer Stone. As if the blood were caught in a vortex, it swept through the center of the stone, and as it came out the other side there was an explosion of bright purple light.

I smiled at the sprites. "Thank you for hearing me. I ask one thing of the Fey. Shed your Light into that Darkness." I pointed at the nest of writhing creatures surrounding Neferet.

The sprites shot away from me. Seconds later purple lights exploded all around Neferet, sending blood and gore skyward.

"No!" Neferet screamed. With her unnaturally distended fingers, she caressed the wounded creatures that slithered back to her, murmuring to them as if they really were her children. Then she straightened. Her anger blazed at me. "You will be sorry you did that!" Neferet began gliding forward, commanding, "Finally, *finally,* kill Zoey Redbird!"

CHAPTER TWENTY-SIX

Zoey

Neferet's command released total chaos. Threads of Darkness moved in a wave of teeth and writhing, muscular bodies toward the stone stairs.

There was a deafening roar, and Aurox rushed from behind the rocks that had been concealing him. He didn't hesitate. He charged straight into the thick of them, goring with his horns, tearing and stomping with his cloven hooves.

He was as terrifying as he was magnificent.

"The betrayer vessel!" Neferet shrieked at him. "Broken! You will forever be broken!"

Unable to speak, Aurox's only response was a roar, as he kept spreading carnage around him.

It was hard for me to look away from him. As I stared I realized that he, too, had changed.

"His horns," I shouted to Stark. "They aren't that sickening white anymore!"

"No," Stark said. "They're black, like Nyx's night."

"And like the *other* bull. The good one."

"Stay sharp, Z. Good bull or not, they're getting past him," Stark told me. "Watch Neferet. The second she's close enough, get that circle cast." Then Stark raised his bow and said, "Kill those bastards of Darkness!"

Arrows rained down on them, all around Aurox. But Stark's aim was true. The bull was not pierced by them, though tendrils of Darkness all around him were skewered to the ground.

"More!" Neferet called into the night. "I need more of my children!"

It seemed that the shadows vomited Darkness. The things swarmed from everywhere.

And still Neferet wasn't close enough.

"Her face! Do it!" I told him.

"Strike Neferet's vanity," Stark commanded as he pulled his bow taut and let fly two arrows at once.

Both sailed in a beautiful arch, falling in perfect timing with one another. Together they sliced her cheeks, scoring bloody, gaping wounds through her sapphire tattoos.

Screaming over and over, Neferet staggered, holding her face in her hands, trying to keep the skin on her cheeks from flapping open.

I'd thought wounding her would at least confuse her tendrils of Darkness, make them pause if she was unable to call out commands.

I'd been wrong.

Wounding her worked on them like spurs on a horse. Suddenly they were everywhere, and Aurox's roar was no longer one of challenge but of pain.

"Zoey! Get back to the Hummer! Lock yourself in!" Stark yelled at me as he shot his last arrow. "I'll follow you!"

"I'm not going anywhere," I said.

He looked up at me and smiled grimly. "Then neither am I." Stark planted his feet wide and held his fists up, ready to battle the tendrils with his bare hands.

Instantly, a longsword materialized before him, glistening with deadly beauty.

Stark's hand closed around the Guardian Sword's hilt, and with a triumphant shout, he began slicing through the tendrils of Darkness that dared try to get past him.

And still Neferet wasn't close enough.

Grimly, I slashed the arrowhead across my other palm. This time deeper, causing my blood to rush into my hand. I held up the Seer Stone. "Sprites of air, fire, water, and earth—come to me!" I blew my blood through the center of the stone, and Fey appeared all around me in the forms of birds and fairies, merefolk and forest nymphs. "No matter the cost, I'll pay it. Just get me to Neferet."

The cost will be
Your true love from thee

I had no choice. Either Stark dies or the world as I know it dies. "You have my oath. I agree!" I said, promising silently to myself, *When this is over, I'll follow Stark. I'll know where to find him. Under the wishing tree . . .*

The Fey bowed their glowing heads briefly in acknowledgment of my oath, then they formed a circle around me.

Go to the Dark Goddess.

I did as they commanded, moving past Stark.

"Zoey? What the hell?"

"Stay there, Stark! Keep fighting them. I'm going to her." I couldn't look at Stark. I knew he wouldn't listen to me. I knew he wouldn't stay up on the stairs where he had a chance against the tendrils. "James Stark, I will always love you!" I shouted.

Then I ran. The Fey surrounded me and moved with me, a solid shield of ancient power, repelling any tendril that approached them. I circled around behind Neferet. And then, using my Fey shield as a battering ram, I hurled myself at her.

The Fey hit her from behind. Blinded by blood and pain, she didn't see us coming. I knocked her toward the grotto. One step, then another.

Hissing at me like she was a cobra, she whirled around and her terrible, long fingers sliced through the Fey closest to her.

It was a water Fey, a mermaid, and the beautiful blue sprite gave a horrible, inhumane shriek of pain and dissolved into the ground.

I gritted my teeth and took another step toward her.

"You little bitch! That is you inside there. Do you think Old Magick will stop me from killing you? *I truly command Old Magick! A mortal cannot defeat me!*"

She struck again, and a fire sprite exploded.

I battered her back another step, and she hacked through a Fey in the shape of a graceful heron.

With only a forest nymph between Neferet and me, I ran at her. Neferet raked her talons through the Fey, who screamed and disappeared, but the dark Goddess was off balance from the uneven Oklahoma sandstones beneath her feet, and she fell.

Finally! Close enough!

"Damien, where are you?" I cried.

"Here!" His head popped up from behind a clump of azaleas to my left. "Air, I call you to our circle!" I shouted, and wind rushed around us.

"I'm here!" Shaunee yelled, stepping out from behind a fire-blackened tree.

"Fire, I call you to our circle!" I felt the heat of her element.

"Children! Stop her! Kill her!" Neferet commanded.

I stood my ground, even as I felt a tendril of Darkness slice into my leg. "Shaylin!"

"Right here!" She jumped and waved from the top of the ridge to my right.

"Water, I call you to our circle!"

"Stevie Rae!" I cried, as I grabbed a snake-creature as it shot toward my throat and bashed it against a rock.

"I'm right behind you, Z, and I got your back!"

I turned. Rephaim's sword sang in an arc around us, while I called, "Earth, I call you to our circle!" I breathed in the scents of a meadow as I completed my casting by calling, "Spirit, I call you to our circle!"

A wide silver ribbon of light crackled into being, connecting the five of us and completely encircling Neferet.

"Do you think a circle will hold me?" Neferet was on her hands and knees. Her face was bloody but already healing. She looked at me and laughed. "You've just made this easier. I destroy this circle, I destroy you. Come to me, children! All of you come to me!"

Her creatures obeyed her. They slithered from all the shadows within the park, a dark tide rising around her.

I ignored her and the creatures she called to execute me. I raised my arms. "Air, fire, water, earth, and spirit—hear me! I am Zoey Redbird. My ancestors danced beneath the sky, evoking you in the name of the Great Earth Mother, in respect and love, themselves caretakers of this land, keepers of the mortal realm's balance of Light and Darkness. Tonight I invoke your aid as a daughter of those ancient caretakers. This Tsi Sgili and her creatures defile us all and create unbalance.

So as the Wise Women before me did, I beg of you, Great Earth Mother and the powers of Old Magick, entrap Neferet and her children!" Imagining myself as a fountain and the elements as streams of power shooting up from the bowels of the earth and through me, I threw air, fire, water, earth, and spirit at Neferet.

The silver ribbon that connected me to the circle rushed from me, closing like a noose around Neferet and her tendrils of Darkness, and drawing them back, together, into the open mouth of the grotto.

"Stevie Rae, help me!" Instantly, she was at my side, taking my hand.

"Earth," she commanded, "close 'em in!" A green glow lit up the rocks all around the grotto. The earth beneath our feet began to shake, harder and harder, until the stones fell free, avalanching to seal the mouth of the grotto.

The silence that followed was incredible. I felt wobbly. My knees were weak. Stevie Rae and I were still holding hands.

"Stark!" I called. "Where are you?" My eyes were already beginning to tear. I knew he wouldn't answer. I staggered, and Aurox caught me.

He was a boy again, bloody but alive.

"Take it easy," he said as he and Stevie Rae helped me sit down. "Everything's going to be okay."

No, nothing is going to be okay.

"Take a few deep breaths, and before you close the circle, borrow some energy from spirit," Aurox said.

I nodded numbly, staring at the silver ribbon that still circled me.

"Z! We did it!" Damien cried as he hurried up to us.

"That was super scary," Shaylin said.

"But awesome," Shaunee agreed.

They were all around me—all of my circle. And we had done it. We'd trapped Neferet. I was the only one who knew the cost, though.

"Yeah, it was awesome, but painful," he said.

I looked up, and through my tears saw Stark. He was standing there, smiling down at me. He had a bunch of cuts on his arms and legs, and he was bleeding like crazy, but *he was alive!*

"Stark! Ohmygoddess!" I was in the process of hurling myself into his arms when the mound of rocks that were supposed to be coaling Neferet inside the grotto began to move.

"Oh, shit!" Stark said. "The tendrils—they're boring holes through the rocks."

I stood, in the center of my circle, and raised my hands again. I noticed there was blood all over them. I didn't care. Stark was alive!

The cost will be

Your true love from thee

The Feys' voices echoed in my mind, and I realized why Stark was alive.

They hadn't meant they were taking Stark away from me. They'd meant *I* was going. It was my turn. This time I had to love my friends and my world enough that I would be the sacrifice that would make it right. I had to exchange my life for entombing Neferet.

"You promised to be sure they're safe," I said to Stark.

He narrowed his eyes. "Z, what are you up to?"

I drew a deep breath, readying myself. I lifted my Seer Stone and started walking forward. *Grandma said it. Sgiach said it. And, most important, Nyx said it. My blood is special. There's ancient power in it, living in the modern world. And I'm going to use my blood to seal that tomb.*

"It won't work." Aurox was suddenly there in front of me, blocking my path.

"Get out of my way," I told him. "And keep Stark out of my way. I know what I'm doing. You were right. Everything is going to be okay."

"No, Zoey. You're strong and wise, but you're wrong about this. You aren't an immortal. No matter what you do. No matter what you're willing to sacrifice, you don't have enough power to hold her. But I do. I was created from Old Magick as a tool of Darkness."

"But you chose Light. You changed."

"Because Heath's spirit within me gave me a choice. I'm making that choice now, out of love. Not just for you, Zo, but for all of you. This is the right thing to do. I know I'm right. Zo, make Stark take care of Skylar for me, 'kay?" He smiled, and I saw Heath within his moonstone eyes. "Oh, and remember the two things I wanted? Got one of them tonight. Nyx spoke to me through you." He reached out and took the Seer Stone from me, putting it over his head so that it dangled, flashing silver, in the middle of his chest. "I am the Old Magick you had to wield."

"And what about the second thing you wanted? What about the girl?" I asked, my eyes filling with tears.

"Next time around, Zo. How 'bout you and me, we make a date for my next time around. 'Cause it's true. The one thing that never dies is love, always love!"

Then Heath disappeared within Aurox's sweet, serious eyes. He turned, lowered his head, and roared an ancient challenge. As Aurox charged the grotto, his body convulsed, shifted, and changed so that by the time he reached the stones and the tendrils that were trying to slither free, he had taken the form of a powerful, beautiful black bull. He gored the rocks, and his body changed again, expanding into a huge black shield that folded over the grotto, closing it, sealing Neferet forever within.

There was a terrible rumbling that became a deafening thunder, coming from the east and the west.

"What is it?" Stark yelled.

I started to say I didn't know, and then I saw the shadow. It spread from the east—an enormous black cloud, taking shape as it grew—horns, mighty chest, and cloven hooves.

"The west! Look to the west!" Shaunee cried.

My gaze went there, and I saw the twin of the other bull taking form, only this one was the white of frost, of death, of the grave.

The two bulls met in the sky above us with a crash that had us covering our ears, even though the sound couldn't be muffled. Pain flashed through my forehead, and I heard my friends cry out with me. I fell to the ground, feeling like my head was going to explode. Stark was holding me. I looked around wildly, and I could see that Rephaim had gone to Shaylin, and Stevie Rae was rushing from Damien to Shaunee. All of them were collapsed in pain with me.

What was happening to us? Ohmygoddess, what now?

Just when I thought I couldn't stand any more pain, the sky flashed with a blinding light, and both bulls disappeared together, taking with them the terrible agony in my head.

Shakily, I sat up.

"Z, are you okay? What happened—" His smile interrupted his words. "Oh, *that's* what happened!"

I frowned. What was he talking about? I rubbed my face. Man, my forehead hurt.

"Ohmygoddess! That's the coolest thing I've ever seen!" Stevie Rae practically squealed.

Still confused, I glanced over to where she was, kneeling beside Shaunee. Shaunee looked as dazed as I felt. Blinking, she turned her head to me—and I understood.

My gaze went from her to Damien and from Damien to Shaylin.

"All of them!" I said. "They all made the Change!"

"All of *you*. You all Changed, Z. Even you!" Stark reached forward and traced a delicate filigree pattern that now spread down around my cheekbones—a *real* Mark for a *real* vampyre.

I looked up, through eyes filled and overflowing with grateful tears, and saw the moon shinning full and glorious down on us.

"Thank you, Nyx. Oh, thank you so much!" I called to the moon.

Zoey Redbird, may you and your faithful friends, eternally blessed be . . .

THE END. REALLY.

AFTERWARD . . .

Nyx giggled. "May I look now?"

Kalona thought she sounded like a carefree young maiden who was incredibly, eternally alluring. He grinned but managed to keep his voice stern, saying, "Not quite yet, Goddess."

"But I want to see what you've been up to!" Nyx said.

"It wouldn't be a surprise if you knew what *we've* been up to."

"Erebus, what are you doing here?" Kalona growled at him.

"I'm not letting you take all the credit for this. It was, after all, me who found the thing ages ago and kept it here, safe, waiting for your return," Erebus said, laughing at his brother's thundercloud look.

"That's it! I simply must look!"

Before the Goddess could open her eyes, Kalona turned her so that she was facing the Otherworld's most lovely lake. He was standing behind her, holding her smooth shoulders in his hands, when she gasped and clapped in delight.

"My boat! The one you carved for me so long ago!" She turned and threw her arms around Kalona, laughing and kissing him. "Thank you!"

Erebus cleared his throat. "What about me?"

Nyx opened one arm, inviting Erebus to share her embrace. "Thank you, too, Erebus, for your unwavering faith in our Kalona."

"Ah, it was nothing," Erebus said, hugging both of them.

Kalona returned his embrace before shoving him teasingly. "Nothing? Maybe for you it was nothing, but I have spent days restoring what centuries of neglect caused."

"Yes, well, when you put it like that, I can say that I know *exactly* what you mean," Erebus said, shoving his brother back good-naturedly.

"Well, I love my surprise," Nyx said, going to the little boat and running her hands appreciatively over the carvings of flowers and stars and moons and other symbols that Kalona had long ago created in remembrance of her. "And you found a pelt and a picnic basket! That does make this gift perfect."

"I found them," Kalona said. Then he glanced at his brother and smiled. "But Erebus suggested the nectar instead of wine, and he went to the mortal realm to gather it for you."

"I gathered it for both of you," Erebus said, returning his brother's smile. "And now I will leave you to your boating. I bribed the naiads to stay away from this lake for the evening, and I have to make yet another trip to the mortal realm to fulfill that bribe." He kissed Nyx gently on the cheek, saluted his brother, and disappeared in an explosion of golden glitter.

Kalona coughed and shook glitter from his hair. "I wish he would stop doing that."

Nyx unsuccessfully hid a giggle behind her hand. "I think the dust of sunlight looks lovely on you."

Kalona went to his Goddess and took her into his arms. "If you like it, I shall ask Erebus to explode more often." He stifled her laughter with a kiss, and then picked Nyx up and gently placed her in the boat on the soft, thick pelt. He pushed the little boat into the lake and then joined his Goddess within, paddling lazily over the shimmering turquoise waters.

"If you would like, we could go back to the lake you loved so well," he said. "Though I would have to ask that you call the elements to conceal us. I visited there earlier. Did you know it is now called Crater Lake, and humans flock to it?"

"I did," Nyx said, letting her fingers trail over the surface of the lake. "I visited there often when you were no longer here." Her eyes met his, and within them he could see a great sadness. "I hoped that someday I might see you there, though I never did."

Kalona put the paddle down and took her hands in his. "It will never happen again. I vow that I have banished my jealousy and anger. I will never make the mistake of listening to those base emotions again and letting Darkness come between us." He kissed each of her hands, slowly, reverently, willing the sadness to leave her beautiful eyes.

"The mistake was not yours alone, my Warrior, my love," she said. "I, too, was at fault. I was so young, so inexperienced. I allowed a secret to come between us."

"A secret? What do you mean?" Kalona's stomach tightened. *What could Nyx have been keeping secret from him?*

"That night, that terrible night that you found me with Erebus. You misunderstood my words to him. I never spoke of it afterward, and I should have, if only to assure you that your brother and I were not betraying you."

"No, we all vowed silence because of what happened that night. It was right to keep that vow," Kalona said, feeling a measure of relief. "And then I wouldn't have listened to you. Then I could only hear jealousy."

"Well, I was wrong to make you and Erebus vow silence, but I do think what we created that night turned out rather well, even if we have been unable to speak of it."

Kalona met her eyes. "Your children the vampyres are remarkable and unusual, and I admit that I have become very fond of them."

"Do you not mean *our* children the vampyres? We both had a hand in their creation."

"I kept my vow, Nyx. I never spoke of it to them, or to any living being," Kalona said.

"I know." Nyx leaned forward and kissed him. "You did not break that vow, even when you were filled with Darkness and rage. That was when I first began to hope that you would find yourself and your way back to me."

"I will never lose my way again."

Nyx went into his arms, resting in complete contentment within the circle of his love and strength.

"I do miss them, though. Our vampyres," he said. "And, of course, my son."

She smiled up at him. "You should visit Rephaim."

Kalona blinked in surprise. "You would not mind it?"

"Of course not! He is your son, mated to a special favorite of mine." Kalona held his Goddess tightly. "I forget that you have never trafficked with jealousy and hatred."

"Nor will I ever, my love," Nyx said. Then her serious expression brightened. "Shall we look in on them, our children?"

"Now?" Kalona's gaze took in the boat, the lazy lake, and the beautiful Goddess.

She smiled. "Yes, now. But we can do so without disrupting your surprise for me." Nyx changed position so that, even though she still rested within the circle of his arms, her back was against his chest. He peered over her shoulder as she leaned over the lip of the boat and waved her hand over the waters of the Otherworld lake.

Magickal lake I call on your crystal might
open to me, bringing what I seek to light.

My wish is to see those who we hold dear
Though far away, I would they were near.

From across the veil of time and space,
Show us our children in their mortal place.

The waters swirled gently, rippling as if Nyx had skipped a stone over the surface of the lake, then they went still and perfectly glasslike. Like the magickal equivalent of a mortal television screen, a scene was being played out before them, in full color and with sound.

"It's Zoey and Stark and Grandma Redbird!" Kalona said. "They're all backstage of the auditorium at the House of Night."

"Shhh, my love," Nyx said softly. "Let us watch without intruding upon them."

"What is Zoey Redbird up to now?" Kalona whispered to his Goddess.

Nyx's shoulders shook in silent laughter. Kalona wrapped his arms more tightly around her and watched, admitting silently to himself how eager he was for news of those whom he had come to think of as his family.

Zoey

"I'm nervous. Ugh, and my stomach's upset," I said, trying not to pick at my fingernails. "Do I look okay? Maybe I should change into jeans. This dress is kinda over the top." I looked down at myself and picked a long orangy-cream hair from my über-dressy dress and glared at the big orange and cream cat who was attempting to look innocent as he purred and rubbed against Stark's legs. "Skylar, you're not fooling me. You're shedding on purpose."

"You look gorgeous, Z. Don't change. Again. You don't have time anyway. And Skylar has long hair—he can't help it that he sheds. A lot," Stark said, and bent to tickle the big cat on the top of his head. Nala padded delicately into the room, sneezed at Skylar, and then, belly swaying, my fat cat took off. Looking very kitten-like, Skylar chased happily after her.

"He's really growing on me," Stark said, smiling after the cat. "And he's not as mean as he used to be."

"Well, don't tell Duchess. Her nose is still bleeding from where he smacked her the other night."

"She's gotta learn to leave him alone. His new collar does say KNOWN BITER." Stark was trying to sound nonchalant, but I noticed that even he was fidgeting with the kilt he'd chosen to wear.

"I think your legs might be better than mine," I said only half jokingly.

"Do not tell your Rooster that, *u-we-tsi-a-ge-ya*. He already struts enough," Grandma teased, patting Stark's cheek fondly. She came to me and smoothed the low, heart-shaped neckline of the crimson velvet dress I'd let Aphrodite talk me into wearing. Then she brushed off another cat hair from the silver embroidered image of the Goddess with her hands raised cupping a crescent moon that rested over my heart. "There, that is the last of Skylar's shedding. And you look absolutely lovely, Zoeybird. This dress becomes the first High Priestess of the new North American High Council."

High Priestess of the North American High Council—when would my stomach stop clenching whenever I heard my now title?

As if reading my mind, Grandma took my face in her hands. "Your title will rest easily with you when you rest easily with yourself. I believe that will happen after you complete what you must today."

"Yeah, Z. You know what you need to do. The sooner you get it over with, the better," Stark said.

I met his eyes, looking for signs of jealousy or anger, and I saw none. All I saw was love and trust. I drew a deep breath. "You're right. You're both right. Let's stop wasting time. It's not going to be that bad."

"Bad, Z? Are you kidding? It's going to be great! Hey, remember— the world is a small place. We're not losing anyone. They're just going to fledge." Stark chuckled and gave me his cute cocky smile. "Get it? *Fledge.*"

I shook my head but managed not to roll my eyes at him. "I get it."

"Zoeybird, you must not think of this as the end of something. Think of it as the beginning of a grand adventure for all of you," Grandma said.

"Okay, yeah, you're right, Grandma. And anyway, we're going to circle one more time before everyone takes off. Let's do this." With Stark on one side of me, and Grandma on the other, I walked out onto the auditorium's stage.

The auditorium was packed, and I could see people standing all along the rear and side walls.

"Where did they all come from?" I whispered to Stark, trying not to move my lips.

"Uh, Z, your mic is on," Stevie Rae's voice lifted from somewhere near the front of the auditorium.

"Ah, hell," I whispered. And then pressed my lips together as my *ah, hell* echoed out over the crowd. Laugher rippled back to me, but it didn't feel mean-spirited. It felt friendly. I blinked, and as my eyes accustomed themselves to the gaslights in the auditorium, I saw that yes, the crowd was, indeed, huge, but it was also smiling up at me. I searched the faces until I found a curly blond head next to another blonde whose hair was long and straight and almost impossibly perfect. I met Aphrodite's gaze. She lifted a blond brow and nodded at me. Then I met Stevie Rae's sparkling blue eyes. She gave me a big smile and a thumbs-up. I let out the breath I'd been holding, cleared my throat, and began.

"I want to thank all of you for coming tonight for this swearing in of the North American Vampyre High Council, especially the humans who are here and who have become such good friends of this House of Night." Detective Marx was easy to find in the crowd—he was taller than almost everyone else. I smiled at him and he tipped an imaginary hat to me. I liked that a half dozen or so uniformed officers had accompanied him, and made a mental note to remember to buy a bunch of tickets to the next TPD fund-raising event. "Today we're going to do something that has never before been done in vampyre society. We're going to make a new beginning of our own, and we're going to include humans in that beginning."

I paused when spontaneous applause broke out, so surprised that I could feel my cheeks get warm.

"So, well, I'm going to start by calling up to the stage the six new members of our High Council." I met her eyes and began with my BFF. "Stevie Rae!"

There were a bunch of *whoohoos* accompanied by arm pumps coming from the seats behind Stevie Rae. I grinned, realizing her family had made the drive up from Henrietta. Stevie Rae kissed Rephaim quickly, then hurried to the stage.

"Aphrodite!"

All of the Sons of Erebus Warriors, led by Darius, stood and applauded loudly as Aphrodite flipped by her hair and gracefully came up to the stage.

"Shaunee!"

"That is right! Good job, Shaunee!" Detective Marx called, as he and the other TPD members, along with Erik Night all cheered and whistled.

"Shaylin!"

I was happy to see that Erik had stood and high-fived her as she walked past him—after Nicole kissed her smack on the lips.

"Lenobia!"

A big cowboy whooped and waved his appropriately white hat as the Horse Mistress, looking ethereally beautiful, made her way to the stage.

"And the last name I call is the first male to be a member of any vampyre High Council. Damien!" I said. And I joined the clapping and cheering as Damien, blushing but smiling, smoothed his impeccably tailored shirt, hugged Adam Paluka, and hurried to join us.

My friends spread out on either side of me, all looking to me for what was to come next. I swallowed my nerves and sat. They followed my lead, taking the seats waiting for them.

Okay, it wasn't like the Vampyre High Council that still reigned in Europe from San Clemente Island. We didn't have stone thrones and big rules about how everyone in the crowd had to act. Nor did we exclude humans from our auditorium/High Council Chamber. Right up front we'd decided to do things way differently here. To start with, we'd decided that our "thrones" would be stools with comfy padded seats that were decorated in the school's plaid of purple, blue, and green on a black background. As I perched on mine, I continued the ceremony.

"Now I want to call to the stage our Vampyre poet laureate, Kramisha, who is also a Prophetess of Nyx. She is going to swear us in as your new High Council. Kramisha, come on up!"

The red fledglings all cheered super loud as Kramisha clomped up the stairs to the stage. She was wearing her favorite six-inch gold patent-leather stiletto boots, which matched her gold bobbed wig. She had one of her lavender-colored notebooks with her, and as she took the microphone Grandma offered her, she opened it and moved into position facing us.

"Is you ready?"

"Yes," said the seven of us.

"Then say what I say, and know that this oath be binding from now until you's dead."

"Uh, or until our first four-year term is up and the North American House of Nights vote us back into our positions," I corrected her quickly.

"Yeah, what Z says." Kramisha nodded, totally unrattled. When she began speaking the words of the oath, her voice changed, was amplified, and seemed as if a silently watching Nyx had suddenly breathed power into her.

> *New times call for new places, faces.*
> *Balance restored, we now look ahead.*

Kramisha paused. Together, the seven of us repeated the binding words of her poem:

> *Our tests were great, but we stayed true.*
> *Our losses were great, but we came through.*

Again she paused and we repeated her words:

> *Tonight we pledge to stand in the Light.*
> *To lead with wisdom, love, and might.*

As I spoke the words with my six friends, I prayed that Nyx would help me, help them, to continue to grow in wisdom, to be filled with love, and to always show others the respect they deserved as I wielded my Goddess-given might.

> *Behold! The new High Council you see!*
> *So we have chosen; so mote it be!*

As we repeated the last lines of the oath, the seven of us stood and, as one, bowed to the crowd, who all erupted in riotous cheers.

"Okay, Z. Now tell 'em the rest of it," Stevie Rae said. "After all, it was your awesome idea."

I nodded, nervous again, but faced the crowd and finished what I'd started. "As you guys know, we plan on being a totally new kind of High Council because we want the world to see a totally new kind of vampyre." The crowd instantly quieted, listening intently. "Part of what I decided, well, what *we* decided, all seven of us, was that we weren't going to stay here, shut away from what's really going on in the outside world."

"And grow cobwebs from our butts," Stevie Rae added, causing laughter to ripple through the audience.

"Well, yeah, something like that," I said, grinning at my BFF. "So, starting tomorrow, your High Council is going to go out into the country, visiting different Houses of Night, listening to the problems and concerns of normal, everyday vampyres and fledglings, as well as the humans who live in their nearby communities." I drew a deep breath, and irrevocably scattered my friends.

"Stevie Rae, you'll go to the north."

"So mote it be," she said, smiling, though her eyes were filled with tears.

"Damien, you'll go to the east."

"So mote it be," he agreed solemnly.

"Shaunee, you'll go to the south."

"So mote it be," she intoned.

"Shaylin, you'll go to the west."

"So mote it be," she said, smiling kindly at me.

"And I will stay here with thee," Aphrodite said, her gaze wise and steady on mine.

"So mote it be," I agreed. I turned to the audience and said, "Merry meet, merry part, and merry meet again. And may you all blessed be!"

Everyone clapped, this time more soberly than before. Obviously, a bunch of people were shocked at the decision my Council and I had made, but I felt good about it. And, judging by the looks on my friends' faces, they felt good about it, too. We'd all seen how messed up things could get when a High Council lost touch with its people. We were determined that wouldn't happen to us.

But I had one more thing I needed to do, one thing I hadn't told my friends about. I turned to them and said, "Guys, before you go, we need to circle one last time."

"Circle? Right now, Z?" Stevie Rae asked.

"Circle yes, and now, kinda. Would you come with me? It's easier to show you than to explain," I said.

"Z, if you need us, we'll always come with you," Damien said.

"I'll pull the Hummer around," Stark said.

"I've already gathered your ritual candles and put them in my basket," Grandma said.

"Fine, let's go. The Herd of Nerds rides again," Aphrodite said.

"I thought the city agreed to build a wall around this part of the park to keep gawkers out," Aphrodite said, frowning at the blacked front of the sealed stone grotto.

"They did. But I asked them to wait until after today," I explained.

"What's up, Z?" Stevie Rae asked.

"Well, here's the deal. Aurox won't leave me alone," I said.

"Aurox? Isn't he over there, keeping Neferet from getting out here?" Shaylin asked, pointing at the grotto.

"He is, but he's also in my dreams," I told my friends.

"What kind of dreams?" Aphrodite asked.

I shook my head. "I don't really know. I can't remember anything from them except that Aurox keeps calling my name, and no matter how many times I try to answer him, I can't reach him. But I know he's there. I know he needs me."

"What do you think it means?" Damien said.

"Well, I think it means he is trapped and I need to free him," I said.

"Wait, no. If you let him out of there"—Aphrodite jerked her chin at the grotto—"Neferet and her disgusting minions will escape."

"Actually, I don't think that's what will happen. I'm not going to let out Aurox's Old Magick. I'm just going to release his soul."

"But his soul's already gone. We saw it that night, right before he charged the grotto, and it was definitely Heath, who definitely got out of that bull's body," Stevie Rae said.

"Yeah, see, here's the thing about that—I don't believe Aurox was soulless without Heath. I believe Aurox developed his own soul because of the choices he made, and that's what's trapped in there," I said.

"And because Thanatos is dead, you're willing to act in her place and help Aurox move on to the Otherworld," Damien said.

"Well, I'm willing to try—if you guys help me."

"Oh, for shit's sake. Circle up, Nerd Herd. What's the worst thing that can happen? Darkness is loosed on the world? Again?" Aphrodite gave a big pretend yawn. "Been there, kicked that ass."

"We'll help you, Z," Stevie Rae said.

"Yea, we trust you," Shaunee said.

"If you say Aurox needs your help, then we're here for you," Damien said.

"Absolutely," Shaylin agreed.

"Thank you. I'm so damn proud to be part of your Nerd Herd," I said, sniffing and wiping my eyes.

"Z, you put the nerd in herd. Circle up before you start snotting," Aphrodite said. "And don't cuss. It never sounds right when you try."

I grinned at her as my circle fanned out, taking their familiar places. Grandma gave each of us our candles. I went to Damien and began where it had all started what now felt like so long ago.

"Air is everywhere, so it only makes sense that it is the first element to be called into the circle. I ask that you hear me, air, and I summon you to this circle." I touched the yellow candle with the lit match, and air whooshed around Damien and me, lifting our hair.

He smiled at me though tears that pooled but didn't quite spill from his eyes. "That's what you said the first time you called air to our circle—that very first time my element manifested for me."

"You remember!" I said, blinking hard so that I wouldn't cry.

"Of course I remember. We'll all remember, Z," Damien said.

Smiling through my tears, I turned to the south and went to Shaunee.

"Fire reminds me of cold winter nights and the warmth and safety of the fireplace that heats my grandma's cabin. I ask that you hear me, fire, and I summon you to this circle." Shaunee's red candle flamed before I could light it. She grinned at me. "Go on, Z. We're here for you."

I kept walking around the circle to Shaylin.

"Water is relief on a hot Oklahoma summer day. It's the amazing ocean that I *have finally seen,* and it's the rain that makes the lavender grow. I ask that you hear me, water, and I summon you to this circle."

Shaylin's blue candle lit easily, and the scent of spring showers filled the space around us.

"I'm glad Nyx gifted me with this affinity," Shaylin said. "I'm glad I am a part of your circle."

"Me, too, Shaylin," I told her.

Then I moved to stand in front of my BFF.

"One more time, Z. Let's do this, and do it right," Stevie Rae said.

I swallowed down the lump that kept trying to rise in my throat and said, "Earth supports and surrounds us. We wouldn't be anything without her. I ask that you hear me, earth, and I summon you to this circle." The sounds and scents of a grassy meadow filled the air. My BFF and I smiled at each other.

Then I moved to the center of the circle and completed the casting, lifting my purple candle to light. "The last element is one that fills everything and everyone. It makes us unique and it breathes life into all things. I ask that you hear me, spirit, and I summon you to this circle."

Spirit swirled around and through me as my circle was enclosed in a brilliant silver light. I closed my eyes and prayed. "Nyx, it won't surprise you to know that I'm not real sure what I'm doing here—I'm only sure I need to be here. Please guide me and strengthen me."

Opening my eyes, I walked to stand before the blackened stones that had been seared together to close Neferet's living tomb. Thinking of Thanatos, and remembering what I had watched her do for Kalona, I held out my hand and said, "Aurox! You must take my hand!"

It happened way faster than I'd anticipated. A blindingly bright globe the color of moonstones burst from the center of the blackened stones. It elongated and expanded until it became Aurox!

"Ohmygood*ness*, Z was right!" Stevie Rae gasped.

"Hi," I said. "Can you see me?"

I can, he said. A brilliant smile lit his face. *You heard me. You came back for me!*

"Yeah, I did. I don't leave part of the Nerd Herd behind," I said.

Part of the Nerd Herd. I like that. I'll remember that.

"Remember something else. Remember that I came back for *you*."

Aurox looked utterly shocked, and then his smile was back. *You really do care about me.*

"I really do," I said.

From just outside the circle, Stark added, "We all really do, Aurox."

Aurox turned his glowing eyes on Stark. *Can we still have that beer together someday?*

"Absolutely!" Stark said. "Next time around."

Next time around, Aurox repeated. Then he looked at me. *Now what?*

"Now you stop keeping your Goddess waiting," I said. "Here, take my hand again."

I'm not sure I'm ready, he said.

I smiled at him. "I'm sure."

He took my hand, and I lifted again, imagining that I was tossing him into the sky. The silver light that had been encircling us funneled through me, and with a great push of energy, Aurox shot upward.

The night sky above us shivered and then parted like an opening curtain to reveal Nyx standing before a beautiful blue lake. Kalona was beside her, smiling down on us. I watched as the Goddess opened her arms to embrace Aurox as if she were a mother welcoming home her beloved son.

"I finally did the totally right thing!" I said, wiping tears from my cheeks.

Before the curtain to the Otherworld closed, Nyx's gaze went to me. The Goddess grinned. She looked younger and happier than I'd ever seen her look. And then, very distinctly, Nyx, Goddess of Night, winked at me.